Skeleton Key

Skeleton Key

A XANTH NOVEL

Piers Anthony

OPEN ROAD

INTEGRATED MEDIA

NEW YORK

Copyright © 2020 by Piers Anthony

Cover design by Amanda Shaffer

ISBN: 978-1-5040-6030-1

Published in 2021 by Open Road Integrated Media, Inc.
180 Maiden Lane
New York, NY 10038
www.openroadmedia.com

Skeleton Key

Chapter 1

SQUID

Squid paused as she passed a quiet pond in a glade, admiring herself in the reflection. She looked exactly like a normal, unremarkable, human eleven-year-old girl who might start turning pretty in a couple more years if she worked at it. Dull brown hair, faded gray eyes, turned up nose. Nobody who was anybody would look twice at her, maybe not even one and a half times. "Great!" she exclaimed, snapping her fingers.

"Hello!"

She turned. There was a nondescript boy, about twelve, emerging from a path leading to the pond. He was calling to her. "Yes?" she answered cautiously.

"Don't worry," he said as he approached. "I'm not going to molest you. I'm twelve, too young for that. Maybe next year."

She simply stared at him, delivering The Look. She had practiced it for just such an occasion. Not that she could be molested by him or anyone; she was pretty much proof against that.

"That was a joke," he said, suddenly uncomfortable.

"Some jokes aren't funny." But she had made her point. "You called to me. Who are you and what do you want?"

"I'm Zero. My talent is to zero in on things. I practice it all the time. Today I am zeroing in on importance, and I got a strong signal, so I followed where it led." He paused, confused. "You don't look like much."

"Well, I *am* not much," she retorted.

"Oh, but you are! At least you're supposed to be."

This was curious. "Supposed to be what?"

"The most important person in the universe. But you look like an ordinary girl."

"Thank you," she said coolly. That was, after all, exactly what she was trying to look like, but he didn't mean it as a compliment. "So your talent must have misfired this time."

"No. It's right on target. Maybe I'm misunderstanding."

"Maybe," she agreed, becoming intrigued. "Maybe I'm going to grow up to be the most beautiful creature, but I'm not there yet."

"That's for sure. Right now your panties wouldn't freak out anyone." That was a not-so-secret weapon women had in Xanth: when men became obnoxious, the girls could lift their skirts and flash their panties, and any man who saw them freaked out until someone snapped their fingers or did something else to jolt them out of it, by which time the girls would be safely gone.

"I'm not wearing any panties."

Zero laughed, embarrassed. He tried to peek under her skirt without seeming to, but didn't succeed. "That must explain it. But it leaves the mystery of why you are so overwhelmingly important. What is your talent?"

"I don't have any talent. At least not a magic one."

"But everyone in Xanth has a magic talent," he protested. "It's in the Big Book of Rules the Good Magician has. Everyone knows that."

"Not me," she said. "The rule is that everyone either has magic, or *is* magic. I'm the latter."

He looked at her more carefully. "Are you sure? You sure look human. Are you a lady elf or something?"

"No. I have no human ancestry at all."

He shook his head, perplexed. "Then what are you?"

"I'm an alien cuttlefish."

"Are you teasing me? Those are sea creatures."

"No. I wear a human form when I'm on land, and in the water too, usually. But it's only a form. That's why you couldn't see under my skirt: it's more apparent than real. My clothing is merely colors."

He actually blushed. He of course had thought his sneak peek attempt was not noticed. Boys tended to be unsubtle; it took them decades to become truly sneaky. That was why women were so effective in managing them. "Show me your real form, then."

"No."

"Just your form without clothing, then."

Another way to get a peek? "No."

"You *are* teasing me! You're no alien creature."

"So my terrific importance remains a mystery."

He laughed. "I admit it. You're a huge mystery."

Then Squid saw something. "Freeze," she said urgently. "There's a stink horn behind you. Don't step on it."

"Oh, come *on*. I won't fall for that," he said, stepping back. "Big joke."

"No," she said, alarmed. "There really is!"

"Ha. Ha." Then his heel came down on the stink horn. It made a foul-smelling noise, and a filthy brown stench emerged from it. "Oops!"

"Run!" she cried. "I'll distract it!"

Zero didn't argue. The noxious cloud was already reaching for his legs. He bolted for the forest. No one wanted to be smeared by such a stink.

Squid went into action. "Nyaa! Nyaa! Can't get meee!" she cried.

Annoyed, the cloud roiled toward her, swelling dangerously. Traces of garbage flashed dully in its bulges, such as decaying eggshells melted by the rot inside them.

Squid dived into the pond and swam, shedding her clothing, which was indeed more apparent than real. The cloud boiled after her, across the surface. The water recoiled from the fetor, forming a dent, but couldn't escape.

She could readily have outdistanced the smelly cloud, but she didn't. It still could reverse and go after the boy. She lingered to tease it more. "You think you're so awful? You're just a blob of nothing!"

The cloud turned an angry, dirty red and forged on after her, extruding streamers of crud. Oh, it was mad!

Then she saw something else. It was a loan shark, attracted by the commotion. That was a real danger; she knew it would take an arm and a leg if she let it. Not that she had arms or legs, but it could still seriously hurt her.

She dived, reverting to her natural squid form; mainly eight long limbs like tentacles. She jetted a small cloud of ink. The shark snapped at the ink, but she was already dodging around and beyond it. She could actually handle a shark, if it wasn't too big, by wrapping her tentacles around it and squeezing it until it surrendered, but right now it was more useful as a distraction.

Meanwhile, the malodorous cloud caught up to the action, colliding with the shark. The shark snapped at it, getting a mouthful of stench. That got its attention, and the two faced each other, neither one accustomed to giving way. That was the distraction she needed, so Squid quietly swam to land, reformed as a girl, and clambered safely out.

She paused to color-in her clothing, so as not to be mistaken for a juvenile nymph. Then she resumed her walk to the next glade, where she had a meeting. The epic battle between shark and cloud continued: she suspected that both parties would regret it. But at least she had saved Zero from a cruel stenching. He was an innocent boy, not deserving of punishment like that.

That reminded her: why did Zero think she was so important? Obviously she wasn't, but it was curious that his magic had led him to her, which was the second minor mystery of her day so far.

Now she wondered about the first one. Her brother Santo had quietly asked her to meet him here privately, away from the fire boat. It was not like him to be secretive. What was on his mind? So she had left the craft quietly, unnoticed, and set out on her nature walk, which had soon turned mildly adventurous.

Then she arrived at the glade. Santo was there. He was a nondescript thirteen-year-old boy, on the verge of early manhood. He could have passed almost unnoticed in a group, and usually did, for the same reason as Squid; he was by no means ordinary, and did not want to attract attention. Three reasons: to start, he was really an unrecognized Magician; he was close to a genius; and he was gay. Their siblings and friends knew it, but were good at keeping secrets. "Good enough, Squid. I was concerned by your delay."

"I got distracted by a boy, a stink horn, and a loan shark. Sorry about that."

He laughed. "I'm sure you handled them efficiently."

"I did. But that reminds me; the boy's talent is to zero in on things. Today it was importance. He said I was the most important person in the universe. Isn't that crazy?"

"No."

Squid did a double-take. "You were supposed to laugh. You know I'm an alien cuttlefish, so I'm weird, but I'm not important."

"It is not a joke," he said seriously. "That's why I needed to talk with you. There is serious mischief afoot, and you're in the center of it."

"Me! I'm not out to make any trouble for anyone. You know that."

"I know it. But you may not have a choice."

"Well, I want a choice," she said stoutly.

He didn't argue; that was not his way. "Talk with Aria."

"Princess Aria from the future? She's my friend, but she visits with Noe. You know that."

Then she paused, because something odd was happening. A presence was joining her, in her mind. *Hello, Squid.*

"Aria! What are you doing in my head? We're friends, but you know my alien nature makes you sick."

Not any more, the princess said. *That is, we remain friends, but I have learned how to be with you, at least briefly. It's important.*

"It must be. What is it?"

You are the protagonist for this story.

Squid rocked back. "What?!" It was tricky expressing both a question mark and an exclamation point together, but she managed it.

You know I can't lie to you when I'm in your mind. You're the main character.

"I know you wouldn't lie to me anyway. Friends don't lie to each other, any more than siblings do. But I don't see how I can believe something so weird."

"Believe her," Santo said, evidently knowing what Aria was telling her.

"But this, this—I'm not even human!" Squid protested. "I *can't* be the main character."

That makes no matter mind. Accept it and move on.

"There's more?"

Much more. Santo will tell you.

"Thank you, Aria," Santo said, again picking up on what he couldn't hear.

Bye. And she was gone.

"Now hold on just a dogbone minute," Squid told Santo before he could open his mouth again. "My credulity is getting overloaded already, but Aria says there's a lot more you have to tell me."

"Yes. That is why I asked you to meet me here. There is much to impart."

"Can it wait? I think I need to sleep on this protagonist business, if it's true. I have no idea how to do it."

"Talk to Jess, when you return to the boat. She was the protagonist for the last story."

"Where Xanth almost got taken over by the big bird, Ragna Roc. I remember. But she's off on a gig."

"We are about to transport her to a new performance site. She will be aboard when we return to the boat."

"Oh." That deflated Squid's argument. She was stuck for the rest of the news. "Okay, let me have it. What am I going to be involved in, that makes me so infernally important?"

"Because you will be the protagonist, it is required that you either participate in, or be aware of, all relevant events."

"You mean what everyone else is doing? When I'm not even there?"

"Yes."

"As if I could keep track of nine other children and scattered adults. This is already heading for a bust. Santo, I can't be in several places at once."

"Hence the addition of a special talent to your repertoire."

"My repertoire! I hardly know what that word means! But from the context I think it means my collection of magic talents. I don't have even one talent."

"You do now. Your shape-changing ability will be improved so that you can emulate any creature and any age, though you won't be able to change your mass."

She smiled. "How about a big bird? Will I be able to fly?"

"Yes, when you learn how. At first you may find it practical mostly to glide."

This was shape-changing of a nature well beyond her present capacity. She was indeed being upgraded. "Is that all?" she asked humorously, as if it wasn't already way beyond any expectation she might have had.

"No. It is incidental. The main addition is attuning."

"Is what?"

"Attuning. When anyone speaks of you, you will hear it, and see it, though you can not affect it, and will remain attuned to the scene as long as their awareness of you remains. It is limited, and they will not know of your presence, but it should be effective for this purpose."

She realized that Aunt Demoness Fornax must have done it, quietly upgrading her as she had done for the others before. But she felt unworthy. "This purpose of completely ruining a story by putting a nothing person into it."

He looked at her severely. He had evidently perfected a Look of his own. "If you don't stop denigrating yourself, I will have to hug and kiss you."

"You wouldn't dare," she said, laughing. "Have you forgotten you're gay, and anyway I'm your sister?"

"You are my sister, and I love you. That has nothing to do with romance, and everything to do with reassurance and support, which you seriously need."

She considered that. . . . then she crumpled. "Oh, darn," she sobbed. "I'm overwhelmed, and I haven't even heard the rest of it."

Then he was holding her while she cried, and kissing her pretend hair, and it did help. There was no one closer to her than her four siblings, and he was the most significant of them, in part because he truly understood what it was like to be different. He knew her for what she was, an alien cuttlefish from the future, and loved her regardless. That counted phenomenally.

"You are worthy, Squid," he murmured. "Of this, and whatever else is to come. Never doubt it."

After a suitable time she dried out. "Okay, I think I'm ready now. You know these things because Fornax is your adoptive mother. Sock the rest of it to me."

"Myst and Firenze are being upgraded too. They will have near Magician class talents, but must not show them unless absolutely necessary. All of you must help each other keep the secret."

"We do that anyway. We always help each other."

"Yes. But we may be severely tested. Something big is about to happen, and we will have to handle it without adult help."

"Something big? What?"

"I don't know. I think even the Demons don't know the whole of it. But it will happen."

"That's scary."

"Yes."

"What else?"

"A special child is about to join us. You will have to help him."

"Who? How?"

"His name is Larry. You must be his nominal girlfriend."

Squid was taken aback, again. "He's human? You know I can't be any human's girlfriend, because—"

"I said nominal. There is a parallel; the way Noe is my girlfriend."

She took stock. "Noe knows you are gay, but she plays along and helps cover for you when that will help. She even kisses you, making it look romantic. And you do like her, but—"

"But there will never be a true romance," he finished.

"So is this Larry fellow gay too? So I need to pretend he's hot for me?"

"Not exactly. He's not gay."

"Then what?"

"He is transgender. A girl in a boy's body. Larry's true identity is female, Laurelai."

Squid digested that. "So it's like a girl dating a girl, only not by preference."

"Yes. The two of you may on occasion need to embrace and even kiss, but it will never be a real romance, only a show."

"Because I'm a cuttlefish and he's a girl and that's nobody else's business."

"Yes."

"Just as you and Noe sometimes hug and kiss in public."

"Exactly."

"Well, if you can do it, I guess I can do it. But why do I have to? I mean, why bother to be a fake couple? Why can't he or she simply tag along with us for a while?"

"Because that will help conceal the secret. So that no one should suspect."

"Suspect what?"

"That Fornax is taking up secret residence within the mind of Laurelai."

Squid gazed at him, amazed again. "Aunt Fornax is going to be with him?"

"With her. She can't associate in that manner with a male."

"With her, then. Why?"

"The Demon Xanth suspects that another Demon is secretly interfering with the Land of Xanth. This is a trap to catch that Demon in the act."

"This is a Demon contest! We should steer the heck clear."

"We support Fornax." He looked at her. "Don't we?"

Squid yielded. Now it was clear why this meeting had had to be private. Squid had to know, but it had to be secret. Who would ever suspect a female Demoness hiding in a male body? And of course the siblings supported Fornax; they owed her everything. "We do. But we need to tell the other siblings, because they will know the moment they touch him/her. We don't want their surprise to give it away."

"We will tell them, quietly," Santo agreed.

"When do I meet Larry?"

"This evening. I will take you there."

"Will I stay with him?"

"No. He has to go see the Good Magician Humfrey, who will assign him to the boat. That is when you will officially meet him."

"So why don't I just wait for that, then?"

"Because you will need to explain things to him, privately," Santo said patiently. "He may not wish to cooperate. You will persuade him."

This threatened to be even more of a challenge. "Persuade him to take a girlfriend when he's not even really a boy, and not gay?"

Santo smiled. "Noe persuaded me. Surely you can rise to the occasion."

And Aunt Fornax, hidden in Laurelai's mind, would be watching. A challenge indeed! "I will try," she promised bravely.

"I am sure you will. Larry will know that Fornax is there, but neither of you will ever speak of it thereafter. Not until the mission has been completed."

"Got it," she agreed.

"Now it is time to return to the boat. You will want to talk with Jess."

"I will," she agreed, remembering.

Santo walked to a rock by the side of the glade. He rolled it to one side. There, behind it, was the open mouth of a tunnel. "After you, important person."

"So that's how you got here unobserved," she exclaimed. "You made a tunnel."

"It's what I do," he agreed.

It was indeed. That was his magic talent, tunneling; only it wasn't limited to small or local tunnels. He could also tunnel between worlds. Maybe between galaxies. That was why he was a Magician.

"Thank you." She got on her hands and knees and crawled through the tunnel, not caring if he saw her nonexistent panties. Apart from being a sibling, why would he care?

The passage was only a few feet deep. Then they emerged at the edge of another glade. But this one was in a completely different terrain. The tunnel had seemed short, but had actually covered a fair trek. All part of Santo's magic.

When they were out, Santo turned and snapped his fingers. The tunnel disappeared. He was through with it.

Ahead of them was Fibot, the Fire Boat they lived on. It looked like a beached rowboat, with a small mast for a sail, but that was deceptive. They walked to it, climbed over the gunwale, and stood on the small deck between the oars.

There stood a small robot dogfish and a small black bird. The robot's face screen flashed. "Welcome back, kids," the bird translated. "What are you up to?"

"That is private, Peeve," Santo said. "That's why we discussed it away from the boat."

The screen flashed again. "Tata is annoyed," the peeve said.

"We will share when we can," Santo said.

"We love secrets," the peeve said. "But not from us."

"We don't mean to tease you," Squid said. "It's just that something came up unexpectedly, and we have to deal with it."

The dogfish's screen showed a star going nova. He remained annoyed.

They walked on to the hatch in the center and climbed down into it, using the handholds.

And they were in the yacht. It was enormously larger than the rowboat, and far more modern. All part of the magic.

"Ah, there you are, back from your walk in the wood." It was Nia, physically twenty-two years old, dark brown hair, gray eyes, so lovely she could make a passing man walk into a tree-trunk without realizing. Mentally she was sixty-two, having been severely youthened by an encounter with a youth spring, but they regarded that as private information. "You missed dinner, but I saved some for you."

"Thank you," Santo said. "We appreciate it."

"You're up to something," Nia said perceptively. Sometimes her true age peeked through; she was far more knowledgeable than her appearance suggested.

"I have a private mission," Squid said. "Santo filled me in on it."

Nia glanced sharply at her. "You've changed. You look the same, but you're different. What is it?"

Squid looked at Santo, uncertain what to say.

"There's a new story beginning," Santo said. "She's the protagonist."

"But please, it's private," Squid said quickly.

"As you wish," Nia agreed. "I'm not one to pry. Not openly, anyway."

They laughed. "Thank you," Squid said. Nia was highly observant, and her talent was to animate a pair of phantom eyes that floated anywhere she wished and observe things. Indeed, she did not need to do it openly.

"Oh," Nia added. "Jess and Magnus boarded while you two were out. We'll take them to their next gig. It's routine. Just so you know."

As Santo had known. "I want to talk to Jess," Squid said.

"I'm sure she'll be happy to see you again."

The two ate quickly, then walked down the hall to the Jess and Magnus suite. Squid knocked.

Jess answered. She was not an impressive woman at first glance. She had dirt brown hair, dull green eyes, and a dull figure. But Squid knew her, and saw a fine person. "Hello, Squid!" Jess greeted her. "It's so nice to see you!"

It came across like a joke, but Squid knew better. It was Jess's curse that nobody took her seriously. To get around it, Magnus had finally renamed himself Nobody. That had worked wonderfully; they were believed to have a marvelous love life. Not that Nia would ever be so crass as to mention what her phantom eyes had seen. But she hadn't denied it when questioned.

"And you mean it," Squid said.

"Of course I do! You know that. That's one reason I like you and the siblings. You have learned to take me seriously."

"Yes," Squid agreed. "I—I think I need your advice."

"Oh, are you planning to become an entertainer? Do come in and talk."

"Uh, not exactly," Squid said awkwardly as they entered and Santo faded discreetly into the background, as he often did. It was almost a secondary talent.

Jess merely waited for her to continue.

"You—you were the protagonist for the last story, weren't you?"

"Yes, undeserving as I was. It was quite an experience."

"I—I understand I am to be the protagonist of the next story."

Jess laughed, then quickly sobered. "Now I'm doing it; not taking you seriously. I apologize." But she glanced at Santo, who nodded from within his seclusion, confirming what Squid said. Jess and Santo had a special mutual respect for each other. "And you have no idea how to proceed."

"Yes!" Squid agreed. "I mean, maybe there's been a mistake, and I'll mess it up. If it's true. It's so confusing."

"I know exactly how that is," Jess said. "But now I understand it better. First, you have to realize that being the main character of a story does not necessarily mean you're important, or that you have to do anything special. You're just an observer, centrally placed so that those who read or hear the story later know what's going on. The viewpoint character. You're like a little recording camera. You can just go about your business as usual and it will work out. Many protagonists don't even know they're protagonists. So it must be simple, if they can do it without knowing. You can surely do it too."

"But, but what if I *am* important? A boy told me I was the most important person in the universe. I know that's ridiculous, but suppose any part of it is true?"

Jess glanced again at Santo, who nodded again. "It just might be true. Stranger things have happened. That suggests that more is going on than we know."

"I guess. But how do I handle it?"

"That's easy. You just ignore it. You must be the person who is fated to be in the midst of significant events, and as long as you see them happen, you have no further responsibility. You're the most important person in this story, pretty much by definition, because without you there wouldn't *be* a story, but you're still just an observer. Relax and enjoy it."

"As men tell the girl who's about to be raped?" Squid asked pointedly.

Jess looked sharply at her. "How old are you?"

"Eleven. But the Adult Conspiracy doesn't address me perfectly, because I'm an alien animal."

"Squid!" Jess said, shocked. "You're a *person*! Never forget that."

"And the boy called me the most important *person* in the universe."

Jess sighed. "I suppose I walked into that one. But important or not, being the protagonist is not rape. It's just a position." She paused, wincing. "Let me rephrase that. It's just an outlook. All you have to do is observe, and that's the gist of it. You're probably best off simply putting it out of your mind. What will happen, will happen, regardless; it's not your responsibility to make it happen, just to watch as it goes by. Everything else is automatic, as the confusing events and thoughts somehow get organized into a coherent narrative. And in due course it will pass, and someone else will be the main character for the next story, and you'll be an anonymous has-been, as I am."

"I hope it's soon," Squid said fervently. "But thank you, Jess; your advice does help. I will try to watch things go by without feeling responsible."

Jess nodded. "There's something else. The protagonist normally winds up happy, no matter how scary it seems before the end of the story. With fame, or glory, or merely a nice boyfriend." She glanced at the bedroom where Magnus must be sleeping. "Something good. So at least you know you'll survive and prosper. That's a nice guarantee that few other folk have."

"Who would want to be my boyfriend, except another cuttlefish? And I don't think I'd want one of those. I've been here too long."

"There will be something. Believe it," Jess said earnestly. "I fell in love with Magnus, but thought he could never love me back, even if he wanted to. Because of my curse. But he found a way. You're a good girl, regardless of your origin or anatomy. There will be someone for you."

"Like maybe a boy who is really a girl and has to fake it," Squid said sourly.

Jess glanced a third time at Santo, who nodded again. "Oh Squid, I'm sorry. I think you have a hard course ahead. But I do believe it will all work out for you in the end, as it did for me. You just have to persevere."

"As if I had a choice," Squid said with resignation.

"I'm sorry," Jess said. "I'm just trying to help." There was actually a tear of sympathy in her eye.

But Squid was fed up. "Don't bother."

"Squid," Santo said. "Remember when I dissed Noe and you chided me?"

Squid remembered, and realized that she had just done the same to Jess, for no better reason. She was abruptly overwhelmed. "Oh, I'm sorry, Jess! I'm sorry." She dissolved into tears.

Then Jess was holding her comfortingly. "It's all right, Squid. I understand. You're under a lot of pressure. It's all right."

Squid glanced blurrily at Santo. "Is it?"

"Yes," he said with an eighth of a smile. "But don't do it again."

Then they all had to laugh, albeit more from awkwardness than humor.

"Who decides who is the protagonist, anyway?" Squid asked. "The Muse of History?"

"I don't believe so," Jess said. "I understand that she was once a protagonist herself, and she didn't choose it. No, it seems to be some anonymous figure who has the mysterious power to do it."

"If I could believe that, I'd have no trouble believing that we are all just figments of some fool's sick imagination."

"Me too," Jess agreed.

They hugged again and parted. Squid did feel better, if only because it was clear that Jess had not only made it safely through her own protagonism, but that she sympathized.

Then it was time to intercept Larry. "I have made a tunnel," Santo said. "To the enchanted-path rest stop nearest the Good Magician's castle where Larry will soon arrive. Are you ready?"

"As I'll ever be," Squid said.

"You will have to acquaint him with the situation, and persuade him to accept you as his girlfriend. I will be there to help, but you are the central figure. More important, you must persuade Laurelai to agree to host Fornax."

"I have to do that? I thought she was already there."

"We know she has to be there, but this will be news to Larry."

Squid sighed. "Already, this is more of a challenge than I like."

"I have a forget spell. You must persuade him; then once it is done, he must forget she is there. The siblings can be trusted to keep the secret, but Larry might otherwise let it slip. But it does have to be voluntary on his part."

"Worse and worse."

"Squid," he said seriously. "I believe that one reason you were chosen for this role is that you are at least somewhat objective, because of your alien nature. We believe you can handle it. Don't disappoint us."

"*We*? You and who else?"

"Me and Fornax."

She knew he wasn't fooling, because Fornax was in effect Squid's aunt and Santo's mother. They were expecting a lot of a minor person. "Oh, blip! All I can promise is to try."

He smiled. "That should be enough. Make yourself pretty."

To impress Larry, she realized. Because boys of any age were always more amenable to pretty girls of any age, even children, foolish as that was. It was so obvious a ploy that no sensible person would fall for it. Except a boy. A girl did not need to be smart, just pretty. She shaped her features to be fine and even, and formed her simulated hair to be verging on lustrous. Now it was no longer dull brown, but glossy brown.

Then the mouth of the tunnel opened and they stepped through to the rest stop. This was a pleasant enclosure beside a placid pond, with milkweeds and pie plants, and a modest wood shelter. It wasn't fancy, but it sufficed for travelers on their way to the Good Magician's Castle. It was enchanted like the path, so that there were no dangers to travelers, and folk could relax and sleep in peace.

There was motion on the nearby path. Someone was approaching. "You're on," Santo said, fading back.

"On the spot," Squid agreed, with resignation. Suppose she blew it? Would there be major consequences for the universe? She tried to suppress the thought, with incomplete success.

The figure came to the entrance to the rest stop and paused. He was an unimpressive, nondescript boy with blue-black hair and eyes.

Squid stepped forward. "Hello," she called. "Are you stopping here?"

"I hope to, if it's not already taken."

"Official rest stops are never taken, only shared. I won't be staying." She smiled, showing dimples and even white teeth. She had her girl form down pat. "Hello; I'm Squid, age eleven, with the ability to change the appearance of my clothing." She made her seeming dress turn green, then red, then back to brown. It was the standard pattern of introduction: name, age, talent. She had not called it a talent, as it was not magic, merely part of the nature of a cuttlefish, but he was free to assume it was magic. That kind of thing enabled her to get along without actually lying.

"I am Larry, age twelve. My talent is to change my apparent physical age, though not my mental age." He demonstrated by becoming two years younger, then two years older. His clothing did not change with him, so it fit awkwardly during the alterations.

So far, so good. "I am traveling with my sibling, Santo," Squid said, indicating Santo, who stepped out of the shadow. "He's thirteen, and makes holes." Santo demonstrated by making a small hole through the trunk of a nearby tree, as if someone had driven a spike through it. This, too, was an evasion; strangers tended to assume that that was the extent of his talent. Then the hole faded, leaving the tree intact. "We stopped by here to meet you."

"Meet me?" Larry asked. "Why? I'm nobody special."

"Ah, but you must be," Squid said. "You're on your way to see the Good Magician, aren't you? Because that's where this path leads. That means you're special in some way."

"Maybe," Larry agreed guardedly. "But not in any way that should concern a pretty girl like you."

She straightened up as if surprised. "You think I'm pretty?"

"Look in the water."

She walked to the edge of the pond and peered in. And was amazed. She wasn't just pretty, she was beautiful! Her hair was a glorious tiara flowing around her face and framing her shoulders. Her face was fair in a manner she had never before achieved. And her body was seductively shapely for her age, with legs even a grown woman would envy. She had succeeded far beyond her expectation. "Wow! I didn't realize." But as she spoke, she realized that Santo hadn't been fooling about the enhancement of her ability to modify her appearance. It had expanded by a magnitude.

"The bleep you didn't. A girl always knows. What do you want with me?"

"First let's get to know each other better. Then we can get down to business."

"Why?" he demanded. "You're about to move on and we'll probably never see each other again. There's no sense in getting to know each other better. We're not about to be friends or associates. Just tell me what you want of me, we'll settle it one way or another, and go our separate ways."

"I don't think so. Sit down, and we'll talk." She sat on the green turf, aware that her lifted knees showed an unconscionable amount of her thighs under her simulated skirt almost to her mock panties. He would pretend not to notice, of course, but he would sit too so he could look without seeming to. As a boy he couldn't help it. Squid and her sisters had verified that many times, teasing boys while pretending innocence. It was practice for when they would become women with potent panties.

Larry sat, but he didn't bother to look. That reminded her that he was actually a girl. "Why don't you think so? I've been walking all day, I'm tired, and I want to eat, clean up, and sleep the night so I'm refreshed for the Challenges of the Good Magician's Castle. So please make it quick and dirty."

She smiled, knowing that the expression now had much more force than it had before her enhancement. "Tell me why you want to see the Good Magician."

"No. That's my business, not yours."

He was not being swayed by her appearance, as any normal boy would be. She knew why, but needed to make him tell her, so he wouldn't know she already knew. "It *is* my business. Tell."

"You've got some nerve! It's nothing that would interest you."

"It interests me. Look, I'm pretty sure you're not what you seem, or you wouldn't be here. I think I'm even less what I seem than you are. That's why we need to talk. The faster you tell me, the faster we'll settle things between us and I'll be gone. So if you really want to be rid of me, that's how, maybe."

"Maybe?" he asked suspiciously.

"When we talk, you'll understand why."

"All *right*!" he exploded. "Anything to be rid of you! But first tell me why you think you're less what you seem to be than I am."

"Fair enough. I look like a girl, but I'm not. I'm an alien cuttlefish from the future."

"Ha ha. Prove it." He thought she was playing a game with him.

Squid gambled that a startling demonstration would accomplish her purpose. She let go of her human girl format and reverted to her natural form: a cephalopod with eight arms with suckers, and two tentacles. "And I eject black ink when I'm in trouble in the water," she said with her un-human mouth.

Now he stared. "I admit it: you surprise me. But cuttlefish don't have lungs; how can you breathe and talk in air?"

"I said I am alien, not local. I have gills for the water, and lungs for the air. I use whichever is appropriate, or both. And I color my skin to look like hair and clothing."

His doubt was suffering. "How did you come here, when this is obviously not your natural environment?"

"My family was touristing in future Xanth, nigh fifty years hence, when suddenly the end came. They barely had time to put me in a carriage in the hope of saving me, before they were lost, orphaning me. I was rescued by two unlikely females, and brought here. Now I have four others from that same doomed future who are unrelated human children, but we all love each other as siblings and would do anything for each other. Santo is one of them."

Larry glanced at Santo. "You're human?"

"I am," Santo agreed. "But I recognize Squid as my sister, and yes, I would do anything for her."

"Even though you know she's really an alien cuttlefish?"

"There's no 'though' about it. If you tried to hurt her, I would hurt you without hesitation."

Larry nodded. "By making a hole through me. I get it. Don't worry; I'm not out to hurt anyone." He looked at Squid. "Please, resume your human form, and answer one more question, and I promise I will tell you my story. I will even look at your panties if you want, though they won't freak me out."

"One more question," Squid agreed, seeing victory on the horizon.

"The two unlikely females who rescued you: who are they?"

"I will tell you if you promise to keep it secret."

"I promise," he said without hesitation.

"One is a basilisk in human form called Astrid. Her direct glance is instantly lethal, so she normally wears a veil. But she's a very nice person, when you get to know her."

Larry smiled. "I'm sure."

"The other is a capital D Demoness named Fornax."

"Fornax! She's notorious!"

"So you know her reputation. But she too is a nice person when you get to know her, and I consider her my aunt."

"And my adoptive mother," Santo said.

"And we would do anything for them," Squid said. "Now you know."

"And I am amazed." He paused, organizing himself. "Very well. It is my turn. I am a girl in a boy's body. My name is Laurelai, but I use Larry for my male form. I am going to the Good Magician in the hope that he can get me into the right body, a female one."

"Are we now talking to Laurelai?" Santo inquired perceptively.

Larry's face smiled. "Yes, now that I have unmasked myself."

Squid nodded. "So you're like me, in one respect: you look ordinary, but you're not at all what you appear to be."

"Exactly. So you are perhaps in a position to understand my situation."

"Yes. So is Santo."

"Why?"

"Because he's gay."

"That's not the same thing. I would like to date a suitable boy, when I am of age, but that's because I'm a girl."

"Don't worry," Squid said, smiling. "Santo doesn't want to date you."

"That's a relief!" She glanced at him. "No offense."

"None taken, of course."

"Santo doesn't want to date you," Squid repeated. "I do."

There was a sudden pained silence. Then Laurelai spoke. "That's why you intercepted me? No way!"

"That's the least of it, but let me explain. Santo has a girlfriend. Her name is Noe. Its mainly just for show, so he doesn't have to keep explaining himself to sometimes hostile strangers with ignorant opinions. They like each other, they understand each other, they make it look romantic, but it's not. It's protective coloration. You need something similar, and I'm it."

"I don't need any such thing! All I need is to achieve my true physical form. As it is, my talent is limited, because when I age beyond puberty the body starts getting these awful male notions I can't stand."

Squid hadn't thought of that before. A girl getting stuck with boy notions when she saw panties or whatever . . . that could be awkward. She couldn't blame Laurelai for avoiding it.

But that was not her concern at the moment. "I think you do need it, because of the rest of it."

"What are you talking about?"

"This is more that is secret."

"I will keep your secret," Laurelai said with resignation.

"There is something big brewing, and they need a hidden Demon to sneak in and find out what's going on, because maybe there's a foreign Demon messing in Xanth."

"I can see that would be a challenge. But what does it have to do with me, or with me having a pretend girlfriend?"

"Fornax needs a host." She waited while Laurelai worked it out.

"A female Demon would need a female host. I still don't see the relevance to me. I'm no good for that, because my body is male."

"But *you* are female. Who would ever suspect?"

Laurelai had difficulty even saying it. "You want me to host a Demon? Because she could join me despite my male body?"

"Yes. And I will be your girlfriend because that will indicate that you are what you look like, a boy. It's all fake, but necessary to fool the enemy Demon."

She shook her male head. "I'd rather just have the Good Magician find me a better body."

"Maybe he will—if you do this chore first. You know there's always a price for his help."

Larry sighed. "So that's how it is."

"That's how it usually is," Santo said. "But there's more."

"Why am I not surprised? You folk are a font of oddities."

"You must never reveal Fornax's presence to anyone outside your body," Santo said. "You can't use any of her powers or give any hint. To ensure that, I will use a forget spell on you so that you don't even know she is with you."

Squid knew he wasn't bluffing; he must have a spot forget spell with him.

"I haven't even agreed to do it!" Laurelai exclaimed. "Already you are making conditions."

"This is important," Santo said evenly.

"I am coming to believe it," Laurelai said. "Very well, let me meet her first. Then I'll decide."

Santo closed his eyes for a moment. "Mother?" he asked of the sky. Then he nodded. "Touch me," he said to Laurelai.

Laurelai stepped to him and touched his hand. And froze, eyes closed. "Oh, my," she breathed.

Squid realized that Santo had made the connection for Fornax, so that she could locate and join Laurelai. The hidden girl was now meeting the hidden Demoness directly. What would be the outcome?

Then Laurelai opened her eyes. "I love her. We are friends already. But there is one thing; I don't want to forget her. I want to be able to commune with her anytime."

"No," Santo said.

"Wait," Squid said. "Laurelai is lonely. She has to be, hiding in a boy's body with no one for company. She's doing us an enormous favor. She deserves this."

Santo hesitated. "Mother?" he asked.

Now the body changed, becoming infinitely more mature and formidable. It spoke. "I am here, son." It was Fornax! "She wants a companion who understands. I was lonely too, for millennia, the loneliest of all the Demons, until I made friends with Astrid, and became aunt to the siblings and mother to one, and married another Demon. I remember. I would like to have another friend."

Santo paused, working it out. "Then a compromise; commune, but never reveal your presence outside your host, until it is time, lest the mission be compromised."

"Agreed."

Then the body relaxed, and Laurelai reappeared. "Thank you," she breathed tearfully.

Then it changed again, and it was Larry. "Did I miss something?" he asked.

"Your kiss," Squid said. She went up and kissed him quickly on the mouth. "We may never do this again except in public," she promised.

"Thank you," he said somewhat dryly.

"Now you will proceed to the Good Magician's Castle," Santo told Larry. "Take your time. Relax for a day. Your appointment there is in two days."

"I will be there," Larry agreed.

"Time for us to go home," Squid said. "Farewell, Larry. We will meet again."

Then Santo opened a new tunnel to the boat, and they went through.

Squid relaxed at last. What a day it had been!

Chapter 2

MYST

In the morning, aboard the boat, Squid remained in the room she shared with Myst. She had been talking for an hour, sharing news of her prior day.

"Wow!" Myst said. "So now you actually have a boyfriend! I'm jealous."

"It's not real," Squid reminded her. Myst was nine, two years younger than Squid, but fully human, so boys interested her just as much as they were supposed to interest Squid. "It's pretend, like Noe with Santo."

"Well, I'd settle for a pretend boyfriend, if he held my hand and kissed me in public. I want to practice for when I'm grown up."

Squid smiled. "You'll get there soon enough, I'm sure."

"I don't know. With your talent upgrade you can flash your panties and make it count."

"I wonder. I was amazed when I saw my reflection. But I'm still underage, and my panties are still fake."

"But outside boys don't know that. Painted-on panties are still potent. Mine aren't. I tried to flash a boy last month, and he just laughed."

"Because you're still a child. They'll work well enough when you need them to." Then something impinged on her awareness. What was it?

"Squid, you're looking funny. Are you okay?"

"Shh. I'm sensing something."

Then in her mind's eye she was seeing a beach. There before her was a plaid panty, lying empty on the sand. This was weird; they had just been talking about panties, and now she was seeing one, somewhere.

"Sensing what?" Myst persisted annoyingly.

"A panty," Squid answered, orienting on it. "A plaid panty."

"Plaid! That's special."

Then Squid was all the way into the scene, at least with her mind. Her body wasn't there; it cast no shadow in the sunshine. But she saw and heard everything: the sand, the distant trees, the waves of the sea, and the sound of their breaking up on the sand. The panty must have been washed ashore.

"Hey! What's that?"

The sound was in the scene. For half an instant Squid thought she had been discovered. Then she saw that two children were approaching. They were about twelve years old, male and female, but similar in appearance.

"It's a panty, Data!" the boy cried.

"Well, don't freak out, Piton."

Piton and Data. Those had to be the skeleton twins; Squid knew of them but hadn't met them. They lived in Caprice, the traveling castle, while Squid lived in Fibot, the boat.

"I'm too young to freak," the boy said. "And it's empty. It has to be filled to work. Panties don't do anything by themselves; they exist to enhance girls. You know that."

"I sure do," Data agreed. "Mine are already starting to work. I wonder who filled this one last? Maybe a mermaid."

"They don't wear panties, silly, because they don't have legs."

"But some can make legs when they go on land. Maybe this one got spooked, and jumped back into the sea when she made her tail and swam away, and the panty dropped to the sand."

Piton dashed up, passing right through Squid's location without contact, and picked up the panty. "Wow! Plaid!"

"Give it here!" Data said, snatching it from his hand. "I want it. It's no good to you anyway."

"Put it on," he said. "I dare you."

"I will. Is anybody looking?"

"Nobody who counts. We're the only ones here."

"Then here goes." Data hoisted her skirt, doffed her own panties, and lifted a foot to put it into the panty. But it hung up on her toes. She tried again, with no better success. "I can't get it on," she complained, frustrated.

Squid, listening in, was fascinated. Not with the panty lore; everyone knew about the magic girls could use on boys to keep them in line. She had heard that in Mundania that effect was not so strong, and men could abuse women. Squid never wanted to live in Mundania, even if she wasn't a real girl. It was just too dangerous.

No, what interested her was the way she was picking up on the scene. Santo had told her that when anyone mentioned her name, she would attune, even if she was far away, beyond hearing physically. But this wasn't that. The twins had not mentioned her name. But here she was, sharing their discovery of the panty.

So maybe Santo had it wrong, or at least incomplete. Maybe the panty was relevant to the story she was supposed to track, and she and Myst had been discussing the subject, so it was almost as if the beach panty had said her name. It couldn't talk, of course, but it was a kind of connection.

"Come on, doofus," Piton said. "I'll help you." He dropped to his knees, took the panty, held it open between his hands, and pushed it toward his sister. She lifted both legs and aimed them for the holes.

And snagged. She still couldn't get it on. "Go ahead. Laugh," she said angrily.

"I'm not laughing. I saw what happened. The holes closed up when your feet came. It's some kind of magic. The panty won't let you get in it."

"Weird," Data said, and Squid agreed. She had seen it too; Piton hadn't done it, the panty had, twisting to block her feet. It truly didn't want to be on her.

"What's the use of a panty that can't be worn?" Data asked as she put her own original panties back on. Why those were plural and the beach panty was single, Squid couldn't say; maybe it was part of the magic. "Isn't that a contradiction in terms?"

"Maybe it's choosy," Piton said. "It's looking for the right girl, maybe a grown girl, and you aren't it."

"That must be it," Data agreed, mollified. "It was made for a mermaid, or something, and won't let any other girl into it." She shrugged. "You know, you have a genius for finding magic things that don't work right. Like that Plan-tain you found last month."

"Plantain?"

"You called it a big banana tree. It was guarded by a huge orangu-tain. I had to distract the creature so you could sneak by and steal some of its fruit."

"Oh, yeah. I grabbed a handful and got out of there. But I couldn't eat them."

"Because they were tains. Like bu-tain, de-tain, sus-tain, uncer-tain, and dis-tain. And you got a bloods-tain on your hands just handling one."

"Yeah. Maybe my luck will change and I'll get something I can handle. Like maybe a pretty girl."

"You would think of that. You've got girls on your feeble mind."

"Well I'm a boy. That's what boys look for."

She laughed. "Maybe some nice girl will be unlucky enough to think you're nice."

"As if you aren't thinking of boys all the time."

"Then there was that Angel Trumpet you found," Data said, changing the subject back. "But it knocked out everyone who heard it."

"I had to throw it away," he agreed ruefully. "But I still think my luck will change."

Then the scene faded, apparently losing its relevance to Squid's interests, and Squid was back with Myst. "Wow!" she said.

"You went all glassy-eyed," Myst said. "You said you saw a plaid panty, and then you tuned out. So I let you be."

"Santo said I was going to have a talent," Squid said. "When anyone spoke my name, I'd be able to tune in on them for a while. But in this case nobody did. But we were talking about panties, and the skeleton twins, Piton and Data, found a panty on the beach, and somehow I tuned in. So maybe the talent is even stronger than Santo knew, just as my form-changing ability is much better than it was. Anyway, I was there on the beach with them, seeing and hearing what they did." She smiled. "Data tried to don the panty, and it wouldn't let her. It snagged her feet."

Myst tittered. "That's funny! Maybe it doesn't like the smell of a skeleton. Those kids are half skeletons."

"Actually all humans are half skeletons," Squid said. "You have skeletons inside you, while I don't. But I know what you mean. The panty might demand a full human girl, so she can't suddenly change into a walking skeleton and leave it hanging."

They both giggled at the thought of a panty hanging loosely on a walking skeleton.

"I wish I had a magic panty," Myst said wistfully. "I'd use it to snag a boyfriend. Like maybe Piton. I think he's handsome."

"He is ready to notice girls, or soon will be," Squid agreed. "His sister thinks he's already too much into that, and he thinks she's too much into boys."

"Well, send him to me! I'd treat him better than that panty thief we heard about, who flashes her panties, freaks out men, then steals their stuff."

Then their dialogue drifted on to other subjects, and the panty was forgotten.

Squid.

Squid, on the verge of snoozing, jerked awake. That was Santo's voice, but he wasn't here.

Then she tuned in on him. He was sitting alone on the deck near the front of the boat as it drifted, gazing at the clouds below. They were going somewhere. Squid hadn't been aware if it, distracted by her changing circumstance. "What?" she asked.

"Squid, I can't see or hear you, but I think you can see and hear me," he said. "If this works, it will verify your talent. Come up here and join me."

Squid hastily did so. She saw Win at the stern, her wind guiding the boat as it caught the fiery sail. "Hi, Win!" she called. "Is Santo on deck?" She knew he was, but preferred not to explain about that yet.

"Up front," Win called back. "Cloud watching."

"Thanks." Squid skirted the fire sail and joined her brother. "Hi, sibling. Fancy finding you here."

"You heard me," he said, plainly gratified.

"Well, you spoke my name."

"Mother told me it would work, but this is the first time, and I wasn't quite sure. I'm glad it did."

She sat down beside him. "Actually it's the second time, I think." She explained about her vision of the panty.

"Now that's really interesting," he said. "Because that's what I was going to tell you about. We're heading for Caprice Castle now, since Magnus and Jess have a week off before their next engagement."

"Wow! I always wanted to tour Caprice."

"That may not be included. We're supposed to pick up Piton and Data. They'll be joining us on a tour for a week while their folks visit Skeleton

Key. Their parents feel they're becoming too isolated, so time with us will help socialize them, because we're in their general age bracket and we're social. But there's a complication."

"There always is," Squid said. "Because this is a story, and complications are good for stories even if they're not much fun for the folk who get complicated."

"Exactly. Data is happy to be social, but Piton isn't. He needs to be persuaded to visit with us."

"Maybe you can talk to him."

"He knows I'm gay. That's a turnoff for him. He's hot for girls and can't understand any boy who isn't. When he gets to know me he should ameliorate, but I can't persuade him to join us."

"Well, I can't either. He knows I'm a cuttlefish."

"Yes. So it will have to be Win or Myst who approaches him. Win is close to his age; she's ten. But we need her to move the boat, so it better be Myst."

"Who is nine," Squid said. "Isn't that too young? Boys don't much want to be with girls until they're older."

"Yes. However, Myst will be significantly enhanced. You must persuade Myst to sway Piton."

"Me! Why do these chores fall to me?"

He smiled. "Because you're the protagonist. It's not all fun and games."

"Fun and games!" she cried indignantly. "Listen, brother—" Then she realized that he was teasing her. "I will talk to her."

"Thank you."

"But if this is an example of the huge event we are preparing for, I'm not much impressed."

"We remain in the setting up stage. I suspect that we need a certain cast of children to enable it. Only when we have them all ready will the main event commence."

"Children? If it's big, the adults should be in charge."

"Adults would be suspected, causing the mission to be compromised. Children are considered innocent."

Squid burst out laughing. "In an oink's eye!"

"I said 'considered.' It may be fallacious, but just as adults keep secrets honoring the Adult Conspiracy, so also children keep secrets they forget when they become adults. So adults think we are innocent, and that has force."

"Oh, sure. I understand. So this is for children. Maybe that's why a child is protagonist."

"Indeed. This is a children's production."

"But you won't tell me what it is."

"Correct. I have little notion myself."

She gazed at him, frustrated, sure that he was not telling her everything. But she remembered that his mother was Fornax, and he was privy to special information that needed to be hidden. "Okay. Anything else?"

"Yes."

"That was meant to be facetious!"

"It's minor, but may actually help. We need a cover story for our close organization of children, which includes non-siblings."

"Brother! That's an exclamation."

He smiled. "I understand."

"Well, let's have it. What's this cover story that's going to further complicate my life?"

"We need to form a dance group."

"A what?"

"A dance group. Classical Mundane dances, mainly. Square, round, triangle, star, line dances. That sort of thing. We'll become an act in Magnus's traveling show."

"A dance group," Squid echoed weakly. "As if we know anything about classic dancing."

"As if," he agreed. "Don't worry; we'll learn with startling velocity."

"Oh, more enhancement? Or do you know where there are dancing shoes that we can put on and they will do our dancing for us."

He smiled tolerantly. "We will call it natural ability that wasn't evident until there was motivation."

"So I will have to get Larry to dance with me, and Myst will have to get Piton. That won't be easy. Girls like to dance, but boys generally don't."

"Consider it a challenge."

"Oh, spit!"

"That's the spirit," he agreed equably.

Sometimes she regretted how hard it was to rile Santo. "I will talk to Myst," she said with resignation.

"Meanwhile, I will talk to Win," he agreed.

Squid returned to her room. Myst was there now. "Anything new happening?" the girl inquired.

"Yes. We're going to form a dance group, square, round, et cetera."

Myst clapped her hands. "Goody! I love to dance."

"But we'll need partners. Boys."

"Blip!" Myst swore. In a couple more years she would be able to say "Bleep!" and later still, as an adult "Damn!" But of course one of the Child Conspiracy secrets was that they knew what the euphemisms stood for. They just couldn't say them aloud. "I knew there'd be a catch. We don't have enough boys, and they won't do it anyway."

"We'll have to recruit a couple," Squid said. "Which reminds me; you have a chore coming up."

"Oh? What?"

"You have to persuade Piton to join us on the boat for a week or two, and get him to join the dance group. His folks think he needs socializing."

Myst laughed. "He's almost a teen. I'm still a child. A pretty teen girl might interest him, but not me. And even a teen might have trouble making him dance."

Squid had a flash of inspiration. "That panty I saw in the vision. He has it. He wants to find out who it fits. Maybe it fits you."

"And maybe it fits a pretty teen girl ten times as well. Try again."

"He'll want to try it on any girl he meets, until he finds the right one. You won't even have to mention it; he'll think of it himself soon enough. And if you should happen to be the one, well, you've got a dance partner, maybe even a boyfriend."

Myst considered. "I don't believe it for half an instant. But you've got me intrigued. The only way I can be sure that panty isn't for me is to try it on."

"That's right. Satisfy your curiosity. What can you lose?"

"My virginity."

Squid froze. "Myst, you're only—"

"Nine years old. I shouldn't even know that term." She laughed. "Gotcha, sister. I do know better."

Squid relaxed. "You got me," she agreed. "I was starting to think like an adult."

"I'll try to talk him into it."

"One favor. Please say my name when you're on the beach."

"Why?" Then Myst remembered. "Your new talent! Then you'll tune in on me."

"Exactly. I'm supposed to track important events, and this may be one of them."

"Okay. But if I do anything I shouldn't, don't tell on me."

"Agreed," Squid said, smiling. "Child's honor."

"We can't let the adults catch on to our secrets. There would be blip to pay."

"There would," Squid agreed.

The boat landed on the beach isle where Caprice was parked. The castle was magnificent with its walls and towers. Piton and Data were still outside, playing on the sand.

Win and Myst debarked and walked toward the twins. "Squid," Myst murmured.

Squid, watching from the deck, went below, now that she had the vision. She was already getting to like this new talent.

"Hey!" Win called. "We're Win and Myst, two of the siblings on the fire sail boat. We want you two to visit us on Fibot for a week or two."

"We know who you are," Data called back. "We saw you blowing the boat in. I'll be glad to get a good ride on it."

"No," Piton said shortly.

Just so. He was the truculent one. "Come, Data," Win said. "Let me show you around the boat. You'll like it."

"I know I will," Data said sociably.

Myst looked at Piton. She opened her mouth.

"Forget it," the boy said unsociably. "Go play with brats your own age."

"I prefer to play with you. Give me a chance."

He sent her a look that could have boiled ice water. "I'll give you half a moment. Then I'm going inside Caprice. Alone."

This was the crux. But she was prepared. "I'll show you mine if you show me yours."

That made him pause. She was young, but the secret places of any girl were of interest to any boy, especially a naughty one. It was mainly curiosity, but compelling. "Yeah?"

"Our talents, of course. Then who knows?"

"Of course," he agreed, disgruntled. But she knew she had him interested. She had hooked him with The Hint. Of course they would talk about talents out here where someone might overhear, but once they got private that might change.

"Here's mine." She dissolved into mist, forming a small cloud as her dress dropped off her vaporous body.

He stared. He knew she would have to reform soon, naked!

"Here's mine," he said quickly, and changed into skeleton form, his clothes hanging loosely on the bones. "It's not magic so much as inherent; Data and I can both do it. But that's our talent." He changed back, and adjusted his clothing.

Myst coalesced back into solid girlform. But a thin lingering curtain of mist concealed the key parts of her bare body. She picked up her panty and dress and put them back on as the mist faded. "Ta-daa," she said.

"Oh." He was having trouble masking his illicit disappointment. The notorious Adult Conspiracy to Keep Interesting Things from Children was childhood's greatest frustration, and they never ceased trying to get around it.

"Let's get out of sight of the boat and castle," Myst said. "We don't want anyone else to see the next stage. Adults might not understand."

"Oho!" Actually the danger was that adults *would* understand.

She definitely had him baited. Squid, observing, had to admire Myst's finesse. She was young, but already talented at managing a boy.

They walked to the far side of a small dune, out of sight of any likely spy.

And encountered a woman walking the other way. Both Piton and Myst were guiltily startled, and Squid knew why: this was an adult woman, and they couldn't afford to have her see or guess what they were up to. Not only that, but she was bomb-shell beautiful, with flaring red hair, crystal bright green eyes, appealing freckles on her face and shoulders, and a soft shade of white skin. She wore a loose robe that no longer even tried to conceal the outline of her phenomenal bosom.

Piton was really too young to freak out, but he was certainly trying, so it was up to Myst to do the talking. "Uh, hello," she said.

"Hello, children," the woman replied. "What are you doing here behind the dune?"

How could they answer that? "Just seeing the sights," Myst said. "I'm Myst, and this is my friend Piton. He's half walking skeleton."

"A crossbreed! So am I. I'm Marceen. I'm thinking about going to see the Good Magician to find out what my ancestry is, or maybe what my magic talent is, because I don't know either and it's about time I found out."

Piton was jolted out of his daze. "Crossbreeds don't always have talents, except changing back and forth between their forms." He shifted rapidly to skeleton, then back before his clothing could fall off.

"That must explain it," Marceen said. "Except that I can't change back and forth, maybe because I don't know what other form I might have. I'm stuck with this form. All I think I know is that I might have some ogre ancestry. Maybe if an ogre met a nymph at a love spring. But that wouldn't explain my ears."

Now both children thought to look at her ears. They were pointed.

"Jenny Elf is the only person with pointed ears we know," Myst said. "And she would never stray near a love spring."

"I know. So it's a mystery maybe only the Good Magician can unravel."

"If you go on around the dune, you'll see Caprice Castle and the Fire Sail Boat," Myst said. "They both travel. I'm sure one of them would take you to the Good Magician's castle, if you asked."

"Oh thank you!" Marceen exclaimed. "I could kiss you both!"

Then, before they could protest, she did both, quickly kissing Myst on the forehead and Piton on the ear. Then she walked on around the dune.

"That was interesting," Myst said. "I'm glad we could help."

Piton did not reply. He had freaked out.

Myst snapped her fingers. "Come out of it," she said.

He recovered. "I'll never wash that ear again." So it had not been a total freak out.

They walked on a bit, making sure that now they really were alone.

"Ready?" Myst asked.

"Sure," he said eagerly.

"I'll match you skin for skin. Show something."

He promptly removed his shirt.

She rolled down the top half of her dress. For a woman that could be impressive, but not for a child. For an instant Squid suspected Myst envied Marceen.

A shadow loomed over the dune. "Bleep!" Piton swore, fearing discovery.

But it turned out to be only an errant cloud.

"We'd better hurry," Myst said. "Just in case."

"Yeah."

"This time I'll lead." She dropped the rest of her dress, standing bare in her panties.

He stared, but did not freak out. He was a little too young for any ordinary effect, and she was a medium degree too young. Blip! Still, his gaze was intense. There was magic, just not enough of it. Yet.

"You too," she reminded him.

"Oh." He laughed, embarrassed. "Maybe I did freak, a little." He dropped his pants and stood in his underpants.

Myst looked almost as intently as he had. She clearly had never seen a boy's briefs before, at least not while in girlform, and did not know quite what to make of it.

To Squid, it wasn't much different from a snug swimsuit. But of course underpants lacked the magic of panties.

"I guess that's it," Myst said, almost reluctantly. "We have Looked."

"I guess," he agreed, still looking at her. Then a faint bulb flashed over his head. "Unless."

"Unless?"

"I've got something you can try on, if you want to. As long as you're mostly bare anyway."

"Unless it's a really pretty dress, I'm not much interested."

Squid smiled. The girl knew exactly where this was going, and was eager for it, but masked her excitement. He wanted to get her bare again, on some pretext. She liked the game of Show Me, but pretended otherwise. What a little actress!

"It's a panty."

"A panty! I've already got one."

"This one's plaid."

"Plaid!" As if that made all the difference, allowing him to think he was playing her.

He fetched it from the pocket of his fallen pants. "Here."

But Myst demurred. "I'd have to get all the way bare to put it on. You're just trying to trick me."

As if she didn't want to be tricked. Beautiful!

"No I'm not! Here, I'll get bare too." He dropped his underpants.

Myst wasn't the only one who stared. Squid was similarly fascinated. There it was, male anatomy. Young, but there. A plain violation of the Adult Conspiracy that they would never tell.

Except that a gnat flew in Myst's eye, and it instantly teared up, making her blink both eyes, so that she couldn't actually see any real detail. Somehow that also interfered with Squid's vision, so she couldn't quite see either. Bleepity bleep!

By the time the vision cleared, Piton had pulled his underpants back up. He obviously wasn't comfortable exposing himself for long. Squid knew Myst wouldn't complain; she didn't want to admit that she had missed her chance.

"I'll hold it for you," Piton said, holding the panty open.

Myst fuzzed into mist, dropping her own panty in the process, floated around the plaid panty, and solidified within it. There was no problem with tangling. It fit her perfectly.

Squid stared. The plaid panty was meant for Myst!

"You did it!" Piton said, amazed.

"Well, I'm a girl and it's a panty."

"But when my sister tried, she couldn't get it on. You're the one it's looking for."

Myst's smile was genuine. "You mean I can keep it?"

He had a second thought. Boys were possessive by nature. "Well—"

"Please?" She twitched her bottom slightly so that the panty moved.

Piton froze in place.

Squid's jaw dropped. He had freaked out! The old panty hadn't done it, but the plaid one had. It was magic!

She continued to ponder it. Empty panties didn't freak out men or boys. Underage panties didn't. But, suitably donned, this one did. It was really special. Squid realized that Myst would never again envy Marceen. She had already achieved Panty Power.

Myst took most of a moment to assimilate the situation. Then she approached Piton as he stood frozen. "You will visit with us aboard Fibot for as long as we need you," she murmured almost in his ear. "You will be my dance partner. You will be my boyfriend."

What a smart boy-manager she was! Maybe the panty was lending her the ability to use it most effectively.

Piton remained frozen, but there was a resistant stiffness to his lips.

Myst twitched the panty again. His staring eyes glazed over. "You will be my boyfriend," she repeated firmly. Then she snapped her fingers. "Come out of it, Piton," she said briskly.

He blinked. "What happened?"

"You freaked out."

"But I'm too young to freak," he protested.

Not quite, Squid thought.

"Not with this panty. Do I need to twitch it again?"

He glanced at it, not quite freaking. Motion made the difference. He got the message. "No."

"Good choice. Now we'll get dressed and go to the boat."

"But—"

She touched the panty meaningfully. He shut up.

They dressed and walked around the dune. Data and Win were walking toward them. "Hey, where did you go?" Data called. "We were looking for you. We met the most interesting person! Caprice will take her to the Good Magician. The boat's about to sail. Are you coming, brother?"

"Well, I don't know," Piton said, reconsidering. "I don't think I want to—"

Myst hoisted the hem of her dress and twitched her bottom hard. Piton freaked out.

So did Data. So did Win. Even Squid felt the power of that naughty flash, but because she was viewing it only mentally, and was not actually human, she managed to maintain her awareness. The plaid panty had not only freaked out the boy, but also the girls. She had never heard of that, regardless of age.

When it came to panty magic, that panty was Sorceress caliber!

Or maybe, Squid realized belatedly, Demoness caliber. What a weapon!

"There will be no more protests," Myst said as she dropped the hem to cover the panty. "We all want to do it."

Then she snapped her fingers, and the three came out of it. They stared momentarily at each other, befuddled.

"Let's get moving," Myst said briskly, not explaining anything. She set out for the boat.

The others followed. There were no protests.

Squid let the vision fade. Now she realized that this was the way Fornax was enhancing Myst; by giving her the Magic Panty. It would do.

"The square dance consists of four couples arranged in a square," Nia said. She was actually forty years older than she looked, and had had decades to learn about such things. "We adults won't be part of your brigade, as we have other business, but we can show you how it's done, especially since you're short two couples at the moment."

The four couples took their places on the floor of the main room of the craft; Dell with Nia, Magnus with Jess, Santo with Noe, and Piton with Myst. Each man was on the left, each woman on the right. Squid regretted that she was not part of it, but her partner was not yet aboard the boat. She would watch and learn as they did.

Nia glanced at the peeve, who perched beside Tata Dogfish. "Start. We'll interrupt you frequently, at first."

Tata's small screen flickered. "Honor your partners," the peeve said, interpreting the signal. Naturally the dogfish had records of all the dances.

Nia held up a hand, for the first interruption. "Honor means this, in this context. Turn to your partners and bow slightly. Like this." She turned to face Dell, who simultaneously turned to face her. They made a small formal bow to each other, then made quarter turns to face the center of the square again. "Do it. We want all four couples to do the motions together, once we get it right, for the larger visual effect. Dances are for watching as much as doing."

Magnus and Jess honored each other. They were familiar with this protocol, but also helping with the demonstration.

Then Santo and Noe did it, and finally Piton and Myst. It was easy enough. The mock formality was sort of fun. True to Myst's panty-inspired directive, the boy was fully cooperating with the dance.

"Honor your corners," the peeve said.

"Your corner is the person of the opposite gender who is corner-wise from you," Nia explained. "My corner is Magnus." She made an eighth turn to her right, and he to his left. They bowed to each other. The others turned similarly. Myst faced Dell, and Piton faced Noe. They bowed.

"Swing your partner."

"Men, put your right arm around your partner's waist, as she puts her left arm around yours," Nia said. "Take her right hand in your left hand. Turn together, clockwise." They demonstrated gracefully. They made a lovely couple, unsurprisingly. Her skirt swung out behind her as she swung. It was a nice effect, and Squid made a mental note to try to emulate it, in due course.

Then the others swung, and the girls looked almost as nice. In fact the four couples swinging together made a larger pattern that enhanced the effect. This was nice dancing!

"Promenade."

"Men, put your right arm around your partner, take her right hand in your left while facing forward together, and slide-step forward together," Nia said, as Dell did so.

When they all did it, the square became a circle as they moved once around. That, too, was pleasant to see.

"Do-si-do with your opposite lady."

Dell and Nia demonstrated the motion with each other, which consisted of holding one's own elbows and making a circle around the other person, without turning around, so they passed back to back. Then they did it with their opposites, Santo and Noe. There was some confusion as eight people advanced to the center, but Nia showed them how to get through without colliding.

The instruction continued, covering the other standard motions. Then they did an actual dance. The four children, whose understanding had been quietly enhanced, danced error-free. It was beautiful.

"That was lovely," Nia said. "You picked up on it surprisingly well. Tomorrow we'll tackle the Round Dances."

Squid and Myst returned to their room to change back into ordinary clothing. "That was great!" Myst enthused. "Piton never said boo."

"You enchanted him," Squid reminded her. "You flashed him with your Magic Panty and gave him the word. He has no choice."

"Oh, that's right," Myst agreed, remembering. "Maybe I should free him. I want him to like me on his own, not because of enchantment. Do you think I should?"

Squid considered. "He's a boy. You can't trust their judgment. Better to keep him captive until he gets to know you better. Then he'll have a chance to get to like you. Then if you free him, he'll stay. Meanwhile, you'll have a good dancing partner."

"That does make sense."

"And when the mood is right, you can kiss him. If he accepts it, you'll know you're making progress."

"But what about the Adult Conspiracy?"

"Kissing is okay, if you stick to his head."

The girl smiled. "Where else would I kiss him?" Then Myst considered. Then she blushed. She was getting a glimmer.

Squid changed the subject. "That is some panty you got. It can actually freak out girls too."

"Yes," Myst agreed. "I was surprised."

"Keep it in mind, in case you're ever attacked by Amazons or something."

Myst laughed. "I will."

There was a knock on the door. "Uh-oh," Squid said. "That must be Santo, with another mission for me to do. This protagonist business is a nuisance."

"You can rest on the bed," Myst suggested. "I'll make sure no one bothers you."

"Thanks, I guess."

"Santo's the most sensible sibling," Myst said. "You're the next. If you find out what's going on, I hope you'll tell me. I'm perishing of curiosity."

"So am I," Squid confessed. "But I still don't see why I'm the main character instead of, well, Santo. He's much more qualified than I am."

"There must be a reason."

That was not quite the kind of reassurance Squid would have preferred.

Chapter 3

ULA

Sure enough, it was Santo. "Noe and I are going with Ula to pick up Firenze. You will need to tune in."

"Can't I just skip this one? I'm sure you both are competent."

"No. You need to record the sequence. I will speak your name, but it is Ula you will need to follow this time, as she tames my brother."

"Santo, this smells like none of my business. I don't want to snoop on the private lives of others, especially my siblings and friends."

"It is necessary. Be ready." He walked away.

"Of all the bleep!" she swore as she turned back into the room.

"So who do you have to spy on this time?" Myst asked, duly intrigued.

"Ula. With Firenze."

"She does like him, and he likes her. Where's the problem?"

"It's that it's not my business. They'll probably be kissing, thinking nobody sees."

"Oooo, naughty," Myst breathed. "They're at least two years older than Piton and I are. Maybe they can get closer to breaking the Conspiracy. He's a hothead who doesn't accept limits well."

"You're not helping."

Myst gave her a savvy glance. "Aren't you curious? It isn't as if you're going to tell on them. It's all sibling secrecy."

"Bleep." Because the girl was right. Squid *was* curious.

Myst wisely left her alone.

Squid lay on her bed, hoping to snooze before returning to duty. Maybe she did, because the next thing she was aware of was her name.

"Squid." It was Santo.

She tuned in instantly. She had to.

Santo was with Noe, standing outside Ula's door. He knocked.

Ula opened it. She was a mature eleven, with orange hair and eyes. "Oh, hello, both," she said. "What's up?"

Santo smiled. "Your talent is to be useful in unexpected ways. We have such a way in mind."

"Oh? Sure, I'll help if I can. What do you need."

"We need you to tame my big brother Firenze."

Ula laughed. "As if he's a dragon? He's a nice guy under that hot head, and I like him."

"You will persuade him to join the crew of Fibot."

"Now wait half an instant! He's okay, but he'd burn up the boat the moment something peed him off. You know that."

"Come with us. We'll talk while we walk."

Ula glanced at Noe. "You know about this?"

"Not a thing."

Ula laughed again, this time without humor. "I think you need to tame your boyfriend."

Noe smiled. "He's untameable."

"At least give me a hint."

"Something big is about to happen," Noe said. "We're forming a dance group. You'll couple with Firenze. That's our pretext for staying close together, so we'll be ready when it happens. That's more than what I know."

Ula nodded. "If I date Firenze, will I be part of your group?"

"Yes," Santo said.

"You said I will need to 'tame' your brother," Ula said to him. "I think that would require feminine wiles I don't yet possess."

"I will explain in the tunnel."

"Okay. But should I wear a dress?"

"Yes."

"One-and-a-half moments, please." Ula disappeared into her closet, and emerged in exactly one-and-a-half moments in a pretty green skirt with a white blouse above, slippers on her feet, and her hair in an orange wave. She did look a shade prettier.

The three walked together off the boat, which was still parked on the beach. They approached the small sand dune Myst and Piton had used, and went around it. Then Santo faced it and concentrated. A person-sized tunnel formed. They entered it.

"We are private here," Santo said as they walked within the tunnel. "No one we don't want to can spy on us here."

That made Squid pause. Santo could make spy-proof tunnels? With a single exception, her? That was impressive indeed.

"I'm impressed," Ula said. "But what is it we need to hide from spies?"

"Our talents are being upgraded," Santo said. "I can do more than I could before, and so can the other siblings. So can you. You can now be highly persuasive. If my brother resists you, kiss him, and he will heed you."

"If he's mad, his head will be too hot to kiss."

"Not only will you be able to do it without getting burned, if you kiss the side of his head you will be able to forcefully cool it."

"That seems like a magic talent. I don't want to lose the one I've got."

"You won't. This is additional."

"Nobody has more than one magic talent!"

"This is why we don't want to be snooped on. Aunt Fornax is gifting us with extras."

"Fornax! But she can't meddle here in Xanth."

"She made a deal with the Demon Xanth. She's allowed." He took a breath. "In fact, she will be with us, personally. One of our party will be hosting her. That's secret, but we need to know so we don't guess it later and give it away. Mum's the word."

Ula whistled. "You said something big is coming," she said, glancing at Noe. "You weren't fooling."

"I wasn't," Noe agreed.

"Back to Firenze. And if you kiss his mouth," Santo said, "he will love you, at least for a while."

Ula paused, visibly taking stock. "I like him, but that's a bit extreme."

"No it isn't. His head must remain cool while he is aboard the boat so he doesn't set fire to the sheets, curtains, and wood. You will keep it cool, by keeping him happy, until he learns the rest of his upgrade."

"His upgrade? All he wants is *not* to set fire to things."

"He can now heat his hands, or his feet, or any part of his body. If some bully tries to grab him, he can heat his arm until the bully's hand inciner-ates."

"And if he holds me, he can incinerate *me*."

Santo smiled. "No. You will cool him wherever you touch him. You will explain about those upgrades to him. He will heed you, as he might not care to heed me."

"Sibling rivalry," Ula agreed. "If I had a younger sister who was immeasurably more intelligent and magically powerful than I, I'd resent her for sure."

"Actually we five siblings do not compete with each other. We support each other completely. All the same, it seems better not to advertise that I am privy to special information."

Ula nodded. "Diplomacy. It helps."

"You do understand," Noe said.

Ula glanced at her. "If I am here to handle Firenze, why are you here?"

"When you get together with Firenze," Noe said, "You will want some privacy. I will make demands on Santo's attention so that he is not in evidence."

"When I convince him to join us on the boat," Ula said, "Then we'll all return to it via a tunnel. That's why you need to stick around."

"You have it," Noe agreed.

"I have it. Now if I can just *do* it. What if I can't persuade him?"

"Kiss him."

"That's right! I forgot about that new power. But it does seem like cheating."

Santo gave her a direct look. "We don't want to cheat. But we do have to have Firenze."

"Why? He might be happier where he is. We all love Astrid."

"Because we need him for the Sibling Conference."

Ula nodded, remembering. "That's where the five of you get together to figure things out."

"And if this new thing is as big as it seems," Noe said, "they'll need to figure it out completely."

"Actually, you friends are becoming virtual siblings," Santo said. "You will join the Conference too."

"Why virtual?" Ula asked. "You five are not related to each other; you're adoptive siblings. Why can't we do that too?"

"Because complete siblings can't be boyfriends or girlfriends," Noe said. "It's mostly a pose for Santo and me, though we do like each other, but it could be real for you and Firenze."

Ula paused, visibly digesting that. She made no further protest.

Squid appreciated why. Just as Myst wanted a real boyfriend, so did Ula. So what if they were children; they would not remain so forever.

The three proceeded on through the tunnel, which led directly to Astrid Basilisk's house, and remained after they exited it. Santo knocked on the door. In half a moment it opened and the lovely veiled basilisk stood there.

"Why, hello, Santo," she said. "What brings you three here?"

"We need Firenze to rejoin the siblings," Santo said.

The veil frowned. "We'd be happy to have him join you. But I don't think he wants to. It's not that he wouldn't love your company; it's the fire hazard."

"I hope to persuade him," Ula said.

The veil frowned again. "If anyone could, you could, Ula. He likes you. But I'm not sure anyone can. He's been depressed lately, and irritable, and argumentative. We have had to fireproof our house, and even so, there have been burns."

"I will try," Ula said. "I may have new abilities."

"Aunt Fornax," Astrid said knowingly. "I will bring him down in a moment." She disappeared into the house.

In exactly a moment Firenze appeared. "What do you want?" he demanded grumpily as his ears reddened. Irritable? He was well on the way to a burn.

Ula stepped forward. She kissed him on the cheek. His head cooled visibly.

"You cooled my head!" he said, astonished. "But that's not your talent."

"I have been upgraded. So have you. Let's get private so we can discuss it." She took his hand.

"Santo, let's admire some scenery," Noe said, taking his hand.

Santo suffered himself to be led. "Can't tell a girl no," he explained. "They don't take it well."

"If she can lead *you*, Ula can certainly lead me," Firenze said, bemused.

"This way," Ula said, drawing him along.

They stopped at a fallen tree. Ula sat down, guiding him to sit next to her.

"What's going on?" he demanded. "You show up here unannounced, and you've got new magic."

"You know the source."

"And what's this about me being upgraded too? I don't feel any different."

"Something big is about to happen, and it seems that we children will be in the center of it, so we need to prepare. Firenze, we need you on the boat. For a sibling conference."

"I can't go there. I'd burn it up. You know that."

"Not any more, I think."

"Yes, anymore! I was always a hothead, and now I'm getting worse." Indeed, his head was reddening again.

She leaned forward and kissed his cheek again. He cooled.

"I can keep you cool. But I must warn you—"

"That you can't keep doing it forever. I know. Much as I like having you kiss my cheek."

"You admit it!" she said, pleased.

"I do. No girl ever gave a blip about me before, not once she saw me heat. You're different. You know I'm a hothead, and you're still nice to me. Maybe it's all an act to get me on the boat, but I'd be satisfied to have you kissing me more."

"It's an act," she agreed. "To get you on the boat. But it doesn't have to be. But that's what I have to warn you about. If I kiss your mouth, you'll love me, at least for a while. So don't let me do that."

"Why not? You could kiss me and tell me what to do, and save all this dialogue."

"Because it wouldn't be fair. You need to make your own decisions, not be coerced into them. I like you too well to mess you up like that."

He considered. "Kiss me on the mouth."

"Firenze, I told you—"

She was cut off as he kissed her on the mouth.

"Oh, my," he said as it broke. "You weren't kidding."

"Neither about the kiss nor the fairness," she said. "I want to talk you into joining us, not kiss you into it."

"I wanted to know whether it was true. It is. Now I want to know why. Sure, maybe there's something big. But that doesn't mean I need to be aboard the boat. Sure, maybe you like me a little. But you shouldn't have to nursemaid me full time. What's really going on, Ula?"

"I don't know. But if it's important enough for Aunt Fornax to upgrade us all, and for her to come with us on the boat—"

"For her to what?"

"This is secret, but you have to know, all of us do. Fornax will be with us, hosted by one of us, I don't know whom."

"But she's not allowed to—"

"Yes she is. She made a deal with Demon Xanth."

"Oh, a Demon bet."

"I'm not sure it is. I think she'll be with us to make sure we don't get hurt, because she loves us. That makes me wonder what kind of threat it could be."

He nodded. "We'd better cooperate. Okay, tell me about these upgradings."

"I can be quite persuasive now."

"You are persuading me!"

"And I can cool you, with my kiss or my hands. And if I—"

"Yes, you demonstrated that. I feel it slowly fading, but I do love you. What's *my* upgrade?"

"You can control it. I think that means you can heat your head without being mad, or cool it when you are."

"Let me see." He sat still while his head reddened and radiated heat. "Yes! I'm not mad, but I'm doing it. And I guess it should work the other way, for cooling. This is great! It means I can be safe now."

"Yes. And you can heat your hands too."

"My hands! I never could do that. Just my head. And usually not by my choice."

"Hot hands. Try it."

He picked up a twig and held it as he concentrated. His hands did not redden, but in a moment the twig burst into flame. "Wow!"

She put her hand on his. "And I can cool it."

His hand immediately cooled.

"Do you know what this means, Ula? I can join you on the boat! And I think I'd like to do that. Except that I don't really know you. You've got a pretty face, and pretty knees under that skirt, but how do I know you aren't just playing me?"

Ula quickly closed her knees. "I'm sorry. I dressed nice to impress you, but I didn't mean to do it that way."

"How can I be sure of that? You set out to impress me, and you are certainly doing that. But as I said, no girl before you ever gave me blip. How can I be sure you mean it?"

Tears trekked down Ula's face. Astrid had said he was argumentative. How could Ula deal with that? Squid feared that this was coming apart after all, because the boy just couldn't accept what he was learning. "I don't know. If you won't take my word, what will you take?"

"And tears are a girl's best weapon. I think I love you, but I don't think I can afford to believe you."

"And I can't blame you for doubting me. Maybe if you knew me better, and I knew you better, then we could really trust each other. But as it is, we can't."

He pondered briefly. "I've known you peripherally for years, Ula, as sort of a background character. I don't have any reason to distrust you. But I know so little about you, really! Maybe if we exchanged histories, we could judge better."

"Maybe," Ula said without real hope. "What's yours?"

I'll show you mine if you show me yours, Squid thought.

"No. Tell me yours first. Most of what I know about you is that you were there on the boat when the first siblings arrived. What about before? I don't think you've talked about that."

"I haven't talked about it because it's so boringly dull. I don't want to bore you."

"Bore me."

She shrugged. "If you insist. I was just a dull girl with a minor talent of sort of helping folk in ways they didn't expect, like having an extra sandwich for lunch when a friend forgot hers, or finding a piece of wire to fix a broken handle before I knew it was broken. It hardly even seemed like magic, and hardly anybody noticed anyway. My parents took care of me, but weren't really good at child caring, as they had lives of their own; I was mostly in the way. So I spent a lot of time alone, not being worth anyone's real interest. I was a background character, and still am." She paused. "Am I boring you yet?"

"No. Your knees drifted apart again."

"Oops! Sorry." She snapped them closed. "Now am I boring you?"

Squid wondered whether the knee drifting really had been unconscious, or whether Firenze really cared.

"Not yet. What changed?"

"One day we were walking home from a sheet harvesting trip, as some really nice ones had grown overnight, when Mother spied an adorable little creature. She picked it up and showed it to Father—and it exploded in their faces, wiping them out. I learned later it was an abombinabowl that existed to do just that; tempt a person into picking it up so it could detonate. It was a really nasty thing. It didn't get me because I was too far away, but I lost both my parents. Next thing I knew I was sent to the School of Hard Knocks, which was the local orphanage. I hated it from the start."

"Why?"

"That's pretty dull to tell."

"Tell."

Ula shrugged. "The first thing the headmistress told me was to behave, or else. I didn't dare ask what that meant because she was so forbidding. Then she put me in a dormitory where the older children exclaimed 'Fresh meat!' and picked on me mercilessly. When I tried to fight back, they threw me in the Cess Pool out back, where cess weeds made an awful stink. I choked, hardly able to breathe, while they laughed. I staggered back to the dorm, but the headmistress intercepted me, hosed me off, then punished me for not behaving and for making a nuisance of myself. She punished me by standing me up against a wall and whipping my back, giving me one long welt. I cried because it hurt something awful, and the other children called me a crybaby. Then I was put to bed without supper, which was how they dealt with nuisances. That was my first day."

She paused again. "I don't have to continue, if it's too dull. I'm not proud of my history; that's why I don't like to talk about it."

Indeed, Squid was appalled. She had had no idea Ula had been treated like that. She had never spoken of it to the siblings.

"Continue," Firenze said tightly.

"Next day I got through breakfast well enough; it was thin gruel, but better than going hungry. For lunch they passed out sandwiches, and I got a good one. But before I could eat it a boy demanded it. When I refused, because I was hungry, he picked me up and threw me back in the Cess Pool. Then the headmistress showed up and punished me for misbehaving again, and I got a second welt on the back. This time I managed not to cry, but they still teased me cruelly. They told me that every year a maiden was sacrificed to the local dragon who guarded the orphanage, and the one with the most welts was the one chosen for that honor. I was now tied for most, as the other children were more savvy about misbehaving.

"That night I made up my mind to escape. I waited until the others were asleep, then sneaked out. I didn't care where I went, just so long as it was far away from the orphanage. And I got lost in the swamp. When morning came I was cold and wet and in fear of the dragon. All I could do was stand there in the muck and cry. A passing mermaid saw me. She told the crew of the flying fire sail boat, who were actually looking for someone else, and they picked me up. They were going to take me back to the orphanage, but I pleaded with them not to, and they voted to keep me as a visitor. All except Grania, who was then in her sixty-year-old form. But she didn't seem to really mind being overruled, and really I liked her best of all. She was like a mother to me, and she treated me very well.

The boat was actually run by two animals. One was a kind of talking bird, called the pet peeve, and the other a robot dogfish who walked on land. He didn't talk, but was very smart, and the peeve spoke for him. Then the siblings came, three of them anyway, and they were okay too. One was a boy who could make tunnels; another was a girl who was really a sort of octopus, but she was nice too. She was my age, and I always liked her. The third was a girl whose talent was to always have the wind at her back, blowing her hair forward around her face, but that was useful for blowing the boat forward."

Squid appreciated that Ula liked her; she liked Ula too.

"So I've been there ever since, and I love it. Sometimes Princess Kadence visits me from the future, and she's nice too. I wish I was a sibling, but I'm not, and that's the way it is. My only fear is what happens when I grow up and have to leave the fire boat and go out on my own. I dread that, because I have no idea how to make it in life." She took a breath. "And that's my story. As you can see, it's not much, because I'm not much."

"May I see your welts?"

Ula was startled. "They've faded some now, but they're not pretty." She turned away from him, then removed her blouse to expose her back.

He looked, and so did Squid. In all the years she had associated with Ula, she had never seen her bare back. The welts were indeed there, two stripes from shoulders to waist. The girl had not been exaggerating; those must have hurt fiercely when inflicted. Which, Squid realized, was the point; Firenze was verifying that the story she had told him was true.

"Thank you."

Ula put her blouse back on and turned around to face him. "So if that turns you off, well, now you know. You called me pretty, but I don't usually show my ugly part."

"I don't think you have any ugly part."

She laughed. "You're being polite, but I appreciate it."

"How do you feel about me, Ula? I know you were sent to persuade me to come to the boat, so we could have a sibling conference, and you are doing a competent job. But apart from that business, how?"

She shrugged. "I guess you don't have to believe me if you don't want to. But I sort of liked you before, and now I like you better. Maybe it's because you are treating me with a respect I maybe don't deserve. I'm supposed to try to get you to be my boyfriend, and make you my dancing partner, though I suspect you'd prefer a girl your own age. You're almost adult, and I'm just a child. But for what little it's worth, I think you're nice, and I wish we could be together, and not just because I kissed you."

"But I'm a hothead!"

"I can handle that, literally, remember."

Firenze pondered briefly, then changed the subject. "Now I will tell you my story." He began, and Squid tuned in on what he was saying and saw it as it must have happened. She had never known her brother's background, and was fascinated.

Firenze had always been a difficult child, but his parents were amazingly tolerant. They constantly bailed him out of the trouble he got into because of his hotheadedness, and moved to new areas when he alienated too many folk in the old areas. They hoped he would straighten out in time.

The problem was his temper. When he got mad, as he often did, his head heated, and little rockets would fly out and explode like fireworks. That did stop anyone from bullying him; all he had to do was butt them with his red-hot head to send them howling. But it also meant he couldn't keep a friend, and of course no girl would touch him. So he was lonely, though too proud to admit it.

Then something changed. Not in him, but in the Land of Xanth. Something was seriously wrong.

"What's going on?" Firenze demanded when he saw how glum his folks were. "Did I do something really really bad?"

"No, son," Dad said. "This is worse that that."

Firenze laughed. "Worse than me blowing my top? That's a laugh."

"No, dear," Mom said. "It is not remotely funny."

They were serious. "Can I help? I know I'm just a ten-year-old kid, but if there's anything I can do to help you out, I'd like to try."

Mom and Dad exchanged a sad glance. Then Mom spoke. "He deserves to know. It affects him too."

Dad nodded. "Son, it is political in origin, but it seems to have gone too far to reverse or even to stop. There are many alternate realities. That is, other Xanths, each differing from ours by only a second or so, very similar up close. The next door Xanth surely has a family just like ours, with a boy very like you. But the farther you go, if you could just walk across them, the more different they become, until at last they are not at all like the one we know. The different realities were protected from each other by the underlying laws of magic. But recently something happened in an alternate reality, one slightly more advanced than ours, at least physically, with stronger magic, and they discovered how to cross the boundaries."

"They can walk across and see the changes?" Firenze asked, amazed. "That must be fun!"

"Perhaps. But it seems that's not enough. They have too many people and want to expand into new territory. They have decided that our reality is a good one to expand into."

"They're going to visit?"

"They're going to invade. They expect to take our land and make us servants. We can't stop them; we don't have the resources. All we can do is pool all our magic and use it to destroy them as they come. It's called MAD: Mutual Assured Destruction. It won't save us, but it will stop them so that they don't bother any other realities."

"I'll fight for us," Firenze said. "I'll burn them!"

"They will have another Firenze, one stronger than you. You can't fight him."

"But then what can I do?"

Now Mom spoke. "You can escape, son."

"And leave you here to be enslaved or destroyed? Never!"

Dad shook his head. "The elders have hashed it out. All we can hope is to save some of the children. There is a cable car line that extends across the realities. We will put you on a cable car, and you can ride to the end, where maybe you'll be beyond the reach of the invaders, and safe."

Firenze was appalled. "But—"

"It has been decided, son. We love you, and if you love us, you will agree to let us try to save you. Before the MAD battle begins."

"But—"

"We can't go with you. Only children can go, beneath the radar, as it were. Adults would overload the reality framework and break the cable."

"But—"

"We don't have much time, dear," Mom said. "We can only hope that you will find a new family to take care of you and love you the way we do."

And that was it. They put him on the cable car, and it carried him out of his home reality while they stayed bravely behind. He knew he would never see them again. He tried not to show his tears.

He looked out the windows of the car and saw the terrain slowly changing, subtly but definitely. Every so often the car paused at a station. He did not get off, heeding the instruction to ride to the end of the line.

But then came a station where two women waited. He thought maybe they wanted to join him in the car, and ride to safety, though they were adult. When the car touched the ground, one of them stepped up to open the door. "All out," she said.

He obeyed, because he automatically heeded an adult, especially one as beautiful as this. "Is this the end?"

"Not exactly, but it will do. This lady will take you home with her."

He looked at the other woman. She was veiled, with dark glasses, but even lovelier than the other. Her beauty simply radiated out around and through the veil. Firenze knew that if he had happened to be a man instead of a boy, he could have been transfixed.

But he knew better than to get off here. He tried to get back on the car, but they blocked him, and the car swung up and away without him. That made him mad, and his head heated, and the little rockets flew out and detonated.

"Behave yourself," the veiled woman said. When he refused, she removed her glasses, closed one eye, and glanced momentarily at him.

He was stunned, literally. Only then did he realize that she was a deadly basilisk in human form. Her gaze with both eyes would kill him; her glance with one merely stunned him. If he wanted to live, he had to obey.

After that they kept him while four other children arrived on succeeding cars, a boy and three girls. Then they took all five children back to their own reality with them. As far as he knew, they were the only ones to survive the loss of their reality.

"Those were Demoness Fornax, and Astrid Basilisk," he concluded. "Aunt Fornax adopted Santo, and Astrid adopted me. I can't look her in the eye, but I love her and am glad she took me home. She saved my life."

"They saved all five siblings," Ula agreed. "They are good people."

"They are." He looked at her. "Now for us."

"Us? Why do I suspect you have more on your mind than chatting?"

"Mother Astrid and Aunt Fornax worked together from the outset to rescue us, and they and their friends have taken excellent care of us despite the challenge of handling a literal hothead, a gay boy, an alien cuttlefish, a child of wind, and a girl who can dissolve into mist at any time. Now I think they want something more of us, and we have little choice but to oblige."

"But I'm not one of the siblings," Ula protested. "I'm just an also ran."

"But you owe the folk of Fibot similarly."

"I do," Ula agreed. "Without them I'd be dead."

"As would we all, without our patrons. And maybe that's the point. I think Astrid, Fornax, and the proprietors of the fire boat got together and decided that you and I should become a couple. They have some kind of huge mission to accomplish, and they need it to be handled by children, and they want the siblings united, and me to be under control. That's your job, and I appreciate that you can do it, if you want to."

"I don't want to control you. I want to be with you."

"Yes. They want to be sure you stay close to me. I think you are the only girl I can safely be with, because I can't burn you, and you have had a rough enough life so that you truly understand what it is like to lose your family and fear for your future."

"Yes," Ula breathed. "I'm just sorry I can't be all the way pretty for you."

"Because of the welts?"

"Yes."

"They are the best part of you. They are like burns, and I have seen plenty of those. They are proof of what you have been through. I hate that you had to suffer getting beaten, but I love what those marks make you."

She gazed at him. "They don't turn you off?"

"They turn me on, in their fashion. My hot head doesn't turn you off?"

"Oh, no, not at all. It is part of what you are, like no one else. And your power of heat, well, it makes me feel safe, because I think you would burn anyone who threatened me."

"I would!"

She considered briefly. "You know, Nia, back when she was old Grania, told me once that what she most needed in her life was to be needed. Dell needed her, and that fulfilled her. I thought about it, and realized that so do I. My talent is to be useful in unexpected ways, but that's incidental. What I long for is to be permanently useful to someone. To be truly needed. But I don't expect that to happen. I'm just a nothing girl."

"*I* need you," Firenze said. "That's the unexpected thing. You're not nothing to me. With you I feel complete, not so much of a freak."

"You're not a freak!"

"Not when I'm with you, Ula. I feel almost normal, for almost the first time. You sustain me."

There was a tear in her eye. "That's just about the nicest thing anyone has ever said to me."

"Then since we are supposed to be a couple, for this mission, let's be a true one. Kiss me."

"But that—"

"It is where I'm going anyway, and I think your kiss magic makes little if any difference now. I think I love you."

"Oh, Firenze!" But still she hesitated. "I am four years younger than you. Too young to love. You don't need a child for a girlfriend."

"Girls generally mature faster than boys, and there are individual differences. By the look of you, you're no more of a child than I am, and I think you will mature physically about the same time I do. Mentally, you're already close. Emotionally, closer yet."

"I suppose," she agreed uncertainly.

Squid, watching, agreed. He was on the verge of manhood, and she was on the verge of womanhood. He was actually pretty handsome when not heating his head, and she was already verging on lovely.

"We each fear our future," he continued. "We don't want to be alone again. But maybe we can make our own future, together, completing each other."

"Yes," she breathed. "Oh Firenze. I think I love you, too." Her orange hair and eyes seemed to be turning golden. "I would give anything for us to be like Dell and Nia, always sure of each other."

"We shall be."

He took her in his arms, and they kissed. Little hearts flew out and orbited them. After most of a moment they paused and gazed at the hearts. Then they both smiled, realizing that it was true.

They were children, but they were in love. They were not, after all, too young.

Squid felt tears in her eyes. She let the vision go, satisfied that she needed to know no more of it. Ula's assignment was done, but it was way more than that.

But she realized something else; each of the siblings was being paired off with a native Xanthian, as if being anchored here. Firenze and Ula, Squid herself with Larry, Myst with Piton Bone, Santo with Noe, even though that was a temporary convenience. All except Win. But Win was now fast friends with Data Bone, and the two were always together. In due course they would surely go boy-hunting together. Was it coincidence, this pairing of the siblings, or did it mean something? She could not be sure that it didn't.

There was also just a touch of envy. Firenze and Ula had found love, and Piton and Myst might be getting there, but what of Squid herself? She was dating a boy who was really a girl. Where was the future in that?

"Blip," she swore to herself.

Chapter 4

CHALLENGE

"Squid."

She alerted immediately to the sound of her spoken name. It was Santo. She tuned in on him. He was resting on his bed in his room in Fibot.

"Don't come to me," he said before she could move. "I am merely alerting you. Larry is about to tackle the challenges of entry to the Good Magician's Castle. He is not speaking your name, but Laurelai is thinking of you, and you can tune in on that. You need to track them until they meet with Humfrey."

She knew that he was receiving information from Fornax, which eased the uncanny impression his information made. "Okay," Squid said aloud, though she realized as she spoke that she didn't need to. Her awareness of the others was supposed to be a private thing. She remained uncertain why she needed to poke into other folks' business, and was sometimes embarrassed by it, but it seemed there was a reason.

She focused on Larry, and sure enough she was on his mind. She had kissed him when they parted, and though he was really a girl inside, he remembered. She suspected it was because there was some male reaction in the male body, and being kissed by a girl stirred that up regardless of his nature. In fact Laurelai had said that she avoided advancing her age beyond puberty because she didn't like the male notions the body got. She doubted that the visiting Fornax would like them either.

At any rate, now Squid was there, observing.

Larry was alone, at least physically; Laurelai and Squid didn't count. He marched toward the castle, and abruptly came across a wall he hadn't seen before. Squid knew he hadn't seen it, because she hadn't; it had appeared in that instant to bar his passage.

He contemplated it, aware that it had to be the first of the three Challenges. Every challenge was passable; the visitor merely had to figure out how. Often they related in some way to the situation of the visitor, but that connection could be obscure. Squid had never undertaken the challenges herself, but gossip about them was common and she had heard plenty of that. Larry/Laurelai had to know the basics, or he/she would not have come here. Squid decided to simplify him in her mind as male, for this purpose.

The wall contained five doorways, all open portals to the continuation of the landscape beyond. Four were blocked by people; the fifth was empty. The question had to be which one led safely through. There was a scintillating curtain across each portal, with the people standing just beyond it. That could be magical or electrical, and surely would mess up any unauthorized person who tried to cross it.

Larry nodded to himself. He approached the first portal, where an attractive almost-young woman stood. She had black hair, blue eyes, and pale skin. "Hello, fair maiden," he said.

"Hello, halfway handsome boy," she replied.

So the folk of this challenge spoke. That helped, perhaps.

"Our hair and eyes almost match."

"Almost," she agreed.

"I am known as Larry, though my real name is Laurelai. I am twelve years old."

"You look like Larry."

"May I ask your name?"

"You may."

Larry smiled. She had answered his question. "What is your name?"

"I am Zuzana."

"And your age?"

"Thirty-three."

Old enough to be his mother. That did look about right, Squid thought.

"My talent is changing my age, so I don't have to stay twelve, though it is an effort to change far or long. What is yours?"

"I can change places with other people, when I choose."

"Physically?"

"Yes."

"Can you do it from far away?"

"No, only when they are close, when I can see them clearly. Distance interferes with my accuracy."

"Thank you, Zuzana." He stepped to the next portal.

Squid was surprised. All he wanted to do was chat briefly? But maybe he was learning what he could, the better to figure out the best way through. That was sensible. Larry was coming across as a pretty sensible guy, or maybe it was Laurelai who brought the more mature female perspective to it.

The second doorway had a solid young man. "Hello."

"Hello," the man replied.

"I am Larry, with the talent of changing my physical age from twelve to something else, for a while. Who are you, and what is your talent?"

"I am Philip. I can see other places in my mind. I can even show them to other people." A picture flashed over his head, of a tree by a pond.

"That's neat. Can you go to them, sort of the way Zuzana can?"

"No. I just see them. But I can see them from much farther away. They don't have to be close."

"I guess when you're bored you just look at something interesting."

"Yes. Like a nude beach."

Larry smiled. Squid doubted Laurelai was much interested in that sort of thing, but she was being sociable. She was good at it.

He went on to the third portal and introduced himself to the middle-aged man there. "And you?"

"I am Tomas. My talent is to change people's moods."

"Oh? Can you change mine?"

"I could, but I'm not supposed to, because that would interfere with your challenge."

Larry nodded. "That makes sense. Thank you for explaining."

"You're welcome. I hope you make it through, even if it is my job to balk you or at least not to help you figure it out."

"Thank you. I know you have your job to do, just as I have mine. We're like players on opposite teams."

"That's a nice analogy," Tomas said.

Larry went on to the fourth portal, and introduced himself again.

"I am Edvard," the portly man said. "My talent is creating food from thin air. What would you like?"

"I'm not sure I am allowed to eat while tackling the challenge. Would that disqualify me?"

Edvard laughed. "Not at all! You can eat all you want, and stay as long as you like. You just can't pass the challenge unless you figure out how."

"I see. In that case, how about a chocolate cupcake?"

The man lifted his hand and made a little conjuring motion. There was a swirl like a miniature storm, and a piece of chocolate formed, condensing from the air. It was in the shape of a cup, of course.

Edvard extended it, and Larry reached for it. They touched at the curtain. There was a flash, and the cup was in his hand.

He took a bite from the rim. "Excellent chocolate."

"Thank you."

Larry went on to the fifth portal, continuing to eat his cake. He touched the curtain with a finger. It flashed, evidently shocking him, because he jerked his hand back in a hurry. There was no passing through that portal.

Squid wondered what Larry was going to do. He had chatted companionably with the four folk here, getting to know them, but how was that going to get him past this challenge? Squid didn't see how. It was supposed to be tuned to the challenger's nature, so maybe she just wasn't properly understanding it. She hoped he was doing better figuring it out than she was.

Larry finished the cupcake and walked back to the first portal. There was the black-haired woman. She was more than twice his age, but attractive enough in her way.

"Hello again, Zuzana," Larry said.

"Hello again, Larry."

"Philip showed me a pretty scene. Tomas helped clarify the nature of the challenge. Edvard gave me a tasty chocolate cupcake. You gave me nothing except a friendly greeting. Would it be inappropriate to ask a favor of you?"

She frowned. "That depends on the favor."

"A kiss."

She was surprised. "Why would you want a kiss from an older woman? You're a child."

"I think it would be a special experience for me. I am still a boy, yes; no one has kissed me in the man and woman style. You are older, but still an attractive woman. You surely know how to do it better than I do. I can learn from you. I would like to have it to remember you by."

Zuzana gazed at him, taking stock. Squid realized that he had paid her a compliment, and a woman noticed. Larry had complimented Squid similarly when they had met, calling her pretty. She *was* pretty, thanks to her enhancement, but still she remembered with pleasure.

However, inside Larry was Laurelai. Why would *she* compliment a woman? Why would she want a kiss from a woman? This wasn't making much sense.

Zuzana decided. "All right. Approach the screen. We can touch only at the boundary."

Larry stepped close to the screen. Zuzana stood directly opposite him. They were of similar height. Both leaned forward so that their lips could touch. They kissed.

Something happened. Zuzana appeared outside the portal, while Larry appeared inside it. Larry instantly jumped away and disappeared beyond the wall.

"Hey!" Zuzana cried. "What happened?"

"We switched places," Larry answered from out of sight. "Thank you for getting me through."

"But I didn't mean to do that!" she protested. "Something odd startled me, and I changed places involuntarily."

"Yes. Thank you again."

"That kiss! It was a grown woman! But you're a boy."

"So it seems," Larry answered.

"You tricked me!" she said indignantly.

"I figured out the rules of the game," Larry said. "Bye." He was gone.

Now Squid figured it out. Larry had changed during the moment of the kiss, becoming years older, and Laurelai had taken over the mouth so as to make a mature womanly kiss. Startled by the contrast, Zuzana had reacted automatically, switching places. And thereby phased Larry beyond the wall, where he quickly got out of sight so she couldn't exchange back.

That struck Squid as close to genius. What a ploy! Only he could have done it. Because the challenge was attuned to him.

"You're smarter than I took you for," Zuzana said ruefully. "I didn't realize when you said that your real name was Laurelai that that meant you were properly female. I thought it was just some kind of nickname. But congratulations. You certainly fooled me."

And pretty much fooled Squid, too. Her respect for Larry/Laurelai increased a notch or two, maybe even two and a half notches.

She re-tuned her vision, rejoining Larry.

He was walking along a path that seemed to be made of chocolate, as if the cupcake had not been enough. This was spongy, so that his shoes left tracks in it. Chocolate cake!

"I get it," Larry muttered. "A Cake Walk."

Now he looked around. On one side there was a corral containing a donkey; on the other a strip mine. Squid recognized it because she saw people walking though it, and their clothing faded out and dissipated, leaving them bare. They hastily retreated and hurried to a nearby sheet tree, to get sheets to wrap around them. She knew Larry would not venture through that, as he did not like to expose his wrong body; it was an effective barrier. But the donkey did not look at all friendly, so that was another barrier. Larry simply had to proceed straight ahead, letting the path guide him. Crumbs of chocolate cake were now clinging to his shoes. He ignored them and kept moving.

It led to what was evidently the new challenge, a huge pile of books. There looked to be about forty-four of them. There did not seem to be any continuation beyond the pile. This was the Challenge.

Evidently curious, he put out one hand and carefully touched the spine of a single book at the bottom. It popped out of the pile, into his hand— and the rest of the stack tumbled into a messy heap. "Uh-oh," he murmured.

Had he messed up the challenge? Squid wasn't sure. The success or failure of a person should not be based on an unintentional accident. That pile had obviously been primed to collapse.

He glanced at the book he now held. *A Pill For Chameleon*. That had an oddly familiar look, as if she had seen it before. Then she placed it; it was a Xanth history volume, or close to it. The first of the recent series was titled something like that. But what was it doing here? Larry seemed similarly bemused.

"So are you going to stand there all day, stupid? Either read it or dump it. Is that so hard to understand?"

Larry turned to orient on the voice. But there was only the corral in that direction, with the motley donkey. "Are you invisible?" he asked.

"I'm right here in your idiotic line of sight, moron."

Larry took stock. "The donkey?"

"The ass, imbecile. Do you see any other animate creature here? Or are you too distracted by the nude lasses in the other pasture?"

Indeed, at that moment there was a feminine scream as a girl discovered herself in dishabille. Squid knew that that was not a turn-on for Larry, as he was actually a woman, but the donkey had no way to know that.

"You're a talking donkey?" Larry asked.

"No, I'm a silent head of lettuce," the animal said sarcastically. "Heehaw! Yes, I'm a Genie Ass. What else could I be?"

"Genius," Larry said, getting it. "A very smart donkey."

"In sharp contrast to the obtuse humanoid you are."

"You're part of this challenge. You must know the proper way through it."

"Of course I know, dumbbell. I know everything."

"And you're not going to tell me."

"Right. I'm here to watch you make an even worse fool of yourself than you look, challenging as that may be. Hee haw!"

"Don't tell me, let me guess," Larry said. "If I open this book, I'll be drawn into its story-line, regardless whether it's the one I want or need."

"Hee-haw!"

Larry set the book down and picked up another. He read the title. *The Sludge of Magic.*

"Most of the sludge is in your head, cretin."

"And if I open this one, I'll be in its story. Which may or may not be my own story."

"The sludge in your skull suggests it is your story, dope."

Larry smiled. "Surely so. But I think I will check some others first."

Squid was coming to know Larry, and suspected that he was starting to play the genius donkey.

"Why bother, retard? You're going to guess wrong anyway."

"Yes. But I might as well make an informed mistake instead of an ignorant one."

That made the smart ass pause. Squid smiled. The more she saw of Larry, the better she liked him, even if their coming relationship would be a mockery.

Larry set down the book and picked up another. "*Cast-off Roogna*," he read.

"Hee-haw! The way you're about to be cast off."

The next one was *Duck of the Draw*, followed by *Knot Gneiss Monster*, *Knight Bear*, and *Bear Apparent*.

There was another scream from the other pasture. "Maybe those should be *Knight Bare* and *Bare Apparent*," Larry remarked.

"Hee-haw! You're getting it, simpleton. But you have a way to go. I know all the titles."

Larry looked at two more. "*Fear Sale. Just Write*."

"You're getting there," the Ass mumbled, plainly disconcerted.

Squid recognized those ones, because she had been in them. *Fire Sail* and *Jest Right*. Those were almost current.

But what was Larry leading up to, Squid wondered.

Then came *A Tryst of Fate*. The Ass hesitated for half a moment.

Larry pounced on the pause. "Why don't you have a smart ass remark? You know all the titles, you said. Is this one unfamiliar?"

"Of course not, fool. It's just that it hasn't yet been published."

"And this one?" Larry glanced at the title. "*Blanket of a Mind*."

"That neither," the Ass agreed reluctantly.

"And this? *The Crock of Spit*."

The Ass nodded.

Now Larry pounced. "What about this one? *Skeleton Keep*."

"What about it?"

"As I make it from your reactions, genius equine, this is the current one, or very close to it. This must be the story I am in. The one I want to stay in. The book I should open."

The donkey gazed broodily at him. "You're not as dull as you look. But you can't be sure. You still have to gamble."

"And I don't like to gamble," Larry said. "Okay, I'll make a deal with you. Rather than gamble on a likely prospect, I prefer to take a certain one. What do you want in exchange for telling me that this is or is not the book I want?"

"Manure!" the Ass swore. "You've got me cornered."

"Maybe."

"My corral is eaten down to zilch, and I'm thoroughly bored with hay and grain. Get me a load of that cake walk."

Larry squatted, scraped together an armful of chocolate cake, and carried it to the corral fence. He dumped it over. The Ass chomped gleefully on it.

"That's the one," the Ass said between mouthfuls. "*Skeleton Keel*, or whatever. It's the current story."

"Thank you." Then Larry opened the book.

Nothing happened.

Larry looked at the Ass.

"Don't look at me in that tone," the Ass said. "It didn't change because you're already in this story. The other volumes would have launched you into the past or future or unknown space."

Larry nodded. Then the fence on the left faded, and there was a path into the strip mine.

"Uh-oh," Squid murmured. "That's not a route he wants."

Larry gazed at it in dismay, then shook his head, gritted his teeth, and walked along it. What choice did he have?

But this was a different kind of path. It soon twisted up into the air, curving as it did. At the height it was upside down. Would it be possible to stay on it?

Then Squid recognized it. It was a Mobius strip! A route that twisted around until it rejoined itself, only upside down. It wasn't possible to get off such a strip except by jumping off; it was endless on its own terms.

Larry shrugged and started the climb. The moment he did, his clothing started to fuzz. He paused, and the fuzzing stopped. He backed off a step, and his clothing reformed. It was a clothing strip as much as a twisted strip. But if he didn't follow the path, he would wash out of the challenge. This was an emotional demand more than a physical one.

Squid understood. A boy or man might not care if nudity was part of it. But this was a girl in a boy's body. She didn't like exposing it, because it was false. But again, what choice did she really have? The challenges were designed to discourage those who weren't really serious about seeing the Good Magician. The first two had been more mental, this one was more emotional.

Larry nodded as if he heard her thought. Then he focused, and aged himself several years so as to gain the discipline of maturity; the body must contribute something to that. He forged ahead. Squid breathed a sigh of relief. He did have the nerve to do what he had to do, distasteful as it might be.

The clothing fuzzed off, and within three moments he was naked. He was also walking at a steep angle to the ground below, and that was increasing. The path was tilting sideways, and he was walking at right angles to it, so that he was now almost parallel to the ground.

Then Larry, distracted by the problem of clothing, noticed. He came to a sudden halt, looking to the side, which was down. Gravity held him to the strip, independent of the scene outside.

Well, so be it. Larry resumed walking, and soon was walking upside down. The strip did not return all the way to the ground. Now he was walking on its outside curve, his head pointing toward the ground below.

There was a sign planted on the ground, with its print upside down, so as to be legible to a person passing it inverted. Squid twisted her head around to read it. THRICE AROUND AND YOU GO AGROUND. What did that mean? Maybe that the Mobius strip was not endless, and that thrice around it would constitute victory.

Larry read it, and smiled. Now he knew he was on track to handle this challenge.

There was something else. There were parallel tracks outside the Mobius track, passing close to it without intersecting. And on one of them there was a woman running. She was nude, because this was all in the strip mine area, but didn't seem to mind. In fact she looked like a nymph, a perfectly formed young woman who didn't bother with clothing anyway. She was simply jogging along, evidently for exercise. She must have been doing it regularly, because her body was slender and fit. It also flexed and bounced in ways any man would find interesting. That was of course a specialty of nymphs. They lived mainly for one thing: to, as they put it, "celebrate" with fauns, the male of their species. Or any other man they spied.

Squid realized that this was one Hades of a distraction. Because nymphs did not wear panties, they didn't freak out men, but they did usually command men's full attention. It could not be coincidence that she was there. She was there to cause Larry to get off the Mobius strip and forfeit his victory.

But there were two strengths Larry had. One was that he was still a boy, not yet fully into the male mode. The other was that he was really a girl. Girls were not usually as fascinated by nymphs.

Meanwhile, Larry was making his second tour around the loop. One more after this and he would be grounded. That was, finished. All he needed was to stay on track.

But the nymph had other ideas. "Hey, young man!" she called. "Come run with me! We'll have a good time together!"

That was interesting. Usually nymphs did not talk. They merely screamed fetchingly as they kicked their bare legs high and swung their long hair about, all things that for some reason attracted male attention. That suggested that this was a fake nymph, maybe a real woman acting the part. Those who came to the Good Magician normally had to pay a year's service for their Answers, or the equivalent. This girl must be doing that, playing a role in a Challenge.

Larry glanced at her. Squid was nervous. Laurelai had said she didn't like to age her body because it got male notions. Now he was in that range, and the nymph was invoking those notions. He was becoming entirely too interested in her.

But Laurelai evidently realized the danger, and youthened him back to about age ten. He took his eyes off the nymph and walked on, ignoring her. "Bleep!" she swore. Yes, she was definitely an actress; nymphs did not swear.

Larry made the third loop without further distraction, and it deposited him at the door of the castle. He had made it!

The door opened. A nondescript woman stood there. "Hello, Laurelai! I am Wira, Magician Humfrey's daughter-in-law. I will take you to the Designated Wife."

Squid noticed that Wira called him Laurelai. That meant she knew.

"To the what?" Larry asked, momentarily confused.

"A foul-up some time ago caused all five and-a-half of his wives of the past century or so to show up together," Wira explained. "Since it is the Xanthly custom for a man to have only one wife at a time, they take turns. Each month one is designated to run the castle and take care of Humfrey, who is reputed to be not the easiest person to get along with. They say that makes less burden for each of them. I wouldn't know; I like my father-in-law. But it is true that the way he uses Youth Elixir to maintain his age at approximately a hundred years seems off; it might be better if he maintained an age of seventy five years or even younger. Then he might appreciate his wives more."

"Oh," Larry said. "I'm sure the Designated Wife is a very nice lady. But it is really the Good Magician I came to see."

"Oh, you will, in due course. But someone has to make you comfortable in the interim."

"Uh, who is the, the Designated Wife?"

"This month it is the Gorgon."

"The Gorgon! But isn't she—"

"Yes, the one whose direct glance can turn a person to stone. Don't be concerned; she wears a full veil, and she's a nice person." Wira smiled. "Way back when, Humfrey did her a favor, which she appreciated, so later she came to ask him a Question. It was 'Will you marry me?' And he made her do a year's service before giving his Answer."

Larry shook his head. "You're pulling my leg!"

"No, it is true. But there was a reason. He put her to work attending the castle; this was before the prior wives were restored to life. By the time the year was up, she knew both Humfrey and his business very well. So she had time to reconsider her question, and to depart if she concluded that he was not as good a marital prospect as she had thought. But she had learned how to handle his moods, and was confidant that this was really what she wanted. So when he agreed to marry her, she was well satisfied. But she is also satisfied now to share the burden with the other wives. The six of them are excellent friends."

"Six? But before you said—"

"Five and a half. It seems that his very first love, when he was young, was MareAnn, whose talent was summoning equines. They met in Xanth Year 948. But though she loved him, she feared that her inevitable loss of innocence in marriage would cause her to lose her ability to summon unicorns. So she held off, and he married Dara Demoness instead, who had absolutely no problem with innocence. She hadn't been close to it for centuries, if ever. Then, much later, in the year 1090, MareAnn spent a tour in Hell, not as punishment, for she was a good girl, but as a holding place. She concluded that Hell was hard on innocence, and she had little of that left to lose, so then she was ready to marry him. So they had a quick, small ceremony, barely half of a normal one. So she considers herself a half wife of 142 years, the time between their meeting and their marriage. She is a full person, just not a complete wife."

Larry shook his head. "And I thought my life was complicated!"

"Not complicated, Laurelai, merely difficult. Every person is unique in his or her own way."

Meanwhile, they had been wending through the castle, and now were in a pleasant chamber where a tall veiled woman awaited them. "Mother Gorgon, this is Laurelai, a querent for the Good Magician."

"Of course, dear," the Gorgon replied. "Tell him she is here." Then she faced Larry. Her veil covered all of her face, especially the eyes. "Fear not; my veil hasn't slipped in years."

Larry froze.

The Gorgon laughed, and the little serpents that formed her hair seemed to laugh with her. They looked cute rather than frightening. "I was teasing. It has never slipped; my little serpents make sure of that. I am glad to meet you, Laurelai. I am familiar with the problem of relating to others, as I really can't look anyone in the eye. Please sit down; Wira will bring refreshments."

Larry sat, and she sat opposite him, leaning forward conversationally. Squid was impressed; her decolletage was not nearly as well covered as her face, and it was finely formed. She was an extremely well endowed figure of a woman, despite whatever her age was. "I need to explain that Humfrey's formal Answers sometimes require some interpretation, but are always accurate and meaningful. I had some difficulty myself, when I came to him with my own Question."

The refreshments arrived: boot rear and peppermint patty cakes. The drink that gave a person's behind a boot, and the cakes that gave the tongue a twinge.

Now Larry smiled, beginning to feel more at ease. "Wira told me."

"So when he tells you to get an alien girlfriend, this is not a dismissal of your case. He knows your nature. If you follow his directions, you will obtain your answer, and be the better for it, as I was for mine."

Larry looked at her. "You know about that?"

The Gorgon smiled, and it was most attractive through the veil. "Humfrey is the Magician of Information, and some of it rubs off on the castle personnel. At any rate, sometimes his Answers lead not to the solutions the querents seek, but to the solutions they really need, which may be rather different. So maintain an open mind; things are not necessarily what they seem."

"All I want is a body to match my nature!"

"Exactly."

Squid couldn't blame Larry for being confused; Squid was confused too. The folk of this castle seemed to know Laurelai's situation, but were hinting that the solution he wanted was not inevitably the one he would get.

"I hope my problem can be solved," Larry said uncertainly.

"Time will tell. Meanwhile, Squid is a fine girl, for all that she is an alien cuttlefish. Give her a fair chance and you will surely be rewarded."

Now Squid froze. They were talking about her! As if her coming association with Larry would not be entirely a pose similar to that of Santo and Noe. Yet how could it ever be real?

"Maybe in time I will understand," Larry said diplomatically.

"You surely will," the Gorgon agreed.

Wira reappeared. "The Good Magician will see Laurelai now."

She led Larry up a tightly winding stairway to a cramped office filled mostly by a huge open tome. Behind it sat an old gnome-like man wearing huge spectacles, the famed Good Magician.

"This is Laurelai, the querent," Wira said.

The gnome looked up. "Of course," he said gruffly. "Come in, querent."

Larry stepped into the tiny office, so that he stood right before the giant book. "I just want to know how I can—"

"Of course," the magician said impatiently. "For your Service you will join the crew of Fibot, the flying craft with the fire sail, and serve there as much of a year as is needful. You will befriend the seeming girl Squid and call her your girlfriend."

"But I don't want a girlfriend!" Larry protested. "I will want a boyfriend, when the time comes."

But the Magician seemed not to hear him. "I say this advisedly: Squid is the most important person you will ever encounter. You must support her completely, and protect her to the best of your ability, even if it puts your life in peril. That is your true assignment."

Larry opened his mouth for another protest, but then stifled it. "Yes, of course."

What? He was agreeing to cater to Squid, even though he knew their relationship was to be more pretense than actual? Because he was really a girl and she was really a cuttlefish. A girl dating a cuttlefish could be reckoned as a joke. It could not be serious. Yet it seemed he was now taking it seriously. Why?

Then she saw something subtle. The five siblings were able to spy the Demoness Fornax when she was near, because they were very close to her emotionally. In fact they loved her. They knew her tiny mannerisms. Squid knew that Fornax was using Laurelai as a secret host for some mysterious purpose. She knew that Fornax and Laurelai were having a private dialogue; that was what the subtle hints suggested.

Fornax must have told Laurelai to agree to what Humfrey was saying. To treat Squid as a very special girlfriend. Laurelai must be telling Larry, who was really a shell operating the male body. So without mentioning the Demoness, Larry was accepting the assignment.

But why was Squid so important? She saw no reason. She was different, yes, because she was not the little girl she appeared to be, but that had not changed. Everyone who knew her knew her nature. Apart from that, she was just nobody.

Then Humfrey looked directly at her. *He could see her!* "The fate of the universe depends on you, Squid," he said.

He was talking to her? While Larry remained frozen in place? Even though she wasn't really here, but was just tuning in on Larry? She had to be dreaming.

"No, you are awake," he said. "Now stop with the childish denial and get with the program. You have a vital job to do."

He could see her, and was telling her that her role was phenomenally important. It seemed crazy, but he was the Magician of Information, and she had to believe him. Somehow she really was the key to whatever was happening.

"Exactly," he agreed.

Squid raised her hands in mock surrender. She would do her best, even if she didn't understand it.

Then Humfrey returned his attention to Larry. "Fibot is sailing here now. Be ready to board." And he turned his tired old eyes back to the giant Book of Answers before him. The querent had been dismissed.

Larry came out of stasis, nodded and backed out of the study. Wira was there. "I will show you to the courtyard where the fire boat will dock."

And Squid shut off the vision, returning to her own awareness. She was on her bed, where she had been lying for safety while tuning into the other scene.

She got up and went to the porthole. There was the Good Magician's Castle, ahead and below. They were slanting smoothly down to land in its courtyard.

She was about to welcome Larry aboard, officially, and become his dancing partner and girlfriend, so that they had seeming reason to stay together without arousing suspicion. In an adventure that seemed to be largely limited to children. If it was so important, why weren't the adults handling it? Nothing was making sense.

She felt as if she were floating in a cloud of strangeness. What was wrong with this picture? She wished she knew.

But what could she do, except play it through, like any other role? She was the protagonist, the viewpoint character. There had to be more of a reason than she had seen so far. If she couldn't really believe it, she could pretend. At least she was good at pretending.

Chapter 5

DANCE

Squid climbed to the sailboat section as the fire sail boat landed. Win turned off the breeze, and Firenze took down the sail. Tending the burning sail came naturally to him, because of his hot hands. Ula was there, lending moral support. When she had brought Firenze aboard the sail had assumed a heart shape; it knew what was what.

The others came topside to watch, including Dell and Nia. They knew this was important.

Squid made herself look exceptionally pretty for the occasion. Then she jumped over the gunwale and landed in the castle courtyard, her simulated skirt flaring nicely to show her legs. Larry stood there, admiring the vessel. Beyond him stood Wira and the veiled Gorgon.

She walked up close to him. "Let's get this over with," she murmured. "Only in public, I promise."

"Thanks," he murmured back.

Then she put her arms around him, drew him in close, and kissed him solidly on the mouth. She knew that no little hearts would appear, but that wasn't the point. The point was that they were now officially a couple.

They finished the public kiss and separated slightly. And stared.

There were no hearts, but there were multiple miniature question marks surrounding them. Slowly they drifted upward and outward, dissipating.

"I never saw that before," the Gorgon said, surprised.

The faces on the deck were similarly bemused. No one else had seen it before either. Maybe it was the first time a misbodied girl child had kissed an alien cuttlefish child. Still, Squid wondered why there were any little symbols at all. Did their appearance mean something? If so, what?

"Sorry to put you through this confusion," Squid said as she guided him to the boat. "It seems to be a complicated time."

"Actually I'm glad to be with you," Larry said. "Because I don't have to explain myself to you, you have a better notion what's going on than I do, and you are familiar with the fire sail boat as I am not. I am happy to leave myself in your hands."

"I will show you around. Then we should talk. There are things you may not like."

"I don't like being in this body. The rest is incidental."

"Maybe."

He halted before they got on the boat. "What do I need to know, that I won't like?"

"I've been watching you. It's a new talent I learned of after we met before. I can tune in on folk who mention my name, or even sometimes if they only think of me. I can see what they do and hear what they say. I saw you do the challenges, and talk with Wira and the Gorgon, and the Good Magician."

Larry smiled. "He mentioned you."

"Yes, I heard that too. It seems I'm the protagonist for this story, so I have to know everything that relates to it. So you have no real privacy."

"So when I poop or pee, you can see?"

Squid was surprised. "I suppose I could. But I'm not out to embarrass you. I just want you to know that I may be with you more than you like. It's not anything I chose; I'm stuck with it."

"I'm embarrassed just being in this body. So if that's it, I can handle it."

"Then let's board the boat." She showed him how to climb over the gunwale, flashing her legs again in the process. That was incidental fun. Then she commenced the cycle of introductions. He was duly impressed by the people, the animals, and the boat itself. By the time they were done, Fibot was on its way through the sky.

"Now you can have your own stateroom," she said, "or you can bunk with me. I used to bunk with Myst, but she got a boyfriend and moved in with him."

"With you," he said immediately. "If that's permitted."

"It is. Fibot has its own rules, and couples can share quarters."

"Even children?"

"Yes. It's not as if children can actually do anything that violates the Adult Conspiracy. We know; we've tried."

He smiled. "Children do. But I can't perform any private natural function without straining the Conspiracy. I hate the whole wrong-body business."

"You're a special case," she agreed. "As I am, albeit a different case."

They settled into her suite. "The next thing is the dance," Squid said. "I hope you like square dancing and its cousins. We'll be partners."

"Actually I do. There's a kind of freedom of expression in dancing that appeals to me."

"Dell and Nia are conducting classes this week. Next week we'll go on tour with Magnus and Jess."

"With who? I don't remember meeting them."

"You didn't meet them. They're taking time off between tours. They're in love."

"Love seems to be going around. I noticed Firenze and Ula."

"Children can love," Squid said a bit defensively. "They com, com, complete each other." She had stumbled, trying to get the term.

Larry smiled. "I think the word you are looking for is complement. One has what the other lacks."

"Yes. He's a hothead but she has cooling hands. He's my brother and she's my friend; I know how hard it was for him, until he met Ula, and how lonely she was. They're perfect for each other, regardless of age."

"I'm sure. But I wasn't disparaging young love. I've had crushes myself." His lips quirked. "On boys."

"And you're not gay. I know. I hope you get your body change, so you can finally be yourself. But meanwhile we have to fake it, for the sake of this mysterious mission."

"If it gets me my body, it's worth it, whatever it is."

"I hope so," she agreed warily.

"I fear you have similar misgivings to mine. We fear the unknown."

"We do." She quirked a smile. "We may actually be kindred spirits despite our physical differences."

"If only I were a boy and you were a girl," he agreed.

Then Santo knocked. "We have met before," Larry told him.

"Yes. As you know, my relationship with Noe parallels yours with Squid. Both are associations of convenience, with a foundation of mutual respect. But my concern at the moment is something else."

"Let's have it," Squid said with resignation. "Your concerns are never easy."

He smiled acknowledgment. "We finally have all five siblings together again, along with five non-sibling associates. We need to have a conference, this time including the others."

"We haven't had one of those in years, even with just the five of us."

"Yes. But we are approaching what may be the most significant mission yet. We need to be prepared."

"Last year we stopped Ragna Roc from taking Xanth over and making it his personal kingdom. What could be more significant than that?"

"This could."

Squid sighed. "You do realize that it might not work with half of us being non-siblings?"

"I believe it will work. It has to work."

"And you do realize that there may be a hidden adult among us?" she asked, carefully not looking at Larry. Because Fornax was keeping Laurelai company.

"That is why I believe it *will* work."

"I'm sure I have no idea what you're talking about," Larry said. He was not allowed to speak of the presence of Fornax.

Santo's smile was grim. "And may it remain that way." He glanced at Squid. "Are you ready?"

She was shocked. "*Now?*"

Santo nodded. "I have already spoken to the others. I will join Noe now. Hold Larry's hand when you strike your match."

"I will."

Santo departed.

"What is this conference?" Larry asked. "What does it have to do with matches?"

"Each sibling has a match. It strikes not flame but position. It will take us to the Playground."

He shook his head. "It seems that I still have much to learn."

"All the non-siblings do. I will see you through it."

"Thank you." He was bemused, again.

Squid pulled a mundane wooden match from her nonexistent hair. She took his hand, then struck the match on the wall. There was no spark.

Suddenly they were in the Playground. There were swings, slides, turntables, and paths for playing tag. "We seem to be the first to arrive," Squid said, letting his hand go and putting the match away.

"The Playground," Larry said, looking around. "For children. We were teleported here. Exactly where is it?"

"It is folded up into a miniature bag that Santo keeps in his room, but to us it seems wide open. All part of the magic. Mainly, it's a private place for us to gather."

Firenze and Ula appeared a few feet away. "Hello, Squid and Larry," Ula said brightly as Firenze put away his match. She had been here before, so wasn't surprised.

"Hello, both," Squid replied.

Ula glanced at Firenze. "Do we have time for a kiss?"

"We'll make time," he said. They kissed, and more little hearts orbited them. Their love remained fresh.

Then Win and Data appeared. "Blip, I wish we had boyfriends," Win said, putting away her match.

"Maybe we can find some here," Data said, looking around.

Myst and Piton appeared. "Wow!" he said as she put her match away.

"If I got on that swing, and swung high, my magic panty would show," Myst said. "Too bad we don't have time for that naughtiness."

"You are an infernal little tease."

"Yes," she agreed as she twitched her hip in a way that made her skirt rise almost enough. "I love it."

Mainly, Squid knew, Myst loved playing eighteen when she was only nine. But it was evident that Piton enjoyed the game too. Flirtation was fun at any age.

Then Santo and Noe arrived. "This brings memories," she said as he put away his match.

Santo was all business. "We are all here? Gather round. Form a circle, couples together."

"We're not a couple," Win said. "We're just friends."

"You're a pair," Santo said. "That will do."

They formed the circle, facing inward. "We all know each other," Santo said. "But for the benefit of the non-siblings, a brief review. The Land of Xanth, on an alternate track, found itself in a situation that doomed it to extinction, about forty-five years hence. There were only five survivors, children who were rescued by Astrid Basilisk and Demoness Fornax, who took them fifty years into the past and arranged for them to be adopted into five families. We five consider ourselves to be siblings despite having no family connection to each other because we share that lost realm and our closeness to Astrid and Fornax; no one else matches those associations. We are an odd bunch, consisting of a hothead, a gay boy, an alien cuttlefish, a windy girl, and a girl who can dissolve into mist. We all love each other, and we love Astrid and Fornax; that will never change."

He paused to glance around. The other four siblings, including Squid, nodded. They were in complete agreement; there was no incomplete about it.

"That does not exclude other relationships," Santo continued. "Firenze has found love with Ula, I have a relationship of convenience with Noe, Squid has one with Larry, Win is friends with Data, and Myst is playing girlfriend to Piton, knowing that when they grow older it may become a true romance. These relationships are close enough so that we consider them virtual siblings too, for this particular purpose. For example the fact that my relationship with Noe is a fake romance does not mean we are not close. I love her and she loves me. We just don't mean to marry."

He paused again. There was no dissension. Squid trusted that he would get to the point soon.

"We discovered also that when we get together and focus, we can achieve a conference that clarifies our situation in a way nothing else can. We can do it only when all five of us are present, and when we all decide. We have not done it recently because only three or four of us have been together at a time. Now something huge is looming; we don't know what it is, only that it concerns the whole of Xanth yet is limited to children. All of our powers have been amplified so that we are better able to handle what we may encounter. The mystery especially relates to Squid, who is the protagonist for this story and the most important person of us all."

Squid opened her mouth to protest, but he stifled her with a caution-ary glance. So she remained silent. Larry squeezed her hand reassuringly, and she appreciated that.

"So now we will enter a conference, trusting that we are unified enough to do it, and that it will clarify our mission. We need to know the right course, even if we don't comprehend all its details. We should have a better under-standing when we emerge." He glanced around. "Are there any questions?"

Larry spoke. "About Squid: she is tormented by this importance attrib-uted to her, which she did not seek, and has no idea how to handle it. Can we help her?"

Squid's feelings were mixed. She normally preferred to speak for her-self, but Larry had phrased her concern perfectly, from a third party per-spective, and she did appreciate that.

"Only by completely supporting her," Santo answered. "When there is anything you think she should be aware of, when you are away from her, speak her name, and she will then be able to tune in on you so that she can see and hear you, though not influence you. That is a new talent she has been given. Then briefly state your concern, knowing that she hears. She will generally not be able to acknowledge you, but will surely appreciate your input."

Now the non-siblings nodded. They understood.

"What are we here for?" Data Bone asked. "I thought it was just for a private place to talk without being overheard by adults, but this is sound-ing more complicated."

Santo smiled, as did the other siblings. "It *is* more complicated. We call it a conference, but that is only approximate. A better description might be a dance."

"I love dancing! But that's not quite it, either, is it?"

"The thing about a classic dance is that every motion is choreographed and every dancer is essential to the whole. If even one dancer misses a step, it can be ruined. But when every part is correct, it can be beautiful, a work of art. So while each individual role may be small, the larger effect can be emergent."

"Can be what?"

Santo made a third of a smile. "I apologize for using a rare term. An emergent phenomenon is something that appears only when certain conditions are met, such as a thought appearing when a brain is activated. It can't exist without the brain, but it is not the brain or anything that can be physically classified; it is new and different and sometimes wonderful."

"The beauty of the perfect dance is emergent," Data said, getting it. She did a little twirl that flashed her legs and was indeed lovely. Squid saw that Firenze, the one normal and unrelated male here, was impressed. So was Myst, but negatively. Flashed legs counted. "So this special conference is like a nice dance. We'll discover more than we anticipated. Thank you."

Others nodded. They understood dancing, and the beauty that emerged from a good and well performed dance. If this was like that, okay.

"In the past we have all touched each of the others," Santo said after a moment. "That is less feasible with ten of us, so we will try it simply by holding hands around the circle. Do not break the chain."

They linked hands. Squid didn't have hands, technically, but she had spent years emulating them, and no one had ever complained. Larry was on her right, and Santo on her left.

"Focus on nirvana," Santo said.

"On what?" Data asked. She was apt at voicing questions others had but didn't ask. That could be useful, Squid realized.

Another third of a smile. "Generic heaven. A state of quiet mental bliss."

They focused. It was plain that the non-siblings were skeptical, but they were doing their best to play along.

And it came, a slow epiphany. The playground around them faded out, and Squid felt as if she were floating into a perfect sky formed of pleasant pastel colors with a gently musical background. She remained aware of her companions on either side, overlapping their bodies as they became misty, and their minds, sharing their thoughts, merging with them to form greater forms and greater thoughts. Then outward to include the ones beyond, Win on the right, Noe on the left, and on around the circle until it was complete. Then, like a flower opening with ten petals, they emerged into the utter beauty of the whole. Together; body, mind, and soul. Self no longer existed, just the larger entity, the glorious flower. Then on to a greater reality, extending to the realm beyond, with more bodies, more minds, more souls, and more beauty. Rapture! They had become the universe.

And it was indeed a dance. They were unified as never before, and synchronized, evolving into new wonder, forming perfect flowers with color, tune, motion, and concept spreading into ecstasy.

And on into weird but nice enlightenment. Squid drifted across the universe, across time, delighted by its every nuance.

Then, somehow, she jumped the track. She got lost beyond the unity and drifted by herself. She felt no alarm, but knew she was in a foreign region.

She oriented on something familiar. In a timeless moment she identified it: her male cousin who had been invited but prevented from joining their visit to future Xanth by a complication of schedule, to his serious disappointment. He was thinking of her, and her talent picked up on it. Actually he was sleeping, dreaming of her with mixed feelings: envy of her visit, relief that he had missed it, and so not perished in the lost land, and grief for her death.

But I did not die, Cuttle, she told him. *I traveled fifty years into the past, and survived.*

It's a good thing I'm dreaming, he replied. *Because that is unbelievable anywhere else.*

She had to laugh. *You are dreaming,* she agreed. *But it is nevertheless true. I no longer exist in your time, but I exist in my own. I'm glad you didn't come, though, because only five of us were saved, and I can't be sure you would have been among them.*

And I am glad for you, he thought. *Yet how is it you are here as an active mind, when always before in my dreams you have been inert?*

I am visiting via a, well, a kind of commune. A mergence of minds. I drifted. I should get back before they miss me.

You drifted into your present future? On another track? To visit me?

So it seems, she agreed.

Accepting that, I am sensing something, he thought. *Something I must tell you, even if you are not really here.*

What is that?

There is danger. A colossal threat. Somehow I sense it as I attune to your reality whatever it is.

There it was again. *Danger?*

You must escape it. No, you can't escape it. You must stop it. I don't know how, but it all depends on you, Squid.

Everywhere she went, it seemed, there were warnings of great danger, coupled with the news that only she could deal with it. But never any details. *I need to know more.*

I don't know any more. But I fear for you.

And that, it seemed was it. *I must go, Cuttle. But it was nice visiting you.*

He laughed. *When I wake up, I won't believe any of it. But I wish you well, cousin.*

Then she lost her footing, as it were, and found herself drawn back to the group mind, and to the playground. The conference was over. She had missed much of it, alas.

"It was a wonderful dance. I love you," Larry said, hugging her.

"You love everyone," she replied. "And everything. That's the way it is with a conference."

"Now I know that we are following the correct course. But we don't know the outcome."

"We don't," she agreed ruefully.

Santo squeezed her other hand. "Where were you?"

"I drifted, and got lost, then talked with my sleeping cousin Cuttle in the future. He was thinking of me, so I oriented on him. We were able to have a two-way dialogue, maybe because he was dreaming."

"And did you learn anything useful?"

She grimaced in the human manner. "Nothing useful. Just that there is great danger that only I can handle. I already knew that."

"Yet, if the news spread even to your future realm, that authenticates it."

"That and a stink horn would make a significant smell."

He smiled, then addressed the others. "That was a conference. Now you know its nature. They aren't all identical, but they do enable us to share identities and come to know each other better. Now we are assured that we are doing what we should, even if we don't properly understand it."

"We do," Data agreed. "That was some experience! I feel closer to everyone."

"It is the unity of siblings," Win said. "Now the rest of you share it."

"This was mainly a demonstration," Santo said. "To be sure we can do it with our larger group. When there is a crisis, we may do it again."

"Now let's go home," Firenze said. "I want to sleep on this."

"We all do," Piton agreed. "How do we get out of here? Strike another match?"

Myst shook her head. "The matches don't work that way. Santo will have a way."

"I do," Santo agreed. "I will make a hole."

He made a hole. One by one they entered it, and emerged in his closet where the Playground purse was stored. Squid saw others looking at the tiny purse in wonder, because it seemed impossible that they could have fit inside it. Actually the Playground was full size: it was the purse that connected to it, a miniature locator. They had not actually been inside the purse.

The others went to their cabins, and Larry and Squid retired to their own cabin. "It is an education to know you and the siblings," he said. "I mean that in a positive way. As a group you have a more challenging history than I do."

"That's why we understand you. We're all different in different ways; we understand difference."

"If I had to remain in this body, I believe you are one I would prefer to stay with."

It was a compliment. But she hoped to grow up to find a man of her own kind. "But we do hope to solve your problem, along with our own."

"We do."

Next day they gathered for dance instruction. "This time we learn the Triangle Dance," Nia said. "I learned it in my youth, but it has never been widely circulated and is virtually unknown by the general public. That means it should be new to most audiences, and that is fine. It's a kind of humorous interlude, a change of pace while the scene is being set for another dance. It should make the audience laugh."

"What's funny about it?" Data asked.

"For one thing, half the dancers are veiled so that their partners don't recognize them, only their gender. They will guess wrong twice before getting it right. When they get it wrong, something spectacularly awkward happens to them."

Three couples set up for the practice: Firenze and Ula, Piton and Myst, and Larry and Squid. The boys were in suits, the girls in identical pretty dresses that emphasized their outlines: slender bodies, smooth legs, richly curling hair. The hair was actually wigs, yellow, red, and black, all similarly luxurious. They were really quite striking. The boys wore small berets of similar colors, so it was clear who belonged with whom.

The girls stood in a triangle, facing outward, while the boys danced around the outside. Then the boys had to face outward while the girls donned thick veils. At this point the audience would be mystified: what kind of a dance was this?

Then the girls exchanged wigs, so that the blonde became a redhead, the redhead became a brunette, and the brunette became black haired. Then they changed places. If the boys thought they knew their partners by their hair or place, they were mistaken. But the audience saw the change, and knew which was which if they cared to keep track. Squid loved this: she didn't even have to fake her hair, because the flowing wig did it for her.

Now the boys turned around to face the girls. "The only way to identify a partner is by a kiss," Nia said, as if announcing for the audience. "They must kiss and say yes or no: is this their true partner? They will say yes, and be wrong and pay the penalty. Kisses are not nearly as identifying as we like to think."

The music started. The boys danced solo in a counterclockwise circle around the maiden triangle, while the girls gestured with their arms and made balances with their legs. Then the music stopped, and the boys halted in their places, turning to face the girls opposite them.

"Kiss the girls," Nia said.

The three boys stepped forward, took the girls in their arms and kissed them, the yellow beret with the blonde and so on. Firenze kissed Squid, and even through the thick veil she felt his hot lips on hers and thrilled to the experience. She felt guilty for that, because she knew he was Ula's boyfriend; it was like cheating. It was all in the mini drama, and they were actors who routinely did such things, but still it was a boy-girl kiss and she thought she shouldn't have feelings. They were siblings! She wondered whether the others had similar misgivings.

Then they stood back. "Right or wrong?" Nia asked.

The boys pondered. The matchings were wrong, by design, but theoretically they didn't know it. They each held a thumb up: right.

"Wrong," Nia said.

The three girls promptly lifted small cups of colored water over the boys' heads and poured them out. Streams of fluid flowed out, far more than mere cups could ever hold, because they were connected to tubes that ran down the girls' arms to a hidden tank, and thoroughly doused the boys. It wasn't real water; it was a liquid-looking thin jelly that did not soak them. But from a distance it looked like a deluge.

The boys seemed ashamed as they brushed themselves off and resumed the dance. The audience was surely laughing.

The music stopped again. Again they had to kiss and tell, this time with different partners. Again they were wrong. Piton kissed Squid, and the naughty boy even pinched her bottom, and she liked it, feeling twice as guilty as before. Would Myst be mad?

But of course Larry was kissing one wrong girl, and then the other wrong one. Were they reacting as naughtily? Should Squid be mad at Larry? It was confusing.

This time the girls held mock stink horns over the boys' heads and squeezed them vigorously. There came that foul smelling noise, and filthy brown smoke gushed out. The boys went into paroxysms of coughing and retching, hamming it up, though the smoke was actually an innocuous fake. Gales of audience laughter, for sure.

The third time they finally got it right. They kissed the girls, and Squid was happy to be back with Larry even if their whole relationship was pretense. Then the boys were rewarded when the veils were thrown off and the girls stepped up for swings. Audience applause.

They all agreed it was one great little dance. "And kissing all the girls wasn't bad either," Piton said.

"But if you pinch me again, I'll make you eat the stink horn," Ula told him severely. "The only one who gets to pinch my bottom for real is Firenze." They all laughed, but it was fair warning. Piton was being too free with other boy's girls.

"Now an announcement," Nia said. "Picka and Dawn Bone have invited Dell and me to visit with them for a week in Caprice Castle, and we have accepted. Magnus and Jess will be there with us too. This is nominally to visit Picka's skeleton relatives on Skeleton Key, which is one of the Sometime Islands, but more just to give us temporary freedom from the incessant burden of children and responsibilities. It's a kind of trial separation for you children too: you are all getting older, verging on maturity, and can practice for the adulthood that will be upon you all too soon. Any questions?"

Santo smiled. "Who will be in charge of the menagerie?"

"Tata Dogfish and the peeve will run the boat, which isn't going anywhere. It will be parked in the sky above the remaining island in Xanth Proper. You children should be able to get along without direction, exercising personal responsibility. The dread Adult Conspiracy still holds: we know you will not do anything we might disapprove of, even if you do make the attempt. If there is a problem, you can vote on how to handle it. We believe you will be up to the chore."

"What will we do?" Data asked. "And I don't mean fighting the Conspiracy. How do we keep from being bored to death?"

"You will dance, dear. We expect you to be thoroughly practiced in all the dances listed in Tata's repertoire. The show tour will start the week we return."

The others nodded. There was a difference between merely learning the dances, and performing them well before audiences. They would have plenty to keep them busy.

"Good enough," Nia concluded. "We go to intercept Skeleton Key tomorrow. Get a good night's rest."

Back in their cabin, Squid and Larry exchanged a significant glance. "They don't know," she said, awed.

"The adults don't know," he agreed. "They think we'll be alone because they want to relax for a week without noisy demanding children."

"This is scary!"

"It is," he agreed.

Squid nerved herself and spoke of another matter. "I hope you won't be mad, but when I kissed the other boys, in the Triangle Dance, I, well, I felt something. And when Piton pinched my bottom, I, I actually liked it."

"I'm not mad. Remember, I was kissing other girls, too. I must admit they were intriguing. I didn't dare pinch anyone's rear, though."

"I'm actually not a girl at all, not a human one. My bottom is just a pair of bunched octopus arms, shielded by the thick skirt. But he was treating me like a real live girl, and I think I felt the way a real girl would."

"He was treating you like an abused girl! Ula won't stand for more of that. You should have slapped his face."

Squid laughed ruefully. "Not in a public dance. The audience couldn't see his hand, but they would see mine."

"Well, when Ula mentions it again, as I'm sure she will, you can say 'Me too,' and that should warn him off."

She nodded. "I'll keep that in mind."

"Meanwhile, I had my own reactions to kissing those girls. I'm a girl myself, as you know. But they acted almost as if it was real, and I almost felt, well, the same. It's weird."

"Weird," Squid agreed. "Maybe they forgot, or don't really understand about you. You look like a boy, so that's how they treat you."

"Maybe. But my point is that just as you reacted, to your surprise, to real kissing, so did I. The male body has its own reactions. It likes kissing girls even if I don't. The mask sometimes becomes real."

"We are well matched," Squid said. "We both understand about pretending."

"It feels like a kind of dance. A dance is not real life: it's a kind of artistic pretense, but it does have its rules and its pleasures."

"We're dancing around the monstrous threat," she said. "We can't say it so we have to glide around it, but maybe the artistry is there."

Larry hesitated. "I, this may seem crazy, but suppose we, well—"

"I think I know where you're going. The Nirvana conference made a difference. Let's try dancing as if we mean it."

"You do understand."

They came together and embraced. Then they danced a few steps, marvelously coordinated though there was no announcer calling out the moves. He held her as though he were a man, and she matched him as if she were a woman. Then they paused, gazing into each other's eyes. Then they kissed, holding it. Then Squid caught his hand and put it on her bottom. That broke them both up laughing, and they split apart.

But the dance had meant something. So had the kiss. Their public kisses had been fakes, but this one was real.

Did that mean their relationship was becoming real, too? Squid shied away from the thought.

Next day Fibot sailed to the chain of islands called the Keys. There was Caprice Castle sitting on an island the shape of a human skull. That would be Skeleton Key.

Picka and Dawn Bone were standing outside the castle. They came to join Dell and Nia, shaking hands and embracing like old friends, as perhaps they were. Then Magnus and Jess joined them. The assembled children just watched. It seemed that the skeleton relatives would join them after the Sometime Island phased to wherever it went when not in Xanth Proper.

"Be good, kids!" Nia called as she waved.

"We'll try," Ula called back, speaking for all of them.

Then the six adults entered the castle. The children boarded the boat. Win took her place at the helm, Data beside her, and blew at the fire sail Firenze raised; the craft angled into the air.

Squid took Larry's hand, nervously squeezing it. She saw Ula and Myst and Noe doing the same with their companions, and even Win's free hand was holding Data's. They all knew that something much worse than a week on their own was about to happen. But all they could do about it was dance.

The boat hovered above the island. Then the island faded out. It did not move, it simply ceased to be there. It was gone, and Caprice Castle and the six adults with it. They would return in a week, but their disappearance was eerie.

Squid shuddered.

Chapter 6

CRISIS

They got together with Tata Dogfish and the peeve. "We need to be sure we're on the same page," Santo said. "Do you two know what is going on with us children?"

Tata's robot screen flickered. "We know that something big is in the offing," the bird said. "But we can't get a line on what it is. You kids have been coupling up and dancing up a storm, but we think you've been hiding something."

"I think that now the adults are gone, we can be more open about it," Santo said. "Something huge is set to happen, and we need to know what it is, but it is hiding from the adults. So it is up to us children to tackle it, because it is important and we can't afford to just ignore it. We are peripherally aware of it, but don't know who or what is behind it."

Tata's screen flashed. "That is consistent with our information," the peeve said. "What else?"

"Squid is the protagonist for this story. She is also the most important person in it."

Both dogfish and peeve were startled. "But she's not even human," the peeve protested.

Santo smiled. "And the pair of you find being inhuman objectionable?"

Everyone laughed.

"Okay, you got us there," the peeve said.

"So at this point you two will probably learn about this matter when we do," Santo said. "Stay alert. We don't know from what direction it will come, but it's incipient."

"We will."

But nothing happened that day. They practiced their dancing, shoring up any weaknesses they found, then had the dinner that Nia had programmed for the Fibot scullery, and retired.

"I hate this," Squid said as she shooed dust bunnies out from under the bed. They hopped away, annoyed. "I wish whatever it is would just happen and be done with it."

"So do I."

"I know we're not really a couple, but would you hold me while we sleep?"

"I am nervous too. Your nearness comforts me as much as mine comforts you."

"Thank you." They held each other and slept.

Next day they practiced line dances, which required no partners except when they split into couples for spot demonstrations. Tata Dogfish flashed instructions, and the peeve translated them. Some lines required high kicking; both boys and girls did it, but the assumption was that the audience would watch mainly the girls because of their flaring skirts. There were intricate foot motions: in some, like the pot-te-bah, the feet hardly seemed to touch the floor. They did intricate steps perfectly synchronized, knowing that more than their magic talents had been quietly upgraded. They were becoming remarkably sophisticated performers.

No threat manifested. Squid was almost disappointed. "Where is this huge danger?"

"It's lurking," Larry said. "I can feel it."

"So can I. But it doesn't strike; it just sits there and torments us."

"Maybe it wants to wear us down, so it will be worse when it does strike."

"We must not let down our guard," Santo said. "It may strike when too many of us cease to be concerned about it."

Next day, they practiced couple dances. There were a number of these, and some of their motions were intricate, with the boys lifting the girls high and slinging them around so that their skirts flared and their legs showed. "We're going to be terrors when we grow up into big girls," Noe said, satisfied. "We really know how to show off our legs."

It was true. They were already close, and the dances brought them right to the verge of the Adult Conspiracy. But what was the larger point of it? Squid wondered. How did dancing relate to the monstrous unseen threat? How did it make her, Squid, so infernally important? She still was not finding much, if any, sense in it.

"I envy you the ability to look innocently sexy," Larry said. "If I had my female body, I would age it into young maturity and flash the whole audience into a freak."

"More fun," Squid agreed.

"I am counting on the Good Magician delivering. I want to use what I am learning to flash the whole world into submission."

"What. Even the women?"

"Myst's magic panties can do it. Why not mine, then?"

"Good point."

"But I just want to have the body, even if I never flash it. I just know it will be more comfortable."

"Maybe it's dangerous to relax," Squid told Larry one evening. "But I'm tired of being constantly afraid. How about this: we take turns. One night I worry while you relax, and next night you worry while I sleep?"

"You are making sense," he said. "Sometimes I almost regret that we can never be a true couple. You are dismayingly practical."

So they alternated nights, and that helped. Squid still didn't like the constant tension, but she was learning to handle it.

On the seventh day Santo had an announcement. "Class, we have graduated. We are making a thing of beauty that should delight all our audiences. Tata will now do a projection, so we can see it through an audience's eyes."

They sat in a big circle, and the dogfish robot projected a magic picture called a holograph to the center. It was them, with their three, four, and five couples, dancing the several types. Squid saw herself, and knew that each of the others saw themselves as others saw them.

They were indeed beautiful, individually and in groups. The dances were phenomenal. The loveliness of the whole was an emergent property, greater than its parts. It was the kind of show no one would ever forget.

When it finished, they burst into applause for the performance, even though it was themselves. Participating in it, they had not seen its larger glory. Now they knew.

Yet, where was the hidden menace, the threat that their dancing existed for, in the sense that it was a pretext for them to stay together so they could deal with it? Their week was over, and nothing had happened. Tomorrow the adults would return and it would be over.

"Maybe we were sufficiently alert," Larry said that night. "That kept it at bay."

"Do you really believe that?"

"No."

They both laughed, but there was no humor in it. Something was, if not wrong, still waiting.

"Hold me."

He did. Their togetherness helped push back the surrounding dread.

"If we were not what we are," he murmured, "I think we'd be perfect for each other."

"A transgender victim and an alien cuttlefish," she agreed.

Then they kissed. There was no passion in it, but considerable comfort.

Next day, the fire boat hovered, waiting for the sometime island of Skeleton Key to reappear. Squid didn't care to say it, but she was quite ready for the return of the adults. Only when they resumed stewardship of Fibot would she feel free to truly relax. Whatever story she was supposed to supervise as protagonist would sink into oblivion, a washout. That would be fine with her.

There was a shimmer on the water, and the skull-shaped island formed. It was back!

But something was missing. "Where's Caprice Castle?" Squid asked.

All of them stared. The island was there, but not the castle.

The boat descended to land on the sand. They got out to walk on the land. It was firm enough. But empty.

Then two skeletons approached, a male and a female. Their genders were clear despite their lack of flesh. The male was larger, and the female had broader hips. She also had one more rib. "Hello, children," the male said. "We are cousins of Marrow Bones. We fear we have unfortunate news." He had no lips, but the sound emerged from his hollow skull. There might have been a time when Squid was spooked by walking skeletons, but that was before she came to know them.

"Where is the castle?" Squid demanded rudely.

"That is the problem, dear," the female said. "We had a wonderful week of visiting, and we toured the marvelous traveling castle. Then one day it was gone. We thought the flesh folk had remembered another appointment and departed, though we were surprised that they left us no word and did not bid us farewell. In fact we were surprised that it could depart our domain, as we are in another shade of existence and travel between the frames is difficult. That was why we rendezvoused during a normal transition. But if you did not see Caprice, then it did not rejoin you. We fear it is lost."

The children gazed at each other with dismay. "It did not reappear here," Santo said after an uncomfortable moment.

"Then we do not know where it went, or why," the female said, her posture exhibiting her regret. "We are sorry we can't help you."

"Could it be hiding elsewhere on the island?" Santo asked.

"No," the male said. "We searched. An edifice that size would be difficult to conceal, and we found no magic screens or invisibility spells. We left no tern unstoned. It is not on Skeleton Key."

Another glance circled the group. Now they knew: the disaster had come upon them. It had not struck them personally, it had struck the castle.

"Do not remain on the land," the female said. "Unless you wish to stay with us. The duration of our visits varies, and this is a brief one. We are about to fade out from Xanth proper."

"Thank you," Santo said. Then they hastily scrambled back aboard the boat and lifted clear of the land.

Just in time. The island faded out, and the water of the bay replaced it.

"So much for our dancing exhibitions," Data said dourly.

Indeed, there would be no tour without Magnus and Jess organizing it. But that was the least of their letdown.

They went below. "What now?" Squid asked. The others seemed too stunned to speak.

"Let's get an analysis," Santo said. "Tata, Skeleton Key returned, but without Caprice Castle. The skeletons don't know where it went. We're pretty sure the people in it would not have simply deserted us. What is your opinion?"

The robot dogfish cogitated a moment. Then the screen flashed. "Agreed," the peeve translated. "They would have returned on schedule unless prevented. They would not have deserted the children. The castle and its occupants were probably somehow abducted and either destroyed or are being held captive."

Squid knew she wasn't the only one who felt a cruel chill. She knew that Piton and Data were especially affected, because their parents were missing.

Santo kept his cool. He was good at that. "Who or what could do this?"

"Only a dwarf Demon or equivalent."

There was a shudder shaking the children as they heard the capital D. They had expected trouble, but not of this nature. It might explain the involvement of Fornax, because it would take a Demon to catch a Demon. "For what purpose?" Santo asked.

The screen flickered again. "Caprice Castle is valuable for travel and storage," the peeve said. "As is Fibot. It may be the initial stage of an invasion of the Land of Xanth."

"Assuming they are captive," Santo said, "how would they be used for an invasion?"

"They might be useful as hostages to gain concessions from the existing government of Xanth. But in the absence of demands, this seems less likely."

Squid saw that Santo was carefully avoiding reference to the other alternative: destruction. "What is more likely?"

"Conjecture: that a collector is active."

"A collector of what?"

"A collector of valuable artifacts, such as a traveling castle or flying boat."

Squid felt an ugly additional chill. "You mean they might be after Fibot too?"

"That seems likely, now that Caprice is secure."

"Why didn't they just grab us when we landed on Skeleton Key?"

"Conjecture: they do not wish to operate in public, as that could stir an immediate backlash. They prefer to collect things when unobserved. Alternate conjecture: they are orienting on things one at a time. Fibot might be the next target."

Santo took it in stride. "What is your advice?"

"Take immediate evasive action for Fibot. Prepare a counter-stroke."

Santo nodded. "Tata and Peeve, proceed with random evasive action for the boat. We children will ponder a counter-stroke."

"Win," the peeve said.

"Right," Win agreed. She and Data headed for the tiller.

"Firenze."

"Right," Firenze said. He and Ula headed for the sail. The others would not feel it, here below-decks, but the fire boat was about to make erratic course changes so that no one outside would be likely to predict where it would go next. Squid wasn't sure how effective this would be if there was Demon involvement, but what else was there?

Santo glanced at the remaining five. "Now what can we come up with to mess up a possible Demon collector?"

Squid and Larry closed in on him. So did Myst and Piton. Noe was already there. They were the war council of the moment. The crisis was upon them.

"I think it is important that there be no hint of any possible Demon participation in our actions," Santo said. "It must be only children, with children's limitations."

The others nodded grimly. Fornax had to remain hidden. However, some of these children had Magician caliber talents, or close to it. They were far from helpless.

"I wish we could know for sure what happened to Caprice Castle and the adults in it," Myst said. "I mean, it makes a difference if they're alive or d-d-dead."

So now the forbidden subject had been introduced. "I agree," Squid said. "Is there any way we could somehow sneak into the Sometime Islands and look? Without involving any adults? Because I suspect that the adults are being watched, while the children are not. That could be why they missed Fibot, this time: no adults aboard."

"Smart girl," Noe said. "That must be it."

Santo glanced at Tata. "Is there a way to sneak and peek?"

The robot screen flashed. "Ion and Hilda, the nine-year-old children of Prince Hilarion and Princess Ida, travel regularly between the sometime realm and Xanth proper, using a route only they know and can traverse. They would likely cooperate, if asked."

Santo smiled. "Which of us would be the best to contact them?"

"Squid and Larry."

"Us?" Squid asked, startled. But as she spoke she realized that it had to be her, because she was the protagonist, and Larry because he was her companion. Also that he was the secret host to the Demoness. Yet she continued her protest, because it reached her mouth before she could stifle it. "We're not important, and we don't have the strongest talents. Nobody notices us."

"Exactly," Santo agreed. "We more noticeable children will do our best to keep the enemy's attention, while you two, unnoticed, do the real work."

Myst, Piton, and Noe nodded. Maybe they simply preferred to remain with the boat.

"We're stuck for it," Larry said.

"So it seems," Squid agreed. "Very well. How do we connect with Ion and Hilda? Will we have to try to protect them from childish mistakes?"

Santo smiled. "Remember, all descendants of Piton and Data's great grandfather Bink have Magician-caliber talents."

"We don't," Piton said. "Because we're half-skeleton crossbreeds. Our magic is to change back and forth." He switched to skeleton form and back again.

Santo smiled. "It may be that you simply have not yet discovered your talents."

That set the boy back. "I wonder."

Santo returned to the subject. "Tata, what are their talents?"

The screen flashed. "Piton and Data are as yet unclassified. Ion's talent is to be immune to all elixirs, including healing. Thus when he broke his legs in an accident, they did not heal, and he must use a miniature flying carpet to travel."

"Broke his legs!" Squid exclaimed. "He's a cripple? This is getting worse."

"He is nevertheless a Magician," Santo reminded her. "Presumably he can eat or drink anything without harmful effect, and may, by touching others, enable them to do the same. The poison of snake and insect bites may be considered potions, so he should be immune to those too. The potential is considerable."

"Point made," Larry said. "If it works on lethe water, or love elixir—"

"It should. No magic forgetting or compelled love."

"I am impressed," Larry agreed.

"Hilda's talent is sewing," the peeve continued.

"Worse yet!" Squid said. "Any girl can sew. It's in their nature. That's not Sorceress level. It's not even magic."

"Clarification?" Santo asked.

"Hilda's sewing is magic," the peeve said. "If she sews a kitchen apron, whoever wears it becomes a phenomenal cook. If she sews a suit of armor, its wearer is invulnerable to attack. If she sews a party dress, the girl who wears it becomes so sexy that her mere glance freaks out any man within range."

"Oh, my!" Myst said. "Did she sew my panty?"

The screen flashed. "Yes."

"I want to meet her!"

"All in good time," Santo said. "At the moment we have to drop Squid and Larry off inconspicuously so that they can intercept those children and perform their mission."

"And how will we rendezvous again with Fibot?" Larry asked.

"That is a question," Santo agreed. "If we could track them, so could the enemy. They need to be beyond tracking."

"There may be a way," Squid said. "I can tune in on any of you who think of me. If you think of me every so often, I will know when you are near, and—" She broke off. "But you may not be near."

"You can safely be aware of us," Santo agreed. "But we can't be aware of you."

"We could have places we visit," Piton said. "When they want to return, they can be at one of those places. If Squid knows of us, she'll know when to intercept us."

"That should do it," Santo agreed.

"Such as near Castle Roogna, where we drop them off."

"Yes. It's a bit haphazard, but it will have to do."

Squid wished there were a more certain way, but they did have to keep the boat hidden from the enemy. However, that was only part of the problem. "And how do we intercept Ion and Hilda?" Squid asked.

"They visit with their mother at Castle Roogna regularly," the peeve said. "They probably play in the orchard, or with the zombie guardians. You can find them there."

Squid was not completely convinced of the feasibility, but thought it was at least a fair chance.

"We will drop you off when we randomly zigzag near Castle Roogna," Santo said.

"So now it has been decided," Noe said. "Now it is okay to cry?"

It was okay.

Squid and Larry retired to their cabin. "At least now we have half a notion of the danger," he said. "And maybe what we can try to do about it."

"That's better than nothing," Squid agreed. "But there is so much more we don't know."

"Amen."

They held each other and tried to sleep.

There was a knock on the door. It was Santo. "We are close to Castle Roogna."

They hastily went with him topside. Firenze hugged Squid as she passed the mast. "Farewell, sister."

Then Win hugged her as they went stern-side. "Good luck, sister."

"Remember," Santo said as they made ready to climb overboard. "We're the decoy. You're the mission." He hugged her and let her go.

Squid was too choked up to answer any of them. She was afraid she would never see them again. But she appreciated their concern.

They climbed down to the land. It was night, but the lighted towers of Castle Roogna showed in the distance. They knew where to go.

They watched the boat sail up and away, a mere shadow in the sky. It carried no lights, as it was hiding. Even the sail was smoky dull.

"I have known the fire boat and your siblings far more briefly than you have," Larry said. "But it hurts me to separate from them in this manner."

"We'll rejoin them in due course," Squid said, hoping it was true.

They held each other in a comfort squeeze, and it helped. The knowledge that they would never be romantic lovers, regardless of their ages, gave them a certain freedom to express themselves. The cuttlefish and the fake boy: they trusted each other because of their significant differences.

Then they set out afoot for the castle. There was enough moonlight so that they could avoid hazards like trees and gulches. Evidently most of the monsters had been cleared out of the vicinity, because of the castle.

They came to a river flowing crosswise to their route, so that it barred their way. "Is it safe to swim across?" Larry asked.

"Let me check." Squid slipped into the water and reverted to her natural form. She sensed plants and fish and one hungry green allegation, but it was too far away to be a danger. Anyway those creatures tended to be more accusatory than physically vicious. "It is chill but safe, for now."

Larry took off his clothing, balled it up, and fastened it to his head. He wasn't concerned about exposing himself to her: it was dark enough to conceal details, and anyway, they had come to know each other well enough so that nudity was not a problem between them. That was one of the advantages of non-romantic acquaintance. Then he waded in and swam across.

On the other side he shook himself dry and dressed. "I wouldn't have dared swim without your assurance." He looked around. "I'm hungry."

"I smelled some beans nearby," Squid said. She walked to the place and picked some.

"No. Those are kidney beans. They can have kidney stones."

"How can you tell?"

He paused, surprised. "I'm not sure how I know, but I'm sure. These are not safe to eat."

Squid got an idea that flashed dimly over her head. "A new talent! could you have one?"

"But no one has more than one talent."

"We siblings have been getting quietly upgraded. I never had talents unrelated to my nature before, but now I do. I can modify my appearance far more effectively than before, and tune in on anyone who speaks my name. You could be similar, with other talents. You are close to the source."

He considered. "You may be correct. In that case we do not want to mention them to anyone not of our group."

"We do not," she agreed. "So we'll pass up the kidney beans, but you can check on any other food we get, just to be sure."

"I will."

Now the castle was close. It was surrounded by orchards with exotic fruit, nut, and pie-trees, a nice place.

Then something moved. It tromped on the ground, coming toward them. There was an awful odor. "Hooze therre?" it demanded.

A male zombie! But she remembered that they weren't enemies, but castle guardians.

Squid stepped boldly forward. "Just two children," she said.

The zombie paused. "Oooh, thee twinnns. Ghoogh bback inssidde."

She realized that the zombie couldn't see well enough to distinguish one child from another. But maybe he could help. "No, we are two other children. We want to visit the twins. Please, tell them to come out here to meet us."

The zombie pondered. This was slow, because of course his head was filled with rotten muck that had once been brains. Only magic kept the zombies going, not the physics or chemistry of living folk. "Yessh," he finally agreed, and shuffled away, dropping traces of spoiled flesh.

They waited. "I realize that the zombies aren't aggressive," Larry said. "But I hope we don't have much more contact with them."

"I understand that predators don't much like their taste," Squid said. "So they make effective guards."

"They surely do."

Soon there was the sound of something approaching. It turned out to be three somethings: the zombie, and two children. A blond boy sitting on a flying carpet, and a dark haired girl.

"So it's true," the girl said. "Children! Who are you?"

Squid elected to answer. "I am Squid, from—"

"You're one of the kids from the future! What are you doing here?"

"You know of me?" Squid asked, surprised.

"Everybody knows of you! Astrid Basilisk rescued you. It's in the Xanth History Book. But you're supposed to be on the fire boat."

"We were there, but then I—"

"Aren't you some kind of fish?"

"A cuttlefish. But—"

"And somebody adopted you anyway."

"Ease and Kandy adopted me. However—"

"So why aren't you with them, instead of poking around our playground?"

Now the boy spoke. "Give it a rest, Sis. She's trying to tell you."

Squid took advantage of the momentary silence. "And this is Larry, who is traveling with me."

The girl looked at him. "I never heard of you."

Larry smiled. "Naturally not. I'm an incomplete nonentity."

"So what do you want with us?" the girl demanded.

There seemed to be no point in pussyfooting. "We are on a dangerous mission and we need your help."

"Why?" the girl asked immediately.

"We can explain," Squid said. "But it's a secret mission, and you can't tell anyone else."

The boy shook his head. "Mom would know anyway. She knows everything."

"And we can't do anything or go anywhere if she doesn't know," the girl said.

This could be mischief. But their mother, Princess Ida, was the Sorceress of the Idea, and it might indeed be impossible to keep their mission from her. But Squid decided to give it a try. "Then maybe we should talk to your mother."

Boy and girl exchanged a glance. "Okay," they said almost together.

"Take us to her," Larry said.

"This way." The boy's carpet floated toward the castle.

They followed. "I'm Hilda," the girl said. "My talent is sewing. My brother is Ion. His talent is immunity to elixirs. Usually men have sons and women have daughters, but there was name reverse wood caught in the Stork Works, and our names got reversed, so I am my father Hilarion's daughter and Ion is our mother Ida's son. We're stuck with it."

"We're Squid and Larry, as you know," Squid said. "My talent is to change my appearance, so I don't look like an octopus. Larry's talent is to change his age."

"Neat. Can he turn 21 and find out what the mean old Adult Conspiracy is hiding?"

"No. He remains a twelve-year-old boy inside."

"Blip!"

Squid had to smile. It was the usual reaction. Every child was frustrated by the Conspiracy.

They reached the castle moat. The moat monster's head reared up out of the dark water. "It's okay, Moatie," Hilda said. "We're taking them in to see Mom."

The head sank back into the water. This was clearly a well trained monster.

They crossed the drawbridge, which remained down, and entered the castle. It was even grander from inside than from outside, with clean floors, sparkling glass windows, and carpeted stairs.

A walking skeleton blocked their way, but heeded Hilda's reassurance. Another well-trained monster. Except of course that they had half-skeleton friends, and their mission was on or near Skeleton Key. So much depended on a person's perspective!

Upstairs they entered a small private chamber. "Mom!" Hilda called at the doorway. "We got company! Squid and Larry."

"That's nice, dear." The woman was sitting in a comfortable chair. She was ordinary looking, for an adult princess, except for one thing: a tiny moon orbited her head. It was about the size of a pong ping ball, but looked exactly like a planet, with green forests, gray mountains, and blue seas.

"I see you are surprised by Ptero," Ida said, jolting both Squid and Larry out of their joint stare. "It is my idea world. Those who travel to it discovered that it is actually full size; its small appearance is because of magical perspective. All people who exist or ever existed or who will exist are to be found on it and its moons." She smiled. "Those moons are not directly visible: it is a bit more devious. There is a duplicate Princess Ida living on Ptero, and about her head orbits another world, Pyramid, with four triangular faces. On that world exists another Princess Ida, about whose head orbits Torus, in the shape of a doughnut. And so on; there are a great many worlds. There are tourists who like to visit some of the more exotic ones."

Squid hauled herself out of her fascination. "Thank you. I think I knew of, of Ptero, but actually seeing it is awesome."

"You must be hungry, dear. Have a late dinner." Ida gestured to a table where four places had already been set. She had been expecting them!

Soon they were feasting on pieces of brownberry pie and boot rear, the standard fare for visiting children. Trust a parent to know what children needed.

"Now the zombies tell me that you came to see Ion and Hilda," Ida said when they finished. "That you are on an important mission and need their help."

"That's true," Squid said uneasily. "But we're not supposed to tell any adults."

"My children don't meet many other children in Xanth. The children who were here grew up and became adults. Ion and Hilda could use some socializing with others in their age range. It would be nice if mine could visit with the siblings and their friends."

She thought this was innocent play? "Maybe sometime."

"It is a child's game that brought you here?"

"Not exactly." This was getting increasingly awkward.

"Something is amiss. Let me look at you." Ida's gaze oriented directly on Squid. "Oh, my! I am familiar with your history, Squid, but did not realize the current situation. You're the protagonist!"

She could tell just by looking? "Yes."

Then Ida looked closely at Larry, and did a double-take. "Oh, my!" she repeated, but did not say more.

How much did she see? The girl inside his body, or a Demoness? "So we—" Squid started.

"Certainly you can travel with Ion and Hilda," Ida said.

Just like that? "I—I have to tell you it may be dangerous."

"Of course it is, dear. But not nearly as dangerous as inaction would be."

How much did she know? With all her orbiting worlds she could have uncanny sources of information. Inaction would leave Caprice Castle in the awful hands of the Demon Collector. But was that all that Princess Ida saw? "So we can go to—?" She didn't want to say it aloud, lest an enemy be tuning in somewhat the way Squid herself tuned in on her own name.

"Tomorrow. Tonight you rest and sleep."

That seemed feasible. "Thank you."

"Thank *you*, Squid. We are bound to help you in any way we can. There is nothing more important."

She knew.

The Castle Roogna facilities were very nice. Ion and Hilda showed them some of its special features, such as the magic tapestry hanging on the wall of the main bedroom, that illustrated any part of Xanth that they thought of in its presence, including aspects of its illustrious history. Such as the rose garden that Rose of Roogna had planted long ago, whose magic roses could tell marvelous things about any person who needed special information. Such as the castle ghosts who were more friendly with innocent children than with cynical adults.

"One thing about our route to the Sometime Islands," Hilda confided to Squid. "It is devious, and no one else can use it. You will have to trust Ion and me to guide you along it."

"We will," Squid promised.

Then they slept, but Squid's dreams were not easy. She had a premonition that something weird was about to happen.

Chapter 7

PORTAL

The four children set out in the morning, buttressed by a good breakfast and backpacks with food for the journey. They took an enchanted path, where there was no danger, but soon stepped quietly off it to follow an obscure winding trail that seemed to lead to nowhere.

Or rather, it led directly to a tangle tree. "Stay in my tracks," Hilda said.

"But that's a tangle tree!" Squid protested. "They eat anything they catch! We can't—"

"We know. You have to trust us, or it won't work."

Squid shut up and followed her. Hilda was after all in her bailiwick; she had to know what she was doing, maybe. Larry was next, and Ion was last, riding his little carpet. "Are we doing the right thing?" Squid whispered to Larry as they drew close to each other.

"They are a prince and princess, Magician and Sorceress," he whispered back. "They have made this journey before."

That wasn't a direct answer, but it was good background information. The twins might be only nine years old, but they were indeed royal, with phenomenal magic.

"Any other thoughts?" she asked him somewhat facetiously, which was a good trick because she was hardly familiar with the word.

"Their mother let them do it."

That had more punch. Squid had never heard of a mother who willingly let her children go into danger. Princess Ida did seem to know what was going on. That did not guarantee that it was safe, but it was an indication. "True," she agreed faintly.

"And we need to complete our mission," he concluded. "This is perhaps the most feasible way."

So it was. She would just have to hope that it was not disastrous.

They came almost within range of the tree's tentacles, which quivered with anticipation of succulent children. One more step . . .

Hilda halted. Squid was glad to stop behind her.

Ion floated up and stopped almost within touching distance of the nearest tentacle. He brought out a little spritz bottle filled with brown fluid. He spritzed.

The tentacle recoiled violently, and so did the others near it. The tree was desperately avoiding them. That was odd, as tangle trees were notorious for consuming any living thing they caught.

Hilda resumed walking, and the others followed. They went right under the tangle tree, passing next to the hideous trunk with its gnarly gaping mouth and saliva sap, but it never touched them. They emerged beyond it and followed the trail.

"What was in that spritz?" Squid asked. She didn't have real knees, technically, but they felt like cooked noodles.

"Essence of stink horn fragrance," Hilda replied. "Just enough of it to make the point. No one is going to follow us on this route."

"Stink horn!" Squid echoed, amazed. "That would do it. But how did Ion get it?"

"His talent is immunity to all elixirs," Hilda explained. "Stink horn aroma is a kind of elixir. He collects assorted ones, as they remain potent on other folk even if they can't hurt him. They can be useful."

So it seemed. The boy's immunity allowed him to handle the elixirs, and to bottle them, saving them for later use. It made sense.

"We were a bit skeptical. We apologize for underestimating you," Larry said diplomatically as they walked through a more open section of the forest.

"That's all right," Hilda said. "Everyone does."

Squid found herself relating. "You're children among adults? They don't take you seriously?"

"Oh, the maids and servitors at Castle Adamant are always polite. But we know what they're thinking."

"That we're spoiled brats," Ion said.

"And maybe we are," Hilda said. "But we don't mean to be. We just don't know any better."

"So we're happier out by ourselves in the wilderness," Ion said. "The trees and animals don't judge us."

"We're common folk," Squid said. "We were concerned that royal folk wouldn't want to associate with us."

Hilda laughed. "You've got the big adventure. That makes you special."

"We like adventure," Ion said. "We don't care who is royal or how much magic they have. We just want fun company, preferably in our own age range."

"I'm an animal," Squid said, turning one hand into an octopus extremity. "I'm not judging you."

"And I'm a girl," Larry said. "I'm not judging you either."

"But we're both children," Squid said. "We hate the Adult Conspiracy."

"Yes!" Ion and Hilda said together.

After that, whatever tension there had been between them dissolved and sank into the ground.

Hilda slowed. "Here we have a choice. The route divides. The faster one is on the left, but it passes through a meet he/her shower."

"A meteor shower?" Squid asked. "We don't want to risk that."

"Not exactly. Sometimes they are falling hes and shes."

"People?"

"We think they step out of their showers and slip, and this is where they land. Bare, wet people. They often aren't pleased to encounter clothed folk."

"I should think not," Larry said.

"And it's worse if one lands on you," Hilda said. "You could get a soapy bare foot in your face. You have to keep your eye on the sky, and be ready to dodge."

"And they definitely don't like it when children see them bare," Ion said. "For some reason."

"Let's not take that route," Squid said. "We're not that kind of sightseer."

"The slower route passes through the portal. Some folk don't like that."

"Does it hurt them?"

"Not really. We go through it all the time, and it's never harmed us. But some people refuse because of the awkwardness."

Squid realized that there was something the girl wasn't telling them. "What awkwardness?"

"Well, clothing doesn't fit right. You have to get new clothes."

"You mean it changes the shape of the clothes?"

"No. Of the body."

"Oh, you mean it makes you look like a troll?"

"Not exactly. You look fine. Pretty, even."

"Is it harmful?" Larry asked.

"Not really," Hilda said. "Just inconvenient."

"Until you pass back through it," Ion said. "Then it reverts you to the way you were before. Then your new clothing doesn't fit. So sometimes we just go bare and save the trouble."

Going bare wasn't as big a deal for small children as it was for big ones or adults. "Well, we can put up with some inconvenience," Squid said. "That's better than getting bashed by a meteor or a falling body."

"That's how we see it," Hilda said. She seemed oddly amused.

What were these kids up to? Better just to call their bluff, whatever it was. "Let's go through the portal," Squid said briskly.

"Coming up," Hilda said, smiling. "This way."

It was a fair distance, and they paused for lunch along the way. There among the sandwiches were several small sealed cans; each child had one.

"What's this?" Larry asked.

"Music," Hilda explained. "In case we need to dance."

Larry shrugged, not electing to challenge that.

Soon they reached the portal. It was a massive gateway, square on the outside, rounded on the inside. The walls were inscribed with magical symbols. It was open; they could see the view through it, just like the scenery on this side. The surrounding trees and brush pressed up so close that it was not possible to avoid it without a considerable hassle. Only the central way was clear.

"I'm slightly suspicious," Larry murmured. "It's as though travelers are being channeled."

"We think whoever made it wanted folk to use it," Hilda said.

"Why, when it doesn't do anything permanent?"

"Who knows what's in the minds of Demons, if they even have minds?"

Demons? "Who made this?" Squid asked. "Do you know?"

"We think some minor Demon who was bored, eons ago," Hilda said. "There's more than one of the portals, and they have different shapes. As if he was practicing his magic, trying different designs, and then lost interest and went home without abolishing it. It's been here as long as anyone knows."

"Well, let's go on through," Squid said. She stepped through the portal.

Suddenly, sure enough, her skin felt funny. She didn't actually wear clothing, just the semblance of it, but it was as if that semblance was trying to change. That was curious.

Then she figured out what it was. She wore the form of a human girl child. Now she had the form of a boy child.

She shifted to her natural cuttlefish form. Then it was apparent: it was male. She had changed genders.

Now Larry walked through the portal. And changed. His trousers bound to his legs so tightly that their stitching started ripping out, and his shirt hung oddly on his frame. In addition, his hair seemed to have grown from short to long.

"What is this?" he asked, looking at himself.

"Take off your clothing," Squid said. "It's not fitting well anyway."

"I might as well. I see a clothing tree nearby anyway." He stripped away his damaged clothing and stood in his underpants, which also had become ill fitting.

"Take them off too," Squid said.

He shrugged and did, as they had already seen each other bare. No child understood why adults were so concerned with bareness, as it was a natural state, and there were no adults here.

"Now look at yourself," Squid said. "You don't need a pool to magically reflect your image. Just look down at your middle."

"And see the anatomy I hate." He looked down, and froze.

"Your body is female," Squid said. "Just as mine is male."

Indeed, Larry's bumpy male anatomy had been replaced by smooth female curves. He was a girl.

"Oh, my," she breathed.

Now Ion and Hilda passed through, he on his carpet, she by foot. They had already removed their clothing.

Ion was a girl. Hilda was a boy.

"Fun, isn't it?" Hilda said. "Now I've got the wee-wee and he's got nothing."

So this was the secret they had concealed. The portal changed the gender of whoever passed through it. No wonder adults avoided it!

Squid looked at Larry. Could he handle this?

Larry took a deep breath, and his chest seemed to soften as it expanded. "Wow! My body is female!"

"Yes," Squid said. Would he stay calm, or would he lose his mind?

"Let me change my age."

"That won't change your gender," Squid said.

But he was already changing, rapidly becoming older. His hips spread wider, his waist shrank, and his chest—

"Wow!" Hilda said.

For now Larry had two beautiful female breasts that quivered delicately when he breathed. He had become an adult woman.

"Where's a pool?" he demanded. "I've got to see myself reflected."

"There's one just down the trail," Ion said. "I'll show you."

The smaller girl form led the way, riding the carpet. The larger girl form followed, afoot. Squid shifted back to human form, complete with male anatomy that the Adult Conspiracy managed to mask with incidental wisps of fog, and fell in beside Hilda. They all went to the pool.

There it was, pristine reflective water. Larry stood by the edge, his feet in the liquid, looking down. "I'm beautiful!"

"You are," Squid agreed. Even though she was not properly human, she now saw things with male eyes, and the girl in the water was lovely.

"Glorious! Now I am truly Laurelai!"

Then it came to Squid: this really was a girl. She had been locked in a boy's body, but it had changed to female. Of course she was happy! This was the answer she had longed for.

Laurelai waded deeper into the pool, then splashed all the way into the water. She swam out into the center. "Glorious!" she repeated.

"That's right: I forgot," Hilda said. "She's really a girl."

"And a beauty," Ion said.

Laurelai swam back to the shore and waded out, blissfully dripping. "Oh, I'm so happy! I must kiss someone."

"Uh—" Squid said.

She grabbed him, hugged him close, and kissed him firmly on the mouth. Such was the power of her beauty that he felt a flare of feeling verging on love.

"The Good Magician said I'd get my wish on this mission," Laurelai said breathlessly. "Oh, how right he was!"

"But I'm male," Squid said. "I don't want to be male. I'm female inside."

"Too bad for you," Hilda said. "Now you're male, same as me."

"But we can go through the portal," Squid said. "And change back."

"I never want to change back," Laurelai said. "This is what I have wanted to be all my life. I want to grow into an adult woman and be that way forever."

Squid realized that he couldn't go back alone: he needed to complete the mission. So he was stuck with the male form, at least until they had finished.

"Let's get dressed," Hilda said. "We still have a way to go."

There was a fair grove of clothing trees: evidently this was a popular place for them. They harvested shoes from a shoe tree, pants from a pant tree, plus underwear from the underbrush, and shirts from shirt trees. When Laurelai donned panties both Squid and Hilda felt their impact despite being too young for the full effect. Then Laurelai reverted to her natural age, and the effect faded.

"I could knit you a better pair," Hilda said.

"Don't you dare!" Squid said. "She's already too dangerous as she is. If she uses magic ones and advances her age we could all freak out."

Hilda nodded. "You could."

Now they were dressed and ready to resume travel. "What's next?" Squid asked.

"There's a village nearby we can stay in," Hilda said. "They know us. I mean, Ion and me. But we'll have to earn our keep. I can knit something, Ion can make sure their water is clean, but each person has to participate."

"We can dance," Squid said.

"That should be okay. They like dancing, and are always looking for new dances."

They walked on. "Something occurs to me," Laurelai said. "We practiced those dances in different genders. I think I can manage the female role, as I have always thought of myself that way, but what about you in the male role?"

"That may be a problem," Squid agreed. "I have always been female, regardless of my form. I'm not really comfortable as a male."

She laughed. "I know exactly how that is! But maybe I can help you. We'll just have to practice to get it right."

"I'm not sure any amount of practicing will make me like being male."

She squeezed his hand. "Exactly. But you can fake it for now."

"You get used to it," Hilda said. "We've been back and forth many times and have learned how to play the roles. Our talents aren't affected, and because we've both been through it, we understand and help each other."

"We will help each other," Laurelai agreed.

Soon they came to the village of Portal. "The villagers don't actually use the portal much," Hilda said. "But they cater to travelers who pass through it, some of whom are sadly confused. Many of them turn around and march right back through it, but some don't."

"In fact some folk pass through it deliberately," Ion said. "Some adult couples treat it like a fun vacation, spicing up their marriages with their reversed roles. They take rooms at the village Inn & Outt. Not that we children understand about any of that mushy stuff."

"And the Conspiracy stops us from peeking," Hilda said, annoyed. "So we can't see what he shows her when he's a she, or what she does to him when she's a he. Or how they make the ellipsis that alerts the storks. But we hear the giggling and know they're having a lot of fun."

"But they are nice rooms," Ion said. "We always like staying here, despite the frustration."

There was a bell on a stand beside the path at the edge of the village. Hilda picked it up and rang it.

Immediately an adult male villager emerged from the Outt. "Ah, Hilda and Ion," he said. "So good to see you again. We have a spring that took a fall, and our girls are looking for new dresses."

Squid worked it out in her mind: a water spring got polluted, so Ion could use a potion to clear it back to purity. And naturally girls wanted magic dresses sewn for them. It was not surprising that the twins were popular here.

"We'll take care of it, as usual, Mr. Inn & Outt," Hilda said. "This time we're traveling with friends, Squid and Laurelai."

The man looked at them. "Welcome to our village and to my hostel, Squid and Laurelai. How do you propose to earn your keep?"

He was clearly a businessman, covering the essentials first. "We can dance," Laurelai said with a smile that brightened the landscape. Her joy at being a physical girl couldn't help expressing itself.

He frowned, evidently immune to such blandishments. "We have plenty of children's dances already."

Squid and Laurelai exchanged a bemused glance. "We are young, but maybe we can do a dance that grownups will like," Laurelai said.

"Very good. You can present it in the village square tonight."

Squid knew that they had better produce, or their welcome would evaporate.

They were ushered into a wonderful suite with beds for four and a table with fresh harvested redberry and blueberry pies and milkweed pods.

"Now we have some work to do," Hilda said. "But you two can stay here and get your dance ready." The twins exited, going out to earn their keep.

"They're pretty responsible, for children," Laurelai remarked.

"Maybe it comes with their royalty," Squid said. "They know how to treat people."

"They have treated us just like other children."

"Yes. We're people too."

"Now let's select a dance," she said. "What one will be easy for us to do with reversed gender roles, and interesting for adults as well as children?"

Squid pondered, and it came to him. "False Step!"

She clapped her hands. "Oh, yes! Perfect." Then she reconsidered. "But we're a little young for it. We don't want it to be a joke, the way it is when children do it."

"Yes. So maybe you can age to teen. I'll try to fake maturity."

"I wonder."

"What are you thinking of?"

"Our talents have been getting quietly upgraded. Maybe my age changing has too."

"You mean you can age farther than before?"

"Maybe. But I'm thinking maybe now I could take you with me."

Squid didn't follow that. "Do you know something I don't know?"

"Yes."

Fornax was with her, and they communicated privately with each other. So there was something, but they should not advertise it. "Take me with you," Squid said.

Laurelai put her arms around him, holding him close to her, face to face, but she was not being affectionate. "Now relax your mind, and let my will be yours. Let me carry you."

Obviously not physically. Squid relaxed as far as he was able.

There was a kind of magical envelopment. Then he did feel as if he were being carried along with her. Not physically, but temporally.

Something strange was happening. He felt his body changing, and felt her body changing against him. In fact her chest was pushing oddly at his.

Then it stopped. She let him go and stepped back. "Our mass does not change, just our age. We reconfigure for the new age."

He looked at her. She had indeed changed. Now her loose shirt was pushing out in front, forming a bosom, and her hips had spread while her waist narrowed. She had done this before, but this time it was more pronounced. She had evidently traveled farther into maturity. She was a full woman. A fascinating one.

"Don't look at me," she said. "Look at you."

Squid discovered that his shirt had become tight across the shoulders and his pants tight in the crotch. He had grown in those areas, while turning lean in others.

But more alarming was his reaction to the sight of her. "I want to grab you and, I don't know what, but I want to."

"You are suffering the complications that prevented me from getting too old, when my body was male. Now you know how it is."

"The Adult Conspiracy! My body wants to do something, but my mind remains too young to know what."

"Exactly. It can be awkward as bleep."

"But I'm really a cuttlefish," he protested. "I don't have human body parts, just emulations. I don't want to, to signal the stork with you, regardless of my age. We're two quite different species."

"I don't think so. Look at your hand."

"My hand? It's just the end of my limbs twined together and colored to look like fingers. It can't pass a close examination."

"Can't it?" She took his hand and lifted it up between them. "This looks like five fingers to me."

"Yes, but the moment I stop the emulation it will look like the tips to two octopus arms with suckers on the sides."

"Well, stop the emulation."

What was she after? Squid let his apparent human hand dissolve into the arms.

Nothing happened. The five fingers remained.

He stared at his own hand. "That can't be."

"Yes it can be," she said. "That's a fully human hand."

He tried again, but again the hand did not change. He seemed to be stuck in the emulation.

"Here is the way I see it," she said. "You're used to emulating other forms, so that you look like something else while still being a cuttlefish doing contortions. You're so good at it that you can fool most folk who don't know you. But now you have taken one additional step: changing the rest of the way to human. You did it before, without realizing. Only when I took you with me five years, and you reacted to my grown body, are you discovering the truth. You have become a teen age human male, with hardly more than one thing on your mind."

He opened his mouth to protest, but Laurelai took Squid's hand, which she still held, and touched his fingers to her newly-grown bosom. He freaked out.

"Wake, Squid," she said, snapping her fingers. "It was only an example so you would know it's true. You're a young man now."

"But how—?"

"Your talent has strengthened. Now you can not only *look* the part better than before, you *are* the part. You're a full shape changer."

He had not run out of buts. "But—"

"And if you emulated a bird, you'd become a real bird, so you could fly. It's not a full Magician talent, like that of Prince Dolph, because you have to work at it and you can't change your mass. Still, it's a really strong ability. But you see, those changes include the feelings that drive those other creatures. Because of the hormones in the bodies. So when I aged us, you started feeling like a grown human male in the near presence of a shapely human female."

He grabbed on to one bit he might belatedly understand. "You aged us both?"

"Yes. My aging talent has been enhanced so that now I can take someone with me, if I'm close enough and concentrate hard enough. I took you with me. You will remain sixteen and I will remain seventeen until I take us back to our natural ages. We won't do it often, or advertise it, but we now have potent additional talents."

So now he was a real human being, sixteen years old. "I think I need to get back to my original self."

She shook her head. "Not yet, Squid. I changed our ages, but it was quite an effort, and probably for you too. We need to save our strength until we have done what we have to do, which is to dance for the villagers. Then we can revert."

"But I'm not used to this! Just looking at you puts me into a tizzy. I need to get away from those hormones."

"Squid, I understand perfectly, I really do. As you know, I've been there myself and felt those uncomfortable feelings. But today you'll just have to bear with it. I'll try to help you, but mainly you'll need strong self-discipline."

He knew that she was right on the whole business. "I'll try."

"Good. Now let's practice that dance."

"But it ends with a kiss! Laurelai, if I kiss you—"

"You'll what?" she asked, not challengingly. She knew the answer.

He struggled to speak the unspeakable. "I'll fall in love with you." There; it was out.

"Would that be so bad?"

"Yes! Because you won't love me."

She shook her head. "I am not sure of that. You brought me into this adventure, you steered me to the course that granted me my fondest wish. I could do worse than commit to you."

"But I'm really an alien female cuttlefish."

She smiled. "We all have our foibles. At the moment you are a young human man. Maybe when you return to your natural species and gender you will be free of such a problematic emotion."

"Are you mocking me?"

"No, Squid. I'm trying to be realistic. You're a good person. That's what really counts."

"You're a good person too. But now you have your real form you'll be able to attract any man you want. You won't have to bother with me."

"Squid, you're forgetting something. To complete our mission, we will have to return to report to the others. That means we'll have to pass back through the portal. We will return to our original genders. Who else will even understand what we have been through here? They'll think it's funny. I think I would rather not try to explain. I would prefer to be with one who truly understands."

"Yes, I appreciate that, though I don't think my siblings would laugh. Still, we're just children, in our real lives."

"There is one more thing. This mission is dangerous; we know that. We may not survive it."

"We may not," he agreed reluctantly.

"If we are to die before we return, I would like to have experienced love first. There may not be another chance."

She had a point. He felt much the same. "So then how do we handle the, the emotion?"

"I think we may be best off to invoke it now, and learn to handle it, if we can. So we don't get torpedoed by surprise later, in public, not knowing its ramifications. That could be dangerous."

"You mean—?"

"Yes." She stepped into him and kissed him.

Squid's world exploded into soft joy. There was no question: he loved her.

A moment or an eon later he found himself staring at a floating heart. Rather, it was half a heart. "What's that?"

She smiled sadly. "Half a heart. I think it's yours. I believe that means that you love me but I don't love you. I'm sorry."

"That's exactly what I feared."

"But Squid, I'm not trying to torment you. I do like you. I just don't love you yet. Women are more complicated than men about such things. Just give me time and it may happen. Meanwhile, we can perfect the dance."

"Kiss and all," he agreed.

They worked on the dance. They were both thoroughly familiar with it, but needed to practice the changed genders. Laurelai had to take the female role, doing the twirls and leg lifts, and Squid the male role, holding her steady. They kept lapsing, but soon they were getting it right. They could present the dance.

The twins returned. "I knitted a bunch of dresses," Hilda said. "Ion cleansed three wells. We have earned our keep. Have you gotten the dance straight?"

"We think so," Laurelai said. "Here, we'll show you."

This time they opened one of the cans, and the music sounded. They did the dance, which really didn't take long. They finished with the kiss, and Squid felt the explosion again. But this time he also felt some response from Laurelai. She was starting to share the feeling!

"That's really cute," Hilda said. "But now I need to make your costumes."

Squid and Laurelai had forgotten about that. Their present clothing was ill fitting because of the age change, and it was getting on toward show time. Could Hilda make that deadline?

"Wow," Hilda said as she conjured material and sewed it. "I'm twice as fast and sure as I was."

Squid's eye met Laurelai's eye; their glances almost collided. Talent upgrading was still occurring. The girl was already a Sorceress; now she was even more so.

Soon the outfits were ready, a nice shirt and trouser for Squid, complete with a colorful sash. A lovely dress for Laurelai, complete with a plaid panty like the one Myst now wore. Dancing slippers for them both.

"But won't that panty freak out the audience when she high kicks?" Squid asked.

"Fear not," Laurelai said. "The flashes will be too brief for that. Just enough to cruelly tease them. This dance was always geared for that. They'll love it."

"We will need a caller," Squid said. "I think you can do that, Hilda."

"Sure. Long as I know what to say."

Squid went over it with him. Hilda was delighted to have the role.

Then it was dance time. Inn & Outt came to the door to collect them, and he led them to the village square, where the whole village was gathered.

There was no applause at their appearance. The cynical villagers first wanted to see whether they really were good enough.

Squid smiled to himself. This audience would not be disappointed.

Now the two of them took the stage. "This dance is called 'False Step,'" he announced. "It is really a story told in dance form. After we demonstrate it, we will teach it to any of you who want to learn it. But be warned: the steps are tricky, as you will see." He saw the dismissal in their faces; they knew how to do tricky steps.

Hilda and Ion came to join them on the stage, Ion floating on her mini carpet. This caused no reaction: they knew and respected her. It was the two new travelers who were on trial.

The four of them took their places. Ion opened a can, and the canned music poured out.

"Laurelai has a problem," Hilda announced, following the script. "She is a winsome girl, but she can't find any boy to match her step."

Laurelai danced forward, age seventeen, pretty as one-and-a-half pictures in her special dress, smiling hopefully. Squid, not yet active, saw all the village men of any age gazing longingly at her, along with some of the girls. Her feet made an intricate pattern so that it was difficult to see exactly when they touched the floor. That was the thing about this dance; it had the trickiest stepping of them all. Now Squid observed the audience in greater detail, and saw the men watching Laurie's legs closely, and the women too, amazed by respectively bare perfection and a step they had not seen before. Already an impact was being made.

"She tries one boy after another," Hilda continued. "But it just doesn't work."

Laurelai danced toward Hilda, and Hilda tried to match the step, but their feet got tangled and both fell to the floor. Ion put his hand over the can, stopping the music. There was laughter in the audience, as there was supposed to be.

"Finally she tries the last boy in the village," Hilda continued as Ion removed his hand and the canned music resumed. "She is beautiful and he is ordinary, so she never noticed him before. And lo! He knows the step!"

Squid started dancing, his intricate steps matching Laurelai's. They came together and swung, and her skirt flared out, almost showing her panty. It was amazing that their legs did not tangle as they danced together.

Then she did a high kick, as he held her in place, flashing the audience too briefly to fully register. They loved it.

It was a beautiful dance, because of the perfection of their meshing; any couple performing it would look great, but they were a class above the ordinary. Finally came the finale as they kissed, and a heart flew out. Laurie had found her partner, and true love at last.

Applause broke out. The dance was a success!

But they were not done. Squid addressed the villagers again. "This is actually a fairly simple dance to do, once you learn the step. We will teach you the false step so that you can do it after we move on. We will start with two volunteers, one boy and one girl, and the rest of you can learn as they do." He smiled. "I'll take the girl."

There was a hesitation, then a village elder indicated a girl. She came forward to stand before Squid, pretty and curvaceous. "Hi," she said shyly. "I'm Renee. I'm thirteen and my talent is to make people younger briefly, or a part of a person younger for longer, like the heart or the mind. But I'd just love to learn this for myself so I can flash boys and make them drool."

Squid considered, and decided not to mention Laurelai's broader talent. For one thing, they didn't want to make it obvious that they were younger than they looked. "That's very good," he said. "Now let me explain the key mechanism of the false step. Once you have that, the rest will be relatively easy."

"Yes!" she agreed breathlessly. Girls like her were very good at being breathless.

He explained the step, had her practice it briefly, then took her in his arms and did it with her. It was far from perfect, but after several false starts she began to get it. Then it came together, because she did know how to dance, and soon had the step. There was applause as they danced prettily, and Renee twirled and did a high kick. She had mastered it, or perhaps mistressed it.

She was of course thrilled, but Squid was quite pleased too. He had taught the step, as a boy to a girl. Did the villagers realize he was actually a girl? It was possible, because the people knew that anyone coming through the portal was gender changed.

Meanwhile, Laurelai was teaching a young man, Rick O'Shea, who tended to bounce around a lot before he got it straight. But soon he had it. Then they put Rick and Renee together, and they showed how they handled the False Step to more applause.

Others followed, until there were enough people trained in the new dance so that they could teach others.

The hosteler Inn & Outt came to them. "You have done marvelously well," he said. "You will always be welcome here when you travel."

"Thank you," they said, almost together.

"I think Renee and Rick have crushes on the two of you."

"Uh," Squid said. "That isn't advisable, because—"

"They know. Our village is not named Portal for nothing. Many of our residents are changed folk. It's a compliment to your performance."

They retired to their suite for the night. What a day it had been!

"Are you ready to revert?" Laurelai inquired.

"More than ready," Squid agreed.

They clasped each other and slid back to their natural ages. Their new clothing no longer fit well, and they had to change, no longer concerned about seeing each other in the process.

"You know, you're a fair semblance of a young man, as a teen," she said. "I could see myself becoming earnestly attached to you."

"Don't tease me! You're a devastating young woman."

"I'm serious. I like you as a boy or a girl."

"Oh, Laurelai! But you know we're really not meant for each other."

"Maybe not. But for now let's enjoy our crushes."

"But—"

She stepped into him and kissed him. That shut him up. Even as a child she had hold of his heart. Maybe it wasn't as serious for her, but what could he do except let it run its course? The future was murky, but this was the here and now.

She joined him on his bed, and held his hand as they slept. That did indeed give him sweet dreams.

Chapter 8

AETHER OAR

In the morning they resumed their journey. "We'll reach the land bridge this afternoon," Ion said. "Then we'll cross to the Sometimes Isles."

"A land bridge?" Squid asked. "I never heard of this."

"Of course you haven't. It's surrounded by Lethe water, and the mist rising from the water has the same effect. I'm the only one who remembers it."

Because he was immune to the water of forgetfulness, Squid realized. That was why he knew a route that no others did.

But Laurelai had another question. "How can any bridge cross to an island that is there only some of the time?"

Ion shrugged. "Magic. It connects to whatever island is there at the time. The islands change, but once we're in the Sometime realm it will be just a matter of finding the right one."

"Sometimes it takes us a while to locate Adamant Isle, because it has moved farther away," Hilda said. "But it's all right because we like traveling."

Considering how well they were treated at Portal Village, Squid could understand. But he had another question. "We assume that Caprice Castle is on a Sometime Island. But we have no idea which one."

"Maybe I have an idea," Ion said.

"What is it?"

"I will trade it for a kiss."

"Are you joking?"

"You kids still don't get it," Hilda said. "When you roam, do as the roamers do. Just about everyone along this trail is reversed. They learn to enjoy its special features. Ion is now a girl. You're a boy. Kiss her."

Squid stood still, uncertain how to react.

"You kissed Laurelai, and liked it," Hilda said. "You can kiss Ion too. And I can kiss Laurelai, if she'll let me."

Laurelai smiled. "Why not?" She went to Hilda and kissed him. Hilda looked surprised, but impressed.

Squid realized that he was making an issue of something that could probably be ignored. They were both changed, but still of opposite genders. He went to Ion and kissed her. To his surprise, she kissed him back.

Hilda clapped his hands. "I win! He did it."

"This was a child's game?" Laurelai asked, frowning.

"A bet. Ion thought Squid wouldn't kiss anyone but you."

Laurelai nodded thoughtfully. "Or that no boy would kiss a crippled girl?"

Squid saw that there was a tear at Ion's eye. The child of nine was a Magician or Sorceress, as the case might be, and a prince or princess, but was lonely. That was a condition Squid understood all too well. "Ion, I'm sorry," he said. "I was acting on a dare. I wasn't trying to tease you. I didn't think of your feelings."

"It's all right," Ion said. "No girl kisses me when I'm a boy, either."

But Squid remembered a similar dialogue between the siblings. "When I'm a girl again, and you're a boy, I'll kiss you again. In public, if you want. That's a promise."

Ion smiled. "I appreciate the thought. I guess you do understand."

They resumed their trek. In due course they came to the end of the trail. Beyond it was a swamp with an island a few yards in.

"Don't touch that muck, even with a toe," Hilda warned. "It's suffused with the water of forgetfulness."

Laurelai looked around. "This is it? It certainly doesn't look like much."

"Yes," Hilda agreed. "That's the way some really important things are."

Squid felt a chill. S/he had been called the most important person extant, but was really just an incidental character. That was indeed the way it could sometimes be.

"The easiest way to handle this is for us just to wade through," Hilda continued. "But only when we're touching Ion, and she's nullifying the Lethe. It will be the same when we cross the causeway. It's why we can use this route and nobody else can. Mom knows it's safe for us, or she wouldn't let us do it."

"That does make sense," Squid agreed. "Usually when I encounter swamp or open water I revert to my natural state and splash on through, but Lethe is something else."

"You bet," Hilda agreed. "You won't want to swim between the islands either, because there are allegations galore just waiting to chomp you."

Squid smiled. "I can handle allegations."

"But the rest of us can't," Laurelai said.

"I'll find a form that can help us all."

They clustered around Ion and held on to her arms, or in the case of Hilda, one of his feet, as it was more accessible. They forged across, and the Lethe did not affect them.

"The nullification remains as long as you don't touch any new water," Hilda said as they strode on to the land of the island.

They stood on the small bit of land. "Now what?" Squid asked.

"We go to the far side."

They walked to the other side. There was the causeway, or land bridge, cutting straight across the open water to another island.

"It is safe to cross this alone," Hilda said, setting out.

They followed. Squid saw a kind of shimmer halfway across, and suspected that that was the boundary between Now and Sometime. Indeed, they could never have made it without the guidance and protection of the twins.

They arrived at the next island. This one was made of candy, but Squid was not inclined to eat any of it. It was too close to the Lethe area.

On its far side was more open water, this time with no causeway. They were on their own. "How do you usually cross?" Squid asked.

"There are ways. Ion floats across, of course: that's one advantage of not being able to walk. I usually sew a small boat that is impervious to predator teeth, and Ion pulls me along by a cord. It's slow, both the sewing and the pulling, but we get there eventually. Or I can sew a swimsuit that completely encloses my body and smells of stink horn. If that isn't enough, Ion opens a bottle of something worse."

Squid hardly cared to imagine what could be worse. "Let me see what I can do." He delved into his memory of oddities, and came up with something he had never tried before because it would have been imitation, not real. But now might be different. "An Aether Oarfish."

"Either Or Fish?" Hilda asked.

"Aether Oar. Tata Dogfish researched it for me once. As in the old magic aether the Mundanes once had, that filled empty space, before they replaced it with the modern Higgs Field that fills in substance. Plus the oar paddle. It's a long ribbon-like fish with something else. It either stays put, or it jumps to where it's looking. Either here or there. Now I won't be able to talk to you in that form, but I will understand you when you talk. But first I have to verify whether I will be real or fake."

"You're real," Hilda said.

"He means when he changes," Laurelai explained. "He used to fake it, merely looking like whatever it was, but now he can actually become it. Such as a real man."

Hilda remained perplexed. "He sure looks like a real man now."

"And kisses like one," Ion added.

"Yes. But it used to be a clever imitation. Now he's actually human, instead of being a masked cuttlefish."

"So maybe now he can be a real Either Orfish?"

"Oarfish. That is the hope."

Squid changed, becoming a flat thin fish about ten paces long. He looked at the island across the water. He focused.

And he was there. He looped his head back and looked behind. There was the other island, with three children gazing in his direction. It had worked! He was a real aether oarfish, who could make the either/or choices. Great!

He jumped back, and changed back to boy form. Unfortunately he had lost his clothing when he changed and was now naked.

Laurelai quickly wrapped his shirt around him like a towel. "You seem to be a success."

"Uh, yes. Uh, thanks."

"We're close enough now to be like siblings, or a couple. We don't freak each other out, and we see to each other's needs. You'd do the same for me."

"Uh, yes." For the rest of his life, if she let him. "Now where do we want to go? If I can see it, I can jump to it, and I think if the rest of you are touching me, I can take you along. But you'll have to tell me where."

"We don't know," Hilda said. "The Sometime Islands change position somewhat randomly; we're never sure which one will be next. So we just hop along until we recognize Adamant, and then we're there. But you're not looking for that, unless that's where Caprice Castle went."

"And we don't know where Caprice is," Laurelai said. "But we'll recognize it if we see it, and it should show up well enough on one of these small islands, because of its high turrets. So random searching should do it, in time."

That gave Squid a thought. "I guess you two just want to go home. We can help you get there, then go on by ourselves to locate Caprice."

Ion and Hilda exchanged a glance. "No," Hilda said. "We want to help you find it."

"We like you," Ion said. "You're fun to be with, and you treat us like friends."

"You *are* friends," Laurelai said. "How could you question that?"

"We needed you to get to the Sometime Islands," Squid said. "But that's just the business side. There's also a personal side. We get along well. For one thing, you understand about getting gender reversed. Few others would."

"To everyone else we're spoiled brats," Hilda said.

"Or royal pains," Ion said. "Except at Portal Village, where they don't really know who we are, and we are careful not to tell them."

"Pains? Not to us," Laurelai said firmly.

"Not at all," Squid agreed.

"And you mean it," Hilda said.

"Of course we mean it," Squid said. "We're used to odd children, being two ourselves. I think the others aboard Fibot would feel the same."

"We'd love to meet them," Ion said wistfully. "We are set apart by royalty and isolation, and of course by our powerful talents, but think your siblings would relate without experiencing either awe or contempt."

"As they related to me," Laurelai agreed.

Squid considered. "If you really want to keep traveling with us, despite the danger, we can introduce you to them when we return." He reconsidered. "*If* we return. We're not fooling about the danger. We've already lost several adults we felt closest to, and whatever took them could probably take us too. And you, if you're with us. So you need to consider whether its worth it, all things considered."

The twins didn't hesitate. "We know your mission is dangerous," Hilda said. "In fact we know that if you fail, we may all be lost, together with our families. So there's no more danger, really, being with you than being without you. Maybe less with you, if we can help you. We're all in this together regardless."

Laurelai nodded. "That's true, when phrased that way."

"So let's go find Caprice Castle," Ion said. "And maybe save Xanth while we're at it."

"Let's," Squid agreed, and kissed her again. Ion almost glowed. She knew there was even less future for her with Squid than there was for Squid with Laurelai, and not just because of the gender reversal, but was giving herself up to the moment.

The decision had been made. Squid was relieved.

"But now another awkward question," Hilda said. "You can zip us from island to island, but that's not the same as locating Caprice Castle. Purely random won't do it, because the castle might even change islands while we search, and appear on one we've already checked. There also may be a time limit, as we don't know what is happening there, on what schedule. How do we find it quickly?"

"That's a good question," Laurelai said. "Too good. I don't have an answer. I didn't really think it through beyond getting to the Sometimes Islands."

"None of us did," Ion said.

Then they looked at Squid.

And it came to him. "I can orient on the scene when someone speaks my name. If anyone in Caprice Castle does that, I can be there, in my mind."

"Will that tell you where it is?" Hilda asked.

Bleep. "No, not necessarily, unless I could rise up to a high turret and look around, and then all I might see would be forest and field."

"And there's no guarantee that your name will be spoken," Laurelai said. But wait—didn't you say that sometimes you can orient on a thought of you?"

"Yes. But I can't be sure that anyone there will think of me, let alone speak my name. They surely have other things to focus on." Because their little mission could not be sure that anyone in Caprice remained alive, she thought dourly. That was their grim purpose: to find out.

Ion smiled. "Too bad you can't think of them, and evoke their thought of you."

Squid laughed, then quickly sobered. "I wonder. Our talents have been upgraded. A little bit of an upgrade there could make a big difference. Let me try." It was as close as he dared come to a hint to Fornax.

He thought of the folk vacationing in Caprice Castle. Dell and Nia, like foster parents to the siblings, especially Nia because of her hidden age. Picka and Dawn Bone, Piton and Data's parents, who were the hosts of that tour. Dawn was actually a princess, with a Sorceress talent; the idea that she could be abducted was especially frightening. Magnus and Jess, with their traveling show, that the children had planned to join before the crisis struck.

Jess. The prior protagonist. That was what Squid had in common with her. It was an important connection. They had discussed it. Enough of one to evoke a thought?

Jess, Squid thought. *I'm thinking of you. Will you think of me?*

There was a faint pulse. Squid pounced on it. *Yes, me. Squid. The cuttlefish girl. The other protagonist. We discussed it. Please, please, think of me!*

The pulse increased. It was definitely a thought, but muted, as if cloaked or suppressed. A thought of her. Maybe confused because Caprice had wards against intrusion. Or because the Squid Jess knew was female, and Squid now was male. That might interfere with the connection in another way.

Squid did not find himself in the scene, but he did have the next best thing: a direction.

He opened his eyes. He pointed. "That way."

After that it was halfway routine. Squid became the aether oarfish, the others grabbed on, and he oared them all on to the next island in the general right direction. When there were two islands in sight, he chose the one closer to the right direction. It wasn't perfect, because the islands weren't always on the line, but they were getting closer, and the signal strength increased.

Until at last they spied the tallest turret of Caprice Castle. "Castle ahoy!" Hilda exclaimed happily.

"That's Caprice," Ion said. "It visited Adamant once, and we met Princess Dawn."

"And Picka Bone," Hilda said. "He was fun. He changed into a walking skeleton, then back to human."

They paused to gaze at it. The castle was beautiful, with its surrounding wall, fortified chambers, and graceful towers. It looked pristine.

But of course it couldn't be, because its occupants never would have deserted the children. Something had to be terribly wrong. What would they find, when they entered it? Because they did have to enter it.

"Can we do this?" Squid asked. Then "Do we have a choice?" And finally "Yes we can, because we have to."

"We do," Laurelai agreed. She took Squid's hand.

They advanced on the castle, half fearing it would fade out, in the quiet manner it traveled. It didn't. The portcullis was up, and the small service entrance door unlocked. It was almost as if they were expected.

That gave Squid a chill, and he squeezed Laurelai's hand. She squeezed back, reassuringly, though he knew she was just as nervous as he and the twins were. They did not *want* to be expected. He looked at Ion and Hilda, in case they wanted to change their minds now that they faced the reality of this challenge, but they shook their heads almost together: no change.

They entered the first hall. It was eerily silent.

"Hello!" Squid called. "Is anybody home?"

There was no answer.

But Squid still felt the direction. Jess was here, somewhere.

They moved cautiously on. Then, in the central court, they found a glassy display case with six standing figures. *The* six.

"Oh, my," Laurelai breathed. "They are in suspended animation."

"In storage," Hilda agreed. "Until they are needed elsewhere."

"What could do this to a Sorceress?" Squid asked.

"Only a Demon or a Dwarf Demon, I think," Hilda answered.

"Can you nullify it, Ion?" Squid asked.

"No. This is not an elixir, but a field that holds them in place. A powerful one."

Squid nodded. Then she oriented on Jess, who stood beside Magnus, both of them fully clothed like dolls or statues, as if there were nothing wrong. But they were not statues. Squid felt Jess's mind. It alone was not frozen, but neither was it free.

Oh, Jess, she thought. *What has happened to you?*

The figure of her adult friend remained fixed in place, her eyes staring over and slightly aside from Squid. But her mind was there. *Touch me.*

Squid put a hand on Jess's hand. Now the contact was significantly stronger. *Oh, Squid, it is you! Your touch is strange, but I feel your mind.*

Squid decided not to reveal her physical change. *It is me,* she agreed.

You know my nature.

Why this? *I do.*

Squid, now that you have found us, bring the others here. Everything is fine. Bring Fibot here. So you can put on a show, with the dancing. Bring everyone. It will be the best time ever.

Something was decidedly wrong, but Squid couldn't quite identify it. *You want to see the dances?*

Yes! To show the universe!

What was she to do, when she knew something was wrong, but not what? She decided to play along. *We do like to dance. We want to impress everyone with our skill.*

Yes! Bring them all, in Fibot. As fast as you can.

That was the second request for the fire boat. *Okay. We'll do that pronto.*

Very good. We'll all join in.

Then Squid removed his hand, and turned to the others. "I have communicated with her. We need to go back and get Fibot and the siblings, and bring them here for a dance show. As fast as we can."

Laurelai looked at her hard, then quirked a smile. "Of course. Immediately."

The twins made no comment.

They exited the castle, then jumped back the way they had come. "I'm glad to get out of there," Hilda said. "It was eerie."

Now Laurelai glanced at Squid again, with that hard look. "What's going on?"

"Did you get to know Jess when you were on the boat?"

"Not really. I saw her only in passing."

"You didn't take her seriously."

"Actually I didn't," Laurelai agreed. "She's pretty much of a joker."

"That's her curse. Nobody takes her seriously."

The girl shrugged. "So?"

"But she is a very serious person underneath."

"Where is this going?" Hilda asked. "We've just visited a frozen castle, and it's scary as bleep. What do we care whether one person is serious or a joker?"

"Jess told me to fetch the others, the siblings, soon, and bring them to the castle soon for a dance, along with Fibot."

"So she's a joker," Laurelai said. "She has to know we won't do that."

"Yes. That's the key. She reminded me that I know her nature. I think it was her way of telling me not to believe anything she said."

Laurelai whistled. "And she said to bring Fibot here."

"Translation," Squid said. "There is great danger. Don't bring Fibot or the siblings here."

Laurelai nodded. "If she's captive by a Demon, and it seems she is, she may be obliged to do the Demon's will, or suffer horrendous consequences. And the Demon wants Fibot here."

"She said what the Demon wanted her to say. But the Demon didn't know I wouldn't believe her. That's how she warned me away."

"Now it's starting to make sense," Ion said. "Why Mom told us that not acting would mean worse danger than letting us go into danger alone."

"But the Demon must have known we were there," Hilda said. "Why didn't it simply grab us and put us in stasis too?"

"Because he's a collector," Ion said. "And maybe a showman. He's already collected Caprice Castle and its proprietors. Now he wants to fill it out with Fibot. They are two of the most valuable objects in Xanth: a castle that travels, and a boat that flies. What a show he could put on then! But he can't just go out and get Fibot, because the boat is hiding, and maybe he doesn't dare do it openly, because the Demon Xanth could catch him. He has to be sneaky. That's why he grabbed Caprice when no one was looking. So he wants us to bring Fibot to him."

"And there's the trap," Laurelai said. "We were supposed to find Caprice. Now we've been recruited to find Fibot."

"Which we must not do," Squid agreed.

"But what will happen to the people in Caprice if we don't bring Fibot?" Hilda asked.

"They'll fry," Ion said bluntly. "It's the hardware he wants; the people are just decorations."

There it was. How could they hope to rescue Jess and the others, without putting even more in peril?

Squid was near tears, which wouldn't do while she was a boy. "So what do we do now?"

"You siblings," Laurelai said. "Don't you have a conference, some kind of way to get at the truth of something, or the right course?"

"Yes! That might give us the answer."

"But to do that, you'll have to return to Fibot," Hilda said. "Do you want to do that, now?"

"No," Squid said. "Oh, I do, because that's like a second home to me, and the other siblings are there, but I don't want to risk it getting caught. I don't know what to do!"

"The next best course is to ask Mom," Ion said. "We knew she knows something about it, and her Sorceress talent is the Idea, and maybe she can steer us straight."

"But she's an adult," Hilda said. "If this mission of yours is supposed to be limited to children, how can we bring her in?"

"Why is it limited to children?" Ion asked.

Laurelai froze, but Squid stepped in. The reason was to conceal the presence of Fornax, whom others would never suspect could be hosted in a male child. Never mind that that child was female at the moment: that would change. So the Demoness could catch the enemy in the act, and nail him. The siblings knew because they were family-close to her, and the near-siblings knew. But the twins, worthy as they might be, were outsiders in this respect. If that truth were spoken, the enemy might hear, and the ploy would be ruined. "We had a sibling conference, and it was decided that only children could accomplish this mission." That was as much of the truth as she felt free to speak.

"That doesn't make much sense to me," Ion said.

"I guess you'd have to participate in a conference to understand."

"Then maybe we need to join this conference."

Which was a perfectly reasonable conclusion. "You're not the same kind of siblings," Squid said with regret.

"But we do need to do something," Laurelai said. "Let's take a vote. All those in favor of going to Princess Ida raise their hands."

Ion raised her hand.

"And those in favor of going to the sibling conference?"

The other three raised their hands.

"I'm changing my vote," Ion said. "I like Mom, but she is an adult, and there must be a reason we're keeping them mostly out. I want to know that reason."

"Four to none," Laurelai said. "Siblings."

"But first let's check in with Dad, so he won't worry," Hilda said.

"When does he ever worry?" Ion demanded somewhat petulantly.

"Oh, he does. He just doesn't show it. He keeps a stiff upper lip, and all that. Mainly, he misses Mom."

"She has to put in duty at Castle Roogna. In case anyone needs to visit a world. Or has a really great idea." Ion glanced at the others. "The idea has to come from someone else, who doesn't know her talent. Then she can agree with it, and it becomes true. But there aren't many folk who don't know her talent now, so she's not too busy."

"Yes," Squid agreed. "Otherwise we could have this great idea about rescuing Caprice Castle with a finger snap, and she would make it true."

"Or my discovering a spontaneous cure for my paralysis," Ion said wistfully.

"Talents have to have limits," Hilda said. "Otherwise there would be no challenge. Or so they say."

"We are in the Sometime vicinity," Laurelai said. "It's true that the two of you should at least check in before getting further involved in our danger."

"Now, we just need to get there as efficiently as we did Caprice Castle," Hilda said.

"I need someone there to think of me," Squid said. "But since they don't know I'm coming, and don't know me, that's out."

"I wonder," Laurelai said. "We don't know how far your talent has been upgraded. Maybe you can send a thought to King Hilarion."

Squid laughed, then sobered, as before. Maybe she could do that, now. She wasn't limited the way the twins were.

"I'll try," she said, and concentrated. *King Hilarion, you don't know me, but I'm with your children Ion and Hilda. Can you think of us, please?*

There was a surprised pause, then a pulse. *My children!*

And Squid got the direction. "That way," he said, pointing.

"It worked!" Laurelai said, delighted.

Squid became the oarfish, and they took hold, and jumped to the next island. From there they reoriented and jumped to another, and then once more.

And there were the pennants of a castle. "Adamant!"

It wasn't as grand as Castle Roogna or Caprice, because this was a small island kingdom, but it was good enough. Soon they were at its front gate, suitably garbed in Hilda's knits.

"Let us in!" Hilda called. "It's us."

"I recognized the carpet," the guard said, smiling. "Welcome home, your majesties."

"And these are our friends who traveled with us," Hilda said. "Squid and Laurelai."

Then they were inside, and King Hilarion was there. Squid recognized him by his kingly crown. He swept his children into his embrace. "Glad to have you back, kids!" He didn't even seem to notice their changed genders.

"These are Squid and Laurelai," Hilda said. "Our traveling companions. We're going to visit them on their flying boat."

His eyes flicked across to them, and lingered half a moment on Laurelai, who was of course pretty at any age. "That's fine. Have a good time. Now I've got a deal to forge." He set them down and hurried away.

"That's it?" Laurelai asked, bemused.

"He's a busy man," Hilda explained, a trifle defensively.

"It's a good thing you aren't in your older phase," Ion said. "He notices."

Squid realized that royal protocols were different from ordinary ones. The king probably had pretty maids to keep him company at night while the queen was away, and she probably knew and accepted this.

They were treated to a sumptuous dinner, served by uniformed personnel, then ushered to an elaborate suite maintained by a bevy of maids. There were extra beds for the visitors, each with its own closet and bathroom, complete with all necessary toiletries. Two maids helped Ion clean up and change. It was a considerable contrast to roughing it on the trail. But the twins obviously preferred the trail.

"Nobody blinked an eye at your gender change," Squid remarked.

"They're used to it," Ion said. "When we travel with Mom we wait for the island to phase in with Xanth. When we travel alone we use the trail. So we can turn up either way."

"Are there no other children here?" Laurelai asked.

"They're not allowed in the castle, lest they make a mess."

They let the subject drop. No wonder the twins were lonely! They had everything except company their own age.

"I was lonely," Squid said. "Until I wound up with the siblings. I've never been lonely since."

"We envy you," Hilda said.

"Suppose we ask the siblings to let you join us? Then you'd never be lonely again either, at least while you're with us. Of course you wouldn't be treated like royalty."

Both children gazed at her with utter longing. No more needed to be said.

In the morning they set off on their journey back. It was routine, in its own fashion. Squid became the oarfish to jump them from island to island, and then they walked north to Portal Village, where they entertained the villagers again in return for their room and board at the Inn & Outt. They had taught the twins a couple of dances along the way; Ion couldn't participate physically, but she could call out the moves for the villagers. Hilda danced occasionally with Laurelai, and plainly loved it.

Next day they reached the portal and crossed back into their original genders. Now Ion was male and Hilda was female. They took it in stride, changing into appropriate clothing. But for Squid and Laurelai it was more difficult. Squid was glad to be female again, but Larry was plainly depressed. They all understood why, and left him alone.

By evening they were near Castle Roogna. They did not enter it, for the sake of secrecy. They went directly to the rendezvous point, and Squid focused on Santo. *Santo! It's me, Squid. We're back. Pick us up.*

She felt his startled recognition. He didn't speak her name, but went to Win and Firenze. "Make a random veer past Castle Roogna. Say no names."

Squid felt their responses, being partly in the scene. They were coming here, and would arrive soon after dark. She signaled the others to wait silently.

It seemed to take forever, but it was only about an hour. Then something obscured the stars nearby. Fibot was silently gliding down.

The boat landed softly, and they hurried to intercept it. "Four of us!" Squid whispered to the silhouette of Win at the stern. The girl nodded.

They scrambled over the gunwale, then Squid led the way to the hatch. Only when all four of them were on the lower deck did she speak, as they were now within the protective shield of the craft. "We're here. Now we can talk."

"Wow," Hilda said. "It's bigger inside than outside."

"Yes. It's a very special craft," Larry agreed. "I was surprised when I first came here."

Santo appeared. "Welcome home, Squid."

Squid hugged him, then indicated the twins. "We have an amazing report and a lot to explain. But for now, this is Hilda, and on the carpet is her twin brother Ion, Princess Ida's children. We need to get them settled in. Then we have to talk."

Santo accepted that. He was always quick on the uptake. "Welcome aboard, Ion and Hilda."

Myst and Piton appeared and were introduced. "I see you're wearing one of my panties," Hilda said. "No, it doesn't show; I just know when my own magic is near."

"Your panties?"

"She sews garments with magic talent embedded," Squid explained. "She made your panty."

Myst was thrilled. "Oooo, I want to know more about you, Hilda!"

"So do I," Piton said. "You must be a princess and a Sorceress."

Squid kept silent, but feared he wanted to pinch her butt. Maybe she could warn him not to, or make sure Myst kept a close eye on him.

"Well, yes," Hilda said. "But I just want to be friends."

"Come with us and we'll show you around," Myst said. "We'll be friends."

Hilda glanced at Squid. "It's okay," Squid said. "Myst's a sibling. You can trust a sibling. She's also your age. I'll take care of Ion."

Hilda went with Piton and Myst. Then Squid spoke to Santo. "Can we get Win down here? I think Ion might like her if he got to know her."

In barely two-and-a-half moments they had put the craft on autopilot and Win and Data were below deck with them. "This is Ion," Squid said. "He's a prince and a Magician, but his talent of immunity to all elixirs prevents any healing elixir from curing his damaged legs, so he rides the carpet. He doesn't want to be known by either of his titles, or by his infirmity, just as a nine-year-old boy. You could make it easy for him to move fast, Win, because of your wind, if you wanted to."

"Maybe I could help too," Data said. "I could turn skeleton and hold him up so he could walk, using my bone legs."

"But you're a girl," Ion said.

"You have something against girls?" she asked archly.

"No," he said, blushing. "It's that you'd have to be almost glued to me to do it, and I'm a boy. Girls don't necessarily like that."

Data laughed. "I wrestle with my brother all the time. I'm a tomboy of a girl. I can handle it. And who knows, I might like getting close to you."

That made him blush again. Squid suspected she had done it on purpose, teasing him.

"We'll get along," Win said. "Unless you don't want two girls all over you."

"He's okay with that," Squid said, smiling. "He knows more about girls than you might think. Talk with him; you'll find it interesting."

The three of them departed together. "Now our private dialogue, we three," Squid said. "This is strong stuff, but maybe you'll know how to handle it."

He nodded, and led them to his cabin. Santo, Squid, and Larry sat down, and the latter two talked about their recent experience.

They let him have it: the twins' talents, the gender reversal, and the discovery of Caprice Castle with the six adults in stasis. Squid's partial dialogue with Jess.

"So you see," she concluded. "We think the Demon wants us to bring Fibot there in a rescue attempt, so he can capture the boat too and add it to his collection. We don't want to do that. But if we don't, the adults we love may be trashed. We don't know what to do. We hope you do."

"The hope is that some Demon on our side, such as maybe possibly Xanth, will catch him and nullify him," Santo said.

"Why didn't such a Demon, if there was one, do it when we were there in Caprice, with the captives?" Larry asked.

"Because no one can identify a hiding Demon," Santo said. "Not even another Demon. The rogue Demon could have been right there in the chamber with you, and you didn't know it. Similarly there could have been a Demon with you, and the rogue didn't know it." He paused, giving them a moment to remember that there had indeed been a Demon with them: Fornax. They kept her secret by never speaking of it directly. "Had the rogue Demon acted to capture you, that other Demon could have caught him, solving the problem. But he didn't act, so the other Demon, if one was there, couldn't act either."

Larry nodded. "Now I understand." Of course he had understood before: he was mainly establishing the rules of the game. "But if we return there with Fibot, and the rogue Demon acts, won't that reveal him?"

"Not necessarily," Santo said. "I understand that Adamant Isle is due to phase in to Xanth proper again tomorrow, so we could conveniently sail there in Fibot, thus entering the Sometime realm, then orient on Caprice. But that is the route the rogue expects, the obvious one. He will see us coming, and be prepared. He has six hostages: he might speak through one of them, like Jess, so as not to reveal himself directly, and threaten to kill them all if we offer any resistance. He could demand that we turn Fibot over to him, in exchange for the release of the hostages. That would be a difficult decision for us to make."

"We couldn't let them die!" Squid said, horrified. That prospect had been bothering her ever since she had seen them in stasis.

"Yes. So we might elect to solicit help, such as from the triplet princesses, Melody, Harmony, and Rhythm, who crafted Fibot. Individually they are full general purpose Sorceresses, but their magic squares when any two act together, and cubes when all three do. That could be a formidable asset." He paused a fraction of a moment. "But I am wary."

"They couldn't stand against a Demon," Squid said. "Even a Dwarf Demon."

"Indeed. And it just might be that the rogue wants us to do that, to bring them, so that they can be added to his collection. We would be playing right into his hands."

"I just thought of something else," Larry said. "Maybe he doesn't want children, just adults. So children are proof against his greed. But if children can be used to fetch in the adults he wants, there's a diabolically neat trap."

"That's why this is a children's mission!" Squid said. "Children are not at much risk, not being worth the rogue's time."

"Yes," Santo agreed. "So we shall have to strike by surprise, to catch him unaware, before he can hurt anyone. That may mean taking Fibot along the route you used. However, there may be a complication."

"We would pass through the portal," Larry said.

"Every child in the boat would change gender," Squid said.

"Could we handle that?" Santo asked. "The two of you, yes, as you have done it before. But I'm not sure I could, and I fear that some others might have a real problem."

"Like Firenze," Squid said. "He wouldn't like being a hot-headed girl."

"Neither would Piton," Larry said with a smile. "Then it would be *his* rear getting grabbed."

"And Ula as a boy would do it, just to get even for when he grabbed hers in the dance," Squid said. "In fact, so might I, just for the fun of it." And it would be fun, for she remembered those boy urges she had had, especially when Laurelai had aged them both to their teens.

"It makes a difference who is grabbing whom," Larry said. "If you and I changed, you wouldn't have to grab, Squid; I'd give it to you."

They laughed together, though Santo also looked thoughtful. They hadn't told him of their increasing interest in each other while reversed. "Still," Santo said, "I am not at all sure that such a thing should be risked. There could be chaos."

"So do we have any other secret routes?" Larry asked.

"I am thinking of the twins' mother, Princess Ida," Santo said. "Her orbiting worlds are legion, and Fibot can readily go among them, as we know. There might be an avenue there."

Squid wasn't sure of that. "I wish we could check out the gender change route without actually doing it. Then we'd know."

"A simulation," Larry agreed.

"There may be a way," Santo said thoughtfully.

They both looked at him. "You've got something on your devious mind," Squid said.

"The Sibling Conference," Santo said. "I believe it can be adapted for more than one purpose. It just might be able to make a simulation, if we all agreed to give it a fair try."

"I wonder," Larry said. "It accepted me and other new members. Would it accept Hilda and Ion?"

"Let's find out," Squid said. "They'd certainly be an asset in this respect."

"Let's," Larry agreed.

"I will present the notion to the siblings," Santo said. "Tomorrow. Tonight we rest."

"Simulation, here we come," Squid said, highly intrigued by the prospect. She took Larry's hand to lead him to their cabin.

Chapter 9

SIMULATION

They were all gathered in the main hall, twelve children plus Tata Dogfish and the peeve. Santo summarized the situation with marvelous precision so that all of them understood. "So we think we should at least try the gender change in simulation," he concluded. "So that we can judge whether we actually want to risk it in real life, or stay the bleep away from it. Are there any questions?"

"Yes," Noe said. "What about those of us who aren't quite certain of our gender, like you, or Larry, or the peeve?"

Squid appreciated the point. Noe, as the nominal girlfriend of a gay boy, well understood how tricky such a relationship could be.

"That is a legitimate concern, and we will answer," Santo said. "I am certain of my gender: I am male. I merely am attracted romantically to my own gender instead of to the opposite one. Should I turn female, I suspect I would then be attracted to other females, though I am not sure. I will want to kiss you, Noe, and discover my own reaction. But should I still be attracted to males, then you, as a male, would be my first choice, because I already know you and love you."

"Thank you," she said somewhat tightly. Squid knew that Noe loved Santo, while accepting that close friendship was the practical limit. He loved her in the manner of a sibling or close friend.

"Your turn, Larry," Santo said.

"I am, as most of you know, a girl in a boy's body," Larry said. "When I changed physical genders, I did not change mental ones. I became Laurelai, my true self, and I loved it. I wish I could always be Laurelai, but that is not presently feasible. At least I can say for the rest of you that mentally you will remain as you are now: only your host body will change.

Boys who become girls will find it awkward to pee, at first, and girls who become boys may be embarrassed to handle their male anatomy for such purposes." He smiled passingly. "Boys who become girls may also be annoyed by the stares they receive from the girls who become boys, and the tendency of boys' hands to touch private parts. It is called payback."

There was a murmur of laughter in the audience, but it was uneasy, at least on the part of the boys.

"And Peeve," Santo said.

"I am genderless," the bird said. "I have been through the portal, long ago. I did not change at all. So it makes no difference to me, literally."

"So you will remain objective," Santo said. "What about Tata?"

Tata's screen flashed.

"Tata is phrased as a male robot dogfish," the peeve translated. "He will become a female robot, with an altered perspective, but will remain objective."

"Any other questions?" Santo asked, looking around.

"Suppose we get stuck in reverse?" Ula asked.

Santo shook his head. "It will be a simulation. It will end in an hour or so, and we will all revert. The only way we could ever be stuck in the roles is if we pass through the physical portal and don't return. That's a risk we can decide on after the simulation."

"The simulation is not actually physical?" Ula asked.

"It is not." Santo looked around. "Any others?"

"Ion and I just want to say that we have switched genders many times, physically," Hilda said. "At first it was startling, awkward, and embarrassing. But we got used to it, and now can handle it either way without stress. So don't let your first impressions be your last impressions: it gets easier. Even fun, at times."

"But one thing," Ion said. "Your clothing doesn't change with you. So wear simple formless smocks, or go nude. It will be easier."

"Nude!" Data exclaimed. "When we're changed? It would be bad enough doing it straight, but in the wrong bodies it would be weird."

Ion shrugged. "Suit yourself. But remember, everyone else will be in the same situation. No one here will tease you for being different."

Data visibly thought about that. "I'll do it if you do it," she challenged her brother Piton.

"You're on, sis. Anyway, we can change to skeleton form if we want. No awkward anatomy there."

She smiled. "Maybe we won't have to."

There were no more questions.

"Then catch up on natural functions and return here in half an hour," Santo said. "We will hold a conference of all twelve children, and the animals too if they really wish to participate, and experience the simulation. We will be free to do what ever we want, during the change, and I think we should be encouraged to explore the limits so we can judge whether we can handle it longer term."

The group adjourned, dissolving into individual discussions.

Squid and Larry went to their room. "Did you mean it, back when you said I could grab your butt?" Squid asked. "Because I don't want to annoy you, but I think I'd like to, at least once, just to find out what the boys get from it."

"Yes. I know what the boys get. I'll even age us into teens if you want."

Squid looked at Larry. "You're such a beautiful girl, when. I don't want to be a boy, but when I am, I think I'm falling in love with you. Maybe it's just the hormones."

"Maybe it is," Larry agreed. "But we don't even know how long we're going to live, because of the danger of this mission. That makes me impetuous."

"We thought about that before," Squid agreed. "Each time I think about it, I'm more inclined to go wild."

"We'll go wild together," Larry said. "Maybe everyone will."

"If they're as mixed up about it as I am, it will be more than wild." Squid hesitated, then plunged ahead. "At least we've been through this much before. Kiss me."

Larry laughed. "Maybe when I'm a girl I'll understand your girl reasoning better." Then he embraced her and kissed her. She liked it, and suspected he did too, even if to him it was more like a girl kissing a girl.

"So do we go naked?" Squid asked.

"Might as well. We can set an example."

"Though if it's just a simulation, our bodies won't really be changing, so our clothes won't matter."

"Apt point," Larry agreed. "But I prefer to treat it as if it is real."

"Okay."

They reported to the main hall on time. The others were doing the same. They might have mixed feelings about this event, but no one wanted to miss it. The majority of them were naked, becoming visibly reassured when they saw the other bare bodies. It seemed that the Adult Conspiracy was unable to balk this aspect, maybe because the intent was not lascivious but practical. That gave Squid some quiet satisfaction.

They spied Hilda and Ion. "How's it going?" Squid asked.

"Myst is great!" Hilda said. "And Piton's not bad. He treats me just like a girl."

Squid had forgotten to warn Piton off. Bleep! "He grabbed your butt!"

"Yes. Isn't it great?"

Neither Squid nor Larry commented. To a lonely girl, any sincere attention from a boy might be nice, however crudely expressed. She hadn't thought of that aspect.

Meanwhile Ion, was with Win and Data, and looked happy. To a lonely boy, the sincere attention of two girls could be just as nice.

"Remember, we need to focus," Santo said. He was one of the nude ones, handling it with aplomb. Noe was beside him, also bare but with less aplomb. "Enter the simulation. The rest will follow. Remember also that we all know each other. We're not out to make fun of anyone. We're out to learn what we need to know." He paused briefly. "Form into a big circle and hold hands."

Squid and Larry were beside Hilda and Ion. They linked hands, becoming part of the big circle.

"Focus," Santo said. "Conference."

They focused. Nothing happened.

Then it did. They were standing in an open field, but personally unchanged.

"Are you sure we're in?" Squid asked. "This is just scenery."

"We're in," Santo said. "Now we travel. Tata, take us along the route the twins used getting here."

"On our way," the peeve said.

The scenery shifted, moving to the side. Now Squid saw the translucent outline of the fire boat, traveling under its own power, sail furled. Squid had almost forgotten that it could do that, so as not to be entirely dependent on sometimes erratic winds. They weren't standing in a field, they were standing in Fibot, which had become almost invisible.

The craft accelerated, and zoomed along the terrain they had twice traversed. In rather less than half a slew of moments it came to the dread portal, and hovered.

"Any second or third thoughts?" Santo asked.

No one spoke. After a generous pause, motion resumed. The boat with all its passengers passed though the portal.

There was a scream. It was Data, discovering herself changed. She now had male anatomy. It seemed the seeming reality had more impact than her anticipation. Win, beside her, was similar.

Squid was male again, and Laurelai deliciously female. Next to them Hilda and Ion were male and female again.

"We're through," Santo said, glancing down at his body. "We can let go now, and mix."

Squid looked at him. He was a girl, actually rather pretty, and beside him Noe was a handsome boy.

"Oh, wow!" Piton said. He was a girl, and Myst was a boy.

Ula, now a boy, forged toward them and grabbed Piton's butt, giving it a good tweak. And paused. "You know, that's sort of fun," Ula said, surprised.

"Maybe for you," Piton snapped. Then he/she paused. "You know, I do have a nice donkey, now."

Squid stifled a smile. That was not the word he had tried to use. It seemed that the dread Adult Conspiracy had not lost its power, even in this exercise of imagination.

"Tata, halt the boat in place," Santo said, and the motion stopped. "Make us invisible." The scenery outside faded to unfathomable mist. "Thank you." Then Santo raised her voice. "We passed through the portal, as you might have guessed. I think we need to get more of a feel for our new bodies, and I don't mean grabbing them. We need to discover how to use them, how to be the opposite gender. How to really come across so that strangers would not know we aren't quite as we look. Any ideas how best to do that?"

"We can practice peeing," Piton suggested. Male Myst slapped her butt, but others nodded; it was actually a good idea, to prevent future embarrassment.

"We can dance," Noe said. "Our regular couples, same dances, just slightly different roles."

Santo nodded. "Good idea, partner. We have enough for a square and some left over, if we count Ion as a dancer."

"I can do it on my carpet," Ion said.

"One square," Noe said. "The others watch. Then a new square with two couples switched out."

"Good enough," Santo agreed. "Form it."

Squid and Laurelai stepped up to join the male Noe and female Santo. Then male Myst and female Piton joined them. Then Ula and Firenze, similarly changed.

"Sets in order," the peeve said as Tata's screen flashed. There was only one set, but it was a generic directive. The dogfish now had softer lines and did look distinctly female.

"Try swinging your partner," Santo said. "That's a good interactive motion."

Squid and Laurelai paused a moment to watch the others. There was immediate chaos as some tried to do it the way they had learned while others tried to assume the opposite role. Myst and Piton actually got their limbs tangled, and landed on the floor.

"Let's try a demonstration," Santo said. "Squid, Laurelai, you know how to do it, right? Show us."

Squid and Laurelai come together and swung, meshing perfectly.

"Now take other partners and show them," Santo said.

Squid caught Piton and folded her into the proper format, then slowly turned her around. She began to get it. "Wow!" she said. "You do know what you're doing."

Meanwhile Laurelai caught Ula and guided him into the proper male position. "Oh, my," he said. "You're some girl!"

"I am," Laurelai agreed happily.

"I mean you look and act as if this is your natural state."

"It is."

Then Squid took Firenze and guided her similarly. "I am learning more than the swing position," she said.

Firenze was fifteen, on the verge of physical maturity as a boy and nudging into it as a girl. Her hips were wide and her chest was softening. "Maybe we can practice after this in clothing."

"Yes!" Squid agreed, because his partner's nudity was forcing unwanted thoughts to manifest.

Then he took Santo, who was quickly getting into it. "How are you feeling?" Squid asked him as they swung.

She did not pretend to misunderstand the question. "I do not want to be with girls rather than boys. Too bad Noe is strictly hetero."

Once Squid and Laurelai had guided the others, the swings went better. "But we should try it in costume," Squid said.

"Definitely," Santo agreed.

They scattered to their cabins to get each other dressed. When they returned they looked far more professional. The boys were handsome and the girls were pretty.

Laurelai held Squid close and quietly aged them both several years. Now they were both knockouts.

"What a difference clothing makes!" Noe said. "You look just like a woman, Firenze, and Laurelai—" He paused. "Oh, your talent is to change your age! You *are* a woman."

"I cheated," Laurelai agreed, not at all abashed.

They practiced swings again, getting it right. Squid, as a slightly older male, was finding the newly minted females alarmingly intriguing. Far from inhibiting those male thoughts, the costumes enhanced them. That surprised him.

"Is it enough?" Santo asked. "Can we decide whether we can handle this for longer than an hour?"

"I'm not sure," Noe said. "I am finding the new girls interesting. I wish I could check some who are not in our group."

"We can, maybe," Hilda said. "We can go on to Portal Village and do a demonstration there. Can the simulation handle that?"

"Let's find out," Santo agreed.

Ion made a quick presentation to the group. "Hilda and I have been there many times as we travel," he concluded. "Always in our reversed mode. But it hardly matters, because most of them are reversed too. They came through the portal, found others like them, and settled down there, not changing back. They're nice folk, and they really do understand."

"Do we have time?" Noe asked. "We're well along in our hour."

"In simulation, time is elastic," Santo said. "We could spend a day and night here, and it would still be within the hour when we emerge."

"A day and night!" Noe repeated, laughing. "In these bodies?"

Others joined him, but some were thoughtful as they gazed around at the clothed dancers. Laurelai was not the only one who seemed to be enjoying the female form, and Squid was not the only one who increasingly liked being with those exploratory girls. It was a novel and stimulating experience, and it could be that others were conscious of the danger of their mission. Why not live life to the fullest while they could?

The vote was solidly to give the village a try.

The boat cruised on along the route. Soon they spied the village, and halted near the bell. "You four should do the honors," Santo said. "You know the people."

Squid and Laurelai got out, followed by Ion and Hilda. Hilda picked up the bell and rang it. The proprietor Inn & Outt promptly appeared. "Back so soon? You must be developing a taste for our cuisine."

Hilda smiled. "This is more complicated. We are with a larger group: in fact there are twelve of us, plus two animals. The others are new to reversal, and wish to interact with more than just their friends. Could we do a dance for you, and show you some steps, and talk with you? You have so much more experience with reversal than we do."

Inn & Outt developed a canny look. "I see you have a remarkable flying boat. I have heard of one that has a fiery sail, and is claimed to be larger inside than outside."

"This is that boat," Squid agreed.

"Would you be willing to give us a tour? We would promise not to interfere with it in any way, and we would be most obliged."

Most obliged. There was something about that phrasing that appealed to Squid in his male form. The village had some very pretty girls; how obliging were they prepared to be? "Let us check."

They checked with Santo, who put it to a vote. They agreed to give the tour.

Soon they were in the village square, boat and all. They put on a demonstration square dance, then split up to take village partners to teach the new moves to. The villagers were plainly thrilled, and were very quick learners. And yes, the village girls were remarkably pretty, and the boys quite handsome. All of them danced well, and rapidly picked up on the new moves. They were putting on their best face.

Squid's village partner was Ruby, an attractive girl and excellent dancer, with waist-length red hair that flounced prettily as she moved. He remained in his older age, and she matched it, which made her truly intriguing. They talked between dances. "I saw you when you here here last time," she confided. "I was really jealous of your partner, who had so much of your attention."

She remembered him from before? Yet this was a simulation, not existing in the real Xanth. Maybe the simulation picked up from his memory of her, though he did not remember seeing her before.

"Laurelai is a nice girl and excellent dancer," he said noncommittally.

"Yes. All the boys like her." She glanced across, and Squid followed her gaze. Indeed, four boys were around Laurelai, and she seemed to be thriving.

Squid suppressed a foolish flash of jealousy. "That's good," he said, feeling the opposite.

She picked up on it. "They want to get that lovely creature to cross the portal with them. They're all genderlings, and so am I."

"Genderlings?"

"Gender switched," she clarified. "Sometimes we like to revert to our original genders to make out, though we don't want to stay that way. Would you like to cross with me?"

Suddenly Squid wanted very much to do that. But that was crazy. He hardly knew Ruby, and Laurelai was the one he wanted most to be with, whatever the gender. So he changed the subject. "Does your name mean anything? Like precious stone?"

She laughed. "You mean, the way naval oranges go to sea and stop sailors from getting scurvy? No, nothing like that. It is short for Rubella, a bad disease that can cause cataracts in babies, deafness, heart disease, mental retardation and other things, if their mothers get it when there is an order out to the stork. My talent is to prevent that from happening. So I visit women who are expecting the stork, and that protects their babies."

"That's a wonderful talent!" he exclaimed.

"Thank you." She looked around. "Oh, they're organizing the tour of your marvelous boat. I desperately want to see it."

Which might be why she was playing up to him. Squid retained a certain female cynicism. But why not? "I will show you around."

"Wonderful!" she exclaimed, kissing him on the cheek. That might be a calculated gesture, but it was effective; he felt as if he floated for a moment.

They joined the tour, which Santo conducted. Then they found themselves in Squid's cabin. Ruby was endlessly enthusiastic about everything she saw.

"The boat is so marvelous," she enthused. "I love every part of it. But you, Squid—I want to know more about you. How did you come by such an odd name?"

He smiled. "It's a literal name. I am an alien cuttlefish. We were visiting Xanth as tourists when something happened and I lost my parents, but was saved along with four other children, and we have been here ever since." This was severely simplified, but he doubted she was really interested in the details.

"You don't look alien. You seem quite human to me."

"I am able to emulate the human form well enough to, in effect, become it. I now feel exactly like a boy."

"Is your romantic interest in girls or in cuttlefish?"

"If I reverted to cuttlefish form, it would be in cuttle females. But when I'm with someone like you, my interest is in you. You are very attractive."

"Thank you," she said, kissing his cheek again. Then she put her delicate hands on his head, turned it to face her, and kissed him again, this time on the mouth.

If the cheek kiss had made him float, the mouth kiss catapulted him into sheerest bliss. "Oh, Ruby," he said, amazed.

"Let's lie down," she murmured, taking his hand and leading him to the bed.

Lie down? Was she tired? Her interest in touring the boat seemed to have faded.

She gently drew him down with her. "You haven't had a girlfriend long, have you." It was a statement, not a question.

"I haven't been a boy for long."

She laughed. "Touche! Let me show you how it's done."

Then she was stretched out against him, from shoulder to knee, and her touch seemed electric. She took his upper hand and set it on her bottom. It was as though sweet fire animated him. Then she kissed him again.

Then he was consumed by passion. He kissed her back as he squeezed her bottom. He had never felt this way before.

He felt moisture on her face. He looked, and saw that she was crying.

"Ruby!" he cried. "Did I hurt you? I'm so sorry. I got carried away."

"Not your fault," she said. "It's mine."

"I don't understand. If I have done anything to cause you grief, I'll stop. I didn't mean to."

She swung her legs up and to the side, bringing them down beside the bed. She sat up. "It's that I can't do it. You're too nice, too innocent. It's not right."

"I'm sorry," he repeated. Then: "What can't you do?"

"I can't seduce you."

He stared at her, "Can't what?"

She took his hand in hers and held it firmly. "That is what I was doing Squid. Seducing you."

"But—"

"Listen to me. We were offered a phenomenal prize if we could seduce one or more of you boat people. Pocket portals. We could have them with us, and invoke them any time we chose. Then we could change gender at any time, not having to go through the main portal. If I was with my boyfriend I could change to a boy, and he could change to a girl, and we could continue our lovemaking that way. Or we could be two girls, or two boys. Or join with others and have a group event. There are many possibilities, and we are eager to try them. If we had the pocket portals."

Squid hung on to one thing for the moment. "Your boyfriend?"

She squeezed his hand. "Squid, we have lives of our own when not being visited. Boyfriends and girlfriends, hot and heavy."

"But children don't get that way," he protested. "We like each other, but we don't know how to do the adult stuff."

"True. I am older than I look. I am a young adult. I know how to summon the stork."

"You know?"

"And I was about to take you there, inducting you into the Conspiracy. To seduce you. You may not know what it's about, but I do, and once we did it, you would be technically an adult. It's a violation of the Conspiracy, yes, but sometimes adults do indoctrinate children. But I realized that it just wasn't right, and I couldn't do it after all."

This was beyond his understanding. "Why? I mean, why do that with a child? When you have a boyfriend you could do it with instead?"

"Because of the promise of those pocket portals."

"But why does someone else want you to do it?"

"We don't know. But there's a Demon in the background who can deliver. We think it is one of their Demon Wagers. So we were ready to do it. Only then I couldn't."

"Are you the only one?"

"No, not at all. We're all ready to do it, hoping that at least one would succeed."

Squid decided to check with Santo, "Santo!" he thought forcefully. "Tune in on me. Better yet, come to me. Something is happening."

He felt Santo's acknowledgment. Then Santo arrived at Squid's cabin, smiling. "Something special?" she asked.

"They are trying to seduce us. A Demon is behind it."

Santo was instantly serious. "A Demon!"

"A Demon wants us to be seduced. To make us technically adult. I don't trust this, so I'm checking with you. Why would a Demon do that?"

"There is one likely reason," Santo said. "Demon contests typically set rules that may make sense only to Demons, not to lesser folk like us. They honor those rules absolutely, not infringing them in the slightest. Often they relate to the manner ignorant mortals may react to particular challenges, in the manner humans might make bets on whether a given ant will turn left or right at the next path intersection. Usually the odds of success or failure are crafted to be precisely even. It may be that children are exempt from capture, according to the rules of this particular wager. Adults aren't. If there's an adult aboard Fibot when it reaches Caprice Castle, the enemy Demon can focus and capture the boat."

"Oh, my," Squid breathed. "Now it's beginning to make sense. We are ants."

"We are phenomenally less than that, to Demons," Santo agreed. "But on occasion useful for settling their bets."

"That would also explain Jess's message to me, in Caprice Castle," Squid said. "She wasn't allowed to say any more than that, and the Demon rules specified exactly what she did say. It was meant to be a mystery for me to fathom if I could, and the conclusion I came to could determine the status of a Demon."

"Demon wagers are almost always for status," Santo agreed.

"I really don't know what you're talking about," Ruby said. "But I gather that this is serious mischief to your project."

"Amen," Santo said. "But now we must stop any other seductions that may be in progress, because as far as we know, it is the enemy Demon behind them. Can you tune in to the others, Squid?"

"I'll try." He was in the background thoughts of the other siblings, and that helped. One was in immediate danger. "Firenze!"

Santo charged off to Firenze's room, Squid following. There she was, being ardently courted by a handsome village boy, and not at all loath. "Break it up!" Santo said.

"Hey, this was just getting interesting," Firenze protested, her head appearing to be pleasantly warm.

"It's a plot by the enemy Demon. Anyone who gets seduced becomes technically an adult, and can then be nabbed by the Demon."

"Oh, bleepy!" Firenze swore in unladylike fashion.

"And you," Santo said to the village boy. "You're older than you look. You're a young adult. You have no business seducing children. Get out of here."

The boy, obviously caught in the act, decided not to argue. He departed.

Then Laurelai, who was at special risk because she was so pretty. "Sorry," Squid said.

"I'm not. If I am tempted to do it, I prefer you."

After that they routed out the others and ended the tour of the boat. "I'm so sorry," Ruby said. "I didn't know it was like that."

"I know you didn't," Squid said. "But I think your conscience just saved our mission. I wish there were a more tangible way I could thank you."

Ruby smiled sadly. "We were carried away by the promise of those portals, but we do believe in doing the right thing. We wouldn't care to profit ourselves at your expense. We thought we would be doing you a favor by introducing you to the wonders of adult ways; now I see that this is not at all the case."

"I am having trouble sorting out my feelings, as well as right and wrong," Squid said. "I like you, Ruby, and not just because you are one interesting girl. I wish we could be friends."

"After I almost betrayed you?"

Squid nodded. "It is that 'almost' that makes the difference. I wish we could meet again when we're in our original genders. Not to do anything seductive: just to enjoy each other's company."

"I think I would like that too. You are really quite a person, Squid. That's apart from your alien origin. I never met an alien before."

"I don't conceal it, but I don't advertise it either. I am really trying to make it as a human girl."

"And you are of course a girl, apart from the portal conversion."

"Yes. Though I confess to being intrigued by the male aspects. Males have interests and desires that females seldom choose to understand."

"Oh, yes! A significant part of my enjoyment of this female form is my knowledge of its desirability to a male. I am better at being female because of my male experience. I know what turns a boy on."

She certainly did. "Oh, Larry would really like to know you! In real life he is the form Laurelai must take, and it's a problem for him."

"We must get together, when we don't have other priorities."

"Yes. Is there any way we can get in touch, some time hence?"

"Short of a magic mirror, I don't know."

Then Squid thought of something. "I have a special ability to tune in on folk who are mentioning me or thinking about me. I can hear them talking. Sometimes I can send them thoughts, if they are receptive. If you think of me every so often, I may be able to respond."

"I will do that," Ruby said. Then she too departed.

Only when it was too late did Squid remember that this was a simulation. Ruby might never think of her, because they didn't interact in real life. Bleep!

They took the boat back though the portal, reverting to their natural or original genders as the case might be, and sailed back to Castle Roogna. Then held another meeting.

"I don't think we can go that route," Santo said.

The others quickly agreed.

"Which leaves the Worlds of Ida. I have no idea how they might lead to Caprice Castle. We will have to ponder."

They agreed, grimly.

Then the simulation ended, and they were back in the real world.

"Let's rest for a day," Santo suggested. "Then tackle our next challenge."

They were glad to agree.

Back in their own cabin, Squid and Larry, now female and male, hugged. "If there any seductions to be performed," Larry said, "We can handle it ourselves."

"Not that we are going to," Squid said. Her mind was still spinning with the revelations of the day, and their narrow escape from likely disaster.

"But if we ever did," Larry said, "I would much rather do it with you, rather than with a stranger. You understand."

"I do," Squid agreed. Her attraction to him was still increasing. There might be future mischief there, considering what they had figured out.

Then they lay down chastely and slept, holding hands. It was enough.

In the night, Squid woke. Had someone called her name? No, someone was thinking of her. It was Ruby! Ruby thought she had dreamed their interaction, but she remembered Squid and wanted to meet her again. They were out of the simulation, but somehow that much had carried through.

Yes! Squid thought strongly.

"Oh, so we did meet," Ruby thought. "Somewhere, somehow. I'm so glad."

Me too.

Then they both returned to sleep.

Chapter 10

WORSE COMING

Squid woke, feeling a malaise. She wasn't sure what it was, as she was generally immune to human ailments.

Larry was still holding her hand. "Squid! Your hand is like ice!"

"I'm not human," she reminded him. "When humans get sick they tend to run a fever; my kind tends to run a chill. It's our way of freezing out bad bugs."

"Is it serious?"

"I'm not sure. A chill is a reaction, not a cause."

"I don't want you sick."

She looked at him. "We're a couple of convenience. You shouldn't be concerned."

"We may not be a true couple," he said. "But we've already been through a fair amount together, and understand each other well. I do care about you, more than incidentally. What can I do to help you?"

She was touched. "Maybe Tata can classify it."

"Tata!" he said immediately, and in a moment and a half the dogfish was there, screen flashing, the peeve perched on his shoulder.

"It is a tentacular virus," the peeve translated. "It tends to get in when her kind is over-stressed."

Squid had been under plenty of stress recently.

"Do you have a treatment?" Larry asked, his worry evident.

"Not aboard this vessel. It's a specialty order. By the time we get it in, she will likely have recovered on her own. She will have to suffer through a siege."

"Is it serious?"

The screen flashed again.

"That depends. Usually hallucinations are impressive but harmless."

"Hallucinations!"

"It's all right'" Squid said. "I have had them before. They normally fade when the chill does."

"We should warm her!"

"No," the peeve said. "The chill is her nature's way of dealing with the infection. We don't want to interfere."

"We just have to let her suffer?"

"In the absence of proper medication, yes."

"Bleep!"

Squid smiled wanly. "Thank you for caring, Larry. I should get by."

Then a panel opened in the wall of the cabin. Beyond it she saw a lovely garden path.

The others in the cabin faded out. She was alone with her vision.

Well, almost. Larry squeezed her hand. She didn't see him, but she felt him, her contact with reality. "I'm going with you."

She laughed. "On a hallucination? Let it be."

"We were together on the simulation. We can do it on the hallucination."

"You're crazy!"

"Do I have to kiss you to make you listen?"

She laughed again. "Don't do that. Tata and the peeve would not understand."

"We'll bring them along too."

He was determined. "As you wish. But it may be a pretty dull excursion."

He maintained his hold on her hand so she could not tune him out. "Just tell us what you see."

"I see a panel in the wall, opening to a lovely garden path. I'm going there."

"Right with you."

She moved up to the open panel and stepped through to the path. "Now I am in the garden. I am breathing its myriad intriguing scents."

"Continue."

"A cluster of red berries is catching my attention. I am picking one and eating it. I like it, so am eating a second, then a third."

"Good appetite."

"And I feel myself rapidly changing, my clothing emulation shredding, leaving me nude."

"Oops, Tata says those must be elderberries, aging you," the peeve said. "You are progressing from age eleven to twelve, thirteen, and fourteen. Better to stop there; three are more than enough."

"Good point," she agreed. "I remain in human form, but now with a thin waist, swelling hips, and lumps of fat on my chest. I have become nubile! It's a good thing that there are no village louts here to goggle at my nudity."

"I'm goggling," Larry said.

"You don't count. You're not a lout. Anyway, you can't see my change."

"Still, when this is over, maybe I'll take you with me on a three year aging so I can properly admire that bare figure."

"It's not as good as Laurelai's when she ages."

Something skittered through the grass. She focused on it, but found herself already losing interest. Why? Now she was interested not in the thing, but in why she had lost interest, because that was suspicious.

"Speak," Larry said.

"Something skittered, but it's not interesting."

"Describe it anyway, so Tata can verify it."

"It seems to be a garden-variety mouse, that seemed interesting only when I didn't know what it was."

"That's an Anony Mouse," the peeve said. "It protects itself from predators by making itself uninteresting to them."

"And I fell for it! Some predator I am."

"Nice girls don't make good predators," Larry said.

She walked on along the path. Then her body started itching. "Bleep! I think I have caught some lice." She scratched desperately, contorting her body to try to get at obscure places, but the itching continued.

"That's a funny kind of Terpsichore."

"A what?" Squid asked.

"Saltation, exertion, endeavor, effort, contortion, movement—"

"Dance?" Larry asked.

"Whatever," the voice agreed crossly.

"Metria!" Squid exclaimed. "What are you doing here in my hallucination?"

"I smelled something interesting, so of course I messed in. It's what I do."

"Well, go do it somewhere else," the peeve said. "This is a private session."

"Never! I hate dullness." The demoness took form, eyeing Larry. "I don't believe I recognize you, young man. Is the alien female cuttlefish trying to seduce you? Your eyeballs are bulging as she distorts her humanoid torso."

"She ate some elderberries, which caused her to age a few years, becoming nubile," Larry said. "This makes her bare gyrations interesting."

"Exactly," the demoness agreed, inhaling in a manner that was more than provocative. "Girls become intriguing when they gyrate, especially when without clothing. Note how portions of her chest project when she bends backwards, and how her bottom tightens when she bends forward."

"I've got an itch!" Squid snapped, horribly embarrassed by this analysis. "I must have blundered through a nest of lice." She was still attempting to reach a frustratingly obscure itch. "I'm not trying to seduce anybody!"

"Just as well. Seduction is best left to more experienced bodies. For example—" The demoness' own torso projected and tightened in a manner that was heating Larry's eyeballs.

"Agreed!" Squid said, not wanting to evince open jealously. "I just want to get rid of the lice." One was now itching her posterior unbearably, but it would have required a worse contortion to scratch it.

"Well, what you need is D Louse, the demon who delouses people."

"Whatever!" Squid said. "Is he close by?"

"He's not here."

Naturally Metria was not being very helpful. "Thanks for nothing."

"But I will emulate him, if you tell me what's going on."

Squid was too miserable at the moment to argue. "Deal."

The demoness dissolved into a small black cloud. The cloud floated across to surround Squid.

Suddenly the itching got much worse. Then it ceased. Squid saw that the lice were desperately leaping off her body.

"What made them go?" Squid asked, hugely relieved.

The cloud separated from her and reformed into the demoness. "Typo," Metria explained.

"Type O?"

"Typo. Lice can't stand that blood type; it makes them all fouled up. They can't even find the right places to bite. So they depart in deep disgust."

"Thank you!" Squid said.

"Now just tell me what's happening here. It's hard to see someone else's delusion directly. I have to key it in."

The demoness had actually come through. Now it was Squid's turn. "I am ill with a chill, and suffering hallucinations. My friend Larry is trying to share them with me, and Tata and the Peeve are interpreting them. At the moment we're on a garden path that leads through the cabin wall." Squid took a breath. "But I thought the fire boat shield was proof against your intrusion. How did you get in, Metria?"

"I am not in the fire boat," the demoness explained. "I am in your hallucination. I came in through the same hole in the wall, which is also a hole in reality."

Squid nodded. "I suppose that makes sense."

"As much as anything of mine does." Metria eyed Larry again. "So Squid has got a human boyfriend now?"

"In a manner," Larry said. "It's a relationship of convenience, because I know she's not actually human."

"I wondered. You, as a typical young human male, don't much care what is inside the form, as long as its external presentation is salacious."

"To a degree, yes," Larry agreed, smiling. He was actually teasing Metria.

Who was starting to catch on. "This is getting dull, so I'm off." She faded out.

Squid relaxed somewhat. She was relieved that the demoness had been satisfied with the immediate situation, and had not caught on to their larger mission, or the secrets about Larry. But she knew that Metria was not necessarily gone when she faded out, so they still had to watch what they said. "Now you have been introduced to a genuine if slightly peculiar demoness." As if he were not already familiar with far more than that.

"I will remember the experience," Larry said.

She looked on down the path. There were two large cans, filled with something. She picked one up, and discovered the ear of a male cow. Evidently the rest of the animal was jammed inside the can. "What is this?" she asked, describing it and its companion can for the others.

"Can A Bull," the peeve reported. "It eats its own kind. And Can't a Bull, which doesn't."

Squid dropped the can. "I don't want any of this!"

She walked on, discovering what looked like two beanie caps with little spinning blades in the top. She tried putting one on, and the blades spun faster, causing the cap to fly, hauling her up along with it.

"A flying cap?" she asked.

"A Propel Her," the peeve clarified. "And its companion, a Propel Him."

"What is this, a junkyard for puns?" she asked, irritated.

"Whatever it is, it is in your mind," Larry said.

"My mind's a junkyard," she said.

"But maybe what you need is in here somewhere," Larry said. "Maybe you'll know it when you find it."

Squid realized that it just might possibly maybe make a modicum of partial sense if she viewed it from sideways and kept her mind mostly closed to a crack. She did have a problem, apart from the one they all faced, trying to rescue Caprice Castle and its trapped adults. She was, theoretically, the most important person in the universe. Probably that just meant she had a grandiose dream of her own self worth, maybe her suppressed wish to really be something rather than nothing. But suppose, for the sake of foolish argument, it was true? What would that mean?

"You're thinking," Larry said. "I can tell, because you aren't talking."

"I am," she confessed.

"Two-and-a half cents for your thoughts."

"You can have them cheaper than that. I fear I have a hard drive ahead of me."

"A hard drive," Larry agreed. "That of course is a trip you don't want to take."

"Ha, ha, ha. I mean a mental one. I am having serious trouble believing something."

"Believing what? That you're a pretty girl?"

She fought against a flush of foolish pleasure. He was trying to lighten her mood, and was succeeding. "I have been told I am the most important person in the universe. Probably that's nonsense, in which case who cares?

But just suppose it isn't? What could possibly explain such a ludicrous thing?"

He stroked his chin. She was seeing him now, even if he did not really see her in her vision. "You're right. If it's nonsense, we don't need to worry about it. But if it actually makes sense, we can't afford to ignore it. Since we don't know the truth of it, it is safer to assume it is true and find out what it means."

She stared at him. "You want to take it seriously?"

"That is the safest course. If we dismiss it, and it's correct, we may somehow be wiping out the universe. If we take it seriously, and it's wrong, all we suffer is embarrassment, and the only other ones to know would be Tata and the peeve. Your hallucination protects us."

"But I thought you'd laugh your head off, like Jess's boyfriend, way back when."

"Squid, I may laugh with you, but never at you."

She found herself suddenly overwhelmed by emotion. He was truly supporting her! "Brace yourself. You've been fishing for a reaction, and now you're going to get it. I'm going to kiss you."

"Not if I kiss you first." He grabbed her and kissed her.

Hearts did not fling out, but some were lurking. They were getting there. "Wow," she murmured.

"Ditto."

"We're a fake couple, but we're starting to feel real."

"We're a couple of convenience. That's not fake."

"But I'm really an alien and you're really a girl!"

"True and true. We can still have a genuine and feeling relationship based on mutual respect."

She let it go, partly because she doubted it was relevant to the present situation, but mostly because she liked the idea of a genuine and feeling association, and loved basing it on mutual respect. He was still pushing her buttons. "I bet you say that to all the aliens."

"Only to the ones I like."

"Are you trying to make me kiss you again?"

"Yes."

This time she grabbed him and kissed him. The little hearts struggled to get out.

"What next?" the peeve asked. "Before you float entirely into the wide blue yonder."

"Trust the bird to mess up the mood," Larry muttered.

Squid looked around. While they talked, their propel caps had been carrying them upward, and now they were floating above the garden. The peeve was flying, and the robot dogfish was swimming through the air. They evidently knew how to stay with a hallucination.

"Where are we going?" she asked.

"That is your decision," Larry said. "It's your hallucination."

So it was. "I want answers, at least an answer to start with. Am I or am I not the most important person in the universe, and if I am, why?"

"To get an appropriate answer," Larry said, "a person needs an appropriate question. Yours are too general and inclusive. You need to get more practical. To break things down into assimilable fragments. What's your specific starting question?"

She pondered half a moment. He did have a point. The universe was too big to start with. "My question is: where can I find the answers?"

There was silence.

She refused to let it wash out there. "There has to be a place. Maybe there's a path to lead us to it."

No one else commented. Why should they? This was her vision, not theirs.

"All *right*!" she said. "I'll get more specific. Tata, where is the place of answers?"

The robot screen flashed. "Maybe the pentagram," the peeve translated. "Or some other gram, such as any N-gram, with a message for points, such as N-points."

"I can't follow that. Does it make sense?"

"Yes. You merely need the mind for it."

"Big help," she muttered. But it might be better than nothing. The universe was vast, and her mind was tiny. "I am assuming we are on a path through the sky, and that it leads where we need to go. That is, the place where I can find the key I need." Then she got a bright idea: she saw the flash. "A keyboard! That holds keys, including the one I need."

Still, there was something missing. "The path!" she exclaimed. "It may be here, but we can't see it. We need to make it visible. To—to outline it."

And the outlines appeared, like hand rails on either side, marking a kind of ribbon in the sky. Squid and Larry set feet on the path and hands on the rails, and were secure in the sky. The dogfish came to land on it, and the peeve perched on a rail.

"Amazing what imagination can do," Larry said.

"Now on to the keyboard," Squid said.

"It should be hanging on a wall somewhere," Larry said. "So you need a wall."

"I need a wall," she agreed. "That means a structure of some kind, here in the sky. Maybe a house."

"A house? Why be limited? It's your imagination. Make it a castle."

"A castle in air," she agreed.

They walked on, the ground now far below. Soon they spied a sign: AIR CASTLE.

Squid had to smile. Naturally it was literal.

It was a lovely little castle, with streaming mist flags anchored on turrets, complete with a moat made from a circular rain cloud. When they set foot on the drawbridge, the moat rocked, and some water spilled out and dropped toward the ground below.

"I always wondered where rain came from," Larry remarked. "Of course that begs the question of where the water comes from to fill the clouds."

The path led on to the outer wall, which seemed to be made of solidified cloud-stuff. The front gate was open.

"All I wanted was a wall," Squid said, bemused.

They entered the front hall. There was another sign. AIR CASTLE SHUT DOWN FOR NIGHT. PERSONNEL WILL RETURN IN MORNING.

"Just our luck," Larry said. "We'll have to make do on our own."

"If this is all in my imagination, how can it be incomplete?" Squid asked.

"Did you ever think about it before?" Larry asked. "Work out the details of such an edifice? Of the personnel required to maintain it?"

"No. So I suppose I can't complain."

"We can find a guest room for the night, and inquire about the keyboard in the morning."

Squid glanced at the peeve. "Does that make sense?"

"As much as any of this does," the peeve agreed.

"Is it safe?"

"As safe as your sanity."

"That's not completely reassuring."

Larry chuckled. "Who can ever know he is sane? We are all at risk."

"Tata and I are sane," the peeve said.

"He's a machine," Larry snapped. "And you're a bird brain."

The peeve was unruffled. "What's your point, girlie?"

"Break it up!" Squid snapped.

"We're just joshing," Larry said. "The peeve *is* a bird brain, and I *am* a girl."

Oh. Squid realized that she was too tense, even in her own vision.

They made their way to an upstairs guest suite. There, to their surprise, was an inset pantry complete with packaged biscuits and cheese, together with bottles of boot rear.

"You must have imagined more detail than you thought," Larry said.

"I think I worked it out just now when I realized it was incomplete."

"It will do," the peeve said.

"Thank you."

Tata and the peeve found a niche and settled down for the night.

They snacked on what offered, then took turns showering, not bothering to hide their bodies from each other. If they weren't a couple, they were close to it, and the Adult Conspiracy seemed to lack force in this hallucination. "A shower does make sense in this context," Larry said. "I wonder where the expended water drains?"

"Down below," the peeve said. "If the folk who love summer showers knew where they came from, they would not be so pleased."

There was just one bed. "I'll take another suite," Larry said.

"Don't bother," Squid said. "I'd rather have you near me."

"I appreciate that. You remain appealing, in your slightly advanced age."

That made her wonder. "What happens here doesn't really count, does it?" she asked.

"Are you thinking what I think you're thinking?"

She blushed. "Yes."

"That we might anticipate the adult state somewhat, and make love?"

She blushed harder. "Yes."

"And there would be no violation, because it's all in a dream?"

Her face was burning. "Yes," she breathed.

"Not to mention that you are a cuttlefish and I am a girl."

"Not to mention," she agreed.

"It is tempting, because being with you like this makes me curious to experience such an aspect of love, that we may never otherwise encounter."

"Yes."

"All we have to do is stop holding back and let nature take its course."

"Yes. Kissing and fondling and being close together. It must lead to something."

"Something wonderful."

"Oh, Larry, let's do it!"

"I want to. Unfortunately there is a caution."

"Bleep! One of those things!"

"It would make us technically adult, and therefore liable to Demon capture."

"But not if we only imagine it."

"Adulthood is an emotional more than a physical thing. We could remember the experience, and become adults in children's bodies."

She knew he was right. "Bleep!" she swore, bursting into tears.

He enfolded her comfortingly. "I am sorry. You know we can't risk it."

She knew. "But it seems so good!"

"That may be the trap. This whole sequence could be another device by the enemy Demon to subvert us, so that he can win Fibot."

"Catching us when we least expect it," she agreed.

"We are up against a devious mind."

"Bleepity bleep!" Her ability to utter such a curse suggested how close she was to maturity. But that certainly seemed to be it. They had to balk their own feelings.

Yet how it hurt! She put her face against his shoulder and cried herself out.

Then they settled down on the bed, chastely side by side, and Squid was soon sound asleep. It seemed she had worn out her wakefulness.

In the morning, Squid saw by her reflection in the shiny bathroom door that that she had reverted to her natural age. The elderberries had worn off.

"You still look very good to me," Larry said. "I can age us those three years if you want."

"No, let's save that for when we need it. That age just makes me want to do naughty things I shouldn't."

"I know exactly how it is."

They ate some more crackers, then stepped outside the suite. There was a new sign on the wall.

RETURN OF PERSONNEL DELAYED. GO ANYWHERE BUT HERE. There was a little map, showing one room of the castle outlined in red.

"They are telling us exactly where not to go?" Larry asked. "Isn't that like dangling candy before a baby's nose?"

"My imagination seems to like trite elements," Squid said. "An open castle with one forbidden chamber."

"I wonder who posts the signs?" Larry asked.

"It could be automatic," Squid said. "Pre-programmed."

Naturally they went directly to the forbidden room. The sign over its closed door said UNAUTHORIZED PERSONNEL ONLY.

They exchanged a four way glance, Tata and the peeve included. "Is that a typo?" Larry asked.

The dogfish's screen flashed. "Maybe the sign maker got muddled," the peeve translated. "He might have wanted to say that we are not authorized to enter."

"Yet if this is all in your imagination, Squid," Larry asked, "how can you be barred? You should be the one deciding these things."

How, indeed? "Let's go in."

They went in. There was a mirror on the opposite wall. Above it was a sign. HERE THERE BE ANSWERS.

"A magic mirror!" Larry said. "Of course."

Then a subtext appeared below the mirror. BUT YOU WON'T LIKE THEM.

"I am wary of that," Squid said.

"I remember a saying," Larry said. "To the effect of 'Ask not what concerns you not, lest you learn what pleases you not.' Something like that. Such warnings are seldom frivolous."

Squid glanced at Tata. "Is this a true warning?"

The screen flashed. "Yes," the peeve said.

"So let's pass it by, at least for now. What I came for was a key to the answers I need. Maybe it's here."

And there beside the mirror was the keyboard with assorted keys hung on its little hooks. The keys were all shapes, ranging from piano keys to key lime pie slices.

Then she spied one that appealed. "A skeleton key!" It was in the shape of a skeleton finger, with the nail grotesquely hooked. "Don't they open any locks?"

"That may be the one," Larry agreed. "Since it was the Skeleton Key island that started off this mischief."

She lifted it from the hook. It lay in her hand, quiescent. "Now if I can just figure out how to use it."

"What, no user manual?"

"Ha. Ha. Ha."

"Then take it with you. It's yours regardless."

She nodded, and tucked it into her emulation hair.

They looked around, but found nothing else in the chamber. "So do we try the mirror after all?" Squid asked.

"Do we? It's your decision."

"I still can't decide."

"Then let's take a break and explore the rest of the castle. We were so eager to come to the forbidden room that we ignored other parts. There might be something important we missed because of that distraction."

She nodded. "That's another way to go wrong. Focus on what we think we shouldn't, and pass by what we would otherwise find."

They left the Unauthorized chamber and methodically explored the rest of the castle. One room held a bright purple ear chained to a perch. A sign said AURICLE.

"A confined ear?" Larry asked.

Squid glanced at Tata. "What is it, really?"

The screen flashed. "It can hear the future," the peeve answered.

"Does it mean Oracle?"

"It is the auditory version," the peeve said. "You ask it a question, and it hears the answer."

"But what good is it to us, if it can't tell us what it hears?"

The bird shrugged. "It's your dream. It doesn't have to make sense."

They moved on. There was a small park on the level roof of an upper floor, with a flowing stream. There was a dam in it, forming a pool. The dam was made of live hamsters. It was labeled HAMSTERDAM.

"Hold me, somebody," Larry said. "I think I'm going to groan."

"I guess I have a sick imagination," Squid said apologetically.

"Other cuttlefish would surely be amused."

They moved on. Elsewhere in the mini park was what appeared to be a clump of trees, but turned out on closer inspection to be a group of police officers.

"What are you?" Larry asked them.

"We are tree cops or a copse of trees, depending how you spell us."

"You police the trees?"

"In a manner. See that you don't litter the park, or we'll have to arrest you."

"We won't litter," Squid promised.

They left the park. The rest of the castle seemed to contain nothing notable.

"So do we or don't we?" Larry asked.

She sighed. "I'm ready to face the mirror. It can't be worse than these puns."

They returned to the UNAUTHORIZED PERSONNEL ONLY room. Squid had half expected it to have disappeared, once they left it without a decision, but it was unchanged. There was the magic mirror, exactly as before.

"You said not to ask about what did not concern me," Squid said. "Lest I learn what I don't like. But what I want to know does concern me. So maybe I'll like that answer."

"Nevertheless I don't trust this," Larry said.

"Neither do I. But what else is there? There may be a reason we have come here, and why the demon was trying to make us forfeit it last night."

"Or the magic mirror could be another ploy to make us forfeit."

"Oh? How?"

"By giving us answers that scare us off, so that we don't rescue Caprice Castle and our friends within it."

That gave Squid two thirds of a pause. Could he be correct?

Then she decided not to be balked by such a guess. "I'm going to ask it."

Larry sighed. "It is your hallucination."

"Yes it is. So I'm going to use it or lose it."

Larry glanced at the dogfish. "Do you concur, Tata?"

The screen flashed. "It is dangerous either to indulge it or to ignore it," the peeve said.

"Fat lot of help you are!"

"We try to oblige."

Squid faced the magic mirror. "Here is my first question. Are there any limits to my questions to you?"

A nebulous face formed within the mirror. "No."

"That's interesting," Larry said. "I understand that usually such devices are so limited as to be virtually useless."

"It's my hallucination. I prefer to have it useful."

"By all means."

"Mirror, am I really the most important person in the universe?"

"Yes, appallingly."

"But this one seems merely obnoxious," Larry said.

Squid had been braced for some evasion or denial, so this set her back half a moment. But she rallied, rather than waste the rest of the moment. "Why?"

"Because the universe depends on you for its existence."

She lost the rest of the moment anyway, unable to speak.

"The mirror does not pussyfoot much," Larry remarked.

Squid finally got back with it. "But I'm nothing!"

"Is that a question or an observation?" the mirror asked.

"Uh, neither."

"Good, because as a question it lacks coherence, relevant as it may be as an observation."

"I want a hammer!" Larry said. "This thing is aching for breaking."

"Go find your own hallucination, dolt, if you want to break things," the mirror said snidely.

Squid finally got organized again. "You said the universe depends on me for its existence. How so?"

"You must struggle with two or three absolute horrors, and if you lose, as seems likely considering your incompetence, the universe is doomed."

She marshaled a thought. "Can you be more specific?"

"Yes."

She nerved herself. "What is the first horror?"

"This." A picture formed in the mirror. It was the figure of a ten-year-old girl whose hair was fluttering in her face.

"That's my friend and sibling Win!" Squid exclaimed. "She's absolutely no horror."

"In fact she's a nice girl," Larry said. "And cute."

The mirror was silent.

Squid tried again. "What is there about Win that makes her such a horror?"

Now the girl in the mirror spoke. "You must kill me, Squid."

"I can't do that! You're my closest sibling and dearest friend."

"Yes. We love each other."

"So why should I ever kill you?"

"Because if you don't, the universe will perish."

"This is crazy!" Squid protested. "I'll do no such thing."

"Too bad." Win faded out.

Squid ground determinedly on. "What's the second horror?"

Now a picture of Larry appeared.

"That's me!" Larry said.

"You're no horror," Squid told the image. "You're my boyfriend."

"Not exactly," the image said, and there was something frighteningly alien in his voice.

"That's not me!" the real Larry said, appalled.

"This—this other Larry," Squid said. "Do I have to kill him too?"

"You can't kill me," the mirror Larry said. "But you need to persuade me not to destroy you."

"I'd never try to destroy you, Squid," the real Larry said. "I love you."

That distracted her again. He had never actually said that before. "Oh, you mean as a friend."

"As a girlfriend. I fought against the realization, but this crisis makes it clear. I want to move us both into adult range and make love."

"But you're a girl!"

"My body at the moment is male, with the male urges I have tried to avoid before. But with you, I believe it would be wonderful! Then I'd like to pass through the portal and be my real female self again, and have you with me as a boy, and do it again that way. I love you whichever way we are. You're the one for me, Squid."

"But we're children!"

"In age, perhaps. Not in spirit."

That was true. She might be only eleven years old, but she was a woman. "But I'm not human!"

"You're a person, whatever your form. You could turn cuttle and wrap your limbs about me and I'd love you that way too."

Squid was silent, because she realized that she felt much the same. She wanted to do it with him, and again with her, and to bleep with the strictures of the Adult Conspiracy, which saw naughtiness instead of love. What really counted was their togetherness, whatever their genders. They truly understood each other.

"Too bad I have to destroy you," the mirror Larry said. "Otherwise I can appreciate the appeal of making out with your cute underage body."

Trust the foul image to demean it. "Get out of here, you fake," Larry said.

"For now," the mirror image said. "But this isn't over. There is worse coming." He faded out.

They looked at each other. "Does any of this make sense?" Squid asked.

"Ask Tata."

The robot screen flashed. "It all makes sense," the peeve said. "We have been treated to a glimpse of the future."

"The future," Squid said. "Where I have to kill my best friend, and that's not even the worst."

"Yes. It is all true."

She looked at Larry. "If that's the future, then what about now?"

"Do you mean—?"

"Yes. At least we can have that much, before the universe ends. What do we have to lose?" She stepped into him, held him close, and avidly kissed him.

He met her as avidly. Now little hearts did fly out and orbit them. It was indeed true love.

But then he paused, and the hearts froze in place. "Unless this whole thing is a trick to dazzle our common sense and make us do it, and ruin our mission."

"Bleep!" she swore.

Then the rest of their reality closed in on her. She had to kill her best friend? And her beloved was going to destroy her? She began to scream.

The chamber dissolved into cloud vapor. Beyond it the castle puffed similarly into formlessness. The floor gave way, and they fell out of the sky.

Squid continued screaming as they dropped toward the land below.

Chapter 11

SEARCH

Then she was back in her cabin on Fibot, still screaming. In two and a quarter moments the others were there.

"Squid!" Santo said. "What's the matter?"

The change in scenario did it. She halted screaming and gazed around, gradually reorienting.

They were all there, watching her with concern. "I had a—a hallucination that we saw the future, and—"

Then she focused on Win. "Oh!" She burst into tears.

"I don't usually have that effect on you," Win said, surprised.

"In my dream I had to—to kill you," Squid said. "Or the universe would end."

The others laughed. "Sister, that must have been some bad dream," Firenze said.

"Fortunately bad dreams are only animate fears," Santo said. "No need to take them seriously."

Larry shook his head. "This one is serious. I was along. So were Tata and the peeve."

Santo glanced at the robot dogfish. "What's your take on this?"

The screen flashed. "It is a true prophecy," the peeve said. "Squid suffered a vision of the future. If she doesn't kill Win, the universe will end."

"I can't kill Win!" Squid said, horrified anew. "I never want to ever even try to hurt her." She was so upset she was starting to lose her shape, her arms dissolving into what others called tentacles. She focused and restored the arms.

"It doesn't make sense," Win said. "We've been friends for half of forever. We never even quarrel."

"Yes!" Squid agreed. They hugged each other.

Santo pondered briefly. "Then we shall have to consider alternatives, and implement them before that future arrives. Fortunately the future is malleable."

Trust him to have the practical approach. Of course they didn't have to wait on the dread future. They could do something in the interim to change it. To unhappen its horror before it manifested.

Squid ran to Santo and kissed him. So did Win. He kissed them back. It had nothing to do with Win being windy or Squid being alien or his being gay. They were siblings. They would never, ever, play each other false.

Then Santo faced the others. "We have clear warning, from Squid's hallucination, which not only confirms that she is the most important one of us, but that the fate of the universe does depend on her. I know this is not anything she sought, but it was thrust upon her, and the rest of us should support her in any way we can."

He paused, in case there was objection. There was none. Santo was the smartest of them, as well as being a virtual Magician in his own right, and they were generally glad to let him do the heavy thinking.

"If we follow our present course, Squid will be required to kill Win, perhaps because of a Demon wager whose penalty for failure will be to end the universe. This forced choice is unacceptable. Therefore we will change our course, trusting that this will put us on a route that avoids any such sacrifice. I believe we need to take a random course, so that our destination can't be predicted. Ultimately we want to bring Fibot to Caprice Castle by surprise, so that Piton and Data can operate it and make it move back into Xanth proper, before the enemy Demon realizes what is happening. The question is how to travel randomly, before we find a route there. Any suggestions?"

"Yes," Ion said from his floating carpet. "Hilda and I have done some traveling, and have some experience in random routing. I suggest that each of us devise an interim destination, which you, Santo, can then tunnel us to. Each can write his or her idea on a piece of paper, and the dozen papers can be mixed up and you can draw one at random, not knowing what it is until you read it. It could be anywhere. Then we all go there and act like regular tourists, appreciating the world we discover. From there, we can try again for Caprice Castle, using a similar ploy. There will be no predicting our route."

Santo nodded. "I like it." He looked about. "Comments?"

"I'll fetch papers and pencils," Ula said. Her talent was being useful in unexpected ways, so this was routine for her. Firenze smiled, appreciating it; he loved her regardless. Her main usefulness now was keeping him under control, and that was fulfilling her as well as him, but she was not limited to that.

They adjourned to the main room, where they sat around the central table and scribbled their ideas. Squid pondered briefly, then wrote "The honey side of the Moon." The thing about the moon was that the side that faced Mundania had long since frozen into a rictus of horror at the awful sights it saw there, and the once pungent cheese had turned sickly green. No one with any sense wanted to be in Mundania, it was not just a matter of its lack of magic. But the side facing away from Mundania remained fresh with milk and honey and was a pleasant place where newlywed couples liked to visit.

Beside her Larry was drawing a picture. She suspected it was of the portal, where he had become Laurelai and been supremely happy for several hours. She understood his longing, and hoped that some day he would be able to make the change permanent. But she doubted anyone else would want to go there.

And what of herself? She could assume many forms, but always female. Yet, for the sake of making Larry happy as Laurelai, could she enjoy passing though the portal again and being male? She thought she might. The folk of Portal Village had learned to get along in opposite genders, so obviously it could be done if other factors aligned.

In due course they all finished, folded their papers, and tossed them into the central basket.

Santo picked up the basket and handed it to Noe, beside him. "Wake shell," he said.

She smiled, and shook the basket well so that the papers were thoroughly shuffled. She gave it back to Santo.

He closed his eyes and reached in. He caught a paper. He unfolded it and read it. "The World of Talent, one of Ida's Moons, where folk go to win a talent. But it's hard to find that world, or to win a talent when there." He looked up. "We have our destination. Whose idea is this?"

Data raised her hand. "Mine. Ever since I couldn't fit the magic panty, I've wanted a magic talent of my own. Maybe on that world I could find it."

"You will have your chance," Santo said. "I hope you win a good one."

"Oh, yes!"

"Now do you want to go alone, or with a companion?"

She was surprised by the thought. "Go alone? I couldn't. I've never been alone. With a companion."

"Who I think should also be chosen by random selection." Santo closed his eyes and reached into the basket again. He drew out a paper, opened it, and read it. "The Honey side of the moon. Who wrote this?"

"I did," Squid said, surprised.

"Then you will be Data's companion."

Squid considered protesting, but realized that the randomness had selected her and she needed to oblige it. Maybe it was because she was the protagonist, and was supposed to be in on the action, or at least observing it. "I will," she agreed.

Santo glanced at Tata. "You have the coordinates of that world, of course?"

The robot's screen flashed. "Yes, of course," the peeve said.

"I will need to study them, to orient accurately on that world, as it is new to me."

Tata buzzed. A ribbon of paper emerged from his mouth, printed out coordinates. Santo reached down and tore it off. "Thank you."

"When do we go?" Data asked eagerly.

Santo smiled. "One more random decision. Timing may be important. Let each of us write a number, any number, and I will draw one and reduce it to a single digit. That will determine the number of hours hence we will make that trip."

That seemed appropriate. They all wrote numbers and tossed them into the basket. Squid wrote 1,000,001, curious how Santo would process it.

The papers were shuffled again, and one drawn. "The number is 666," Santo said. "We add those together and get 18. Then we add those, and get 9. We will depart, in nine hours from now."

So Squid's number would have condensed to 2. She was satisfied with the longer wait.

Back in their cabin, Squid turned to Larry. "Would you—?"

He put his arms around her. She had the comfort of knowing that if they managed to change the future with respect to Win, it should also change with respect to Larry. They lay together on the bed and slept.

There was a knock on the door. It was Data. "It's time."

So it was. Nine hours, just like that. Squid went with Data to the main chamber. The others were there. "We will tunnel there now," Noe said. "Then anchor in private air, cloaked to be invisible. The two of you will be on your own. But if there is trouble, strike your match and we will come to you quickly."

Squid nodded. "I hope we don't need to."

"When you find what you seek, then strike the match."

"Yes."

"Go topside. We are about to tunnel. Santo is already focusing."

Which was why Noe was doing the talking. Small local tunnels were easy, but interplanetary tunnels took a lot out of Santo. Which was also why the boat would anchor for a while, to give him time to recover, while she took care of him. The two might never be a romantic couple, but they plainly needed each other.

They climbed to the topside. Win was at the helm, with Firenze at the fire sail, Ula beside him.

And there ahead appeared the tunnel, big enough for Fibot to sail through. It looked to be only a ring, but beyond it was a completely different world. The World of Talent. It was in shades of gray.

The wind accelerated, catching the sail, which brightened into a round sheet of flame. The craft moved forward, through the ring, and suddenly they were in the gray world. Squid knew they had actually traveled light years, jumping from Xanth to Talent. Santo did not show off his talent, he just used it when required, but it was as powerful as that of any other Magician.

That triggered another meander of thought. When Santo was grown, he would have a man as his romantic partner. Squid wondered whom that would be. The siblings would remain close to him, regardless.

The boat cruised to a landing on a gray sand dune. The wind died out. "Bye," Win said.

Larry hugged Squid one more time, and let her go. "Take care of yourself," he said tensely.

Then Squid and Data climbed over the gunwale and landed on the dune. They were on their way.

Squid glanced back. The boat was gone. She knew it remained close; it was that it was invisible, now that they were off it. But it would soon find a better anchoring place.

She heard voices, and realized that others aboard the boat were talking about her. Which was to be expected. She tuned it down to a background babbling and ignored it.

"Well, it's just you and me now," Data said.

Squid felt doubt. She hardly knew this girl. "Maybe we should have let you pick your own partner. You and I have not been close."

"No, I think random is better, considering the importance of our mission. I confess to being a bit jealous of you and your boyfriend, even if he's not really into being male. I could take care of that pronto, if I got him alone five minutes. I'm jealous of Firenze and Ula too, and even of my brother Piton and Myst. She's only nine, and he thinks he doesn't take her seriously, but she's got that panty. That gives her control, and it's not just a matter of freaking him out. She can take him anywhere she wants to go, and she'll be getting ideas soon enough. I've already got the ideas; I want a boy of my own."

"Maybe you'll find one here."

"More likely I'll find one on Skeleton Key, when this is over. If I brought him to Caprice Castle, he'd be able to assume fleshly form while there." Data smiled. "The flesh has some things that skeletons don't. Things I could play with."

Squid found herself blushing. "Uh—"

"Like ears and lips. Good for kissing."

"Oh."

"I'm teasing. But I do want to play with the other, too. Why should my brother have all the fun?"

Squid realized that this girl was indeed a tease. She liked pushing the Conspiracy limits. And why not? She was on the verge of nubility, anticipating the crossover. Squid had been seriously tempted with Larry, especially when she got aged three years, and with Ruby, when Squid was male. "Why, indeed," she agreed.

"But mainly I miss my parents. They were good ones, and I want them back."

Safer ground, perhaps. "I know how it is."

"You do?"

"I lost mine in future Xanth. All five original siblings did. Now we have other families, and they are great, but it's not the same."

"You have other parents?"

"I was adopted by Kandy and Ease. She can change into a board when she wants to, and he uses her to bash monsters. They both enjoy it. But there are ways in which I feel closer to Aunt Astrid, the basilisk, and to Aunt Fornax."

"The basilisk! And Fornax! The evil Demon?"

Squid smiled. "She's a Demoness, but she's not evil. We all love her, and Astrid."

Data nodded. "I guess you do understand about losing your family."

"Oh, yes."

"I knew you five siblings were close, but I guess I didn't really understand why. You all lost your families in the same disaster. You truly understand each other, emotionally."

"We do."

"I thought having a skeleton daddy and a flesh princess mommy was really unusual. But they're a normal couple compared to what you siblings have."

"And we do want to rescue them," Squid said. "Once we figure out how."

"Yes. So let's be on our way." Then Data paused. "Except I have no idea where to go now. I didn't think that far ahead."

"Maybe my skeleton key will help." Squid reached into her hair and drew the key out.

Data stared. "I thought your hair was fake!"

"It is. But I can keep things in it."

"Such as a key you got in a hallucination?"

Squid nodded. "That does seem odd. The dream expired, but the key didn't. I didn't realize how weird that was until now."

"Someone must have wanted you to have it."

"I guess so." Indeed, this could be more of Fornax's quiet involvement, making a dream key become real when the dream ended. It was not the only gift the Demoness had quietly given her.

Squid held the key up. "Now I just need to figure out how to use it."

"No problem. I know about skeleton things. Just ask it."

Could it be that simple? "Skeleton Key, where should we go?"

The key twitched in her hand, surprising her, but that was all.

"Well, you have to give it something to orient on," Data said. "Such as 'Where is there a useful talent?'"

"Where is there a useful talent?" Squid asked it.

Now the key jerked in a specific direction, pointing.

"On our way," Data said, stepping forth in that direction.

There turned out to be a gray path there. They followed it. Soon they came to an alcove with a pedestal. On the pedestal was a statue of the head of a bald man.

"This is a talent?" Squid asked.

"There's a plaque. TALENT: GROWING INSTANT FUR."

"This bald head could use it."

"There's a button," Data said. "It says DEMO."

"Demonstration," Squid agreed. "It seems it wants you to know its nature."

Data pushed the button. Abruptly fur grew on the head. In two thirds of a moment not only the pate but also the face, neck, and shoulders were thickly covered with brown fur.

"Um, that's a bit much," Data said.

Squid read the print below the plaque. STANDARD DISCLAIMER: THE PRICE OF THIS TALENT IS FIVE PERCENT OF YOUR SOUL.

"Part of my soul!" Data exclaimed. "Outrageous!"

"What would a pedestal want with part of a soul?" Squid asked.

The gray pedestal shifted and became a hunched green gnome. "It would free me from this captivity and let me go home," he said. Then he reverted to the pedestal. The head on it was now bald again, and all was gray. The demonstration had been made.

Data shuddered. "It's a punishment, or something. He's caught until someone buys his talent."

"This must be a punishment planet," Squid said. "What a horror!"

"I feel guilty, but I don't want this talent," Data said.

"Neither do I," Squid agreed. "Not that I'm looking for one."

"At least now we understand how it works. I'm sorry I suggested it."

"At least it is purely random. No one would have predicted that we'd come here."

"Well, now that we are here, we should follow through. I hate the system, but maybe a bit of my soul will buy the freedom of some suffering creature."

Squid held up the key. "Skeleton Key, where is there another useful talent?"

The key twitched a new direction. There was a path there. Maybe the key was indicating the path rather than the talent.

They walked on. This path led to an enclosed field. The plaque by the gate said STUD FARM. WE GROW FINE STUDS FOR STUDDED TIRES.

"Do we even need to see the demo?" Data asked. "This is obviously an export market."

"Maybe those studs go to Mundania, where I understand they use tires," Squid said. "In any event, this is not exactly a talent."

Data peered more closely at the plaque. "THIS IS NOT A TALENT, IDIOT," she read. "IT IS JUST A FARM ALONG THE WAY. KEEP WALKING."

"Oh."

"My appreciation for this planet is not growing," Data said.

They came to another pedestal. This one had a goblin and a crow side by side. The talent was listed as MERGER.

Data pushed the Demo button. The two creatures moved together and merged, becoming one. It looked like a winged goblin with the beak of a crow.

"Actually that could be a useful talent," Squid said. "You could form new hybrid creatures."

"Maybe so." Then Data looked at the price: 25% OF YOUR SOUL. "Ouch! That's too much."

They went on. The next pedestal showed a cute elf girl and a fierce male griffin. Was the griffin about to eat the elf? The plaque said ACCOMMO-DATION.

Curious, Data pushed the Demo button. The elf and griffin came together, and became the same size. They embraced. Then a patch of fog blotted them out.

"Oh!" Squid said. "The talent is to make an accommodation spell. You know, where any two creatures of any size or nature can come together and signal the stork."

"And the demo blotted out the detail!" Data complained. "The bleeping Adult Conspiracy strikes again. We still don't know how two people do it, let alone a griffin and an elf."

"It's like the last one," Squid said. "Only instead of making a crossbreed directly, you can do it by enabling them to breed. That could be a valuable talent."

"If you want to crossbreed with monsters. I'll stick with humans or skeletons."

Squid smiled. "I suppose. Technically, I am a monster."

"Technically, so am I. Still."

"Still," Squid agreed.

They moved on. Now they saw two others walking the opposite direction. They turned out to be young male trolls.

"Uh-oh," Data said.

"Not all trolls are mean. But we can handle them if we have to."

"We can."

They walked on. Soon they met the trolls, as the path was only two persons wide. They stopped.

"Well, now," one troll said, eyeing them lasciviously.

"Two pretty human girls," the other said, licking his thin lips.

"Two children," Squid said. "We aren't looking for trouble. We're just passing through, looking for talents, same as you are."

"It's no trouble," the first troll said. "Take off your clothes."

"Please, just let us pass," Data said.

"Sure, after we're done with you. We know what girls are for."

"We're underage," Squid said. "And we don't want to do anything with you."

"As if you have a choice," the second troll said. "You should know better than to travel alone."

Then both trolls reached out and grabbed both girls.

Squid shifted to cuttlefish form, her pseudo-tentacles wrapping around the youth and pinning his arms to his sides. Data shifted to skeleton form and poked a finger bone at her youth's face.

Both trolls seemed stunned. They had had no idea they were dealing with shape changers.

"Next time you encounter a girl," Squid said. "Treat her politely, so she won't do this to you." She wrapped a limb around his head, stuck a sucker on his cheek, and twisted his neck just hard enough to hurt.

"Or this," Data said, and clapped her troll on the ear with a bone-hard fist. A little lightning bolt of pain zapped out.

Then they let the boys go, tossed them to the side of the path, and walked on. The trolls made no further sounds. Surprise, pain, humiliation? It hardly mattered.

"That was almost fun," Squid said as she shifted back to human form.

"Almost," Data agreed, shifting back to flesh and adjusting her messed up clothing. "It reminds me how ogres teach young dragons the meaning of fear."

"A useful lesson."

Now the path came to a several way split. A sign said GOOD TALENTS AHEAD, IF YOU CAN GET THERE.

They considered the choices. One path led to an underground tunnel. HERE THERE BE GOBLINS.

"Goblins can be worse than trolls," Data said. "The ladies are nice, but the men are ugly and mean and believe in what they call gang bangs, whatever those are, and there can be hundreds of them. We couldn't fend them off long, and would survive only as long as they found us amusing to play with. Then they'd dump us in their cook-pot."

They considered the next path. This one led up the steepening slope of a mountain where hungry-looking flying dragons circled. "That's not promising either," Squid said. "They can crunch flesh and bones with equal relish."

A third path led down to a pervasive bog where the colored fins of loan sharks showed, as well as the snouts of allegations. Squid could swim well, but doubted she would get far through that swarm of horrors.

A fourth path led to a cliff that dropped off into a dark void. They didn't much like the look of that one either.

The fifth path traversed ordinary terrain, but was labeled CHOOSE YOUR DISABILITY. What did that mean?

There were several objects parked at the path entrance. One was an old fashioned Mundane wheelchair. Another was a white cane. A third was a pair of ear muffs. Another was simply a big question mark. Another was a pane of glass. What did they mean?

"I think we'll have to try the demos," Data said.

"Yes." Squid touched the glass.

It exploded. Suddenly she was in agony. She screamed, but the hurting didn't stop. Only when she fell back out of the area did it ease.

"That's not a pane," she gasped. "It's pain. Maybe a pun, but we don't want it."

"We can use the path, but be in terrible pain," Data said. "Somehow I think I'd feel it in my skeletal phase also, and your flesh is vulnerable regardless of your form."

"I think so. Maybe a masochist could handle it, but not me."

Data touched the question mark. "Oh!" she cried. "I am hopelessly confused. Why are we here? What are we doing? I can't make sense of anything." She dropped the question mark and looked around. "I think I lost my mind for a moment there."

"It's a mental question," Squid said. "Mental illness. I don't think we want that one either."

"We don't. We need our minds. But now we're getting a notion what 'disability' means. That there is something wrong with us, physically or mentally. I don't think I can handle what we've seen so far."

"Me too. Of course we can quit and return to the boat."

"You can if you want to. I'm going on, one way or another."

Squid was coming to like her attitude. The girl was more than skin and bones. "I don't like quitting either."

Data picked up the ear muffs and put them on. "Where did all the sound go? I can't hear anything."

Squid still heard the calls of the dragons on the mountain, and the swishing of the sharks in the bog, and there were birds trilling in the nearby woods. "You're deaf."

Data gazed blankly at her. "I see your lips moving, but what are you saying?"

Squid reached across and pulled the ear muffs off her. "You're deaf," she repeated.

"Oh, that's the disability! Now I understand."

"I suppose we might make it through without hearing. But I suspect that there will be warning sounds we need to hear. Things like a basilisk hiss, or a spoken warning. I don't want to gamble on it."

"I like your reasoning. And your attitude."

Squid smiled. "Me too," she repeated.

"In fact I think I like you, now that I am coming to know you. I was jealous of the way you have a boyfriend, but I see you're your own person."

"Thank you." Squid looked at the remaining two objects. "My turn." She picked up the white cane.

Suddenly she was blind. Completely without sight. "Uh-oh. I can't see a thing. I don't like this." Already she was beginning to panic. She dropped the cane, and her sight returned. It was an enormous relief. She had not realized how dependent she was on sight. She simply could not function without it. "I can't do this."

"I see," Data said. "No pun. Let me try the chair." She sat in the wheelchair. "Oh, my!"

"What is it?"

"My legs are paralyzed. I can feel them, but I can't move them."

"Can you use your arms to move the wheelchair?"

Data tried it. "Yes." she put her hands on the rims of the wheels and pushed forward. The wheelchair moved. "But I can't stand being paralyzed, again no pun. I've always been mobile in both my forms. This is not for me." She used her arms to heave herself up and out of the chair, and stood beside it, her legs restored.

"I think we have just eliminated all the choices."

"Maybe not. Maybe you could handle the chair."

Squid shrugged. "I saw how Ion handles it. The wheelchair may not be as versatile as his floating carpet, but the principle's the same. I can't say I'd like it, but I think I could handle it, at least for a while." She went to the wheelchair and sat in it. Her legs lost volition, but her arms still functioned. She wheeled herself forward. "Yes, this I can do."

"And I think I might be able to handle blindness, for a while." Data picked up the white cane. "But I will need your guidance, if you retain your sight."

"And I could use your help, if you retain your legs," Squid said. "I can move this on my own, but it would be twice as effective if you pushed me. That would help guide you, too."

"An hour ago I would have doubted that. But now I think I trust you." She reached toward Squid. "Where are you?"

"Stand still. I will come to you." Squid pushed the wheels and made her way to Data. She caught the girl's hand and guided it. "Here is the chair."

"Ah, yes." Data put both hands on the handholds behind the chair. "I think we're a team. Let's do it."

"Let's." Squid looked ahead. "The path is clear, but there's a steep drop-off on the left and a bog on the right. We need to be sure to stay centered."

"You're the guide." Data pushed the chair smartly along the path.

"Oops, there's a door ahead, with a spring to keep it closed. The path goes right to it. I don't think I can get the chair past it."

"Yes you can. Guide me to the door, and I'll hold it open for you."

"Straight ahead about ten more paces."

Data pushed her there and stopped. "Now where?"

"Feel your way around the chair. The door's right before it."

Data felt her way, and found the door. She opened it and held it open. "Go on through."

Squid turned the wheels and propelled the chair through the doorway. It just fit. But on the far side was a step. "Uh-oh."

They discussed it. Then Squid saw a thick board lying to the side. "A ramp! We can make a ramp."

Data felt her way to the board, and placed it carefully on the step. Now Squid was able to ride across it and get to the path beyond.

Data resumed her position behind the wheelchair. "Where to?"

"The path continues to a foggy field."

"Makes no difference to me."

They entered the field. The fog surrounded them, misting out the scene. Squid was unable to see the path ahead. "I don't like this. I am effectively blind, and can't tell you where it is safe to go. It's not safe."

"Maybe I can use my cane." Data circled the wheelchair and tapped the ground with the end of the cane.

That worked, but progress was slow. "It will take forever to get any-where," Squid complained.

"Yes. But it would be a shame to quit after coming so far."

Then there came a voice. "Hello! Anybody there?"

Someone else was lost in the fog? "Hello!" Squid called back.

"So I did hear something! Who are you?"

"We're visitors to this world, looking for a talent."

"So am I. Any luck?"

"Not so far. Now we're lost in the fog."

"There is fog?"

"Don't you see it?"

"No. But then I wouldn't."

This was curious. "Can we meet and talk?" Squid called.

"Sure. I'll be there in a jiffy."

Indeed, in exactly one jiffy a girl appeared from the fog. She was about their age, or a little older, with short dark hair and obscure eyes. Overall she was fairly pretty.

"Hello," Squid said. "I'm Squid, and this is my friend Data."

"I'm Nicole."

"You say you can't see the fog?" Data asked.

"That's right. I'm blind."

"Oh, you chose that disability too?"

Nicole laughed. "I didn't choose it. I was delivered with it." She flicked her wrist, and a white cane appeared. "I came here hoping to win a talent for sight, but that didn't work out."

"You didn't find it?" Squid asked.

"Oh, I found it, after much searching. But I didn't take it."

"Why not?"

"The price was half my soul."

"Ouch!" Squid said.

"So now I'm ready to return to my home world of Puzzle. Next month they will come to pick me up. Meanwhile, I've just been exploring. I've been over all the paths. I already have the disability, so am unaffected by theirs. I know where most of the talents are."

"You do?" Data said eagerly. "We're looking, but we got bogged down here."

"What talent do you want?"

"I don't know. I'm window shopping so far. I'm not eager to give up part of my soul."

"I know exactly how that is. But they aren't all that expensive. If you'll settle for a nice minor talent, like conjuring a wet blanket or making a sun burn, you can be done in next to no time."

"I've got an idea," Squid said. "Guide us to some talents, and we'll help you get home faster. We have a way to travel."

"That's a deal! I'm tired of this world." She considered. "How about a cold snap? You snap your fingers, and the air within the range of the sound gets horribly cold so that ice even forms. It can stop a dragon or a troll, and it costs only five percent."

"A cold snap," Data said. "That would be fun to try on a lecherous troll."

"Yes. Coincidentally I just encountered a pair of young trolls, and thought I was in trouble, but they were excruciatingly polite. I was so surprised."

Squid laughed. "We know why. They tried to molest us, but we set them back with a warning."

"Oh? What's your secret?"

"We're not exactly what we appear to be, if you could see us. We look human, but I'm an alien cuttlefish in the form of a girl, and Data is half walking skeleton."

Now Nicole laughed. "You're shape changers! Oh, I wish I *could* have seen that!" Then she turned about. "Follow me." She set off along the path she knew, heedless of the fog.

They followed. In barely two-and-a-half moments they were out of the fog and at a pedestal. The plaque said TALENT: COLD SNAP.

Nicole pushed the demo button. A loud snap sounded, and shards of ice appeared in the air above the pedestal. Squid felt the chill of the air as it flowed out.

"I'll take it," Data said. "Five percent doesn't seem so expensive any more."

"Put your hand on the pedestal," Nicole said. "And say you are taking it."

Data did so. And straightened up. "Oh!"

"It just took part of your soul," Nicole explained. "That's a jolt. But now you have the talent."

"I can't wait to try it out. But first I want to see again."

"We're near the edge of the disabilities section. This way."

They followed her to another sign. EXIT. The moment they passed it, Squid's control of her legs returned, and Data looked joyfully about.

"Are you ready to go home, Nicole?" Squid asked as she stretched her restored legs.

"More than ready."

"Fibot," Squid murmured, knowing the craft was tracking them.

The boat silently appeared, floating beside them. Nicole did not react, as she could not see it.

"We made a deal with Nicole, here," Squid said as Santo came to the rail. "She is blind. She helped us find a talent, and we promised to take her home."

"Hello, Nicole," Santo said. "I am Santo, Squid's sibling. We will take you to your home world, but you must promise not to talk about it to others. We are on a private mission."

"That's fine," Nicole agreed.

Piton and Myst appeared. "Well, now," Piton said, eyeing Nicole's form. "I'll help her board."

"The bleep you will," Myst said.

"*I'll* help her board," Data snapped. "Keep your grabby hands to yourself."

Data guided Nicole to the gunwale and helped her climb over. Then Santo questioned her about her home world, and Tata determined the coordinates. Santo opened a tunnel, and they sailed directly to it.

Chapter 12

PUZZLE

"I believe it is better if our guest learns no more about us," Noe murmured to Squid. She was speaking for Santo, who was recovering from the effort of making the tunnel through space. "It is no reflection on her merit as a person. This amounts to another random location, and we should keep it as private as we can."

"I'll see that she's okay, and we can quietly fade from the scene," Squid said.

The boat settled to a landing on the ground beside what appeared to be a giant hedge maze. Squid helped Nicole step down to the ground. "Do you recognize your home world?"

"Oh yes! I can smell it. I can find my way home readily enough. Thank you for the lift."

"Thank you for helping us find a talent for Data. I know she's pleased with it."

"She's welcome."

"How is it that you don't have a magic talent?"

"Oh, I have one: it just doesn't show. It is to be fortunate in my encounters with strangers."

"So we were a function of your talent! We never knew."

"It's minor. I'd give it up in a moment in exchange for sight. Not that I wasn't glad to meet you."

"We'll be on our way now. It has been nice knowing you."

"You too. Bye." Nicole set off for her home, tapping the ground confidently with her cane. She was used to being blind, and evidently could handle it well enough when in familiar surroundings.

Squid returned to the boat. Noe met her on the deck. "We believe this is a suitably random planet. Let's see what we can find here, as long as we're here anyway. Santo is still recovering, though he will soon be up and about."

"We really don't know much about Puzzle Planet, do we? It's just where a chance acquaintance lives."

"That's what makes it random. Tata has researched it. It's interesting in its own right. There are amazing puzzles here."

"What we need is a puzzle about how to find Caprice Castle without alerting any Demons."

"Yes. It is possible that puzzle is here."

They went to the central observation room, where the landscape was spread out beneath them as they slowly traversed it. Squid saw a huge garden maze formed by living hedges. Its passages were so intricate she started to get dizzy just trying to trace them with her gaze. "It might be fun to walk such a maze, and try to figure it out," Squid said. "But to what purpose? How would that get us any closer to Caprice Castle?"

"If the center was an access to a castle of our choice, we might choose Caprice."

"Oho! They have that kind of prize here?"

"They may. The prizes have to be worth something, as an inducement for folk to use them. This seems to be a tourist world, attracting visitors from many others, so the prizes have to be worthwhile."

Squid nodded. "I suppose that does make sense. Who is going to tackle their puzzles?"

"You are the protagonist."

"Oh, fudge!" But Squid realized she was probably stuck for it. She was supposed to be where the action was. "Let me get a good night's sleep. Then I'll see what I can do."

"Good enough." Noe went to see to the sleeping Santo.

Squid went to join Larry. She realized that she had been quietly tense while away from him.

In the morning they held another general meeting. "Tata has researched his archives for information on this world," Santo said. "It turns out there are many puzzles of many kinds. We happen to be in the maze section. The mazes are formed by hedges and are in different shapes, such as faces, fish, dinosaur, shield, mundane tractor, windmill, deer, wagon, clock and so on. Each is a challenge to navigate, and there are dangers along the way.

If a person gets eaten by a dragon, he is simply dumped out of the maze; actual danger would be bad for the tourist industry. Those who make it through to the center win that maze's prize, such as the ability to emulate other faces in the face maze, or to tell time with marvelous accuracy in the clock maze."

He paused for a breath. "Our interest is in a castle shaped maze, because the prize there is private transport to the actual castle represented by the maze. It seems that one resembles Caprice Castle." He smiled. "It also seems that some tourists seek private trysts that their partners don't know about, so such transport enables them to meet each other safely. We may pretend that this is the type of interest we have, but actually we want to get to Caprice with one of the skeleton children and steer it out of the Sometime realm. So we plan to assemble two teams of five each, randomly selected, and try two mazes. That way any spying party won't realize what we're really after. They will think it is just for diversion."

"Diversion?" Noe asked, prompting him.

"The second maze is in the general shape of an attractive woman. A corn maiden."

They all laughed. They were children, more than half of whom were girls. They were not interested in private trysts with lovely women. But someone spying on them from afar might not realize that.

After that they drew lots for two parties of five each. Squid joined with Piton, Myst, Firenze and Ula, while Larry went with Data, Win, Hilda, and Ion. Squid's party went to the woman-shaped maze, while Larry's party went to the castle-shaped one.

Squid found them in a corn maze, the paths winding curvaceously through thickly growing corn stalks. Soon they came to a split. Which way?

"There are five of us," Ula said. "We can take more than one path."

"But what about the next split?" Firenze asked. "And the one after that? We could get hopelessly separated and lost."

"Also, if there is danger, we can defend it better together," Piton said.

"Shall we vote?" Myst asked. "Or do we have a leader to decide?"

Squid knew that if they wanted a leader, she'd be selected, being the protagonist. "Let's vote," she said quickly.

They voted, and decided to stay together. It might decrease their chances of finding the right path to the center, but it was safer. In any event they were more like a decoy team, and it didn't really matter whether they won or lost. They just had to be a good distraction in case they were being observed.

There was a weird howl ahead. "Uh-oh," Ula said. "I have heard that sound before. Corn dogs. This is a corn field. They'll be after us within three moments."

"Corn dogs?" Myst asked. "Aren't they something you eat?"

"Not when they're wild. They prefer to eat you."

"I can handle them," Firenze said. He strode forward, his hands heating visibly.

"Don't get too hot, dear," Ula said, sounding insincere. It was almost as though she were suggesting something. Her job was to keep him reasonably cool.

Firenze smiled grimly. "I won't." But his hands were heating.

In just under three moments the pack of corn dogs appeared. They looked like dogs made of corn cobs, with yellow corn kernels for teeth. They charged.

Firenze shot out his hands, catching two dogs by their corn silk tails. The silk shriveled with the heat. The dogs yelped and backed off. Then they rallied, making ready to charge as a pack.

"I wouldn't," Ula said to them. "My man's a terror when he gets riled."

The dogs ignored her and charged Firenze as a unit. He put down his head and charged right back at them. Sparks flew as his fiery head singed their corn silk fur. Their corn teeth popped into popcorn, each one sounding a melodic note: pop music. They howled, this time in pain and panic.

That gave the dogs the message. They fled, some of them limping.

"Sorry I had to do that," Firenze said. But he didn't look chagrined.

"I'm sorry too," Ula said. But she looked positively smug. They understood each other. She didn't mind him heating in a good cause.

"That's a neat talent," Piton said.

"Yes, now that he has it under control," Myst said.

Just so. And the control was Ula. Squid was pleased that the girl had finally found her place in life; she would never be lonely or in fear again.

They walked on, alternating left forks with right forks, uncertain where they were going. Then they came to a section where several corn stalks seemed to have been ripped out of the ground, leaving holes. "We can get past that," Ula said.

"Nuh-uh," Piton said. "I have heard of those. They catch people who don't know their butts from holes in the ground. They're corn holes. I don't know why they're so bad, but I know we don't want to mess with them. We need to take another route."

"He's right," Firenze said. "I've heard of them too. We don't want to go near them."

The girls shrugged. "We can take another path," Squid said.

They backed off and took another fork. But that one led to a section where a net made of corn silk dropped over them, entangling their arms and legs while making a musical sound. It was a corn-net. They were hopelessly confined.

"Dear," Ula murmured.

"Got it." Firenze's head and hands heated up, burning through the strands. In moments they were free. Squid had never seen him so happy: he was now an asset to their group, instead of a liability. All because of Ula.

The path opened out into a larger chamber. There stood another creature of the corn, a horse with a single spiraling horn. "A uni-corn!" Squid said, delighted.

But this one was not friendly. He snorted and clove the earth with a fore-hoof as he oriented his horn for an attack. He strode toward them.

"Myst," Piton said as he covered his eyes. "Don't look, the rest of you."

But Squid managed to watch peripherally, feeling obliged to track the action.

Myst turned around and hoisted her skirt, flashing her magic panty as Firenze, Ula, and Piton looked away from her. The unicorn saw it and froze, freaked out.

They walked around the stunned creature. Only when they were well beyond him did Myst snap her fingers, breaking the spell. The unicorn came back to life and resumed guarding the corn.

"Great show, girl," Piton said.

"Just doing my bit to help." But Myst was practically radiating pleasure. That panty was indeed useful.

They came next to a section where a number of corn plants seemed to have gotten tangled together while growing. They looked odd, but the path continued on by them and there was no obvious danger. So Squid walked on—and paused, bewildered. "What am I doing here?" she asked.

"We're in the corn maiden maze," Ula said. "Don't you remember?"

"I—I suppose. But it's so confusing."

Piton stepped up to join her. He paused. "Are we on the right path? I feel lost."

"Corn-fusion!" Ula exclaimed, getting the pun. "The stalks are twisted together, and in their presence folk are cornfused."

Firenze groaned. "Awful pun. Real corny."

"Fittingly," Ula agreed. "We'd better bypass this section too."

They drew back, and the minds of Squid and Piton cleared. It seemed the challenges weren't just physical.

At last they did make it to the center. There was the prize: the lovely Corn Maiden herself. Her hair was fair corn silk, and her shoes were made from corncob husks, but were quite delicate. She wore a green skirt made of corn leaves that flashed hints of her thighs as she moved. "Hello, puzzlers," she said. "I am Cornelia, the prize of perfect love, as you can see by my crop-top." She spread her arms so that they could see the abbreviated blouse she wore, made of corn, that barely contained her full bosom. "But you look like children."

"We *are* children," Squid said.

"Then you will want Maizy. She's a-mazingly good with children." Cornelia put two fingers to her mouth and made a shrill whistle.

A second woman appeared, wearing a child-party dress and hat, also made of corn. "Hello! I am Maizy, for children. Let's have a popcorn party!"

Suddenly all of them were interested. Soon they were feasting on corn pudding, pop corn, and corn squeezings that made a tasty non-alcoholic drink.

"And here is my sister Maisy, who grows mini-mazes made of maze," Maizy said. Maisy appeared, and proceeded to grow tiny mazes whose outlines and paths the children could readily see. These were much easier to solve than the big ones. "But beware the unicorns, lest they corner you with corny puns." Indeed there were miniature unicorns in the mazes.

Seeing them happy, Squid settled down by herself and tuned in on the other group. Larry was thinking of her, so it was easy to join him as he stood before one of several gates to the castle.

It was apparent from the outset that they had a worse challenge. The castle maze was an actual castle, each room and hall a challenge to enter, with special and sometimes formidable dangers. It had five entrances, and one of the group stood before each entrance.

"Squid, if you are tuning in on me," Larry murmured, "I will give you a summary. We made our way across the moat via the drawbridge, and through the surrounding gardens, but now we face the real challenge: getting into the castle itself. It seems that each entrance is a puzzle, and each of us is trying a different one, hoping that one of us will find a key to entry that the others can also use. I am contemplating this one, which has a series of levers and slides I need to work in the correct order to unlock it. It frankly baffles me, and I think the other locks are similarly baffling the others. This is a formidable challenge, yet only the beginning. I wish you were here to hold my hand and encourage me; then at least I would feel up to the challenge."

Squid got an idea that flashed brightly over her head. *Youthen it!* she thought strongly to him.

Larry looked up, startled. "I got that thought, but that's crazy. My talent affects my own age, or that of those I am touching. Living things. The inanimate is ageless. Are you teasing me?"

Our talents are being quietly enhanced. Try it anyway.

Larry shrugged. "I will humor you, girl, but you will owe me some kissing when we get together again, for trying something so obviously foolish." He put his hands on the complicated locking mechanism and youthened himself, trying to take it with him.

Larry went from age twelve to age eleven, then to ten. And the lock changed with him, becoming more primitive and simpler to operate. He stared at it half a moment, then continued. He went to nine, then to eight, then to seven. And the lock simplified until it became an elementary slide and catch, something a child could figure out. He gazed at it, amazed. "It's working!"

Do it!

"Do what? Oh." He slid the bar across and lifted it out of the catch.

He pushed, and the door swung open. Then he relaxed, reverting back toward his regular age, eight, nine, ten, eleven, twelve. The lock reverted with him, becoming as obscurely complicated in its maturity as before.

But now the door was open.

"Hey, folk," Larry called. "Mine's solved."

The others quickly joined him, as none of them had succeeded in unlocking their doors. "We have entry," Win said. "Nice going, Larry."

"I had help."

"No need to be modest," Hilda said. "You used your talent to help all of us."

But be modest anyway, Squid thought at him.

"Thank you," he said modestly.

"Is it safe?" Data asked.

"That seems unlikely," Ion said. "But I can check it for poison." He floated his carpet through the doorway and into the dark interior chamber beyond. "No poison vapor," he called back. "The air is clean."

"Booo!" It was a ghost, a floating sheet with blank eye holes.

None of them were frightened. "So it's a haunted castle," Hilda said. "Ghosts can't hurt us, because their only substance is just enough vapor to make them visible, and to blow a little sound."

"Not necessarily," Ion said. "There are ways ghosts can cause serious mischief."

"Too bad Myst is not in our party," Win said. "She could mist out and get to know the ghosts on their own terms."

"Well, let's get on with it," Data said impatiently. She marched into the dusky chamber, stepping on the wood board floor.

"Hooo!" a ghost cried, dancing in front of her.

"Oh, get out of my way, spook," Data said, pushing through it.

Then she screamed as she dropped down out of sight.

"I knew it," Ion said. "Fake flooring."

Win stopped just before the place where Data had dropped. She put her hand on a board, and it passed through the wood. The floor was illusion.

"Bleep!" It was Data's voice, coming from deep below.

Win put her face to the floor, and through it. "There's a little light so I can see. She's in a well, or at least a deep cellar," she said. "She changed to skeleton form so she didn't get hurt, but she can't get out."

"I will get her out," Ion said. He floated his carpet to the spot, then sank through the floor. Three-and-a-half moments passed.

"Oh, you naughty boy!" Data squealed from below.

"I was trying to pick up your hip bone." He sounded embarrassed.

"I changed back. That's not bone there."

Squid smiled. Data had of course timed her change to make him take hold of soft flesh instead of hard bone. She had made him goose her.

There was more dialogue as they got things organized. The carpet was sized for one, so they had to get close together to stay on it. Then the carpet rose up out of the floor with Ion sitting on it and Data wrapped around him, her dress hopelessly askew. Their position could have been mistaken for something else, had they been adults. But of course it was just their way of both fitting on the carpet.

"Thank you for rescuing me," Data said, and kissed Ion on the mouth. He blushed purple.

"Let me help you dismount," Larry said, putting his arms around Data to lift her from the carpet and set her on the safe part of the floor.

"Thank you too," she said, and kissed him also. "Squid's lucky."

Now Larry blushed, for her half-bare body was up against his. She was back in teasing mode.

Then Data turned to the others. "Ion was right. There are ways ghosts can cause physical trouble, such as by casting a spell of illusion to show floor where there is none. If I had landed on my flesh bottom I'd have been hurt." She unhurriedly adjusted her dress to properly cover up that flesh.

"Ion was right," Hilda agreed. "He usually is."

"We have to get rid of those ghosts," Data said. "We were lucky that I was the one who fell through, so I could convert and save my assets."

"And very nice assets they are," Larry said.

Data eyed him saucily. "Are you angling for another kiss?"

"He wouldn't dare," Win said. "Squid would know."

The others laughed, but it was true: Squid already knew. Data was a flirt, and the boys did not know exactly how to handle her. Especially when one grabbed a hip bone that turned out to have flesh on it. Data had probably done that on purpose, to catch Larry also. Even the ghosts seemed to be amused.

"I can take care of this," Win said. She oriented, then revved up her wind. She could blow at hurricane force if she needed to. It blew the ghosts away, literally, or at least prevented them from manifesting, as they had no vapor to play with.

When the ghosts were gone, their illusions faded. Now the chamber was revealed as largely floorless. It was mostly a cellar hole.

"I can take care of that," Hilda said. She got to work sewing, and soon had a long band of cloth. She tossed that across the chamber, where the end caught near the far door and stuck. "This is magically strong cloth," she explained. "Spelled to be easy to hold on to. We can crawl along it to get to the other side without dropping."

Data tried it. "You're right," she said as she hung on the cloth. "It makes my body feel light so that I'm not getting tired." She handed her way on across the chamber. The cloth really did have magic properties. Hilda didn't look it and didn't brag about it, but she really was a Sorceress.

The others followed, one by one, except for Ion, who simply floated across on his carpet. That was, of course, more of Hilda's handiwork. Soon they were all standing before the door to the next chamber.

This door was not fancily locked. Data pushed it open, and paused.

There before them stood a zombie, marvelously rotten. "Ghoo aawaay" it said through its decayed tooth and rotten lips.

"I don't like zombies," Data said. "They're so icky. Not clean, like skeletons." She flashed her skeleton form briefly, then had to pull her clothing back into place. She was having a ball, getting away with repeated flashes of flesh. Squid knew she'd be deadly when grown.

"That is their nature," Larry agreed. Squid was annoyed; he was paying too much attention to Data's little show.

"We could simply bash through them," Ion said. "They are not great fighters."

"And get ick all over us," Hilda retorted. "When would we ever get to wash it off? Ugh!"

"Good point," Data said. "Maybe boys don't much mind getting icky, but girls have higher standards. We like to be clean, at least in our bodies."

"Amen," Win said. "Which gives us a three to two majority: no bashing zombies."

"I may have a way," Larry said. "I may be able to age one into extinction. That could persuade the others to leave off."

The girls considered, but didn't have anything better to offer. "I'll make a sanitary napkin," Hilda said. "To clean you off, after." She produced cloth and started sewing. She seemed to have an inexhaustible supply of cloth, needles, and thread as part of her magic.

Squid smiled. A sanitary napkin to make them sanitary? She had heard that some folk, notably in Mundania, had a rather different use for that kind of napkin.

Larry advanced on the zombie. "I know you don't have much of a brain left, Zom," he said. "But maybe you can understand this: I can destroy you in a horrible manner, and will, if you don't clear out of here. So save yourself; get out of here now and let us pass uncontaminated."

"Hhaah hhaah, hhaah," the zombie laughed, hacking forth some spoiled phlegm, and advanced on him.

Larry caught hold of the zombie's diseased arm, holding it carefully so it didn't tear off. Squid admired his nerve; he was doing what he had to do. Then he aged them both. Larry was twelve, and the zombie could be any age. But it would change proportionally. Larry turned thirteen, then fourteen, and fifteen. The zombie deteriorated visibly. "Give up?" Larry asked.

"Nneverr!" the zombie rasped, spitting out a decayed tooth, then collapsed into a rotten pile.

Larry let go and youthened back to his normal age. He faced the next zombie. "Your turn."

The zombie's sick eyeballs gazed at the pile of garbage that was the first one. Then it backed off. It had gotten the message. Even a spoiled brain understood destruction.

Then the other zombies backed off. They might be rotting, but they didn't want to perish sooner than they had to. They had been bluffed out. It might not have worked had their minds been less rotten, but that was a liability of the condition.

Hilda handed Larry her napkin. He took it and wiped himself off. It was marvelously effective: not only did it clean him, it eliminated the smell. "Thanks. I needed that."

Hilda blushed with pleasure. Squid nodded; they were learning how to get along.

The third chamber contained walking skeletons. "Well, now," Data said. "I'll distract them while the rest of you pass by." She paused, considering. "Um, Larry, this might work better if you could age me to nubility, at least for this scene. Can you do it when I'm in skeletal form?"

"I'm not sure."

"Okay, then, do it flesh form, and then I'll change."

"I will have to be very close to you to do it safely. It doesn't matter if a zombie goes wrong, but I wouldn't want to risk hurting you."

"Be close," she agreed. She stepped into him and put her arms about him, holding him close.

Larry concentrated and aged them both. They were both twelve; in less than half a moment they were thirteen, then fourteen, and fifteen. Both became young adults, physically, and Data was a voluptuously pretty girl.

Larry abruptly let her go and stepped away, "Hey, I'd like a couple more years," she protested.

"I can't risk it," he said. "I'd violate the—never mind."

"Violate what?" Data asked with assumed innocence.

"The Adult Conspiracy. We're children, even if our bodies mature temporarily."

"But that's the idea. Skeletons are just as distractable as flesh folk, when they see nice bones. I need nice bones to be sure of getting their attention. Two more years should do it. It's not as if we are actually going to do anything; I'll be turning skeleton."

"She's got a point," Hilda said.

Larry reluctantly returned, and Data embraced him. They aged to sixteen, then seventeen. He didn't change much more, but she continued to fill out impressively, plastered against him

"That should do it," Data said. She disengaged, then removed her ill-fitting clothing and stood bare. Both Larry and Ion were staring, unable to remove their gaze. If she'd been wearing panties they would have freaked out. As it was, Larry was dangerously near a freak.

The girls, too, were impressed. "I hope I grow up to look like that," Win murmured. "I'd blow men away, and not with my wind."

"Me too," Hilda said. "But I don't think I'll look like that. Even when I'm of age."

"I wonder. Suppose you sew a dress of fascination, like that panty? Your exact proportions wouldn't matter. You could be as impressive as you ever want to be."

"Maybe I could," Hilda agreed thoughtfully. Squid was sure she would succeed in fashioning truly seductive outfits for herself, in due course. Clothing did tend to make the woman.

Data danced about, luxuriously stretching her age-enhanced body. Now Larry and Ion did freak out. "Oops, sorry," Data said insincerely. What a flirt!

"Get on into skeleton form," Win said, not much amused.

Data changed, becoming a dancing skeleton. Her bones were extremely shapely, but no longer as compelling for flesh folk.

Myst snapped her fingers, and the two boys recovered. Neither commented.

Data's skull eyelessly eyed the skeletons. "Do you like my dance?" she asked, and went into one of the ones they had practiced. Squid had not realized how sexy some of their dances were when considered for that. The hip and chest bones might be bare of flesh, but were quite suggestive of it, especially the way she was moving them.

Three male skeletons converged on her. "Oh, we'd love to knock you up," one said.

Squid remembered the lore. Skeletons did not signal for babies the way flesh folk did, whatever that was. Instead when a couple was ready, the male would kick the female in the tail bone so hard she flew apart, her bones scattering wide and far. That was called knocking her up. Then he would pick up a number of the smaller ones and assemble them into an animated bone baby. Then he would help the adult skeleton reassemble herself from her remaining bones. She would be only slightly the worse for wear, and soon enough would grow new bones to replace the missing ones. She would also take care of the baby skeleton. It was very romantic, though for some reason flesh girls did not especially like getting knocked up. Their tailbones weren't set up for it.

Data went into her act. "Yes, but only one of you," she said. "You must choose who gets to kick my butt. Which of you is it to be?"

That set the skeletons back. They had expected to scare off the intruders, but instead Data was coming on to them, and she was surely provocative as Hades. A discussion broke out, which escalated into a quarrel, which in turn became a fight. They all wanted desperately to kick her butt. Soon bones were flying, as the skeletons broke each other apart.

But not all the skeletons were involved. Half of them were female, and they did not much like having their males distracted by an alluring visitor. They advanced on the children, blocking their way so that they could not get by during the distraction.

This was mischief. What to do? Piton, similarly aged, could have distracted the females, at least long enough for the others to get past. But Piton was in the other group. Could one of them emulate him? Ion was out, as he could not dance. That left only one male. It would have to do.

Larry! Squid thought.

"I hear you," Larry murmured. "Do you have an answer?"

I may have. But you may not like it.

"Those lady skeletons need to be stopped, or we'll wash out of this challenge. What's your idea?"

You must emulate Piton, and attract the ladies.

"But I'm solidly flesh!"

Ask Hilda to make you an outfit that will cause you to resemble a skeleton. Then do a strip tease dance. They should love it.

He pondered briefly. "I will try." He went to Hilda. "Can you make me an outfit that makes me resemble a skeleton?"

"Oho!" she said, appreciating the ploy. "Coming right up."

In a moment and a half she had sewn him tights. He looked at them dubiously. "Will these fit me?"

"Yes. They stretch."

He looked around. "There's nowhere to change."

"We can't hang up on that," Hilda snapped. "Those bone girls are almost upon us. Here, I'll do it." She started stripping away his clothing.

"But—"

"I change my brother all the time, because he can't do it himself. I know what you males have. I don't know how it works, or why the Conspiracy wants to hide it, but it's no news to me."

Let her do it, Squid thought.

Outvoted, Larry stood and let Hilda change him. Soon he was in the tights.

"Now put your clothes back on, so you can do the strip tease," Hilda said.

He quickly did so. "But I don't look different."

Hilda laughed. She produced a compact mirror sewn from shiny cloth and held it up to his face.

Larry stared, and Squid appreciated why: his head was now a hollow skull. His whole body looked skeletal; Squid had seen it when the briefs got on. His natural flesh had disappeared, replaced by his bones. The tights made his flesh invisible, but his clothing covered it up. Only his bony hands showed beyond the sleeves.

Squid suffered an imaginative chain of thought: suppose a girl thought she was donning hot pants to freak out boys in the way Myst's panty did, only it was skeletal tights? What an impression she would make!

Hilda retreated, giving him the stage, such as it was. She had done her part. Squid made another mental note: this girl really was worthwhile. She was not only a Sorceress, she could handle people when she needed to.

Now dance! Squid thought. *Arrogant male mode.*

Larry nodded. Some of their dances had exaggerated male and female roles, the males being like grandiose princes, the females like haughty princesses. All exaggerated posturing, but always fun. The role was easy to assume, because it was part of the dance.

The three lady skeletons were right there. "Back off, ladies," Larry said arrogantly. "Give me dancing room."

Caught by surprise, they backed off. Larry began the elegant little dance, "The Taming of the Skew," wherein several ladies sought to outdance a proficient male.

The skeletons eyelessly stared as Larry strutted, as well they might; he had the dance down pat, and his seventeen year old body was impressive, whether fleshly or skeletal.

Then the three materialized bone-flour dresses and started dancing themselves, mirroring his motions. *They knew the dance!*

Larry got into the swing of it. His legs pumped as he tapped the floor, facing the three. They tapped the floor in time, making a staccato. Their bodies, covered by the dresses, looked almost human.

Squid found this fascinating. She had never imagined skeletons doing it, but why not? The dance had male and female roles, and they were male and females. The bodies might differ, but the roles did not.

Larry whirled, and removed his jacket, baring his skeletal ribs and backbone.

The three females twirled and threw off their blouses. On flesh folk this could have been highly impressive, because men noticed women's bare chests. Actually it was impressive in a different way, as the bare ribs were exposed.

Larry continued dancing, next removing his trousers, exposing his gyrating hip bones. The skeletons removed their dresses, showing similar bones.

Squid realized that not only was she fascinated, so were the others in that castle chamber. The dance had become real. Win, Ion and Hilda had sidled by and were at the chamber's far door, but were facing back to watch.

Finally Larry was all bare bones. So were the ladies. The dance required that he select a female to be his romantic partner, but of course he couldn't take it beyond that. What was he to do at this point?

Data had finished her dance, leaving a pile of male bones behind. "Mine," she said, taking Larry's arm possessively. The three skeletons looked disappointed, but did not protest. Data had demonstrated her worthiness. Data led him to join the others at the far door. "Get on through," she hissed. "Before they catch on."

Squid's respect for Data grew. The girl was a flirt, but she had done what was needed, when it was needed. She had a sensible head, or skull.

They hustled through the doorway, and came up against a sign: HERE THERE BE DRAGONS.

"Uh-oh," Win said. "They won't want to dance."

"I will handle this," Ion said. He produced a small bottle and opened it. Vapor puffed out. "Stay behind the mist. It won't affect us."

The dragons charged, revving up their fires. They plowed into the vapor. They inhaled it. And fell to the floor, sound asleep.

"That was fast," Data murmured appreciatively as she shifted back to flesh form, then glided evocatively to Larry. "Youthen us."

He did, and soon they were age twelve again, and back in their normal clothing. Larry stuffed the folded briefs into a pocket. "But you know,"

Data murmured, "If you ever break up with Squid, look me up. I like the way you handle yourself, not to mention getting to be seventeen."

Squid kept her thoughts to herself, suppressing her momentary fury, knowing that she and Larry were not about to break up. She was coming to appreciate Larry even more: he was coming through for them, and not responding to Data's overtures.

The fifth room had a sign HERE THERE BE TIGERS. Sure enough, there were several of them sleeping on the floor. One step into the room would rouse them.

"Do you have tiger snooze potion, Ion?" Data asked.

"No. It didn't occur to me that I would ever encounter tigers. They're more of a Mundane threat."

"Maybe I can handle them," Hilda said. "Let me sew a cape."

"A cape?" Data asked.

"A special one, a limbo cape." Hilda quickly sewed more cloth, forming a brightly colored swatch. The others were silent, having seen what her sewing could do.

Hilda stepped into the chamber. Immediately the tigers roused. One charged.

Hilda held the cape out before her, like a Mundane matador. The idea that this flimsy material could stop a tiger seemed ludicrous, but there was no time to warn her away.

The tiger leaped into the cape. And disappeared.

The others stared. What had happened?

"Limbo," Hilda explained. "A sort of nowhere. It will take them long enough to get out of it so that we can safely reach the next room."

Oh.

Another tiger charged, and disappeared. After that the other tigers hesitated. They weren't stupid. They didn't like being disappeared.

"I will lead you across, one by one," Hilda said.

She did so. She started with Ion, on his carpet. When a tiger threatened, she brandished the cape, and it backed off, snarling.

Larry was next. This time a tiger did charge. Hilda swept the cape before it, and it disappeared. After that the remaining tigers stayed clear. They were safely through the challenge.

The next chamber had a man at a desk. What sort of threat was this?

"Come in guests," he said. "Have seats. I am Comper, director of the puzzles. We wish to forge a bargain."

This was different. "Folk," Squid said to her own group. "They want to bargain with the other group." She also sent a thought to Santo, in Fibot.

"Find out what they want," Santo said.

Find out what they want, Squid told Larry.

"What do you want?" Larry asked the man.

"You just performed a remarkable set of dances with the skeletons, unlike anything seen here before. We are familiar with the dances; it was the manner you accomplished them that impressed us. We recorded the sequence, and wish to have it as a promotional ad for the planet. What do you wish in return?"

Squid relayed that to Santo.

"Private access to a castle whose name begins CAP," Santo said, cautious about giving the full name so that their secret could be kept.

Squid relayed that to Larry. "Access for our whole group, including the ones at the Corn Maze and in our traveling boat, to a castle whose name begins with CAP."

"Done!" Comper said. "Follow the green line."

Just like that?

A line appeared, leading away from the chamber. They followed it, and in due course it came to the central courtyard of the castle. Another line led in from the corn Maze, and a third from Fibot, with Santo and Noe walking. They all met in the courtyard. Squid knew that Fibot was actually there too, cloaked for invisibility.

A new line appeared, this one blue. A sign said TO CAP CASTLE.

"To rehearse," Santo said. "We will steer the boat inside the castle. Piton and Data will use their knowledge to guide it out of the Sometime region back to Xanth Proper. The rest of us will give them any help they need."

They all nodded. Then they entered the boat, Win took the helm, Firenze took the sail, and they started moving.

Chapter 13

CAPRINE

The boat followed the blue line into a blue cloud, and out the other side. And there was the castle ahead, with a high pennant showing a handsome goat! Squid was bemused: who had hoisted that oddity?

They went directly to it, landing in its courtyard. Piton and Data stepped off the boat and entered the castle.

Only to return two thirds of a moment later. "This isn't Caprice," Piton said grimly.

"But it looks like Caprice," Squid protested. "It has a similar skyline."

"It's Caprine," Data said. "They have a common floor plan."

Oh for pitiful sake! Santo swore mentally. "I thought to protect our destination from others, but that allowed imprecision. We're in the wrong castle.

Two people followed Piton and Data to the courtyard. "Greeting, visitors," the male said politely. He was an exceptionally handsome young man, brown of hair and eye. "I am Burt Buck, and this is my associate Nancy Nanny. We're in charge of tourist visits."

"How may we best serve you?" the woman inquired. She was equivalently appealing, with long fair hair and a figure to make folk notice. Obviously they had been selected to make favorable impressions on visitors.

Santo hesitated, obviously unwilling to be impolite or to give away their real mission. Then he acted. "Squid, Larry, talk to our hosts. Perhaps we will want to visit for a day or so." He departed.

So it was in their hands. But who knew? Possibly some good might come of this misconnection. Squid knew that her job was to distract their hosts, and learn what they could about this castle, while Santo organized the others for the resumption of their search. He was always efficient. He knew that Squid and Larry could be trusted to keep private matters private.

"We—we thought to visit another castle," Squid said. "But there was a confusion of names, and it seems we got the wrong one. We apologize."

"If you seek a vacation castle," Burt said, "You can't do better than Caprine. We have all manner of entertainments."

"By day and by night," Nancy said, glancing at Larry in a way that could hardly be misunderstood. Adult women really knew how to make an impression on a male. Any male.

"We're children," Larry said.

"Not by Caprine standards. We are Human/Caprine crossbreeds here, adult by age three. Our law governs in this castle. You may do whatever you like here, without reference to your home standards. That is one of the things that make this a popular resort."

Squid suspected that this was the case at many vacation resorts. "We have reason to maintain our innocence," Squid said.

"As you wish," Burt said easily. "No one need do anything here they do not wish to do. Our business is pleasure."

"Endless pleasure," Nancy said, eyeing Larry again. Now this made Squid nervous. There was more to this situation than was being revealed.

Santo, she thought. *Let's get out of here now.*

"Get on board," Santo said from below decks, knowing she could hear. He did not question her judgment; probably it echoed his own conclusion. He was smarter than she, and working things out faster.

"I think we need to be going," Squid said. "It has been nice meeting you, Burt and Nancy, but we have elsewhere to go."

"As you wish," Burt repeated.

"We will always be here, should you change your minds," Nancy said.

No resistance? Squid did not trust that either, perversely.

The two of them climbed aboard, waved to the two Caprines, and nodded to Win and Firenze, who were in place. Santo had it already organized, accomplishing it while they talked with the Caprines.

The wind revved up. The square sail flared brightly. The boat lifted, rising out of the courtyard and over the castle. Then it angled into the sky.

Soon there was another castle in sight ahead, with a similar outline.

They tried to steer around it, but there seemed to be only one channel in the air, leading down to it. So they landed in its courtyard.

Two people came out. Squid and Larry went to meet them.

"Hello, travelers," the man said. "I am Boris Boar, and this as Sonia Sow. Welcome to Porcine Castle."

Oops. Santo caught Squid's eye from the deck. She knew what to do: engage the pair long enough for the boat to reorient and depart again.

Their dialogue was much like the prior one. Boris and Sonia were handsome and lovely, respectively, and eager to have tourist type company, proffering entertainments that were unlikely to be had in Xanth proper, age no barrier. These were pig crossbreeds, quite personable in their human guise, but not what their own group was looking for.

Squid and Larry soon bid parting, and there was no opposition from the hosts.

"As you wish," Boris repeated.

"We will always be here, should you change your minds," Sonia said.

Exactly like the others. They were speaking from a common script.

The boat sailed again. "Let's see whether there is another like those," Santo said. "There may be a pattern."

Soon they came to another castle, similar in outline to the others. This turned out to be Bovine, with Bruce Bull and Cora Cow, both personable in human guise, and speaking from the same script.

They continued through Ovine, with sheep folk, Equine with horse folk, Lupine with wolf folk, Canine with dog folk, and Feline with cat folk.

"I think we have the setup," Santo said. "We are in a loop of similar tourist castles, none of which are exactly what we want. Any thoughts?"

"Yes," Ula said. "Is this what Caprice Castle is slated for, once it captures enough people?"

The others stared at her. Once again she had come up with the unexpected but useful idea. This could indeed be where Caprice was going.

"I think we should investigate Caprine more thoroughly," Santo said. "There might be clues we can use to rescue Caprice, once we get there."

The others agreed.

"However," Noe said thoughtfully, "The Caprines may have seduction in mind, to commit us to their life. We shall have to be on guard."

"We must not tell them no outright," Data said. "We should seem amenable, merely cautious about committing, so that they believe they are making progress."

"We can flirt with them," Piton agreed.

"But not too seriously," Myst said.

Santo turned to Squid. "I think this is a job for you, as listener."

"Got it," she agreed.

"Murmur Squid's name every so often," Santo said to the others. "Or at least think of her, so she can tune in on you. That way all of your individual experiences will be noted. Then we may be able to put them together and arrive at a sensible conclusion."

They turned the boat around and retraced their route until they came back to Caprine. They landed.

Burt and Nancy came out to greet them. Squid and Larry met them. "We briefly visited several other castles," Squid said. "All of the folk there seem nice, the Porcines, the Bovines, the Ovines and all, but none of them interested us the way you Caprines do. So if we stay at any castle, this seems to be the one. We are not ready to stay, but would like to learn more about you."

"Welcome to do so," Burt said. "The only thing we insist on is that each visitor be paired with one of us, so that all interactions are personal."

And the visitors would be separated and isolated, maybe more amenable to persuasion. But discovery was a two way process. "We can do that," Squid said. "I myself am tired and will soon retire to our craft to rest, but the others will take you up on your kind offer."

"That will be fine," Nancy said graciously.

Squid turned and beckoned to the boat. Two more children came out: Santo and Noe, to her surprise. Santo must really be curious! She introduced the two couples to each other, and the two Caprines ushered the two visitors into the castle.

Two more Caprines emerged: Brian and Nadine. Squid beckoned again, and two more of theirs emerged: Firenze and Ula. Squid introduced them, and they entered the castle.

Then Barry and Nila met Piton and Data.

And Benny and Nola met Ion and Hilda.

That seemed to be enough, with eight from the boat matched with eight from the castle. Squid and Larry retreated to Fibot and settled down in their room. Squid was ready to attune, and Larry to make notes on what she told him.

Almost immediately, it started as Santo murmured Squid's name. She tuned in on him. "You are gay?" Nancy said to Santo. "But you were with a lady friend."

He had told the goat girl that? Santo was really going for candor!

"Precisely," he agreed. "She is my female friend, not really my girlfriend. I do not have a romantic relationship, though I do like her very well."

"Then let me invoke my portal."

"Portal?" Squid was as surprised as Santo sounded. Was that a coincidence of terms?

"Nancy!" Santo exclaimed, surely for Squid's benefit, to be sure she understood what was happening. "You turned male!"

Indeed, the goat girl's dress now hung awkwardly on a handsome buck. "I turned male," she/he agreed. "You may call me Naldo."

"This is amazing!"

"We have a number of special devices we have picked up over the years, among them a collection of portable portals," Naldo explained. "They enable any person to change gender at will. I remain female in essence, but am making this demonstration so that you can better appreciate what we offer. If you elect to join us here at Caprine castle, a PP will be yours."

"But I don't want to change gender."

"But you have a lady friend who plainly likes you very well: it showed in her manner toward you. You also value her: that also showed. You could use the portal to convert her to male, if she is amenable, as she well might be, when I suspect you would like her very well indeed. She surely understands your preference. If the two of you joined us here, the portal would be yours."

Santo was plainly shaken. This was wickedly tempting for him, for Noe as a boy might very well be his ideal partner. She knew him and loved him, and would do just about anything for him, including this.

"I will consider it," Santo said. That was their agreement, not to say outright no, though Squid knew Santo would never betray their mission for personal gain. But what an offer for him!

"Now as I said," Naldo continued smoothly, "I am female, and am not interested in any long term relationship as a male. But perhaps I can proffer you a taste of what offers. If your friend Noe used the portal to change, she might be inclined to do this with you." And Naldo abruptly kissed Santo on the lips.

Santo looked as he were about to faint. The prospect of having Noe as a boyfriend evidently astounded him. Noe had turned male before, but Santo had turned female at the same time, so nothing had come of that. But this was different. He kissed Naldo back, and the goat boy met him with a certain simulated passion.

"You fight dirty," Santo said with rueful appreciation.

Squid appreciated that. They were pulling out key stops, and getting to Santo in a way no one else had done before.

"We are desperate to increase our genetic base," Naldo said. "A gay relationship would not do that, but you might elect to contribute, in the interest of our welfare. We will welcome you regardless. We understand you are a formidable Magician."

"I do have a talent, but have not been classified as a Magician."

Naldo glanced at him cannily. "Because you are gay, I suspect. There is a prejudice."

How much of this type of understanding could Santo take?

Santo evidently had a similar concern. "Your interest in recruiting us is so strong that you, a temporary male, are relating to me in a way you would not normally do? Male or female, you are straight."

"You appreciate candor. Our need is desperate. Yes, I am female and straight, but I will do what I need to do to persuade you to join us. We believe that you are the key decision maker of your group."

"No need for you to be uncomfortable," Santo said. "Why not bring Noe here and let her try the portal?"

Naldo walked to a button on the wall. "Please bring our visitor Noe to us in room sixteen."

"Almost immediately," a male voice agreed.

And close to that time, Burt and Noe arrived. "We have had an interesting dialogue," the buck said. "Noe is a remarkable person."

"It is about to become more interesting," Naldo said. He faced Noe. "I am Naldo, a male aspect of Nancy. I converted via one of our portable gender portals. We suspect that you might wish to use it."

"I have been through a portal," Noe said. "I was male for some time. I prefer female."

Naldo lifted the portal and invoked it. He became female, her clothing in disarray, revealing potent aspects of her shapely body. "I understand. But how would you feel about turning male for your friend Santo?" Nancy asked.

"He was female at the same time I was male. That did not improve our relationship."

"You alone shifting gender."

Noe stood still, suddenly catching the drift. "Maybe." She turned to Santo. "Is this something you might want?"

"Yes," Santo said.

"Then let's find out." She took the portal. "Do it," she told it.

Then Noe was male, clothing distorted. "Do you want me to kiss you, Santo?"

There was no hesitation. "Yes."

Noe stepped into him, embracing his body. Then he kissed Santo's mouth. Then he drew back slightly. "I love you."

Santo seemed about to faint. "And I love you, Noe. I think I always did. But your body was wrong. Yet would you actually care to make that a permanent state?"

"For you, yes. Only for you."

"I could do it also when you are female," he said. "Only for you."

"Yes," Noe-male breathed.

"Join us, and the portal is yours," Nancy said.

Santo reoriented with a visible effort. "We have another mission we must attend to. But after that, I think we would be interested."

"The offer will remain open indefinitely," Nancy said. "Keep the portal, for now, while you are here. You may wish to experiment further."

Squid would have remained tuned, but now there was a new interest. Ion had gone with Nola Nanny, and Hilda with Benny Buck. It was Hilda who had sent a thought Squid's way. "You do know that I am nine years old, and not about to violate the dread Adult Conspiracy?"

"I am a young adult, in human terms," Benny said. "A mature male, in caprine terms. You are an amazing Sorceress. That fascinates me."

"It's my magic you like, rather than me?"

"So far, yes. But I shall be glad to get to know you, and I think I could love you if things went that way. It is not that I don't like you personally, so much as I don't know you sufficiently. I have never known a Sorceress before, of any age. However, as a doe goat you would be very much of age. Are you interested in having a boyfriend?"

Squid knew that Hilda was quite interested, because she had been largely isolated socially by her status as a princess and her need to help and protect her brother. This might be her chance to find out what a real boyfriend would be like, without generating any scandals in her home kingdom. "That depends on how far the boy wants to go." She was a child, but not ignorant, and wary.

"Holding hands. Kissing faces. Talking. Doing things together, such as touring the castle. No adult stuff. At present you are my assignment, and I will do my best to please you, help you, and safeguard you, with no expectations beyond the day."

Squid was impressed. This seemed like complete candor.

"An ad hoc boyfriend?" Hilda asked.

Benny glanced at her. "That is an advanced expression."

"Ad hoc. It means for this special purpose. You may have a regular girlfriend, but today you will treat me that way."

Benny nodded. "You're savvy."

"That annoys you?"

He laughed. "Not at all! It impresses me. Now I know I want to learn more about you. For the record, I am between girlfriends, and turned on by intelligence. I just didn't expect to encounter it in a child."

"And you are not a child."

"I am not. But you won't be a child much longer, and you may, in due course, become the kind of woman I want to have, though I fear you are well beyond my league. I am no prince, Magician, or genius. I am just an ordinary guy, the kind who would fetch your shoes in your realm. So I am realistic. This relationship is limited and temporary."

Hilda nodded. "I am interested. But first, I want to talk about my brother Ion. He is a Magician, but unable to walk, which is why he uses his little magic carpet. I worry that a pretty girl might fascinate him, but that her interest would never be real because he is lame. I don't want to see him hurt."

"He wants to walk, but can't? We have healing elixir."

"Here is his problem: he is immune to all elixirs. This is great when they are bad ones, but he can't turn it off when they are good ones, such as healing potions. His Magician status prevents him from being magically healed. It's ironic. Also a turnoff for girls. I know he would love to have a girlfriend, a real one, not one assigned by our parents. But how can he ever trust a girl from outside? He's not as assertive or cynical as I am, and he's, well, male. He's more likely to get harmed, at least emotionally. If she didn't want his magic, she'd want his status as a prince. He couldn't believe anything she said. He's a Magician, and he knows how to use his talent, but he's a babe in the woods socially. I know this hurts him, and I hate it, but there it is."

"And it would please you and make you more willing to be my ad hoc girlfriend, if you knew your brother had a similar relationship," Benny said. "One you could trust."

"You got it."

Squid was coming to appreciate Hilda more. She was putting it to the goat.

"I like your concern for your brother," Benny said. "It is possible we have an answer."

"What, a girl Ion can really trust? I don't trust that, and I'm a girl."

Benny laughed. "You are definitely a girl! I think I like even your distrust of your own gender. You are the kind of person whose respect must be earned, and I like that. I will do my best to earn it. Let me see whether I can find an avenue."

Squid, after having seen Nancy in action, was not about to underestimate Benny. The selected companions were clearly experienced in handling visitors. But she didn't see how he could come up with a girl for Ion they could trust. Squid, too, was female, and was wary of the devious ways of women. Especially grown ones.

Benny walked to a mirror on the wall. "Mirror Central, Benny Buck here. I need information."

So it was a magic mirror! What else did these odd castles have?

"Mirror Central here. What is your concern?"

"My memory says that a year or so back, there was a human girl who came to this planet, Animalia, as a tourist, and stayed because of our clean environment. She had a talent but couldn't use it because she couldn't safely go outside. Is she still here?"

"Vinia Human, age ten," the mirror said. "She took up residence in Equine Castle because she likes horses, though she can't actually go out and ride one. We are unpolluted, but that is not sufficient for her health."

Girls did like horses, Squid knew. That sounded authentic.

"What specifically is her problem?"

"She is highly sensitive to even the most dilute toxins in the environment. Her room is kept constantly purified, because even our fairly pristine air can set off her allergy. She is a virtual prisoner, and lonely because of it."

"That's the one," Benny said. "What is her talent?"

"Telekinesis, or levitation. That is, she can lift and move close objects up to her own weight with her mind. But she can lift and carry with her hands, so hardly uses her magic."

"We may have an answer for her. Please send a shuttle to pick up a party of four here at Caprine and conduct us to Equine for a visit. Notify the equines that we are coming."

A party of four?

"In process."

Benny returned his attention to Hilda. "Now, let's join with your brother and his companion, and go to the courtyard for the shuttle."

Oh, of course.

"You know, Ion could shield that girl as long as he was close to her," Hilda said. "He has a naturally antiseptic environment because of his magic."

"This is ideal."

What did they have in mind? Squid wondered. She was already discovering that the Caprines had a good deal more technological magic than had first been evident.

Hilda and Benny went to the room where Ion was being flattered by Nola Nanny, a remarkably comely and personable doe. Squid's distrust accelerated. This girl was in the process of wrapping Ion around her little finger. Even young boys were subject to the charms of grown women. So far, Ion was holding out, depending on his mistrust of women in general to protect his vulnerable feelings, but he was surely losing ground. Nola, like the other companions, was clearly older, perhaps adult, and experienced in handling folk.

"We're going to see Vinia at Equine Castle," Benny said. "She just may be the girl for you, Ion."

"I was working on that role," Nola said. "I am a perfectly competent temporary girl."

She was indeed, Squid thought.

"A permanent girl," Benny said.

"That would of course take precedence." Nola shrugged. "If she doesn't work out, I will remain for temporary duty."

As Squid saw it, that duty was dangerous to the mission of the children.

They went to a high turret where there was a large basket. The four of them climbed into the basket. Nola managed to flash her nice thighs at Ion as she climbed, surely no accident. Those were definitely not children's legs. Of course, Ion looked as he hovered beside the basket. Had he been grown he would have freaked out: as it was, he merely heated somewhat.

Why, Squid wondered, was Nola trying so hard to impress him, if she was about to be out of the picture? It must be back-up, in case the girl didn't work out. These folk left nothing to chance if they could help it.

Ion was the last to board, guiding his carpet to the place beside Nola. She caught his hand and held it firmly.

When they were settled in the basket, two griffins flew in. They caught the ends of cords attached to the rim and flew up. In two-thirds of a moment, the basket lifted. In four-thirds, they were swinging above the castle.

"Wow!" Hilda said. "This is fun."

"It is part of the lifestyle," Benny said. "There are dances each night at one castle or another, and of course, the neighbors attend."

"Dances," Hilda echoed.

"The women dress up," he said. "Actually Nola is quite a dancer."

"I enjoy it," Nola said. "Some of the men of other castles are pretty dashing."

"We dance too," Hilda said. "We might put on a show for you before we go."

"It would surely be well attended," Benny said.

They chatted as they traveled, and Squid saw that Benny's interest in Hilda appeared to be genuine. She was certainly interested in him, though careful. He had a quick mind, and Hilda seemed intrigued though still reserved.

"Tonight, the dance will be at Equine Castle, coincidentally," Benny said. "You and I can be partners."

"Those horse women can really prance," Nola said.

Ion looked sad. It was clear he would have liked to dance, but it simply wasn't possible for him.

"I'm sorry," Nola said immediately. She lifted his hand to her mouth and kissed his fingers. "I did not mean to be thoughtless." Ion visibly melted.

Oh, she was skillful!

Soon they arrived at Equine Castle, with its pennant showing a splendid horse. Squid realized belatedly that each castle flew its mascot picture: they just hadn't noticed.

The basket landed, and the two griffins settled down in the courtyard to rest. The passengers debarked and were greeted warmly by Hero Horse and Mona Mare, an attractive couple. In fact none of the folk on this world seemed unattractive; it was almost as if they were all in show business. Their small party was ushered into the castle, and to a chamber where a girl waited.

She was plain rather than pretty, but her body looked healthy. She was ten, a year older than Ion, but smaller. "Hello, Vinia," Benny said. "This is Ion, who as you can see, is unable to walk, so—"

"Oh, Ion!" the girl said. "I can help you stand and walk." She went to him and put her hands on his shoulders, gently lifting him. To Squid's surprise he came right up, off the carpet, and his legs dropped down until they touched the floor.

"You're lifting me!" Ion said, seeming surprised. "But I don't feel anything."

"It's my talent, telekinesis. It lifts every part of your body so you don't feel awkward." Then she glanced around. "Oh! Maybe I shouldn't have done that. Shouldn't have touched you. I just wanted to help."

"Keep doing it," Ion said. "I've never stood before, not like this. Am I tiring you?"

"No, I can do it indefinitely, as long as you're close. Touching is best, but I can do it from a short distance less precisely. But I mean I shouldn't have just put my hands on you as if we knew each other. I just got carried away."

"You can touch me anytime," Ion said. "Can I actually walk?"

"Well, it would be more apparent than real. I can make your feet move, but it's like working a marionette on strings. I don't think you'd want that."

"Try it," Ion said.

"We can walk together." She held his hand, and the two stepped forward together, perfectly synchronized. "I am making your legs do what mine do; it's easier to have you copy me than to pull each string directly. But you don't have any control yourself, so—"

"Stop apologizing!" Ion said. "I love it!"

She was taken aback. "You do? I thought you'd feel, well, used. I'm not pretty or royal or anything. I don't want to embarrass you or—"

Ion drew her into him and kissed her, shutting her up. She was plainly astonished. Then it was his turn to have a second thought. "Maybe I shouldn't have done that. I do have control of my upper body. I apologize for taking advantage—"

This time she kissed him, to shut him up.

When the kiss broke, they stood there, staring into each other's eyes. Then they kissed a third time, more lingeringly. And a little heart floated up.

"I think we have a match," Benny said.

"We do," Nola agreed.

"Now wait half a moment," Hilda said. "They hardly know each other. He's a Magician and prince, while she's just a common girl. Maybe she just wants to use him for status. Why should he settle for that?"

Vinia turned her head to face Hilda. "He needs me," she said joyfully. "And I need him. Right here with him I can finally breathe free. We're using each other. I don't much care whether he's royal or whatever. I just feel so great being near him. I'd like to stay close to him forever."

"We're a couple," Ion said. "The rest doesn't matter."

"You know you need someone to dress you each day," Hilda reminded him. "To help you in the bathroom. There are endless little chores."

"I can do that," Vinia said. "I'm a servant class girl."

"Not any more," Ion said. "Can we dance?"

"We can dance," Vinia agreed happily. Then the two of them danced, facing each other, perfectly synchronized. It was impressive despite the knowledge that the synchronicity was because Vinia was actually doing both parts.

"You're both satisfied?" Hilda asked. "You're sure?"

"We are," the two answered together as they continued dancing.

"And you really do like each other, regardless of what anyone else thinks?"

"Hilda, she's the real thing," Ion said. "A girl who needs my magic just to exist in the outside realm. There's an element of truth mist around me, part of my inherent nullification of falsity: it doesn't affect me, but it affects others near me. You know that. It's why the maids who attend to me are always completely candid about what they think of my helplessness, especially when I accidentally poop my pants because of my paralysis. They would falsely flatter me if they could, but they can't. It's why I'd rather be out traveling with you than staying at home in the palace. Vinia is not deceiving anyone. She really does need me. And I need her. To bleep with what anyone else thinks."

"I'd be glad to clean up your poop," Vinia said. "I know how it is. I get so sick when I venture out of my sterile room. I vomit and poop and collapse. I'm such a mess. But with you, I'm perfect. That is, I mean—"

"I know what you mean," Hilda said. "We've been there, done that. Being a prince's consort isn't all flowers and applause. It's covering for him when he messes up. I just wanted to be sure you understood."

Vinia smiled. "Suddenly I love poop."

Hilda turned to Benny. "You set this up. You knew about Vinia and what she needed, and her talent. You found the perfect girl for Ion."

"Yes," he agreed. "Isn't this what you wanted?"

For an answer, she kissed him. It was a surprisingly mature smooch. Her heart was plainly in it. She really did care about her brother, and was truly grateful for what Benny had done. That was rapidly translating into a kind of passion.

"I presume this means we're on for the dance tonight," Benny said, taken aback but pleased.

"For longer than that, if you're interested."

"For the duration of your stay here at the castles, then."

"Longer, maybe. I think I'd like to take you home with me."

Now it was his turn for caution. "But you are a princess and Sorceress. You may be destined for a prince or Magician when you grow up. You won't want an association with a nondescript crossbreed to embarrass you."

"And I may be destined for whom I bleeping well choose. Who will tell me no? I am long beyond embarrassment."

"Suddenly I have a thought. That little flying carpet your brother rides on—you sewed it!"

"I did. What of it?"

"That's awesome! You truly are a Sorceress."

Hilda's eyes narrowed. "Are you changing your mind?"

"No. Just marveling at the wonder of you."

She glanced sharply at him.

"He's not teasing," Ion said. "He can't quite get his mind around the fact that a girl child can have such enormous power. Mostly you don't show it."

"Well, it's part of the package. Can you handle it, Benny?"

He nodded. "When you kissed me, you felt like a warm person despite your youth. I always thought a Sorceress would be cold, aloof, and frighteningly adult. It's a fair mental adjustment, but I'll try. Let's see how it works out."

"I prefer warm to aloof." She squeezed his hand. She plainly had control of the situation.

Squid came out of her reverie. "I need to report to the others. There's heavy stuff on the bargaining table."

"There is," Larry agreed. "You have been telling me all along, but we need to tell the others. We really want what they offer. You and I could use those portable portals, for example."

"They have a big dance tonight at Equine Castle. We should all go, if they let us. Then we can have a conference."

"Yes."

They held a meeting of those on the boat. Firenze and Ula had returned after pleasant chats with their Caprine hosts that did not amount to anything serious, and so had Piton and Data. Data, however, was interested in Barry and wanted to see him again.

They updated the others on what Santo and Noe had learned, and on Ion and Hilda's progress. "There's a general rule of three I have heard," Larry said. "It may be a guideline. It is that if three binding deals are made, the whole group may be committed to a larger whole. The portals and the girl for Ion may represent two deals. We may have to be wary of one more."

"Meanwhile, I think we should attend that big dance," Squid said. "To get more of a feel for the situation, and just to have some fun. We can maybe demonstrate some of our dances, and learn some of theirs."

"Let's do it," Myst agreed. "Can we contact them about it?"

"If we go into their courtyard, they will meet us," Squid said. "We can ask them."

Chapter 14

ANIMALIA

They guided Fibot to Equine Castle, then debarked, leaving the boat in the charge of Tata and the peeve. It promptly turned invisible. It would respond to any of the children, but not to strangers.

Equine Castle was well lighted and gaily decorated for the dance. Griffin shuttles and other craft were arriving from other castles. Hero and Mona were there, handsomely garbed, to greet each arrival in style.

Squid approached them. "I am Squid, and this is my companion Larry. We obtained an invitation to the dance."

"Of course, Squid!" Hero said warmly. "Caprine sent word. Your associates Ion and Hilda are already here with their escorts, and Santo and Noe are en route. Everyone's welcome! Come in and horse around!"

Meanwhile, Mona was welcoming Larry similarly. In fact she embraced him and kissed his cheek. Squid suppressed an irrational surge of jealousy, instead focusing on a rational understanding, because the woman was amply endowed in all the right places and her embrace put them all up flat against the target. But of course the horse woman had no real interest in a visiting child; it was just part of her manner with tourists. She was very good at making visitors feel wanted.

Soon the other members of their party were welcomed, and they were ushered into the giant ballroom where folk of every type congregated. They were the only children there; the others were crossbreeds and tourists, not only adult but showing it with their low blouses and high skirts. Squid suppressed more jealousy; she would get there in time.

"There you are!" It was Ion, on his feet. Squid was startled despite having seen his introduction to Vinia. And of course Vinia was right beside him, shyly smiling. Neither could have been there without the other.

Squid took charge. "Folks, this is Vinia, Ion's companion. She enables him to stand, and he enables her to breathe. They are clearly meant for each other." She named each of the ones from the fire boat so that Vinia could identify them, though of course Ion would keep her current.

"It's so nice to meet you," Vinia said faintly. She plainly felt out of her depth. Squid realized that social events like this one had simply been beyond her reach before. Yet she was delighted to be here.

Then Hilda and her goat boyfriend appeared. "And with Hilda is her companion Benny," Squid said smoothly, and introduced the others again.

Refreshments were freely available, boot rear for the children, stronger stuff for the adults, with abundant cookies.

The dance began. Squid saw that many couples consisted of one attractive crossbreed with one ordinary human tourist. They held each other close, and between dances a number of them adjourned to other rooms. It seemed that there was more than dancing going on here. That was of course one of the main attractions of this castle, and this world.

They joined the dancing, and Squid was not the only one impressed by how well Ion and Vinia coordinated theirs.

Santo and Noe appeared, suitably garbed. "We should do a dance demonstration," Santo murmured to Squid. "That will efficiently introduce us to all of them." It seemed he had something in mind.

Squid and Larry went to Hero and Mona. "We happen to be a dance group, among other things," Squid said. "We would like to do an exhibition square dance for you, in appreciation for your hospitality. We have our own music."

"A children's dance," Mona said appreciatively. "I will put it on the schedule. It should be a nice contrast."

So it was that easy. But of course these folk catered to the tourists in whatever ways they could, and what children could do was limited.

Before long it happened. "We have special guests from beyond Caprine Castle tonight," Hero said grandly. "They will now perform an exhibition square dance, for your pleasure."

There was token applause. It was plain that the adults were humoring the children and did not expect much from them.

Squid caught Santo's eye. He quirked a smile. This audience might be surprised.

They lined up with four couples: Squid with Larry, Santo with Noe, Piton with Myst, and Firenze with Ula. They were all suitably dressed, and the girls had flaring double-circle skirts.

"Sets in order," Win said, though there was just the one set. She was not dancing this time, so was available as the caller. The dancers were already in order, of course. "Honor to your partner. Honor to your corner. Swing your partner. Promenade." They followed her instructions perfectly. Squid knew she was not the only one loving this. It was good to be back in the square.

They went through the full dance, perfectly timed, their steps aligned as they sashayed to the music. They were good, and knew it.

When they finished, the applause was hardly token. It rocked the hall.

Hero and Mona strode forward. "We had no idea!" he said. "You are expert! Could we prevail on you to do another dance? The people are truly intrigued."

Thus encouraged, they performed a circle dance, then the Triangle, which evoked a roar of laughter. Their show was definitely a success.

After that they were deluged by others wishing to dance with the children. Squid danced with several young men in turn, and actually enjoyed it. She saw Larry with Mona, of all things, and that woman could really make her skirt flare. Firenze wound up with a cowgirl who was just as flashy. All of it was fun.

Hero came to dance with her. "We know of square and round dances," he said. "And of course couple dances. But you children amazed us, and we appreciate that."

"We may amaze you more," Squid said, bringing up something Santo had mentioned to her. "Four of us would like to meet privately with you and Mona while the dance remains in progress, so that it is not evident. We have a serious matter to discuss."

"If it is as serious as your dancing, we are more than ready."

"But off the record. We trust you can keep secrets."

"We are good at that, yes." Probably an understatement.

"Then usher Santo and his companions Noe, Ion, and Vinia into a private chamber when you can do so without attracting attention. I will not join you."

"Not you? There is an intriguing mystery about you, Squid, more than the oddity of your name."

"I am odd. I am an alien cuttlefish in human form, somewhat the way you are a horse in human form."

He laughed. "Our ancestry is equine, and the majority of our heritage is that of the horse, but we are unable to change shape. We are essentially human in body and mind, merely not universally recognized as such."

"I am recognized as such, but am not. Observe my hand." She split it into two green limbs with suckers just long enough for him to see before she reverted it to a human hand.

"You amaze me again! Are the others of your group like you?"

"No, I am the only cuttlefish and the only alien. But two of our number have skeleton ancestry, and they can change between forms. Others have other secrets."

"It should be an interesting dialogue."

"We hope so." Then another man cut in, and Hero departed. She tracked him with her mind, and saw that in due course he did discreetly usher Santo and Noe out of the hall, while Mona did the same with Ion and Vinia. So they were on.

Squid excused herself and went to rescue Larry from flashy women he surely had little real interest in. They got boot rear and cookies and sat at the edge of the hall. Larry would run interference for her while she tuned into Santo.

She was just in time. "Your associate Squid tells me that you have an important private matter to discuss," Hero said.

"Yes," Santo agreed as they took seats. "But in the interest of fairness, I must tell you that our friend Ion here is diffusing truth elixir into mist. We will all be speaking with absolute candor. If this is not your preference, you should break off this dialogue now."

Hero glanced at Ion and nodded. "Squid surprised me in more than one manner." He glanced at Mona. "Squid is an alien cuttlefish in the form of a human girl, and I suspect that is only part of the mystery of her. These children are significantly beyond what they may seem."

"I was gathering that," Mona agreed.

Hero returned his attention to Santo. "Which I think is that truth mist in operation. I am normally more circumspect. My role as host requires it."

"We are on a serious mission which must remain private," Santo said.

"We do honor confidences. That is to a fair extent our business."

"There are secrets some of our clients would kill to protect," Mona said. "But they know that we would never betray them. Our given word is absolute."

"That was our impression," Santo said. "We hope you are able to help us."

"We do what we can for our guests, not all of it for general news."

"So we gather. We are trying to rescue parents and friends who have been abducted, we think by a Demon, along with their castle known as Caprice. This is one that travels softly and silently to any location desired by its proprietors. We came to Castle Caprine by accident, confusing the name, but think we may be able to make something of this."

"A Demon! You are in deeper trouble than we can help with."

"Two of our number were residents of that castle, and know how to operate it. We hope that if we reach it by surprise, they can move it out of the trap before the Demon can interfere. At that point the Demon would risk exposure of his machination, as it is in the territory of another Demon, and may have to give up his ill-gotten item."

Hero whistled. "You are in a league beyond ours! Demons are dangerous."

"Yes. What we would like from you, if it is feasible, is a hidden avenue or route to Caprice Castle, so that we can not only get there, but do it swiftly and by surprise. We may be able to deliver something in exchange that is worth your while."

Hero considered. "There may be an avenue, though it could be more challenging than you care for. But I should provide the background, as it is devious. Our suite of castles were set up some time ago by an interplanetary consortium interested in hidden power. They obtained volunteers who desired a good life, to unite with assorted breeds of animals to produce crossbreeds who looked and seemed human, but who were more than half animal. I for example, am about two thirds equine, one third human. The human form and mind dominates, but I am not recognized as human. I am an animal, just as your associate Squid is. All our associates are similar, with their respective breeds. This was done to enable us to be obliging hosts without the limitations of humans, such as age."

"There is no Adult Conspiracy for us," Mona said. "We can have relations with children, or provide children for tourists who wish to have relations."

"You are a—" Noe started.

"Please don't say it," Mona said. "We are not proud of it. But this is the nature of our assignment. That is not the only way we cater to tourists with specialized tastes. We hate it, but we do it."

Squid realized that animals did not have the rights humans did. Human tourists could do anything they wanted with human-looking animals, and the animals were obliged to cooperate. Specialized tastes indeed! It was a devious form of slavery.

Ion and Vinia were silent, staying out of the dialogue, but Squid could see Vinia react to the term "specialized tastes." She had to have a notion what these folk were enduring.

"It is our fondest ambition," Hero said, "to increase our human component to the point where we are more than half human. Then we will qualify as human, and become protected by human standards."

"That's why you're angling for more settlers!" Noe exclaimed. "To get more human as a community. A half human crossbreed who marries a full human person would have children two thirds human."

"That is why," Hero agreed. "The rest of our life here is good. We simply would rather cater to a higher class clientele."

"Now we more fully appreciate your motive," Santo said. "We were concerned that it could be something more nefarious."

"You would have to join the Adult Conspiracy to appreciate the details of what we do. But I think that, even as children, you can understand that we are obliged to do things that would normally revolt us, and would be forbidden elsewhere. Things that you would not care to do even in exchange for an otherwise virtually perfect life. We can't revolt or even protest; we have no standing as humans. But if we achieved a human majority, then we would be in a position to bargain for improvement."

"I believe we can help you," Santo said.

Hero and Mona gazed at him with muted hope. It seemed that they had been disappointed many times before. "We understand that you are a very intelligent person, and a remarkably powerful Magician, though your expertise is not in our area," Mona said.

"My talent is physical rather than social," Santo agreed.

"And that you are capable of bargaining," Hero said.

"Yes," Santo said. "It is not that we bear you any malice, but our situation is difficult, and we are desperate."

"You sound like us," Mona said.

Hero nodded. "Make your offer."

"We want, I think, three things from you," Santo said. "The portable portals, Vinia for Ion, with her staying with us, not he with you. And a safe secret route to Caprice Castle."

"The first two are feasible: the third is a challenge, as I mentioned, but perhaps possible," Hero said. "What do you offer in return?"

"Just one thing. A direct physical connection to Portal Village and its neighbors, where they have many residents and tourists eager for new things. I believe a fair number of them would be interested in coming here to Animalia to mix with your people, perchance to stay and join with your men and women to form families." Santo quirked a smile. "They may have some tourist appetites, but they are settlers ultimately interested in establishing worthwhile lives, if they find the right partners. I doubt that they are prejudiced about crossbreeds."

"Ooh," Mona breathed. "We could give them such a time, and we have the partners when they want to settle."

"They are completely human," Noe said. "Their crossbreed children would be more than half human, as I mentioned."

"Would any of them be interested in connecting with more than one of us, so that there would be more children?" Hero asked. "Our assorted castles would be quite ready to adopt such children. Foster homes can be good homes."

Amen! Squid thought. The siblings had found wonderful homes and families.

"I suspect some would," Santo said. "To them it might seem like multiple romances without the attendant responsibilities. They would, of course, want to be sure that the children were well cared for."

Squid thought of Ruby. She was adventurous, and might find Animalia fascinating. There were surely many others.

"The children would be honored as elites, because of their plus-human heritage," Mona said. "They would be the hope for our future."

Exactly, Squid thought. Santo's real offer to the Animalia was the chance to have such children. Not one or two, or six or seven, but maybe hundreds or even thousands. All of them with full human rights.

"We are interested," Mona breathed. "I believe that in this respect I can speak for all of Animalia."

"Let's rejoin the dance," Hero said. "So that our absence is not noticed. We will see if we can find a guide for the trail you desire." It was his way of agreeing to the deal, off the record. All of this was unofficial, but highly meaningful.

"It may be best if we do not meet again," Mona said. "Someone at Caprine Castle will talk to you in a few hours."

"Understood," Santo said.

Mona came and kissed Santo with such feeling that he couldn't help responding. He put his arms around her and kissed her back. Noe, far from being jealous, was observing the technique the horsewoman employed. Santo was gay, but evidently could be moved by a skilled and lovely adult woman. Noe clearly meant to learn such skill herself.

Without further ado, they left the chamber, and rejoined the dance as two couples who had perhaps needed to freshen up between efforts.

Squid was impressed and hopeful. Had they quietly forged the deal that would give both parties the things they most wanted? After coming to the wrong castle because of the confusion of names? That might be the most wonderful surprise.

An hour later a cowgirl approached Squid in the dance. "We have your guide," she murmured. "His name is Fox. He is from Castle Vulpine." She moved on without further explanation. It was as though they hadn't talked.

The dance night ended and the dancers dispersed, a number of new couples having formed. That was of course much of the point of such a gathering, to facilitate many meetings by many people. The tourists evidently liked the novelty.

Squid and Larry joined with Ion and Vinia, then Santo and Noe. They walked out to locate Fibot.

There in the courtyard was a disheveled young man. "I'm Fox," he said.

"Join us," Santo said, without otherwise seeming to react. He lifted a hand, and Fibot appeared. They climbed over the rail, Fox included, and went below decks. It happened in part of a moment, without any commotion.

"Within this craft it is private," Santo said. "We can speak freely. Will you tell us something about yourself?"

"I'm synesthesiac. I see sounds as colors, and so forth."

The other children formed a silent circle around them. "How does this enable you to follow a path?" Noe asked.

"I see things in ways others don't, so can pick out a path they don't see."

"Ah. The way some folk can see a picture others can't, because they perceive colors differently."

"Something like that, yes."

"And can you select the path to a particular destination?" Santo asked.

"To a degree. I need a sound or sight or smell to go by. It gets faint away from its source, but I can tune in and follow it."

"The way dogs do?"

"Not exactly. It has to be my kind of essence. Dogs smell what's there. I smell the sound, or feel the sight, or hear the texture, which is a different thing. All things give off these alternate signals, which aren't apparent to ordinary folk."

"So you can perceive a signal that others can't," Noe said. "And if we gave you one of Caprice Castle, you might be able to follow it there."

"Yes. But such routes can be devious, sometimes dangerous."

Noe glanced at Data. "Do you have something from Caprice?"

"I found a thimble there, and saved it, because sometimes it's useful," Data said. She produced a miniature silver cup the size of the end of a finger.

"Show it to Fox."

Data handed it to Fox. He took it, looked at it, sniffed it, listened to it, and ran a finger around it. "This smells musical."

"Can you trace it to its source?" Noe asked. "Considering that Caprice Castle has moved around a lot."

"Yes. The source remains in touch. I can trace it wherever it is."

"Then I think we have our guide," Santo said. "But I suspect we will have to make our own deal with you."

"I want only one thing," Fox said. "The love of Dori Doe."

"Who, or what, is that?"

Fox smiled. "An Animalian girl. I love her, but she wants nothing to do with me. They agreed to make her do this mission with me, to give me a chance to win her. If I fail, then I lose her."

Noe shook her head. "A girl forced to keep company with a man is not going to be very friendly."

"Yes. She will serve, but be angry about it, and will take it out on me. So, if you can make her like being on this mission, I'll be satisfied."

Noe took it in stride. "We'll see what we can do."

A tall order, Squid knew. But they would have to try.

"Where is Dori?" Santo asked.

"She's at Caprine Castle, of course. She is Caprine."

Oho! A female goat was properly a doe rather than a nanny. So the Caprines selected names for the tourist tastes, and tourists thought a female goat was a nanny, but this one was not that type. Squid realized that the Equines had to have known that, and known that Dori would be easy for visitors to Caprine Castle, like themselves, to pick up.

"Meanwhile, we'll give you a tour of our boat," Santo said, glancing at Squid.

Who else? She was the protagonist, and probably the one best able to fathom the nature of a new person. Squid stepped forward. "Hello. I am Squid, the alien member of this mission."

Fox looked at her. "I'll say! Your voice smells of a distant ocean. Your arms look like twined tentacles. There is a wet blue aura about you. I like you already."

Squid laughed. "I guess we'll get along. This way, please."

She took him through the boat, introducing him in passing to the other children and to Tata and the peeve, both of whom mightily impressed him. Finally she took him to his assigned cabin.

"I have a room to myself? Is it that you know no one else could stand my company?"

So this man had social insecurity, unsurprisingly. Squid briefly pondered and concluded that a forceful frontal approach was best, considering his isolation and uncertainty. "Stand still while I kiss you."

Surprised, he did so, and she did so, borrowing some of the technique she had just observed in Mona Mare. She felt the way it impressed him, not so much romantically, as he had no romantic interest in her, but because of its tangible demonstration that she cared about him on some level.

"I've never been kissed by an alien cuttlefish before," he said, amazed. But it was her human aspect that had wowed him despite her youth.

"We can stand your company," Squid said. "We just thought you'd prefer a private room."

"I'd rather have company."

"We'll see what we can do," she said, echoing Noe. "Now rest. We'll be at Caprine Castle soon, as they are our hosts, and will see about picking up Dori Doe."

He nodded. She left him there and went out to join Santo and Noe. "He is prickly, but impressed by Fibot and its creatures. He will need a roommate."

"Who does he want?"

"Dori Doe, of course. But he knows that's foolish."

"What is your sense of him?"

"He's an outsider because of his nature, but a reasonably sensible person. He'd probably be a good fit for our group, except—"

"Except that he is adult, and we must all be children."

Squid had nothing against children, being one herself, but she hoped that after this adventure she would be free to be with adults also. Adults did have their qualities.

The boat was landing at Caprine Castle. "Now you must tackle Dori," Santo said. "Noe will go with you."

Squid and Noe debarked. There in the courtyard stood an astonishing lovely young woman. Her features and form were classic, her honey colored hair so voluminous as to resemble a cloak, her expression one of justified confidence. This was no outcast or wallflower; this was a woman among women.

"Hello," Noe said. "We are—"

"I know who you are, Noe and Squid," Dori said. "Girlfriend of a gay, and alien cuttlefish. You dance divinely. Let's get on with it."

Squid was impressed. This woman was not only supremely self-possessed, she had done her homework.

They boarded the boat, then paused topside as Dori admired the softly flaming sail. They could be private here, and they wanted to know more about her before going into the main hold.

"You will be working with Fox," Noe said. "He would like to room with you during the mission. We understand if you prefer other accommodations, and we will honor your preference."

"No, put me in with him," Dori said. "He knows better than to touch me without my express consent."

"You are annoyed with him," Squid said, "yet willing to room with him?"

"I can handle him. He's not a bad person, and has a remarkable talent. Much better than mine, which is to see smells. That's why he is interested in me."

"If he's a decent person with a good talent, why are you averse to him?" Squid asked.

"Because I want to marry a full human and have recognized children. We all do."

"How did the Animalia get you to join this mission?" Noe asked. "I inquire because we are obliged to make you amenable to working with Fox if we can, and we appreciate why you may be annoyed by being drafted for this."

"You promised us contact with a whole village of interested full humans. I am eighteen and ready to form a family. I should be able to nab a good real man there."

Noe chuckled. "You could nab a good man anywhere you went. Men are much affected by appearance."

"The more fools, they," Dori agreed. She clearly understood the power she possessed apart from her talent.

"What may we offer you to facilitate your comfort?"

"A girlfriend. That is, a friend who is a girl, and conversant with this remarkable boat of yours."

"We are all children," Squid said. "Bound by the Adult Conspiracy. Some of us are half your age. Will a child do?"

Dori smiled, and it was like the sun rising on a perfect morning. "But you are not ordinary children."

"Not," Squid agreed. "There is Data, who is half skeleton, age twelve."

"It's not marriage, but still I would prefer a full human."

"You are crossbreed yourself, but don't want a crossbreed companion?"

"Crossbreeds are considered inferior. You have surely felt that prejudice yourself, Squid. I know that is bigotry, but I want to be as close as possible to full humans."

"I am not a crossbreed," Squid said. "I am an alien masquerading as human. But I think I understand your position."

"I think you do."

"Then there's Win, age ten, full human. She's one of the original sib-lings, as I am."

"I know of you siblings. Is she the one with the wind at her back?"

She did know about the siblings. "Yes."

"She'll do."

They were standing amidships, and the boat was at anchor, so Win was not on duty at the helm at the moment. "We will introduce you to her."

Squid sent a thought to Win. *Visitor needs a friend.* She got Win's men-tal acknowledgment. They knew about assigned friendships that could become real. Squid herself had been that route, with Princess Aria.

They descended into the main craft. Win appeared, her hair fluttering in her face as usual. "Hello."

"You'll do," Dori said. "You may be a Sorceress."

"Oh, no, I'm just a nondescript girl."

"Who could blow away Caprine Castle if you had reason."

"Oh, I wouldn't!" But neither did she deny it. Win preferred to use only as much wind power as was needed for the task at hand, such as propel-ling Fibot.

"Show me around the ship." Dori turned briefly to Noe and Squid. "Thank you for your attention." She had dismissed them.

They watched the woman and the girl move on. "She's a charmer," Noe murmured ironically.

"But no man will ever tell her no," Squid said.

Squid tracked them mentally until Win took Dori to the cabin she was to share with Fox. "Hello, Vulpine," Dori said. "I am going to take a shower and wash my hair. You may watch but not touch." She proceeded to do exactly that, not concealing her splendid body at all, and he did watch without trying to approach her. It was clear that she had him utterly fascinated, and obedient to her whim. He knew that if he annoyed her in any way, she would be gone. He wanted to keep her close.

If only all women dominated all men similarly, Squid thought. What a different world it would be! As it was, the girls had only their panties and personalities, the former immediate, the latter much slower. Dori was rather like an animated panty with her power to amaze men.

They caught up with Santo. "They have delivered our guide," Santo said. "Now we will do our part, because it may not be feasible when we complete our mission."

Santo and Noe went out to talk with Brian and Nadine, who represented the interest of the Animalia in this respect. They set a time for the tunnel: noon next day. Animalia had until then to assemble its representatives, who would use the tunnel two by two. Squid could tell that many hardly believed it, but they would become believers at noon.

They retired to the boat. Dori kept company with Win, and absolutely fascinated every male on the boat except less so with Santo and Larry, for special reasons, and had an effect on the females too. They had a communal dinner, but the boys hardly ate, and Fox didn't even try. Ion was in a seeming trance, putting Vinia badly out of sorts, and it was no better with Firenze and Ula. And Hilda's Benny.

"Enough of this nonsense," Hilda snapped, and started sewing. In about two and a quarter moments she had made a large transparent veil. "Put this on," she told Dori.

The doe shrugged and did so. The veil settled over her head and fell down around her body like a gossamer net. She remained fully visible, beautiful as ever, but the males resumed normal activities. The veil had somehow deleted the allure. Squid was impressed again by Hilda's magic sewing ability. What else could she make, when challenged?

"Thank you!" Vinia breathed. Ula plainly echoed the sentiment.

Hilda just smiled. Her Benny was now free of the distraction.

"This is fabulous," Dori said. "It enables me to become a normal person. May I keep it, Hilda?"

She actually appreciated the effect of the veil! Squid realized that the doe could remove it any time she chose, so it really cost her nothing.

"Sure," Hilda said. "Glad to have helped."

Dori wore the magic veil thereafter. She really did like it.

Next day, a throng formed in the castle courtyard, as pairs of the other persuasions assembled. All of the folk were attractive representatives of their kind, surely by no coincidence.

Then Santo opened a man-sized tunnel between Caprine Castle and Portal Village. The Animalia were amazed. It looked like a simple ring in the air, but those who looked through it saw a completely different terrain.

It was in fact a direct connection to a different planet. It was also another example of the awe-inspiring kind of magic the children had.

Santo and Noe retired to the boat, as maintaining the tunnel was a special effort for him, and Noe knew exactly how to support him. Now it was up to the others to follow up.

Squid and Larry were the first to go through, partly to demonstrate to the Animalia that it really worked and was safe, but mainly to contact the villagers.

"I must talk with Ruby," Squid said. "I know her."

Ruby appeared, now looking fully adult, as she was not pretending to be a child. She was a very fine figure of a woman. "Have we met?"

"I'm Squid. You almost seduced me when I was male, but your conscience stopped you." She sent a mental confirmation.

"Oh! Squid! You changed genders!"

"Yes. Get us into a private room with you. We have a deal you will truly want."

In a moment the three of them were private. Then Squid produced her mini portal and became male.

"Squid!" Ruby repeated. "I thought it was all a dream!"

"It was a dream, but also real. Here is Laurelai."

Larry used his portal and became the lovely lady.

"You have mini-portals!" Ruby exclaimed in sheer wonder.

"Here is the deal," Squid said. "You can have pocket portals like these, to keep and use. In exchange you must meet and interact socially with attractive crossbreeds in their own castles, to see if any villagers would like to marry them. The crossbreeds want to have children who are more human than animal."

"Well, I don't know. Crossbreeds have an imperfect reputation."

"Meet them and see. What they offer is fabulous, and they are good people in their own right." Squid used the portal to revert to her female gender, and Laurelai reluctantly did the same. Then they handed the two portals to Ruby.

They rejoined the villagers, and Ruby quickly explained the deal. Meanwhile, Squid and Larry went to the tunnel, stepped through, and beckoned. Two equines stepped up, Hero and Mona. Squid took Hero by the elbow and guided him through, and Larry did the same for Mona.

"Here are Hero Horse and Mona Mare," Squid said formally. "They are equine crossbreeds of good reputation. Meet them, talk with them, satisfy yourselves that these folk are worthy of your attention."

"Well, now," Ruby said, eyeing Hero.

"Well, now," he agreed, and swept her into his arms. In half a moment they were kissing. It was his way, and it was generally effective.

Mona was doing similar with a male villager. That was even more effective. Then both couples fell to animated talking, getting to know each other.

Squid walked back to the tunnel, stepped through, and waved in another pair. These were two Bovines, a cowboy and cowgirl. She didn't know them personally, but knew they could do the job. Indeed, soon they were charming two more villagers.

Then a third pair, Caprines, a buck and a nanny. They, too, readily melded.

"When you said crossbreeds, I had a mental picture," Ruby told Squid breathlessly. "But this is something else. These folk are wonderful!"

"They are," Squid agreed. "But because they are more than half animal, they have no human rights. They want to change that."

"They want to breed with full humans!" Ruby said, catching on.

"Yes. Some of your men can breed with a number of their women if they want to. The object is to get more majority-human children."

"We have some men who would really like that, if the girls are pretty."

"They are."

"Not all our men are handsome, however."

"But all your men are full human. That makes them attractive to the fractional humans. The same is true for your ordinary women."

Ruby nodded. "This is phenomenal! Of course we want to know more about it."

Squid raised her voice, calling to them all. "Your attention please. This access will be open until noon tomorrow. You may freely cross both ways. Get to know them, villagers, learn what you have to offer each other, but be sure to be home before noon unless you decide to stay. Meanwhile, Animalia brings you a gift of four portable portals the village can keep and use regardless."

Half a dozen villagers crossed immediately. They were welcomed by appealing Animalia. Very soon several couples disappeared into the recesses of Caprine Castle. Squid knew from their minds that they had Adult Conspiracy intentions. That was, after all, the point. To some villagers, it might be mere entertainment, but to the crossbreeds it was a chance at fulfillment.

Then Squid conducted Ruby across to Animalia. Ruby was amazed by the castle and the throng of attractive folk. "This is just the contact point," Squid clarified. "Each species has its own castle, and they are all in on the deal. There are many, many to choose from, and they are all physically appealing. They cater to the tourist trade, and you are tourists."

"We cater similarly," Ruby said. "I think we will understand each other."

"I think so too." It certainly looked like success on this part of their mission.

It was late by the time Squid and Larry retired to the boat, which remained invisible, but by then they were hardly missed. Hundreds of villagers and Animalians were making their acquaintances. It was like a huge party.

Would it all work out in the long run? It was impossible to know for sure, but it did seem likely.

Chapter 15

TRAIL

In the end, quite a number of villagers from several local villages elected to cross over to join attractive and accommodating crossbreeds who were eager to get to it. They didn't require marriage, merely the effort to get babies, and some village men came to understandings with half-a-dozen or more assorted Animalia women. A similar number of Animalia crossed to the villages to be with their chosen villagers; the men were dashing and the local girls were thrilled. Overall, all parties seemed well satisfied.

Santo could not promise to open another tunnel at a later date, because he could not be sure he would be free or even alive, but agreed to do it if he could. For one thing, all the available portable portals had been given out, and if they wanted more they would have to make another connection. It was a tacit part of the deal.

So the transferees were gambling that if they changed their minds there would be a chance to return, and the villagers were gambling on the chance to get more invaluable portals. Dori would be on the village side, ready to choose the right villager, after the mission was done. A number of men had expressed interest, even while she wore the veil. Fox was gambling that he would be able to win her before they returned.

The tunnel shut down at noon without fanfare, and Santo went to sleep. Squid, tuning in, noted that Noe had used her mini portal to convert to male as she slept with him. She did love him, and gender was secondary. The portal made it feasible for them to have a complete relationship. Squid's own roommate, Larry, used their portal to become Laurelai, and Squid was satisfied to remain female herself. They were after all children; when time passed and they became adult, they would have to decide the nuances of their relationship.

They had to wait at least a day while Santo recovered from his inter-planetary effort. In that time, Hilda and Benny circulated socially. Benny was winningly affable, impressing the girls, but he made clear that Hilda was his choice. "She's a Sorceress," he said, as if jokingly. "And full human. I can't do better than that." Hilda clearly loved it, knowing that he meant it. She had already sewn him a hat that made him look debonair. She could hardly wait to come of age.

Ion and Vinia also circulated, he proud to be on his feet, she thrilled to be safely mixing. That couple was never going to break up. The other children welcomed Vinia, especially after Hilda explained. She was indeed perfect for Ion, and he was perfect for her. He was a prince and Magician, but his family would welcome her also because of the way she fulfilled him. He might one day be a king, with her at his side.

When Squid and Laurelai circulated it got interesting. The others had seen Laurelai before in the simulation, but then they had all been reversed in gender. To meet her when they were normal, and Squid remained female, was a novelty. Laurelai had aged herself three years to be fifteen and the very picture of dawning maidenhood, phenomenally lovely. Then they encountered Win with Dori Doe, already eye-hauntingly beautiful.

The two faced each other, taking stock. Laurelai had glossy blue/black hair and eyes and a fair young figure. Dori had voluminous honey-colored hair with matching eyes and full figure. They were two types, opposite in coloration but similarly impressive.

Then Dori spoke. "You are Squid's friend. You need her."

"I do," Laurelai agreed. "She understands me."

"Squid is special."

"She is."

They were speaking as if Squid were not standing right there with them. Squid was not offended: rather she was interested. Dori was an assertive woman; what was she leading up to?

"I would like to be your friend too." Dori glanced at Win. "These things are not exclusive in your culture?"

"They are not," Win said. "Squid and I are friends and siblings. We would never play false to each other."

That was true, but it also iced Squid's heart for a moment. What of her vision of having to kill Win? How could that ever be reconciled with their abiding commitment to each other? She had never come to terms with that future horror.

"Then let me kiss you," Dori said. She closed the distance to Laurelai.

How would Laurelai react to that? Squid knew that she was not the only one seriously curious. Laurelai normally wore a man's body, but she had no romantic interest in women.

Laurelai met her half way. They came together, embraced, and kissed each other on the lips. It was beautiful both as an image and as a gesture.

"You are not what I expected," Squid told Dori.

"We crossbreeds vary as much as purebreds," Dori said. "That is partly to offer greater range of choice to tourists, some of whom actually have more than our forms in mind. I am one of the rare ones with a magic talent. It makes me independent."

The four of them retired to a nook and chatted, getting to know each other. Dori was candid about her nature and experience. As an animal with strongly appealing form but with no human rights she had had more adult experience with men than most women her age, and it had started well before she left girlhood. She couldn't go into detail in the presence of children but it was clear she was far from innocent. It was a life she intended to escape as soon as possible. Yet she came across as a nice person and surely a worthwhile friend.

"After this is over," Laurelai said, "and things return to normal, I hope we can get together again. I suspect we will appreciate you even more as adults than we can as children."

"Don't be eager to lose your childish state," Dori said. "It is precious, and can never be restored once it is lost." And, of course, she knew.

In due course they retired, and Dori spent the night with Fox. Now they understood that she had nothing to lose, but held him at bay because she did not care to commit even briefly to him. Squid knew, because she tuned in; the two never touched each other, literally.

Laurelai reverted to age twelve and changed back to Larry. "I'm glad I met Dori in my female state," he said. "She would have tongue-tied me as a male, even as young as I am."

"She would," Squid agreed.

"Tomorrow, she will help Fox follow the trail to Caprice Castle. Then, we'll be up against the finale."

"And I will have to kill Win!" Squid exclaimed. "I hate that. I don't believe it, I don't accept it, I can't abide it, but that vision seemed dreadfully true."

"Or the universe will end," he agreed. "I can't make sense of it, but fear it."

"I'm nobody. How can I be called the most important person? Ludicrous!"

"If the fate of the universe really does depend on you, you are that important."

"That's utter nonsense."

"It is nonsense," he agreed. "There must be some explanation that makes sense of it. We must be misinterpreting the signals."

"We must be," she agreed, clinging to that hope. Then she dissolved into tears, and he held her as long as it took.

Next morning, Santo was ready. Noe explained the procedure: "Fox will locate the scent of Caprice Castle, and lead us to a window, which is a kind of portal to another world. He does not make the world or the window, he merely sniffs them out and uses them to follow a scent. Dori can see smells, so can spot them from farther away than he can. They will work together. Fibot will follow. The trail may be devious, as it follows other rules than the ones we know, but it will inevitably lead to our destination, Caprice. We really won't have much to do until we get there. Then Piton and Data will move the castle back to Xanth, as it can travel there on its own power. It is all very simple, we hope. Any questions?"

"Yes," Squid said. "I have had bad dreams of my role in this. As far as I know, I shouldn't have a role; it's all Fox and Dori, then Piton and Data. So how do I figure in?"

"I said, we hope it is all very simple," Noe said. "Not that I believe it will be. I think of the trail as like the string of a necklace. The episodes along it are like the beads. A necklace needs both string and beads. Fox will trace the string. You must be a bead. Only with your participation will the necklace be complete."

That did make sense. But what a bead! She would have to kill her friend and sibling? Or else? But what could she do except follow the course and try to change it when she got there. "Thank you," she said sadly.

"Squid," Santo said. "I wish this dreadful burden were not yours. But when Demons play, mortals are largely powerless. I know you will do the right thing when the time comes."

"What if the right thing is to kill Win?" Squid cried. "How could I ever do that?"

"I know you would never choose it," Win said. "We siblings would never harm each other. But if it takes my death to save the universe, then I am ready."

"Oh, Win!" Squid hugged her and burst into tears. In a moment the other siblings joined her in tears, and some of the others.

But what could they do? They all were victims of the awful game.

And maybe her vision was wrong. It had occurred when she was ill, and might be a delusion. That was about all Squid had left to cling to.

Before long things settled down. "We are all ready," Noe said grimly. "Except for one detail. Fox, Dori, Benny, you are adults. We believe that the rules of this Demon game mean that children are exempt from capture. Only if there is an adult aboard Fibot when we reach Caprice Castle can they spy and capture us. You will lead us to it, but you will have to debark before we enter the castle. You can then track us to Xanth, and we will pick you up and welcome you. We do not mean to strand you alone, only to play the game the way we have to. Do you understand?"

"Understood," Fox agreed.

"When this is done, I hope to be your friend also," Dori said.

"I would like that," Noe said. "Now it is your turn, Fox."

"My turn," Fox agreed. "Let me see the thimble again."

Data produced it. Fox took it and sniffed it, then handed it to Dori.

"Green," she said, and gave it back to Data.

"Thank you," Fox said.

Squid remained silent, as did the others. This was a curious way to start a major quest. Did either of these visitors really know what they were doing?

It was Dori who started the action. Fibot remained in the courtyard of Caprine Castle, invisible. The doe went to the deck and looked around. "I see a very faint smell of that thimble, that way," she said, pointing upward.

Squid and Laurelai were beside her. They saw nothing, of course.

Win generated her wind. Firenze activated the fire sail, which was now in the shape of a question mark. Fibot was cautious too. The boat slid smoothly up at that angle.

There were several Animalia at the edges of the court, including Hero and Mona, quietly watching. When the boat became visible and took off, they waved.

"I like those folk," Larry said. "I hope we do see them again."

"Me, too," Myst murmured, and Firenze nodded. It was a hopeful but slightly sad parting.

"That way," Dori said, pointing again.

The wind changed. The boat altered direction. They sailed out over the forest. How could a smell from another planet be there, whatever its color? But Squid kept her mouth shut.

Soon they came to a rocky field. "I see several wisps of smell there," Dori said. Squid saw nothing, and knew the others were similarly blank.

Fox stepped in. "Now I see a green smell radiating out from a center. That must be a window."

"It must be," Dori agreed.

"Land me there," Fox said to Win. "I will verify it."

Win guided the craft to the ground. Fox jumped down and walked to an undistinguished spot. "I need a ladder," he said. "It's too high."

Hilda floated a small stepladder on Ion's little carpet, as Ion no longer needed it. She set it up where Fox indicated. The others stood in a circle around it and watched.

Fox climbed it, reached the top, and disappeared. First his reaching arms, then his head, then the rest of his body, climbing into nothingness. It was weird.

The others stared.

In half a moment Fox's feet reappeared from above, found the ladder, and the rest of him joined them. He descended to the ground. "It's a window," he reported. "But there's a complication. It opens on a city on, I think planet Earth. There are people on the street. We will be noticed."

That had never occurred to Squid. She had somehow supposed that their journey would be private.

"I can wear the veil," Dori said. "But I will still be visible, and seeming to appear from nowhere. That will be hard to explain."

"Worse," Fox said. "Most are men, perhaps heading for a sporting event. They look like crude types."

Dori nodded. "Aren't they all!" She pondered briefly, no more than two thirds of a moment. "Maybe I should remove the veil. I am not dependent on magic to make a man pause."

"A dozen men may gather. Men become bolder in groups. They don't speak a language I recognize. You could be in trouble."

"I could be," Dori agreed. "Maybe Hilda could sew me a cloak of invisibility."

"I could," Hilda said. "But I am not completely expert in those. It would block your sight out, as well as theirs in."

"Unless I exposed only my eyes."

"Then they would seem to be floating eyes, like a ghost."

"Maybe I can help," Larry said. "As Laurelai. To distract them from you, while you look for the green smell."

"Then you could become a target," Dori said.

"Then maybe I can help," Squid said. "I have a sense of meaning from folk I meet, so could read their thoughts and maybe counter them."

"Or Dori could use a portal to change to male form, to be less distracting," Larry suggested.

"Forget it," Dori said. "I have tried male. I'm no good at it. All my reflexes are female. I'd mess it up royally. Nobody respects a man who flashes panties or leans forward to show his upper chest."

"This is already getting complicated," Noe said. "Maybe we need another window, one that is more isolated."

"They exist," Fox said. "But can be far apart. We might lose the trail. Better to find a way to follow this one."

"Then let's be a distraction," Squid said. "If we get in trouble, Fibot can pick us back up."

"There is another risk," Fox said. "Windows tend to be temporary. This one might last a year, or one minute. Best not to delay."

"Then let's get moving," Squid said. "Larry, let's change ages too."

He nodded. They retreated to Fibot and to their cabin, where Larry efficiently stripped and changed gender with the mini portal, then held her while they both aged about five years. Then they did their hair and put on female dresses, Squid too, though she didn't really need to. They returned to the courtyard as two teen girls.

"We'll need the ladder there," Fox said. "It's about the same distance above the pavement."

"We'll fetch it after us," Dori said.

The group boarded the boat, except for Fox. He went up on the ladder, disappeared, drew the ladder up so that it also disappeared, then dangled a ribbon behind for Fibot to orient on. The boat was invisible too. It could navigate any aperture of any size: that was part of its magic. From aboard it, it simply seemed that the world outside briefly distorted.

Win blew the craft through the spot indicated by the ribbon.

Suddenly it was a dramatically different world outside. It was a city street, such as existed in the dreary world of Mundania. Tall buildings rose on either side, odd vehicles cruised on the pavement, and the edges were thronged with people.

There was no sign of Fox. Then the ladder appeared and dropped down to the concrete, and Fox appeared, climbing down it. "There must be a bit of a tunnel between realities," Noe said. "He perched there until we passed."

"Our turn," Dori said. She climbed over the gunwale to the ladder and descended.

Laurelai followed. Then Squid. Soon all four were standing on the street.

And were suddenly the center of attention. "Pretend to ignore them," Dori said. "I see a whiff of green smell ahead. This way." She started walking.

"Kool ta taht!" a man explained. "Tahw a kcar no taht ebab!"

Their language was utterly foreign, but Squid was able to pick up the essence from the man's one-track mind. "He's admiring Dori's form," she said. "Though he seems to think she's a baby."

"Some baby!" Laurelai said.

"Now the distraction," Dori said. "You follow the green, Fox. We'll rejoin you when you verify the next window."

"Got it," Fox agreed, walking in the direction she had indicated.

Dori angled away from him, and Laurelai and Squid went with her. A contingent of men followed them, not interested in Fox. The distraction was working!

"Eerht sebab!" another man said. "Ylsuoiciled gnuoy, oot!"

"They like us young, oddly," Squid said.

"Oh, men do," Dori agreed. "That's why the Adult Conspiracy exists. If it was up to the men, girls of any age would be signaling the stork for babies."

"That must be it," Laurelai said. "They don't think *we're* babies. They just want to get us to signal for them, because they can't do it by themselves."

"If we only knew how," Squid said.

A man confronted them, blocking their way. "Yeh, llod, woh tuoba a ssik?" he said to Dori.

"This one thinks you're a doll," Squid said. "He wants a kiss."

"He wants more than that," Dori said. Then, to the man: "Get lost, donkey gap!"

"Oho!" he said, needing no translation. He grabbed for her.

Dori leaned forward and drew open her upper decolletage, providing him a deep peek inside her bra. "I hope this magic works here," she said.

The man froze in place, freaked out.

"Well, now," Laurelai said as a man reached for her. She spun about in place and hoisted her hem to flash her panties.

He, too, freaked out. So did several others.

One grabbed for Squid. She could form her body as she chose, to a degree, and had exaggerated the configuration of her chest. He too freaked out. She was pleased; that was her first freak out.

So their female assets were effective here. Good enough. Meanwhile, Fox was well on down the street, and had found a spot that radiated green smells, according to Dori. He turned and gave them a high sign. It was a window!

"S'tahw siht?" a new voice demanded. The three turned to it. It was a man garbed in blue with copper buttons and flat feet.

"Uh-oh," Squid said. "He thinks we're—"

"Serohw," the blue man said. "Gniticilos yllagelli no eht teerts."

The three stared blankly at him. Squid was only just beginning to process the thoughts. "He thinks we're doing something wrong."

"I know what he thinks," Dori said. "We're in trouble."

"Ton dewolla ni eht riaf ytic fo Tsew Hsaw. Er'uoy rednu tserra."

Then other blue men appeared, and clamped linked metal bracelets on them behind their backs. They were hustled helplessly into a wheeled vehicle and taken to a barred cell. The bracelets were removed, but they were locked in. There they were left alone for a while.

"They think we are ladies of the evening," Dori said.

"We are girls. But it's not evening yet," Squid protested.

"Never mind. It's a misunderstanding we are not in a position to clarify."

Squid shared a glance with Laurelai. Apparently it was some adult kind of thing. Meanwhile, what were they to do? How could they ever return to Fibot when they were locked up here? Their diversion had gone disastrously wrong.

It was about to get worse.

Blue women appeared. "Pirts hcraes," one announced.

They stared at her blankly.

"Yrruh pu. Teg tuo fo ruoy sehtolc."

"Uh-oh," Squid said. "They want us bare."

Then Fibot appeared in the cell behind them. They needed no urging; they scrambled over the gunwale and tumbled into the boat as it returned to invisibility. Squid saw the blue women staring. Their quarry had disappeared!

The boat sailed between the bars and out of the building. "How did you find us?" Laurelai asked.

"I know you, especially Dori," Fox said. "I sniffed your trail. Dori's scent is the color of light honey."

"That makes sense," Laurelai said, laughing. "Mine would be blue/black."

"It is," Fox agreed.

"Now don't misunderstand," Dori told him. "This is purely relief at being rescued, not any commitment." Then she threw her arms about him and kissed him so firmly that his feet almost lifted off the deck.

When she let him go, he fell back into a chair. "It will do," he gasped. Then: "Maybe it's time to tell you."

"Tell me what?"

"I am not a crossbreed. I live in Vulpine Castle because I did an errand for them and they invited me to stay. They have been good to me, never teasing me about my synesthesia the way others do. But I am actually a visitor. I am full human."

Squid spotted Tata Dogfish observing. *True*? She thought to him.

True, he replied mentally.

Dori stared at him. "I just naturally assumed—"

"Everyone does. I am happy to be considered a Vulpine. That's why I adopted the name."

Her eyes narrowed. "The Vulpine girls, the foxy ladies. They can be very attractive, and cunning in their pursuits, and they are looking for babies. They keep you company?"

"They would if I asked them. But my interest is elsewhere. I would prefer to be with someone in a position to relate to my liability."

"Liability? But you use it to track things anywhere!"

"I discovered the magic component later. Still, few truly understand the way you do."

Dori let it drop. But Squid knew that they had just passed a most significant point. Fox was after all marriageable, by Dori's definition, and he wasn't committed elsewhere. And she did understand about sensing things in a different manner, even if for her it was only seeing smells.

They sailed through the new window, which had not closed during the delay. Squid knew she was not the only one to breathe a silent sigh of relief.

The next was a forest world, or at least they were among grand trees. Squid and Larry reverted to their natural ages, he to his natural gender, and debarked. Fox and Dori were sniffing out the trail, which seemed to wind among the trees.

Larry and Squid walked by one of the trees, a huge spreading one of indeterminate species. "How do you do, nice visitors," a voice came.

They paused and looked around, but saw no one. "Uh," Larry said. "I hear you but I don't see you."

"You see me. I am the tree."

They looked at it. It seemed perfectly ordinary, in trunk, branches, and foliage. "Uh, hello, Tree," Squid said. "What kind are you?"

"I am a Pleasant Tree, of course. It is so nice to have company."

A pun. But of course puns abounded everywhere except maybe drear Mundania. "It's nice to meet you," Squid said.

Then Fox whistled. He had found a window.

"We have to move on," Larry said. "But it was indeed pleasant to meet you."

"Mutual, I'm sure," the tree said pleasantly.

They went to catch up to Fox and Dori. There was the spot with green smells emanating, though only the two of them could see them. "We'll go fetch Fibot," Squid said.

They walked back to where the boat was parked. Several others were out among the trees, unwinding after the nervousness of the prior planet. "They found a window!" Squid called. "All aboard!"

The others came in from the forest and boarded the boat. Then Squid and Larry directed Win and Firenze so that the wind and sail could operate. Soon they came in sight of the window.

Maybe too soon, because Fox and Dori were kissing again. The first kiss must have had an impact. Squid was glad to see it.

This window was low to the ground, almost on it. They sailed through it, emerging in what looked like an orchard. Fruit trees abounded, and it looked like the nicest place yet. Of course that could be deceptive.

"Let's take a break," Noe suggested. "I'm happy to take a brief walk."

The others agreed. They debarked, while Fox signaled the boat, so that Tata and the peeve could guide it to follow him.

"Oh, look!" Data said. "A stocking tree!" She ran to it and harvested a nice pair of stockings. She put them on, and they made her legs look like age 16 instead of age 12.

"Oooo," Win said, taking some herself. They added about five years to her legs. Then Myst tried a pair, and her legs went from nine to fourteen. All three girls were thrilled. There was just something about having sexy legs. The stockings did not stay up perfectly, but it was easy to pull them back into place.

The trail was becoming clearer, according to Fox. It was not clear to anyone else. It started down a broad avenue between trees, but abruptly diverged to the side, looped three-quarters of the way around a tree trunk and set off in a new direction. It came to a clearing where a number of donkeys were grazing. They were all in pairs.

Larry groaned. "This is a pun world. Those are ass sets."

Then a male troll appeared, evidently attracted by their exclamations as they donned their stockings. "Well, now!" he said, grabbing hold of Data.

Data snapped her fingers. The troll froze in place, literally, ice flaking off his hide.

"Hey, it works!" Data said. "My Cold Snap!"

That was right. Her talent from the World of Talent. Squid was glad it was serving her in good stead. Of course Data could have turned skeleton and escaped the troll, but this was so much more satisfying.

The trail continued to a deserted building, at least on the inside. A man was hanging on the wall, on his back, busily copying one pad of paper to another. "Uh, sir, what are you doing?" Larry asked.

The man glanced at him. "I'm copying material, of course. I'm a backup."

Larry stifled most of his groan. "I hope we find the next window soon," he muttered.

Then they spied figures running around aimlessly. They were classic numbers, I, II, III, IV, and V. Each had little legs. What were they doing?

"They're roaming," Larry gritted. "Because they are Roaming Numerals."

"Let's move on," Squid said. The others were glad to agree.

But their trial of puns was hardly over. They came next to a section overrun by small snakes. They did not look threatening, but it was impossible to avoid them. In fact they oriented on the girls, slithering toward their feet.

"Get away, get away!" Data exclaimed as the little reptiles surrounded her. Then she screamed. "Eeeeek!"

Because two snakes had slithered up her legs. She slapped at them, but they avoided her and wrapped themselves around her thighs. She couldn't use her cold snap on them because it would have frozen her legs too. Then they clamped their little teeth on the tops of the sagging stockings, pulling them back into place.

"They're garter snakes!" Noe said. "They hold up the stockings!"

Data had opened her mouth for another multi-E scream, but stifled it. "So they are," she agreed. "They're doing a good job, too. No more sag."

Now Win and Myst stood still while garter snakes slithered up their legs and secured their new stockings. Their legs looked sexier than ever.

And when Piton looked too suggestively at Win's legs, her snakes eyed him and hissed. They were guarding the stockings and their wearers from any possible molesters.

"You can look at mine," Myst said.

He did, and there was no hissing. It seemed that the little snakes knew what was what. He was her boyfriend. But he didn't try to touch the stockings, lest he get bit.

Meanwhile, the boys were finding something of interest to them, a club tree. Firenze took one and hefted it, and Ion took another. Oddly, the clubs did not make them look more threatening. In fact Ula and Vinia, beside them, were startled when the boys took them by the elbows to help them.

"I get it," Larry said. "These are Gentleman's Clubs. They make men act like gentlemen in the presence of ladies."

"I wonder," Ula said, intrigued. She went to a neighboring tree and harvested a slender lady's club. And immediately became more solicitous of Firenze.

"And Gentlewoman's Clubs," Larry said. "Making disreputable girls act like ladies."

Ula turned to him as if about to make a sarcastic comment, but instead complimented him. "You are very perceptive, Larry. It must be the woman in you." Then she glanced at the club as if chiding it for overruling her. But she didn't drop it.

Benny left Hilda's side long enough to pick a slender cane. But he immediately walked so fast that it stirred up a dust storm in his wake; leaves and twigs swirled. He quickly threw it away. "That's a hurry-cane," he said. "It was making me hurry so fast I was about to leave devastation behind."

"That could be useful," Hilda said. "Let me sew a bag for it so we can save it." She sewed rapidly, forming a long thin container. Then Benny gritted his teeth, picked up the cane, and jammed it in the bag before he could rush off. The cane was quiescent; Hilda's magic pacified it.

Fox paused. "The path is fading out. It was stronger, but now I am not seeing it. I'm not sure what happened."

"You're being too limited," Dori said. "Use your other senses."

Surprised, he tried it, listening to a dull background noise. "I hear something purple."

"Listen for something green."

"And something yellow. Red. Blue." He smiled. "Green!" He headed off on a new trail.

"You are helping him," Squid said.

"It's just a woman's intuition, filling in what the man lacks." But Dori was plainly pleased.

Squid tuned in on Fox, and became aware of what he was seeing. She paused, amazed. Not only did she see green sounds passing rapidly by, she smelled faint green wafts and heard furrowed columns. There were other sounds, feelings, and colors; everything was giving off emanations. It was an entirely different realm.

But Fox was focusing on the green sounds. She joined him in that concentration. There was a kind of path formed by the color, distinguished from the myriad other colors.

There was too much there, too different from her normal perceptions. Squid withdrew, feeling greenly dizzy. Her world returned, but now with a trace of otherness. She was satisfied to let Fox do it.

The new trail led to what looked like a dragon's den. That was best avoided, unless there was no choice.

There seemed to be no choice. "If I leave the trail, I may not be able to pick it up again farther along," Fox said worriedly.

And there in the sky was an approaching shape. The dragon!

Ion hurried forward, closely paced by Vinia. "I can pacify it." He lifted a little bottle, applied a sprayer nozzle, and blew out a small cloud of vapor.

"All the same, I think we'd better get elsewhere," Fox said. He stepped back.

Ion stood his ground, and Vinia with him, necessarily, though she looked uneasy. The dragon glided down to land, ignoring them as clearly no threat. It was medium-sized, which was big enough to incinerate the boy with a single well-stoked breath of fire. It inhaled, taking in the vapor.

And fell asleep.

Fox stared. He had not seen Ion's magic before. "I stand corrected."

"He's a Magician," Vinia said proudly. "He is immune to all elixirs, and he collects some for incidentals like this."

"I will remember," Fox said. He stepped forward, cocking his ear, resuming the trail of green sound.

The trail led on into the dragon's cave. Fox followed, Dori pacing him. When it became too dark to proceed safely, Hilda brought out a swatch of cloth. It illuminated, lighting the way. "I, too, collect incidentals," she said.

The trail led down to an underground pool, and into it. "I don't like this," Fox said. "Anything could be down there. I'd better seek another path."

"We've put too much effort into this one," Squid said. "Fibot can take us down. Fox, can you hear the green from inside the boat?"

"Maybe."

Come in, Fibot! Squid thought. And in four-and-a-half tenths of a long moment the craft was there with them.

They piled in, and resumed the quest from the observation deck as the boat slowly descended below the surface of the dark water. "This is some craft," Fox said admiringly.

"It is," Squid agreed. "We are only borrowing it until we rescue the real boat proprietors."

"From a Demon?" That was obviously impossible.

"So we fear. But we have to try. Otherwise we have lost regardless. Maybe the Demon rules allow it, depending on how we approach it."

"You are nervy children."

"I suppose we are," Squid agreed. "Our core base of siblings are all effective orphans, and we have had to make compromises to get along. Nerve seems to be part of the package."

"I am doing this because it gives me a chance to win Dori. But I think had I known more of you siblings, I would have done it for you."

"Thank you." She was coming to appreciate the man more, now that she understood his magic.

Fox focused. "Yes, I can make out a green sound through the water. May I converse with your helmsman?"

"That's Win. This way." Squid led him back topside, where the screen held back the water.

"Really impressive," Fox said, observing it. Then, to Win: "Ahead and slightly to the left."

"Port-side," she agreed and the craft made a graceful turn.

There was a smaller cave there. "Uh-oh," Fox said. "Too tight for a craft this size."

"You forget that Fibot can handle any dimension," Win said. Sure enough, the boat moved through the tighter cave without difficulty.

"Most impressive," Fox said. "Now bear upward. I hear an air filled cave ahead."

They glided up, and emerged into the air cave.

"It is here," Fox said. "The next window."

The shield faded and they stepped out into the cave. Fox led them to a human skeleton. "This is the chest," he said, indicating the rib cage.

"Piton. Data," Squid said. "Your department, I think."

The two skeleton crossbreeds joined them, along with Myst. "That's not our type of skeleton," Piton said. "The bones are wrong."

"In fact it's a chest in the form of a skeleton," Data said.

"The window is inside it," Fox said.

They tried to get into the chest, but the bones were metallically solid and didn't budge. "Well, Fibot can handle that too," Squid said.

"Except that the window is locked," Fox said. "It is made out of bones, and if you force it, that may destroy it."

"Let me check," Myst said. She dissolved into vapor and suffused the chest, causing Fox, Benny, and Dori to react with surprise again.

After a while minus a couple of moments, Myst floated clear of the chest and reformed as a girl. "It is definitely locked," she reported. "There's a keyhole, but no key."

Squid smiled. She brought out her skeleton key. She inserted it between the bones to find the keyhole, and turned it. There was a snap, and the window opened. But it remained encased by the chest.

They returned to the boat, and Win blew it toward and then into the chest. The craft passed between the bones, and through the open window.

They emerged into a storm. Winds buffeted Fibot, threatening to blow it into a jagged mountain. "The trail is forward," Fox said. "If we can stay on it."

But the storm was too strong. The boat was being pushed away from the trail. The shield went up, but the wind blasted the shield so that the boat could not make headway.

"I think this is a job for Super Child," Win said. "Douse the sail, tie me to the mast and let the shield down."

"That could be dangerous," Santo warned her.

"Are we going to follow the trail, or not?"

Santo shrugged. "Be ready to restore the shield in an instant," he told the peeve. "If she is in trouble."

"Got it," the peeve said, perching on the dogfish who would actually control the shield.

Squid and Larry went topside with Win. Firenze had already folded the sail, leaving only the standing mast. Squid used cord to wrap around Win, binding her to the mast. "I don't like this," Squid murmured. "It looks as though I am tying you so I can—" She stifled the rest of it.

"Squid, don't worry about it," Win said. "I know you wouldn't kill me without good reason. We've been friends and siblings ever since we met."

"I don't want to kill you at all!" Squid cried, and dissolved into tears as she hugged her and the mast.

Win patted her back. "It was only a bad dream anyway."

Squid hoped that was the case. But she had a sick premonition that it wasn't.

When Win was secure and all other hands were below decks, the shield faded. The winds buffeted the boat worse.

Then Win turned on the wind. Originally it had been a mere nuisance, the wind always at her back, blowing her hair forward in her face. But it had been quietly enhanced to near Sorceress level. The wind blew forward, first a breeze, then a gale, then a hurricane. There was no push back, just the powerful blast of air, still increasing.

Until at last it blew away the storm. There was only the air rushing forward, carrying everything before it.

The storm was gone, but the boat wasn't moving, as there was nothing to propel it. Win could not ease up, because then the storm would return. She could not blow the boat itself forward, when the sail was not spread.

"Oarsmen," Santo said.

"But we'll be blown away!" Firenze protested.

"No. Win's wind is narrow at the source, broadening only with distance. You can come up behind her and to the sides, out of the main thrust."

"Got it," Firenze said. He headed topside, along with Piton, Benny, and Fox. Two older boys, two men.

They ducked down, staying clear of the torrent of wind, and took their places on either side of the boat. They lifted their oars, then stroked them. There was no apparent water surface, but the boat nudged forward. It was working. The storm still raged, but they were in a kind of cone cleared by Win's wind, and it could not get at them.

They increased their strokes, rowing harder, and forward progress increased. They were now moving smartly through the alien welkin. "Still ahead," Fox panted.

Until they came to a crease in the sky. They crossed it, and were in another environment. The storm was gone.

In its place was a logjam. Logs of every size were jammed together in a giant tangle.

Win's wind eased and quit. "What now?" she asked.

"The trail goes through it," Fox said.

"My turn," Firenze said. He went to the prow and leaned forward so that his head was in front of the boat. Then he turned on the heat.

"Wow!" Benny said. "That's what I call a real hothead!"

The girls had come topside when the wind abated. "That's his talent," Squid said. "It was once his curse, but now it is under control, thanks to Ula." Indeed, Ula was there with him now, helping to steady him so he wouldn't fall in front of the boat.

Firenze's head got hotter, turning red, then white. "Nudge the boat forward," Ula called back.

Win resumed her place at the helm, and Piton went to haul up the sail. It caught fire, burning brightly in a pentagon outline. The wind caught it, and the boat nudged forward.

Firenze's head touched the closest log. The wood burst into flame.

The head touched the next. That too flared up, dissipating into ashes.

In fact Firenze was burning his way through the logjam, forming a charred tunnel the boat used.

In due course they emerged from the far side.

Only to discover a broad plain under a low ceiling, as though it were a space between too giant plates. It was supporting an army. There were hundreds of grim armed men. A number of them carried torches of the type that looked to be designed to set fire to boats.

"The trail leads dead ahead," Fox said. "Right through that contingent."

"We can't fly over it," Santo said. "We can't go around it. And I doubt we can fight it."

"Something there is that really, really doesn't like a trail," Noe said.

The soldiers spied the boat. A bugle sounded a green note, and they marched forward.

"My turn," Hilda said, busily knitting. Soon she had what looked like a flag, only it was in the shape of a giant panty. "Who is big enough to put this on?"

"That must be me," Dori said. "Panties work best when worn by grown women with mature behinds."

"I'll add some elastic," Hilda said, sewing some more.

The army was almost upon them. Dori almost leaped into the panty, donning it over her skirt, and the elastic tightened it around her middle. Then she went to the mast. "Douse the fire," she told Firenze, who was back with the sail. The fire flickered out. Dori took hold of the dry material. "Now hoist me up."

Firenze worked the cords and the sail rose, carrying Dori with it. She squirmed around to present her backside to the army. Then she bent over, stretching the fabric tight.

The closest men freaked out so hard they fell backwards. They knocked down the next row, which was freaking out similarly. They were like dominoes, freaking and falling in an ever-widening semicircle. Before long the entire army was on the ground, gazing sightlessly up at the upper plate.

So were the men and boys of the boat.

"Now that's what I call a panty flash," Dori said, satisfied. She climbed down. "May I keep this too?" she asked Hilda. "Along with the veil?"

"Keep it," Hilda agreed. "You earned it."

They woke the boys and men of the crew and resumed their forward motion. Beyond the fallen army was the next window.

They sailed through it. There was a pleasant island covered with bushes and trees. In the distance rose the graceful turrets of a castle.

Data stared. "That's Caprice!"

The others in turn stared at her. "You recognize it?" Noe asked. "You're sure it's not another Animalian castle with a similar outline?"

"I'd know it anywhere. Ask Piton."

"It's Caprice Castle," her brother agreed.

"It is solid green," Fox agreed.

They had arrived.

Chapter 16

CHAOS

"Stop right there," Santo said. "We must reorganize before we go any farther."

"Indeed we must," Fox agreed. "As you explained before, it is not safe for an adult to approach that castle."

"It may not be safe for a child, either," Noe said. "We're really just guessing. But Squid, Laurelai, Hilda, and Ion were there before, in their changed genders."

"We really don't know what rules the Demons are following," Squid said. "It's just our best guess that children are immune."

"It does make a certain sense," Dori said. "All they can do now is try it and see."

"So we three adults will depart your group now," Benny said. "And if you escape with the castle, Fox will track you down for a later reunion." He paused. "But that leaves a question, Hilda. Do you wish to go with me now, or the siblings?"

Hilda grimaced. "Bad phrasing. What I wish is one thing. What I must do is another. I wish I could be with you, Benny, but the siblings may need me."

"I understand. When we get together again, then you can decide whether to introduce me to your royal family. I will understand if you decide not to." He smiled a bit wanly. "I am, after all, a pretty ordinary guy, a crossbreed without a known talent."

She ran to him and hugged him. "Oh, Benny, I have decided that! If I live, I will live with you."

"More than that, I can't ask." It was a simple statement, not especially emotional, but Squid felt the surge of emotion within him. He was close to loving her, and not simply because of her royalty or her Sorceress talent or the fact that she was completely human. He had come to know her as a person, and he liked that person. She would become his ideal woman when she matured. The main thing that restrained him now was her youth, though of course time would take care of that. If she elected to stay with him, he would devote his life to serving her interests.

"I'm not adult," Vinia said. "But neither am I a sibling. I don't know where I should be."

"With me," Ion said firmly. "I need you for every step I take."

She looked at Santo, wanting his stance. Ion did have his magic carpet, so could manage without her, physically.

"Stay," Santo said. "He does need you, and you need him. This is the countryside: without him you would soon be choking."

"I would," Vinia agreed gratefully. Squid knew that her love was already absolute.

"Next question," Noe said. "As we approach the castle, do you two skeletons go in first, alone, to see if you can take it out of here?"

"Why should we?" Piton asked. "The presence or absence of the other children shouldn't make any difference, and you don't want to get stranded here if we move it out. We're sure not going to bring it back here for the Demon to grab again if we do get it out."

"Apt thought," Santo agreed. "So, then, we thirteen children will enter the castle, where Piton and Data will see about moving it out. We will not dilly-dally; moving it is our first order of business. Once we save it, we can see about the welfare of the six adults trapped in it. They may be okay the moment the castle is clear and their stasis abates. We hope so. Any other thoughts?"

"What gender, this time?" Larry asked. "Now that we have a choice."

"As we are now," Noe said. "The fact that we can now change genders at will does not mean that we have to. We should be in our most familiar bodies."

"And our adult thoughts," Fox said. "Just that we outsiders admire your talents and your courage, and wish you success."

"And if you succeed, and we rejoin you," Dori said, "We may want to remain close to you and your associated adults as you achieve adulthood yourselves. You are remarkable folk, regardless of your youth, and an amazing group, not merely because of the royal or Magician caliber members. You are something special. Even your animals, to which I also relate." She glanced at Tata Dogfish and the peeve.

"Thank you," Santo said, quirking a smile. "We agree you are some animal, Dori Doe." There was general laughter.

Then the three adults stepped back, and the boat started moving. They waved to each other as they passed out of sight. It was no secret: the children had come to like these adults, and appreciated their assistance on the trail.

They wove between the trees, not advertising their presence, until they came close to the castle. Surprise was the key element.

"I just had a nasty thought," Ula said. "Suppose it is Fibot the Demon is after, to add to Caprice? They are similar devices in some respects."

"We considered that," Squid said. "But if the Demon can't act unless an adult is aboard, it doesn't matter."

"I mean, suppose it's not the presence of an adult that triggers the take-over, but the presence of Fibot?"

They looked at her with dismay. Once again Ula had come up with the unusual perspective. Could she be correct?

"And if we anchor in the castle courtyard," Win said, "We'll be making it easy for them."

The craft stopped moving.

"But if we don't," Myst said, "And we see trouble coming, we'll have to scramble worse to reach the boat, to escape."

"If we can escape, at that point," Piton said.

"Vote," Santo said. "How many say to land in the courtyard?"

The decision was to land in the court, though it was plain that none of them were entirely easy about it.

The craft resumed motion. It sailed up over the castle, then down into the central courtyard, landing softly.

"Do we go in together, or single file, or only some of us?" Squid asked.

"Together," Larry said, taking her hand. "And in couples or clusters. No one alone."

The others agreed, forming exactly such units.

They exited Fibot together, leaving Tata and the peeve in charge. They walked to the nearest entrance to the castle proper as a close group of clusters. There they paused.

"If this goes wrong," Santo said. "I just want to say that it has been an honor to associate with you. All of you."

"Ditto," Firenze said, smiling.

"Ditto," the others echoed.

Then Santo put his hand on the lever and turned it. The door opened.

The castle was silent, as before. They gathered in the front hall. "Piton, Data," Santo said. "Do what you know how to do. Myst will help you. The rest of us will go silently admire the frozen figures Squid, Ion, and Hilda will show us."

Piton and Data disappeared down a hall, Myst following Piton. Squid stepped forward to lead the others to the central chamber where the folk had been in stasis. Were they still there?

And there they were. Six adult figures in a glassy display case. Picka Bone and Princess Dawn, the proprietors and Piton and Data's parents. Dell and Nia, proprietors of the fire boat. And Magnus and Jess, guests. All fine people. All trapped.

Jess, Squid thought. *We have come to rescue you.*

The figure did not move, but the woman's mind came awake. *Oh, Squid, you didn't!* There was anguish in the thought.

We did. All of us. With Fibot.

But I thought you understood. You are in great danger here.

I did understand. You were warning us away. But we had to come anyway.

But why, if you understood?

That was what she could not say: that this was a setup for Fornax to catch the culprit Demon in the act. If that Demon struck. *We just had to try to rescue you and Caprice. We couldn't let you be captive forever.*

Oh, Squid, Jess repeated sadly.

Then the castle moved. They felt it lifting and floating in the air. Piton and Data were doing it!

"We're flying!" Data called. "We've got it on manual so we can move slowly. No fading out and in. Now we're going over water."

Oh, Data! That was a different thought, probably Princess Dawn, horrified about the danger to her daughter.

There was a jolt as the castle abruptly halted.

"Oops!" Piton called. "Something's gone wrong. We're stalled over the sea. Caprice is not responding any more."

The display case dissolved. The six frozen figures came to life. "Bleep!" Dell swore. "The trap has sprung."

The children stood as if freaked out, neither moving nor speaking. Squid realized that the trigger had not been the presence of an adult, or the arrival of Fibot, but the movement of the castle. Or maybe there were several triggers.

But Squid was ready. "Trap?" she asked, though she already knew its nature.

"They figured that when the skeleton kids came, all the children would come, and bring Fibot," Princess Dawn said. "That's the other prize. That's what they were waiting for. Now they've got it."

Squid needed to keep them talking, so she could verify the exact nature of the trap, knowing that Fornax was listening. "Who was waiting?"

"D NA and R NA, Dwarf Demons," Jess said. "They can't operate freely in Xanth proper, so they set their foul snare in the Sometime region nearby and waited for the castle to bring Picka Bone to visit the skeletons. But the boat didn't enter Sometime proper, so they missed it. Now they've got what they sought, by tricking you into coming back. Caprice and Fibot both, together with the folk to operate them as a functioning exhibit. Oh, if only you had stayed away!"

"Who and who?" Squid asked.

"Demon NA and Robot NA," Magnus said. "The Not Announced twins. They're collectors. They set up displays and charge others to come see them. Now they've got a fine set."

"I don't see any Dwarf Demons," Squid said. "Where are they?" She was playing a role, of a kind, getting things out into the open. There was still too much obscurity.

Dell and Nia stepped into the center. "We are here, animating local hosts," Dell boomed in a voice quite unlike his own. "Dwarf Demon Not Announced." He had a presence that radiated outward like a dirty boulder dropped into a polluted pool.

"And Robot Demon Not Announced," Nia said in a voice completely different from her own. "Now line up, brats, so we can label you as supplementary exhibits." Her voice was like overgrown fingernails tearing up ancient mildewed blackboards.

Now was the time. "Oh, go away," Squid said. "We're not your creatures."

Both Demons stared at her as if amazed by her effrontery.

"Who sez?" Dwarf demanded.

Squid stood her ground, or in this case, floor. "I say. I am Squid."

"You and who else?" Robot scratched.

Now Larry strode forth. "She and me," he said. Then he burst out of his male body and expanded into an effulgent queenly display. Only because Squid had long known Fornax and was able to relate to her was she able to see her and understand her thoughts. "Demoness Fornax, popular name for the condition of Anti-Matter." She gestured, and the two lesser Demons cowered back. "In the name of the Demon Xanth, whose property you have stolen, I am arresting you and sentencing you to eternal degradation."

The children, caught in the middle of this strange interchange that only some of them could follow at all, retreated quietly to the edges of the room. Could these really be Demons manifesting in local hosts?

Squid thought to them, so that they would understand some of what was happening. *Capital D Demons are vastly greater than any human form can emulate. We are seeing only the tiniest fraction of their essence, like single motes of dust in a galaxy of hundreds of millions of stars. Their appearance and dialogue are approximate, as I translate them for you. In reality they are not remotely this crude. They are forces of nature, eternal and infinitely powerful. Just as Fornax is Antimatter, Xanth is the force of Magic. They existed long before we gave them names.*

The two minor Demons looked at each other. "It was a counter-trap," Dwarf said ruefully.

"That's why they returned after being warned away," Robot agreed. "They brought a hidden Demoness to catch us."

"But where did she come from? That's a male host."

"Not really," Squid said. "Larry is the male body of a female person. Fornax stayed with the female, Laurelai."

"So the trap is sprung, and we have our culprit," Fornax said, satisfied. "Now you children can take your toys home, the miscreants are dealt with, and the mission is accomplished." She gestured, and the two Dwarf Demons vanished.

But then her body twisted and stretched as if being deformed like taffy, as it became male again. "Not yet," Larry's voice said.

"What?" Fornax asked, wrestling the voice back.

"I am the Demon Chaos," Larry's voice said. "Begone, slattern."

"There is no Demon Chaos," Laurelai's voice protested.

"You think? Then what of this?" A bolt of lightning speared out, curved overhead, and returned to strike the body, which became completely male.

"Calling backup," Fornax's voice said through the smoke as the body fuzzed. The Demons were fighting over the host!

"Here," Magnus said in a new voice. "I am the Demon Nemesis, lord of Dark Matter. Unhand my wife, blackguard."

More lightning speared out, and Larry reappeared. "I don't care who you are. You are in my power."

"What is this?" Nemesis asked as Fornax reappeared in Laurelai. "Does this idiot really think he can stand off two Demons?"

"I am going to abolish you," Chaos said, reappearing. "All of you. I just needed to attract you to my lair."

A new form appeared: that of a donkey headed dragon. "What is going on here?" he demanded.

"I am Chaos. Who are you?"

"I am the Demon Xanth. You have been raiding my demesnes, stealing my magic, and I am putting a stop to it, now that we have caught you red-handed." Indeed, as he spoke, Larry's hands turned red.

More lightning shot out, framing the room. "You have it backwards, ass face. You, all of you, have been raiding *my* demesnes, and now at last, I shall put a stop to it. All I needed was the pretext, at long last, and you have provided me that."

Squid was silent now. This was amazing! It seemed that four full Demons had manifested here, and the new one was treating the established ones with contempt. How could this possibly be?

It continued. More Demons arrived, until there were ten of them. Nine familiar ones, according to the memory Squid was provided, and the stranger who called himself Chaos.

Nemesis assumed the role of spokesman, the other Demons allowing it. "We do not lightly tolerate the arrogance of ignorance. On what basis do you assume the right to assert yourself among us?" This was only approximately the import of his communication, but Squid was obliged to interpret it in her minuscule-mortal terms, and to continue sending a mental translation out to the other children so that they could grasp it too. They were like atoms observing a battle among dragons.

"I am the original Demon," Chaos ranted. "The rest of you have been impinging on my territory, carving out your pirate demesnes, all of them stolen from mine. For millennia I have suffered your insults, but now I can abolish all of you in one fell swoop and return reality to its pristine original state. You fell into my counter–counter trap, and have committed yourselves to the fray. All of you are doomed."

"You didn't exist," Nemesis said. "Now, you appear and think to have things your way? Unlikely."

"I existed long before you did, Dark Matter," Chaos said. "Now I will show my strength. Observe."

The room dissipated, along with the castle surrounding it. There was not open sky, but open space. They were looking out at the universe, the myriad galaxies spinning around their axes. Squid realized that she was seeing an accelerated picture, so that motions that took millions of years to happen in regular life seemed to be happening immediately. "This is the abomination I will destroy."

"Not while I exist," the Demon Earth said. "I am Gravity. I hold things together, at every scale."

"Then hold that together," Chaos said. He pointed at a distant minor galaxy. It suddenly exploded, its strings of stars unwinding. "See? No gravity."

Earth focused, and the galaxy rewound itself.

"And that one." Chaos indicated another, on the other side of the universe. It, too, flew apart.

Earth focused again, and it came back together.

"And those." Three more galaxies tore themselves apart.

Earth concentrated, and they held together. "I can stop you," Earth said. "Gravity is my bailiwick. No outsider can overrule me in my own domain."

"But you must stay focused, or you will lose it all," Chaos said.

"I can stay focused as long as you can. We're both Demons."

"That is only one aspect," Demon Jupiter said. "Regardless whether galaxies hold together, matter still does, because of my Strong Force. It holds the fundamental atoms together."

"Yes, that," Chaos said. "Observe." He looked at another galaxy. A portion of it dissipated into fine mist. "No strong force. No solid matter."

Now Jupiter focused, and the galaxy mended.

"And those." Six more galaxies started to dissolve.

Jupiter concentrated, and their decomposition ceased.

But Squid saw that Earth was still focusing to maintain his gravity. Chaos was opposing two other Demons in their domains simultaneously. That would be unimaginable, were it not actually happening.

This continued, until all the other nine Demons were concentrating to hold on to their domains. Chaos could not destroy them, but neither could the other Demons retain them without continuously concentrating. It was like holding down a table full of papers in a stiff wind: it could be done, but it absorbed a person's whole attention.

The Demons were at an impasse. Chaos could not destroy the works of the others, but neither could they stop him from attacking. He was as strong as all the others combined. It was pointless to continue striving when there could be no decision.

"Compromise," the Demon Xanth suggested. "A Demon Wager in the standard format, designed to be absolutely fair, decided by the random chance of the actions of an ignorant mortal. All parties to abide by the decision, whatever it may be. The issue is the fate of the universe: whether it continue as it is, or be abolished."

"Agreed," Chaos said. Squid was surprised, but then saw that it made sense. This gave him a fifty fifty chance to prevail, with much less effort. It was better than a perpetual impasse.

"Make it three trials," the Demon Neptune suggested. "Of different natures."

"Agreed." Clearly Chaos wanted to get the matter settled.

"Two out of three wins the issue."

"Agreed," Chaos said. "Select a suitable mortal and venue."

"I propose Squid, here in Caprice Castle," Fornax said. "She has perspective beyond the ordinary, because of her nature. She understands different sides."

Squid's body seemed to turn to ice. *No!*

"Agreed."

But of course she didn't have a choice. She had known it from the start of this story, when she had been selected to be the protagonist. The fate of the universe depended on her, regardless of her wishes. "I am mortal, but I'm not ignorant," she argued desperately. "I have seen the wager being set up. I know the stakes."

They ignored her. "And give her a weapon," the Demon Mars said. His was the Electromagnetic Force. "One that will not betray her and will always be ready at hand, so she can defend herself from surprise attack."

"Agreed. But her opposition must have a similar weapon, to keep it fair."

A wall filled with mounted knives appeared before Squid: big ones, small ones, swords, daggers, dirks.

"I don't want a knife!" Squid protested.

The knives were replaced by clubs of every size and description, all neatly mounted for the display.

"Or a club!"

The clubs faded, to be replaced by Mundane pistols, rifles, shotguns, machine guns, and specialty firearms.

"Or guns!"

The wall went blank. "What, then," Mars asked. "You must choose a weapon."

Squid thought fast. "The question," she said, "with insight to make it the right one for the occasion. And it's fine if my opponent has a similar weapon. And when asked, it has to be honestly answered."

"The Word as a Weapon. Good choice. Done."

Then the scene dissolved, and Squid found herself alone in the castle. No Demons, no captive adults, no children. Just the bare halls.

How was this a contest? She didn't even know how to make the castle move. So maybe she was ignorant after all, in a way that counted.

She walked through it, finding nothing but eerie emptiness. What was she supposed to do or understand or accept or oppose? She had no idea. Was it that there was something she had to find, and if she failed, she'd lose? At least she could look.

She could not sense them, but knew that the Demons and the mortals were watching. None of them could affect her decision or indecision in any current way, by the rules of the Wager, but their fates and her own depended on it, whatever it was. So of course they were paying attention.

She found nothing on the ground floor or the cellar. All was quiet and barren. So she mounted the steps to the upper floors, checking every chamber. Nothing. She didn't know what she had expected, if she had expected anything at all, but it certainly wasn't this.

Nothing was left except a circular stairway to the highest chamber, so she climbed that. Finally, she came to the topmost turret and gazed out the stone loophole that passed for a window. The castle hovered above the sea. It was a long way down. This was a kind of embrasure, with crenels or gaps in the battlement. She could easily jump through a crenel and plunge down into the water and swim away, but that would mean abandoning the Wager and forfeiting the issue. She could not do that.

So what was left? She had searched the castle, and if there was anything to find, she had failed to find it. Had she already lost the first trial? Well, she would just have to look again.

Then she got a notion. Why not use her awareness of people? Others had to be thinking about her.

She tried to tune in, but there was mental silence. Her ability to tune in on other minds was blocked, probably because she had to figure this out on her own. Except for one faint signal. Someone was, maybe bound and gagged, trying to call to her, but stifled. Where?

She oriented on it and got a direction. It was actually close by, in a stone storage cell down the stairway just below the turret. The mind was struggling with horror, perhaps at being confined. Now there was also a weak murmur, as of a stifled sob. Someone was trapped. This had to be what she was supposed to find.

Squid saw a closed stone door, the kind that could be opened from the outside but not the inside. She took hold if it and pulled. Slowly it opened. Inside was—

"Win!" she cried gladly, seeing her friend standing there.

The girl shook her head. "Not exactly. You should have left that door alone."

There was something off about her voice. And her mind.

Then Squid recognized the horror of it. "The Sea Hag!"

"I am not happy to make your acquaintance," the Hag said.

"But you were banished to the Void, where nothing escapes!"

"I was freed by a Demon, and given this fine young body. All I have to do to keep it is eliminate you."

Now Squid understood her vision. It was not her friend Win she had to fight, but the horror that had taken over her body. Win was still in there, of course, but cruelly suppressed by the evil spirit that now governed her body. That was the stifled sob she had picked up on: Win. The Hag seldom, if ever, let go of a body before it was old, crippled, or dead. Win was doomed. It would actually be a kindness to kill her.

Kill me, Win begged. *I can't stand this horror.*

Squid appreciated her position. The Hag would make her body do appalling things. After Noe had been possessed by the Hag a year ago, she had wanted to commit suicide because of the foulness of the memory, even after the Hag departed. But could that be all? Was killing the body of her friend the test of her mettle, the sacrifice necessary to preserve the universe? That could not be right.

"No. I'm not going to fight my friend."

"As if you have a choice, my precious. *I* will kill *you.*" And the Hag leaped at her, fingers extended in claws.

Squid softened her limbs where the fingers clutched, so that they slid off. She turned to the side, so that the Hag lunged on past her and came up against the opposite wall. She clung there half a moment, reorienting.

"What else did the Demon promise you?" Squid asked, remembering her weapon of the Question. This might be relevant. "A nice young body isn't enough, if the universe ends."

"I will be Queen of Xanth," the Hag answered, as she had to.

"You can't be Queen, either, if the universe ends."

"He will save just enough of Xanth for me to govern. This nice body and my little kingdom. That's enough."

"But—"

"Enough of this stalling!" the Hag screeched. "I'm going to blow you away!" and a blast of air came from her, pushing Squid against the wall. She couldn't approach the woman, couldn't get hold of her.

That was right; the Sea Hag could use the host's talent. She could blow with hurricane force if she chose. She could literally blow Squid out of the castle, or blow her into a wall so hard it killed her.

This was dangerous. Squid needed time to figure things out.

Squid fled back up the steps, but the Hag pursued her, preceded by her wind. Could Squid somehow get behind her, where there was no wind? That might be her most likely chance.

She reached the parapet. Now the crenels of the battlement seemed unconscionably wide. It would be all too easy to get blown through there!

"Got you cornered, you alien creature," the Hag said. "If you have any last words, stifle them. I've got a kingdom to win." She revved up her wind, ready to blow Squid away.

Squid ran to the side, trying to circle her, to get behind. But the Hag kept facing her, aware of that danger. The Hag had hundreds of centuries experience dealing with enemies, because everyone was her enemy, for good reason. No chance there.

Now was the time, her only chance. "Why do you think the Demon will honor his word to you, and give you a kingdom?"

And the Hag had to answer honestly; it was part of the weapon of the Question. "Because it is fair payment for my service to him in eliminating you. It is easy enough for him to do. A mere detail. He's a Demon."

"But suppose he is lying about that detail?"

"Why would he?"

And the key question. "Would *you* lie in such a situation, to get your way conveniently with no continuing obligation?"

The Hag paused. Of course she would lie, and she judged others by herself. So by her own definition, the Demon's promise was meaningless. In her distraction, the wind died down.

Squid flung herself across the space between them and wrapped her arms around the body. Then, before the Hag could react, she heaved her to the battlement and leaped through the crenel, carrying them both into the air.

"What are you doing?" the Hag screeched. "Killing us both?" It had never occurred to her that Squid would *want* to jump off the parapet.

"Maybe," Squid said as they fell.

Then they hit the water and plunged below. Squid maintained her hold on the other, so that they both went deep.

The Hag was from the sea, but she was in a host that could not breathe water. Squid, being a cuttlefish, could. So while the Hag struggled vainly for air, Squid breathed the water through her gills. She could handily outlast the other body, waiting for it to drown. She was killing her friend. Even if Squid let go of her now, there would not be time for the body to reach the surface and breathe before it drowned.

At last, seeing the hopelessness of it, knowing that she had lost the fight, the Hag elected at least to save her spirit. She left the body and drifted away through the water. She would be returned to the Void, a loser. Squid had won.

Except that in the process she was also killing her friend.

But she didn't have to. Had the Hag done her homework she would have learned that Squid could breathe both air and water simultaneously. Now she breathed the water in with her gills, put her mouth to Win's mouth, and breathed air out, giving her mouth-to-mouth respiration. And swam for the surface, taking them both there.

Their heads finally popped above the water. "Thanks!" Win gasped. "For both! You got rid of the Hag, and you saved my life."

"We're siblings," Squid said, "and friends. How could I do less?"

Then they swam for the castle. Squid knew she had won the first challenge. The key had not been to kill her friend, but to get rid of the Hag.

When they got there and climbed onto the pavement in front of the entrance, Win kissed her, stepped back, and became Santo.

Santo? How did he relate? The next challenge was upon her with no respite between them. Had Win been real, or a simulation? Did it matter?

"Why are you here?" she asked him.

"Your challenge: I know what it is," Santo said as they entered the castle. "You have been given the power to change me."

"Change you?"

"To hetero."

"Why would I do that?"

"To save the universe."

Oh, no! But as she searched within herself, she knew that it was true; she had been given special magic for this purpose. The question was not whether she *could* do it, but whether she *should*.

"Santo, you have a better mind than I do. Let's discuss this rationally."

He smiled. "Let's."

"Santo, I don't want to change you. I love you the way you are. Your orientation is a fundamental part of you. You would not be the same person with it changed."

"Precisely. I don't want to change either. But the choice is not mine. It's yours."

Squid focused on it. "If your changing meant saving the universe, would you do it?"

"Of course."

"Would you *want* to do it then?"

"No. But the sacrifice of one person is a very small thing compared to the universe. For one thing, all my friends are part of it, and I would not want to sacrifice them." He laughed. "In fact it would not be much fun without them."

"So I have to do something to you that neither of us wants, to save the universe?"

"So it would seem."

"How would Noe feel about it?"

"As it happens, I have asked her, since with the mini portals we can now change genders. This is not at all the same, yet there is a parallel. She answered that she loves me as I am."

"Did you ask her whether she would rather leave you alone and let the universe go, or change you and have you as a hetero?"

He smiled again. "I did not think to ask her that. Our dialogue was before the Demon Chaos appeared."

"But you must have a notion how she would have answered."

"Yes. She would prefer me as hetero. But she would regret the necessity."

"You love her?"

"Yes, as a friend. And when she uses the mini portal, as a lover, for all that we have not done that at our age. But the question is not what we have done or would do at present, but what we would prefer for the future."

"You are marvelously rational."

"Thank you."

Then a notion came to her. "Santo, I believe I have the answer. My trial here is to determine how to save the universe, when I don't know what is right or wrong in this specific case. I want to save the universe *as it is*, not as the Sea Hag or someone else might want it. If I changed you, that would be in a small way a different universe. So I believe the correct decision is not to change you."

"If you feel that is right, that is your prerogative."

"Oh, Santo, I don't know what is right. I am deeply unsure. But it is what makes most sense to me."

Then she faced away from him. "My decision is not to change him."

There was a quiver in the environment. The decision had been made.

"Oh, my," Santo said. "I am told that is wrong."

"Wrong?"

"I am informed that life itself is a process of change, so that to maintain the universe as it is we must embrace change. This is the answer the Demons agreed on."

"Well, I disagree."

He quirked a smile. "So do I. However, it was your prerogative to make the decision. It is theirs to judge whether that decision is correct. You have done so, and they have done so."

"I think the Demons are Ethics-challenged. In fact, Wrong."

"But their Will governs," he said sadly.

Squid was chagrined. "So I stand at one to one, by their reckoning. I had better be right on the third challenge."

"By their definition."

"By *my* definition. Right is right, regardless who differs."

Santo spread his hands. "At any rate, I thank you for leaving me alone, though the universe pay the price."

Then he faded, and in his place stood Larry.

"And you were the worst one, in my vision," Squid said. "I had to decide whether to kill my friend, or change my friend. What do I have to do with you, my boyfriend?"

"I am not your friend," Larry said in the voice of Chaos. "Neither am I Laurelai, whom Demoness Fornax animates. I am animating this form of this host in order to have an even dialogue with you."

The Demon actually wanted to talk with her? The amazement continued to pile on. "And what do I have to do to you?"

"You have to convince me to spare the universe."

Squid stared at him. "But that's the object of the three trials! I have to win the third one in order to tilt the victory to the other Demons so you won't destroy the universe."

"You can win it by convincing me. That is the challenge."

"Convincing you to let the other Demons win?" she asked incredulously.

"Yes."

"How could I ever hope to do that? Apart from the fact that you are on your own side, by definition, you have all the resources of the universe you wish to destroy to draw from, while I have only my tiny juvenile alien cuttlefish brain. It's inherently unfair."

"It is fair, because for this purpose I am limited to the intellectual, informational, and emotional resources that you yourself possess. We are evenly matched, by the decree of the Demons you support."

She gazed at him, confused. "I'm not certain I believe this."

He smiled. "Then default and let me win. That is your prerogative."

"The hell!" Then she paused. "I used a bad word. How can that be, when the Adult Conspiracy limits children to good words or euphemisms?"

"The Adult Conspiracy is suspended for this engagement as an artifact hostile to serious reasoning. You are limited to your own resources, not that outside restriction."

"That I *really* have trouble believing! You mean that I could violate the Conspiracy with impunity?"

He smiled again. She rather liked that smile, despite knowing he was the ultimate enemy. "In the interest of saving your universe, you could do so, yes. But you are not obliged to violate it; that is merely an option you now possess."

"Except that I have done so already, by swearing."

"Indeed. That is hardly the beginning of what you could do, if you chose."

Squid was foolishly intrigued. All her young life she had chafed at the Adult Conspiracy, and wanted to abolish it. Did she really have the chance? Maybe she should discover its secrets right now, since if the universe ended, it would be too late.

And there was something about Chaos. Maybe it was the host he was using, her boyfriend, about whom she had become remarkably serious. "Show me."

"Show you what? My side of our debate?"

"No, not yet. Show me the other side of the Adult Conspiracy. What I have been forbidden to know."

He considered. "I said that my horizons were limited to yours, for this engagement, but I realize now that that is not strictly true. I do know what the Conspiracy hides, having observed all life forms as long as they have existed. But I am uncertain how this relates to our discussion."

"I don't know either," she confessed candidly. "But if I'm going to vanish along with the universe after this, I just want to know what I have been wondering about all my life. I want the answer to the big secret. It's simply stupid curiosity."

He nodded. "Simple, perhaps. But sensible, given your position. I will show you. Take my hand."

"Your hand? Can I touch you without losing my argument?"

"Squid, this is a Demon contest. It is inherently fair. I will not betray you in any manner. Only when our dialogue is done will I render my decision. You direct that dialogue. I am obliged to answer your questions honestly, whatever they may be. Your current question is about the nature of the Adult Conspiracy. I will answer to your satisfaction. To do otherwise would be to default, and lose my case."

She gazed at him. "It is getting hard to believe that you really are a Demon. You seem like a nice guy."

He laughed. "I am trying to be nice. It is a struggle, because I have always been hostile to all the given forms of the universe, life included. But I can't answer your questions honestly unless I relate honestly."

She took his hand. "Show me," she repeated.

"First I must age you and this host. Fortunately it is a power this host already has."

"Yes, we have aged three or five years. I have become fourteen, or even sixteen. I had odd urges then, that I don't understand now."

"How old do you wish to become?"

"Older than I was. Make it ten more years. To age twenty one, for me."

"And twenty two for this host," he agreed.

Power animated his hand, and Squid felt herself rapidly aging. Then she was there, her body fully developed and rather pretty. Larry was handsome too. "What next?" she asked, getting excited.

"We kiss."

"What has a kiss to do with it?" Actually she had a strong suspicion, but wanted a clear answer.

"It stirs the feelings."

"Oh." She stepped into him and raised her lips for a kiss. He met them with his own. Suddenly she felt a surge of love. So she kissed him again. And again.

Then they were lying on a soft green bank, and their kisses were building into something else. Their bodies were heating as they pressed tightly against each other. They were about to signal the stork!

That made her pause. She wanted to know the secret, but not to have the stork bring her a baby. She froze.

"Is something wrong?"

"Yes," she said with real regret. "I think I don't want to do this after all."

"Then you don't have to."

"Thank you for understanding." She kissed him again, then separated. Their ages reverted. "I think I have not answered your question."

"I think I changed my mind. I will wait to grow up for real before I do anything as significant as bringing a baby here."

"I don't properly understand, but you impress me nonetheless. You just made a difficult decision."

"That's life." She wasn't sure she had done the right thing, considering that she had no certainty of existing beyond his dialogue. "I guess I have to do what I feel is right, regardless." But what was really getting to her was how much she had liked the kissing, and had wanted to take it further. It wasn't just that he looked like Larry; she knew he was the enemy Demon; but still couldn't help liking him. Did that make any sense at all?

"That's odd," he said.

"Are you reading my thoughts?" she demanded.

"My parameters are limited to yours. You are to an extent the template for our connection. You relate to the minds of others. It seems that I do, too. So I know that you liked kissing me, even though you are aware that I am your opponent."

What use to deny it? "True," she said tightly. "I agree it's odd."

"What is similarly odd to me is that I liked it too."

Now she looked hard at him. "Are you teasing me?"

"Teasing? That is a new concept for me. I was not trying to do it, but would have liked to, now that I understand it as a form of flirtation."

"Flirtation!"

"I am learning that there is bad teasing when mean folk do it, but also good teasing when friends do it. I would like to be your friend."

"You're my enemy! You want to destroy me and the universe."

He pondered briefly. "The universe, yes. You, no. I would rather kiss you."

"But if you destroy the universe, I go with it."

"Unless I make an exception for you alone."

"As you did for the Sea Hag?"

"Yes. But in the end she thought I would betray her."

"And would you have?"

"Yes, because that was her standard."

"And what of my standard?"

"You are honest, and keep your bargains. With you I must be honest, and keep mine."

"I accept no such bargain. I will not betray my friends. I choose to survive only if the universe as I know it survives."

"Yes," he agreed sadly. "I have to respect that, as I am coming to respect you."

That got to her in a weird way. "Let's flirt," she said, and kissed him.

"Oh, Squid, I wish—"

"I know. It's impossible. I guess I was only teasing."

"It is effective. May I tease you back?"

"Anything you want." Because his mind indicated that he really did want to be with her. "Flirting is part of the game of Love, even if it is only window-shopping instead of the real thing."

"Thank you." He kissed her. She kissed him. He kissed her again.

She had to call a halt before she lost control of her rushing feelings. This was the other side! She drew away. "I can't do this. It is the verge of betrayal of my mission."

"Were we to meet in other circumstances, would you be interested?"

What could she say? Yes, he was the enemy. Yet along with his incalculable power, and arrogance when dealing with other Demons, there was a quality in him that appealed to her. Maybe it was that he, too, was an alien assuming human form. That he, too, found the passions of the human condition to be curious yet intriguing. Or that his interest in her was new and unfeigned. He had observed the whole of life, yet never participated in it. Now he wanted to, because *doing* was not at all the same as observing. He was in that sense a novice much like herself. Honesty compelled her, apart from the requirement that she answer candidly. "Yes."

"May I make a request?"

She was startled. "*You* are asking *me* for permission to talk?"

"By the strictures of this Wager, you direct the interview. Your will governs. Were I to attempt to violate any part of it, no matter how minor, I would forfeit my case."

"You Demons don't fool around, do you!"

"We do not."

She laughed, more in confusion than in humor. "You may make your request."

"I ask you to teach me Love."

"Teach you—" she started. "But haven't you already seen every act of love that anyone anywhere in the universe has ever performed?"

"Yes. But I have not experienced it directly. There may be a difference."

"There certainly may be! Emotion is apart from observation. I guess it's an emergent phenomenon."

"Agreed."

"You actually want an eleven-year-old child to try to teach you about something the Adult Conspiracy has determinedly hidden from her?"

"The Conspiracy does not exist in our dialogue," he reminded her.

"Yes, but it has kept me ignorant about the details."

"Has it prevented you from experiencing the emotion, apart from those details?"

Squid considered, remembering her encounters with Larry. If she didn't love him, she was close to it. If only he weren't in truth a girl!

"No, not really. The feeling is there."

"Then I ask you, please, to share this feeling with me, so that I may come to understand it. You are free to decline without prejudice to your case."

What the hell! He was asking her to do something she discovered she desperately wanted to do. It was crazy, because Chaos was the enemy, intent on destroying the universe and reducing it into sheer nothingness. She had no business giving him anything at all, least of all love. Yet at the same time he really turned her on. Larry was a decent boy, considerate of her concerns, honoring the boundaries. There was no sharp edge to him, no danger. Chaos, in contrast, was all edge, lethally dangerous. He was the ultimate Bad Boy, nothing but horrendous mischief. Why was she so infernally attracted to him? It made no sense at all. But suddenly she really wanted to make it with him in whatever way she could.

"One stricture," she said breathlessly. "Those details you know about, that I don't? Don't let me do them, physically. Keep it on the emotional plane. So that I remain a child, technically."

"Agreed."

"You can read my mind, right? Feel my emotions? They may not be your own emotions, but you can feel mine. Vicarious experience. That's how I can show you love, to the extent I am capable of it."

"Agreed."

"The flirtation is over. Now we are getting to the real thing." She put her arms about him, her lips to his, and let herself go.

Suddenly she was cruising into deep space, plastered against him, her lips hungrily pressing into his. Her emotion of love expanded until it burst out of her heart, coursed through her body, and overflowed into his. They floated up off the floor into the sky, radiating beams of heat that not only transformed the air around them, but melted their bodies together until they were one. Sheer joy transformed them as they shone like a star gone nova, illuminating the galaxy in their vicinity.

Then they sank slowly back to the mortal realm, the brightness fading but their love still strong. They became two bodies again, quietly warming each other as they relaxed. She knew he had honored his promise to keep it strictly emotional. But what a wild emotional trip it had been! Marvelously forbidden love.

"Something like that," Squid said. "Only with the details included."

"Now I understand. I wish we could include the details."

She laughed. "Ask me again in five or six years when I'm of age."

"I will."

"Not if the universe is gone. But stay tuned."

He did not pursue the matter further. "What's next?" he asked.

Suddenly she got an idea. The bulb flashed over her head so brightly it illuminated the castle walls that had returned. "I question you."

"What a flash! I will answer."

"What is the earliest thing you remember?"

"Dimension. The one you call Demon Saturn. He brought dimension into existence, so that the universe had space and time instead of being a formless void. I hated him from that moment."

"Nothing before that?"

"Nothing mattered before that. The universe was in total entropy, its ideal state. It was pristine."

"Nothing?"

"Complete randomness. No organization at all. Until the Demons came to mess it up with their foul organization. Mass. Energy. The Strong Force. The Weak Force. Gravity. What horror!"

"And eventually Life."

"Worst of all. An infection."

She did not pursue it further. She had her answer, maybe. It was time to apply her insight.

"Now, I will make you a picture," she said. "I need thin black cardboard, a ruler, a piece of chalk, and a pair of scissors."

"Here." Suddenly there was a sheet of it before her, with the ruler, scissors, and chalk.

"Thank you." She got busy with her simple tools. First she drew a triangle on the cardboard, using the ruler for a straight edge and the chalk to mark the outlines. It was not perfect, but did not need to be. Then she cut the triangle out. She used it as a model to trace four other triangles, and cut them out too. Now she had a pile of five.

"I am wondering what you are doing," Chaos said. "I sense great purpose in it, but frankly, I'd rather be flirting. You showed me a kind of feeling I have not experienced before."

"Flirting? So would I." She loved being able to be so candid. "But I have a job to do." She set the triangles down on the floor, arranging them so that their outer edges touched, forming a rough circle, and their inner points projected toward the center. The result was a light central space in the form of a five pointed star. "Do you see that star?" she asked.

"Yes."

"Now suppose we remove a triangle." She did so, leaving a sadly distorted central shape. "And another." She took away an opposite triangle. Now the star had pretty much disappeared. "And the others." She picked them up. "What picture is left?"

"No picture. You have removed its outline."

"But all I did was subtract the black background. Why isn't the star still there?"

Chaos shrugged. "It was never there. It was an artifact of illusion, defined by the absence of cardboard."

"Yes. Now do you remember how you answered my question about your first memory?"

"It was of the Demon of Dimension interfering with perfection."

"And before that there was really nothing."

"Nothing but pure chaos, yes."

"So you really came into existence as a conscious entity only when the other Demons appeared on the scene."

"My consciousness was not necessary before that occasion."

She took a breath. "I have a theory that may interest you."

"What you have to say does interest me."

"It is that your very existence, as you know it now, came into being at the point that Saturn, the Demon of Dimension, did. Because that's when you needed awareness, to defend your demesne."

"I suppose that is true. Does it matter?"

"It may. Consider my picture of the star on the floor. It exists only because of the surrounding triangles. Without them, it's gone."

"Agreed. It is another emergent phenomenon."

"Without the other Demons and their demesnes, you have no existence. You are defined by them. You are the absence of them."

"Oh, I am there, just not conveniently defined."

"As the star is there on the bare floor. No one knows or cares about it, unless the triangles define it. Without the triangles it might as well not exist."

"That's true."

"Without the other Demons to define you by their absence from the floor of the universe, you might as well not exist. You need them and the universe to define yourself. Without them, you and I could not be having this dialogue."

Chaos nodded. "We could not," he agreed. "I will be sorry to lose your presence."

"And I will be sorry to lose yours, though if I don't exist it won't matter much to me."

"The Demons are like triangles," he said thoughtfully. "I am like the space between them."

Squid tried to fight back a tear, but it flowed anyway. "Oh, Chaos, I don't want to lose that space! I think I love you!"

He gazed at her. Then the scene faded.

"Squid!" Win cried, hugging her. "You did it!" Then, to the others: "She's awake, after three days."

For half a moment, she was confused. "Did what?"

"You convinced the Demon Chaos to let the universe exist! Don't you remember?"

"I was just talking with him. Nothing was decided."

"Yes it was," Nia said, taking her turn to hug. "Three days ago you satisfied him that he preferred the presence of the universe to its absence, and I think it was at least in part because he liked you."

"Well, I liked him. But what has that got to do with the price of beans?"

They all laughed, which was when Squid realized that they all were there, the children and the adults and the castle. And the universe.

"You never did really appreciate your importance," Laurelai said, looking radiant. "You didn't give up when you lost the second round. You saved the universe, and us with it. What a scene when you flirted up that storm!"

So they had indeed been watching. Well, so be it. Chaos had asked her to teach him love, and she had tried. It wasn't real, any more than the Simulation they had all done with the Villagers. She really didn't regret it.

"Let's take a walk," Laurelai said.

"A walk?"

"As far as our cabin will do. Someone wants to talk with you."

What now? "Who?"

"You'll see."

Squid realized that she had not been sleeping in her cabin, but in the infirmary. She had truly been unconscious. She went with Laurelai to their room, perplexed.

"We've all been working it out," Laurelai said. "We want you to know that this is fine with us and with Fornax. We're all in it together."

What was fine? But surely they were about to tell her.

"He gets Larry by day," Laurelai continued. "Dawn to dusk. I take over by night. You can change gender then if you want to. We can be girls together, or boy and girl, maybe increasingly as the years pass and we mature."

"Uh, okay," Squid said, hardly following the relevance.

"And we've made a deal with the skeletons, Piton and Data's relatives, to have a regular square on Skeleton Key where Caprice Castle and Fibot can have a home port. Things got complicated with Skeleton Key, and now they'll be simplified. The castle and boat will each have a built in pass so they can leave and return to the Key at any time. In return we'll take the skeletons anywhere they want to go, when they want to visit Xanth Proper. Piton and Data can stay with the siblings and still have skeleton friends. It seems ideal."

"Okay," Squid agreed. It was amazing what the others had worked out while Squid was tuned out.

"We're forming the Skeleton Key Dance Ensemble. Thirteen children and three peripheral adults. Enough to form two Squares, to start with. It's really a planned community, accessible only by invitation, but we'll tour Xanth and meet many others as we do our demonstration dances."

"Okay," Squid said again, beginning to get a picture of the whole. It looked like a very nice future.

Then Laurelai transformed into Larry. "Now for the piece of resistance," she said, deliberately mispronouncing it as she faded out.

Squid smiled as she looked at Larry. "You'll never believe who you remind me of."

"I believe," he said, his voice carrying evocative timbre.

"Chaos!" Squid cried gladly. "I thought you'd gone."

"Not far from you," he said. "Without you I am just a space. With you I am learning love. I can hardly wait until we both mature."

"We have some serious flirting to do," she said, hardly caring about the rest of his nature.

Then they were kissing, and she knew this was just the beginning.

AUTHOR'S NOTE

This is the 44th Xanth novel, and it could be the last. Not because I'm tired of it; but because I am old, 83 at this writing, and my life is getting complicated. Let me explain. I eat right and exercise, staying reasonably fit, but my wife of 61 years, Carol, is fading, and in the past decade I have taken over making the meals, washing the dishes, and spot chores where standing is required, as she can't stay long on her feet. I go shopping with her, and we take along the wheelchair so that it can be used at need, as increasingly it is. For decades, she ran the household, but advancing age required compromises, and now it is my turn.

So my writing schedule works around the needs of our family. I don't expect to write as much in a typical day as I did when we were younger. I don't actually have to write at all to maintain our lifestyle, as we are financially comfortable. I write because it is my reason for being, but I no longer have to make deadlines. I also read the books that interest me, and buy and watch the DVD and Blu-Ray videos that are on sale and intrigue me. For example I saw the entire Star Trek series, the original and the followups, on sale at a bargain price, so bought them. But then came the question: when would I watch them? Trying to assimilate hundreds of hours in one long binge would be wearing and unfair to the material. My wife suggested an answer: watch one episode a day while I wrote my novel. When I'm in a novel I tend to get absorbed in it and everything else suffers: I'm a workaholic, or more properly a write-a-holic. I have to schedule other things to be sure I get to them at all, when I'm writing. You know, like eating and sleeping and answering fan mail. So this might enable me to watch the episodes in a paced manner without sacrificing my novel. Would it work? This was the test.

I started writing this Jamboree 2, 2018. (I use the Ogre Months, which are more expressive than the Mundane ones.) I played half an hour of Mahjongg tiles, watched one episode of Star Trek, then wrote the novel. It went well, and by the end of the month I had written over half the novel, 52,600 words. Then in FeBlueberry, I got the flu, with a fever of 101 degrees Fahrenheit, and lost any writing initiative. When I lose interest in writing, you know I'm sick, because writing is my life. I resumed in a few days, but then Carol got the flu.

It put her in the hospital for nine days. Sometimes when I visited she never woke up: the drugs they had her on kept her knocked out. Once she phoned me: they had moved her from the Inverness, Florida hospital to Tampa. What? It turned out that it was a confusion: she was still at the local one. But you can see this was not an easy time, and when she returned home she was on oxygen and had to use a walker and have physical therapy. She could no longer mount the stairs to our bedroom, so I unfolded the sofa/bed in the living room and joined her there each night. Fortunately our daughter Cheryl was there to help us, or we would not have been able to cope. She is now taking over some of the things like shopping and laundry.

Then during one of my exercise runs—we live on our little tree farm, and our drive is three quarters of a mile long, so I alternate days running out for the newspapers or using the adult trike—I tried to kick a fallen pine cone clear, missed it, stubbed my foot into the drive, and fell, landing on my face, getting scrapes, a black eye, and bruised ribs that wiped out my exercises for about three weeks, and made coughing, sleeping, and sometimes just standing up painful.

We put a picture on my HiPiers.com web site, and fans agreed that I looked awful. I think they were referring to my blood-masked face on that day, rather than my normal appearance. At my age a fall is no minor matter. So my writing schedule suffered further, and I wrote only half as much in that month. I finally finished the novel in Marsh. I was also in the third season of *Star Trek The Next Generation*, and enjoying it, an episode a day. So my experiment was working despite other problems.

Then there was the Xanth movie option. They were considering doing both a movie and a TV series, and it hung like fire for almost three years as the option got extended, and extended again. But alas, at the end, the studio had a new boss, and the new one axed the project of the old one, like a new alpha male killing the offspring of the old alpha male, saying Xanth was sexist. Xanth mirrors and parodies the attitudes of Mundania, so there is sexism there, but hardly approval of it. Folk see what they choose to see. Some say that because in *A Spell for Chameleon,* she varies with the time of the month, that's sexist. Ugliness, like beauty, is largely in the eye of the beholder. Now I am left with three novels to market, as I held up #42 *Fire Sail* and #43 *Jest Right* pending the verdict on the movie option, because a movie could make a phenomenal difference to their salability.

And my dentures. My original teeth have been mostly trouble throughout my life; I remember when my wisdom teeth came in, they arrived complete with cavities. It's not a matter of hygiene: I take care of my teeth. But cavities came in from below, with no connection to the surface; can't brush that away. So now it was the time for my lower denture, as I got the upper one a year or so back. A months-long hassle, and I lost weight because I couldn't properly chew. As I type this, I still have pain chewing, but things are slowly improving. Teeth, like old age, are a lady dog.

And I am breaking in a new computer, and this is my first novel on it. The problem is that it doesn't have my variant of the Dvorak keyboard, so my touch typing reflexes make myriad errors, such as ; for ', so the word "doesn't" comes out "doesn;t." Yes, a geek checked it; it's a Known Problem that they may or may not eventually get around to fixing. My annoyance doesn't count; I'm only a user.

So my life as I wrote this novel was hardly sanguine. And you wonder why at times I feel more at home in a fantasy realm, where problems are more straightforward, like Demons, nickelpedes and fire-breathing dragons? Now you know.

At any rate, I do plan to write another Xanth novel next year, though I don't yet know its title or its nature. Probably it will have new characters and settings, as the ones in this novel have been around for about three novels. We now have a fair idea whom the sibling children will marry when they grow up and turn traitors to children everywhere by joining the dread Adult Conspiracy.

There may be some readers who don't like the fact that both gay and transgender characters are in this novel. They were suggested by readers, and I prefer Xanth to be inclusive rather than exclusive. Some may take exception to the awareness of sex by children. This echoes Mundania, where the very subject of sex is considered taboo for children. They don't practice it, but they know it exists. This is reality, and even fantasy can acknowledge it. Some may object to the idea of an eleven-year-old girl getting seriously romantic. Well, children do get crushes, and I am not at all sure there is much of a difference between a young crush and mature love. When I was eleven I had a crush on a girl that was unmatched emotionally by anything other than my later marriage, and I suspect that even today, over seventy years later, aspects of that girl define my interest in romance, despite the fact that my interest was not returned. I never disparage young love. So, bluntly, if you don't like this kind of realism, read something else.

Now my credits to those who suggested ideas and puns. I don't use all the puns sent by all the readers: some send hundreds, and I prefer to give newcomers a chance before filling up the volume with repeaters. Some just didn't quit fit in this story. Some were too complicated for my narrative. They remain in my suggestion file, and may be used in a future novel.

First, a credit to a book, *The Amazing Book of Mazes*, by Adrian Fisher, which I used for inspiration in my chapter on the Puzzle Planet. It truly is amazing what can be done with hedges and walkways, though you won't find sexy corn maidens as prizes here in Drear Mundania.

Title *Skeleton Key*; Ion and Hilda, reversed; you know, men are supposed to have sons and women have daughters, as signaled by the first letters of their names, so Ion is the son of Princess Ida, and Hilda the daughter of Prince Hilarion; auricle hears the future: person with synesthesia—Misty Zaebst

Marceen—Tina Barker

Plantain growing tains—Heather Harris

Angel Trumpet—Jema Schunke

Panty Thief; Gentleman's Club, Gentlewoman's Club—Alexander Sellers

Laurelai—Laurelai Bailey. I am not now, and have never been transgender, so my presentation of this condition may be clumsy. But this is fantasy, and the rules differ. Gender portals do not exist in Mundania, unfortunately.

Dancing Shoes—Emilio Ross

Abombinabowl—Mitch the Mad Hatter

School of Hard Knocks—William Adams

Zuzana, Philip, Tomas, Edvard, with their special talents—Tomas Lauman

Strip mine, Hard Drive, N-gram, N-points, keyboard to hold keys, Roaming numerals—Clifton R Liles

Cake Walk, pun titles *Duck of the Draw, Knot Gneiss Monster, Knight Bear, Bear Apparent*, Demon NA, Robot NA—Tim Bruening

A Tryst of Fate, Blanket of a Mind—Leigh Anne Harre

No tern unstoned—Dale Davis

Genie Ass; Talent of immunity to all elixirs—Naomi Blose

Mobius Strip, meet he/her shower, typo as a blood type, talent of growing instant fur, stud farm, cold snap—Mary Rashford

Sidetrack—Stefano Migneco

Dust Bunnies—Sam Doherty

Talent of sewing garments imbued with talents—Susan Taylor

Kidney beans with stones—Douglas Brown

Renee, making folk briefly younger—Renee Fourman

Rick O'Shea, cops or copse—Kari Lambert

Ruby—credit lost, frustratingly.

Naval Oranges go to sea—Richard Van Fossan

Elder Berry, Anony Mouse—Tom Pfarrer

D Louse—Bear Rollins

Can A Bull, Can't A Bull, Propel Her, Propel Him—Jestin Larson

Hamsterdam—Joshua Davenport-Herbst

World of Talent—Emma Archambault

Talent of combining two creatures into a crossbreed—Kenneth Adams.

Creating accommodation spells—Ann Marie Mohrmann

Have a wheelchair bound person in Xanth—Lester Gregg, Jr.

Have a blind person in Xanth—Nicole Valicia Thompson-Andrews

Conjuring a wet blanket, making a sun burn—Sara Cornelius

Crop Top—Jonathan Holland

Maisy growing mazes—Javier Valdez

Talent of seeing smells—Linnea Solomon, who was age 11 when she sent this in 2015; she may be older now.

Pleasant Trees—Steve Pfarrer

Ass sets—John at Mazes.com

Backup—John Knoderer

Garter Snake—Terence Vickers

Hurry-cane—Cal Humrich

And my credit to my proofreaders, Scott M Ryan, Anne White, and John Knoderer. They chase down the errors that grow on the page after I do my editing of the manuscript.

If you enjoyed this novel and want to know more of me, you can check my website at www.HiPiers.com, where I do a monthly blog-type column, have news of my new projects, express my ongoing opinionations, and maintain an ongoing survey of electronic publishers for the benefit of aspiring writers.

More anon, when.

ABOUT THE AUTHOR

Piers Anthony has written dozens of bestselling science fiction and fantasy novels. Perhaps best known for his long-running Magic of Xanth series, many of which are *New York Times* bestsellers, he has also had great success with the Incarnations of Immortality series and the Cluster series, as well as *Bio of a Space Tyrant* and others. Much more information about Piers Anthony can be found at www.HiPiers.com.

THE XANTH NOVELS

FROM OPEN ROAD MEDIA

INTEGRATED MEDIA

Find a full list of our authors and
titles at www.openroadmedia.com

FOLLOW US
@OpenRoadMedia

CPSIA information can be obtained
at www.ICGtesting.com
Printed in the USA
JSHW030826140121
10810JS00006B/4